Instruc ...

LET AUGMENTED REALITY CHANGE HOW YOU READ A BOOK

With your smartphone, iPad or tablet you can use the **Hasmark AR** app to invoke the augmented reality experience to literally read outside the book.

1. Download the **Hasmark app** from the **Apple App Store** or **Google Play**

2. Open and select the (vue) option

3. Point your lens at the full image with the and enjoy the augmented reality experience.

Go ahead and try it right now with the Hasmark Publishing International logo.

STICKS
in the
CLOUDS

A NOVEL

WILLARD HOWE

Hasmark
PUBLISHING
INTERNATIONAL

Editor: Allison Burney
Cover Design: Anne Karklins anne@hasmarkpublishing.com
Book Design: Amit Dey amit@hasmarkpublishing.com

ISBN 13: 978-1-77482-128-2
ISBN 10: 1774821281

Taxi

ACKNOWLEDGMENTS

This writer thanks the following authors and websites for valuable source material:

Against All Hope, a Memoir of Life in Castro's Gulag, by Armando Valladares.
Encounter Books, San Francisco, CA ©2001

Amnesty International, USA, amnestyusa.org
5 Penn Plaza, New York, New York 10001

A Taste of Cuba, by Beatriz Llamas, illustrations by Ximena Maier, translated by Claudia Lightfoot. Interlink Books, Northampton, Massachusetts ©2005

A Woman Unafraid, the Achievements of Frances Perkins, by Penny Colman.
Atheneum MacMillan Publishing Co, New York ©1993

Celia Sanchez, the Legend of Cuba's Revolutionary Heart, by Richard Haney.
Algora Publishing, New York ©2005

Cuba, a Journey, by Jacobo Timerman, translated by Toby Talbot.
Alfred A. Knopf, New York ©1990

Cuba, Going Back, by Tony Mendoza.

University of Texas Press, Austin, Texas ©1999

Cuba, photographs by David Alan Harvey, essays by Elizabeth Newhouse. National Geographic Society, Washington D.C. ©1999

Dancing with Cuba, a Memoir of the Revolution, by Alma Guillermoprieto, translated by Esther Allen. Pantheon Books, a division of Random House, New York ©2004

Exposing the Real Che Guevara, and the Useful Idiots Who Idolize Him, by Humberto Fontova. Sentinel, a member of Penguin Group, New York, New York ©2007

Finding Mañana, a Memoir of a Cuban Exodus, by Mirta Ojito. Penguin Books, New York, New York ©2005

Hard Landing, by Thomas Petzinger Jr. Times Books, a division of Random House, New York ©1995

Havana USA, Cuban Exiles and Cuban Americans in South Florida, 1959 - 1994, by María Cristina García. University of California Press, Berkley, CA ©1996

Haydée Santamaria, Rebel lives series, edited by Betsy Maclean. Ocean Press, Melbourne, Australia ©2003

Prisoner without a Name, Cell without a Number, by Jacobo Timerman, translated by Toby Talbot. Alfred A. Knopf, New York ©1981

Singing to Cuba, by Margarita Engle. Arte Público Press, Houston, Texas ©1993

The Exile, Cuba in the Heart of Miami, by David Rieff. Touchstone Books, New York, New York ©1993

The Soccer War, by Ryszard Kapuscinski. Alfred A. Knopf, New York ©1991

Truth Recovery Archive on Cuba
www.cubaarchive.org

Which Side Are You On? Trying to Be for Labor When It's Flat on Its
Back, by Thomas Geoghegan. Farrar, Straus & Giroux, New York ©1991

Wings of the Morning, by Orestes Lorenzo.
St. Martin's Press, New York, New York ©1994

Wins, Losses, and Lessons: An Autobiography by Lou Holtz.
Harper Collins, New York, New York ©2007

A special thanks to Suzanne Berg, for an insightful critique.

And to Kathy Mott, for support and encouragement.

A special thanks to my teacher, Molly Daniels-Ramanujan, University of
Chicago fiction writing workshop.

For Catherine and Jennifer

CONTENTS

PART ONE

"What is chiefly needed is skill, rather than machinery."

Wilbur Wright, 1902

CHAPTER ONE

Matt Lavery leaned against the wing of the blue and white twin Cessna and looked at his watch. Two hours had passed since he landed on South Caicos. It was supposed to be another routine charter. He was to pick up four passengers and fly them back to Fort Lauderdale. Arriving just before sunset signaled the beginning of the night curfew.

The island was located at the farthest perimeter from the base, and Matt was concerned that he might not have enough fuel to make it back. A fuel stop in Nassau would require a night flight home under an instrument flight plan, an illegal act since South Tropic Airways didn't have approval for overwater night-operations but Wally wouldn't mind.

Wally Martinez, Matt's boss, and the founder of STA, tended to view the Federal Aviation Regulations as mere suggestions. Besides, part of the FAA's mandate was to promote air commerce, and how could you promote air commerce by making it next to impossible to make a profit?

No, Wally won't mind, Matt thought, but I do. He was tired of being out there with no support, tired of being on call twenty-four hours a day, Wally being too cheap to hire another pilot. He was tired of calling Wally at the back bar at the Ramada whenever he needed something, and he was tired of all those passengers: bail bondsmen and lawyers with gold Rolexes and leisure suits, South Florida druggies with cowboy boots and hundred-dollar bills; Colombians, Haitians, and Bahamians, with their dirty, sweat-stained T-shirts and questionable passports.

Of course, it was all legitimate. Nadine booked the charters, calling Wally at the back bar for a quote, and Matt flew them. Whatever his passengers did for a living was none of his business. But there were times when the smell of foul play was as pungent as a garbage strike in August. And besides, wasn't there something out there called guilt by association?

Matt glanced at his watch again, looked down at the pager attached to his leather belt and felt the urge to throw it into the prickly island scrub. He was wearing beige khakis and a white cotton shirt. He felt the warm beads of sweat dripping from his armpits and the heat from the white conch-shell concrete burning the soles of his shoes. He looked down and stared at the crushed seashells and macaroni-like crustaceans, forever entombed. Then he looked over at the airport tiki bar. The barstools were made of bleached gray driftwood and weathered green canvas. Dry palm fronds lay over a rusted, corrugated tin roof. Gnarled bougainvillea with pink and purple blossoms outlined the indigo paint-peeled clapboards and flamingo-colored shutters. Matt imagined the entire bar, with all its glass bottles of booze, flung into oblivion with the arrival of this year's hurricanes. Mother Nature, with harmless names like Agnes, Bruce, or Camille, could drop a nuclear bomb on this little piece of paradise faster than you could spit. He hoped he'd be long gone by then but just where, he wasn't sure.

Matt looked out at the blue ocean shimmering beyond the limp and lifeless palms. His friends back in the grips of a freezing Chicago winter would be envious to work in paradise, where every day is like a vacation.

Matt noticed that no one at the tiki bar was on vacation. From the looks of the patrons, he expected to see a fleet of Hell's Angels Harleys parked nearby. They were bad boys with rotted teeth, beards, and tattoos. Crime had found a home in the tropics.

A few months ago, Matt stopped off at the Cockpit Bar and Grill on his way home from work. The bar was a refuge for charter pilots and airline flight crew on layovers. Maynard Smith, a Bahamas Air captain, told him the story:

A few weeks ago, just after midnight, a DC-3 full of marijuana landed on South Caicos. The runway was illuminated by the headlights from a Toyota Land Cruiser. Nothing too unusual these days, but what was so disturbing was that Percy Watson, the senior Customs official in the Bahamas, was found the next morning, seated at his wooden desk with his throat slit, not just from side to side but clean around. Blood covered the desk and chair where Percy sat, slumped over, surrounded by framed photographs of his wife Jolie and their children and grandchildren. His white uniform shirt glistened crimson, blood caked in the links of the silver chain around his neck which held the cross of Jesus. A ceiling fan revolved above the crime scene. The only witnesses were the portraits of the Queen, Jesus Christ, and JFK that hung on the wall.

Percy was a legend among pilots and boat skippers who made their living in the heart of the Bermuda Triangle. He not only displayed the quintessential warmth of a true islander but was unique in another way: Percy couldn't be bought. If he wouldn't take tips from the pilots or boat skippers, he certainly wouldn't take bribes from the drug cowboys. To turn the other way and pretend not to see could net a Customs official more in a weekend than he'd make in an entire year at his official post. Percy was a grandfather to eleven children and an elder in the Turks and Caicos Anglican Church. He always knew where you could find a spare room for the night, a set of tools, or how to contact the overseas operator.

Matt just shook his head when Maynard finished the story. "Those bastards. Percy wasn't even armed. Why didn't they just land on Cat Island or Bimini? Fergie would have welcomed them with open arms."

"Yah, mahn," Maynard said. "Dis is true. Poor Mister Watson, due to retire in six months' time. Was going to live like a king at his brother Alvin's sugar cane farm on St. Kitts. All the boys are chipping in, trying to give his miss a little lift. Governor's going to send Mister Ferguson over to take his place."

Matt reached into his wallet, took out a ten-dollar bill and gave it to Maynard.

"Sorry man, that's all I've got."

Matt sipped his beer for a while and thought about what he'd just heard. Ferguson, that imperious, Idi Amin wannabe, with gold chains around his neck and gold Rolex around his wrist. Fergie wouldn't let you go until he'd had his fun. There were always fictitious transient fees, security fees, weekend and holiday fees, all for the Queen, of course. But Fergie would behave himself when Mike was around.

Mike O'Neil ran a thriving dive business on Bimini and used South Tropic exclusively. Matt liked to fly the divers over on Saturday mornings. Everyone was always in a festive mood. Mike's business was booming, and Wally enjoyed a steady stream of income. Mike would usually be there on the tarmac to greet the divers as they deplaned. He was a big, strapping, Magnum P.I. type, an ex-Marine who always wore a Hawaiian shirt, Ray-Bans and a baseball cap. Matt wasn't sure if Mike paid Ferguson off. Sometimes Fergie would feign island hospitality, but Matt knew that, deep down, he was a pathological bully, intoxicated by his status as an official.

Matt watched the sun over the western horizon turn blazing orange. He was beginning to wonder if there had been a mistake, like the time Nadine booked that charter to Georgetown:

Matt had flown down to Georgetown, in the Exuma chain, and waited for his passenger to show up. He was booked to fly cages full of live tropical birds back to the States. When he finally reached Nadine back at the office, she was in tears.

"Oh Matt," she cried, "I screwed up, big time. The man with the birds just called and he's furious. He said he's been waiting for you for three hours."

"Three hours? I've been here for three hours and the sun's starting to go down."

"I know," Nadine said. "He's waiting for you in Georgetown, Guyana."

"Guyana?"

"South America. It was my mistake for not checking. Wally's going to be furious."

"Well, what should we do?" Matt said, pressing the phone closer to his ear.

"You might as well come home. He said he'd never fly South Tropic again and threatened to sue if anything should happen to his birds. Then he hung up."

"OK. I'll have to make a fuel stop in Nassau. I should be home by eight. And don't worry about Wally, Nadine. I'll smooth him out tomorrow."

The next morning, Matt climbed the stairs to the second floor of the Sunny South Air Terminal. He could hear Wally yelling from behind the closed office-door at the end of the hall.

"That charter was worth two thousand dollars! Dammit, Nadine."

"I know, Wally, it was my fault. I'll make it up to you. You can take some out of my pay each week."

"Dock your pay?" Wally laughed. "That's ridiculous. It would take years to—" He was starting to calm down. Then a look appeared on his face, the hint of a grin. "I have another idea." Just then Matt burst into the office.

"Another perfect day in paradise," he said. Nadine sat at her desk. Tears pooled around her eyelids. "Nadine, you look lovely," Matt said. Then he looked over at Wally, who was obviously hungover. "You too, Wally. Now what's this all about?"

"You know what it's about," Wally said. "Another screwup like that and we'll all be out of a job."

"Maybe, maybe not," Matt said.

"What's that supposed to mean?"

"I was looking over the Georgetown charter in the book last night. Nadine called and gave you the details before she booked it, right? The only mistake she made was listing the wrong Georgetown, and who can blame her? We operate in the Bahamas, not South America. If it was Georgetown, D.C., how's she supposed to know?"

"Yes, we know it was *her* mistake," Wally said, pointing a finger at Nadine.

"But the type of cargo, the fare quote and the other details, she cleared all that with you first, Wally."

"Yeah, so what?"

"So, the birds, it turns out, were tropical starlings, strictly low-altitude creatures. The Cessna's unpressurized. They would have died up at altitude from asphyxiation. Every one of those darling starlings would have suffocated, and you'd have *another* lawsuit on your hands, Wally, big time. So, you see, Nadine, totally by accident, saved all our precious jobs. I'd say she deserves a raise." Matt was trying to pull the smile off his face.

"Very funny, mister. Let's not let something like that happen again or I'll be forced to close a lot more than this door." Wally ushered them out of his office and slammed the door shut.

The sounds from the tiki bar were getting louder and angrier, like the prelude to a brawl. One of the thugs banged his fist down on the bar, and a roar of laughter trumpeted out across the tarmac. Matt looked over and saw Ferguson, his gold tooth reflecting the setting sun like a flashbulb.

Matt was aware that he was, to some extent, hiding behind his Ray-Bans and holding onto the wing for support. He wanted to make himself inconspicuous, shrink down and connect with the conch creatures at eye level. Or better yet, climb back into the Cessna, fire up the twin Continental engines, roar down the runway and lift off, retracting the gear but staying down on the deck, building speed. Then pull back in a climbing chandelle, letting the nose drop through the horizon in the middle of a 180-degree turn. He'd dive down low and come screaming across the airport, blow the tin roof right off the tiki bar, beat Mother Nature to it, and send those bearded bastards running for cover. He'd fly home just before the curfew, drive his Jeep over to the back bar at the Ramada and drop the keys, with a final "clink," into Wally's Dewar's on the rocks.

Matt looked at his watch again, then looked up to see a cloud of dust rising from the back of a tan Toyota Land Cruiser as it wound its way around the perimeter road.

The Land Cruiser swerved around the small terminal building and blew fine bits of conch gravel out to the side as it fishtailed and came to a screeching halt next to the plane. Matt felt his heart race. The driver and two other passengers in the back seat wore tattered T-shirts and faded, oil-stained denim pants with tears in the knees. They were speaking Spanish and laughing and one of the men had an AK-47 strapped around his shoulder. The driver started unloading beige canvas duffels from the back seat while the passenger in the front seat got out and walked toward Matt. He wore a fine, European suit of clothes with Italian leather shoes and black wraparound sunglasses.

"Buenas tardes, Capitán," the man said.

"You're late," Matt said, looking away.

"An unavoidable delay," the man said. "Jorge Roca." He reached out to shake Matt's hand.

"Have them stow the duffels behind the rear seats and put the smaller ones in the wing-lockers. We've got to move. We're not authorized to fly over water at night, and we have to stop in Nassau for fuel." Jorge Roca held out his hand in a halting way.

"That will not be necessary, I assure you, Capitán," he said, looking over at one of the men and nodding toward the Land Cruiser. The man came back to the plane carrying a red five-gallon jerrican and six feet of black rubber hose. Matt noticed a maroon scar across the man's upper arm. Roca issued more quick instructions in Spanish. Matt saw the man take a stepladder from the Land Cruiser and climb up on the wing of a Beechcraft King Air that was parked nearby.

"You can't do that," Matt said.

"No te preocupes, señor," the man said. "Ees a friend of ours, no hay problema."

"The hell there isn't," Matt said, his blood pressure rising. "For one thing, you're about to mix Jet-A with Avgas; the engines will quit right on takeoff." Jorge Roca barked at the man in Spanish. The man ran over to a Piper Seneca, unscrewed the fuel cap on top of the wing and fed the rubber hose down into it, ignoring Matt's protest.

"Besides," Matt said, "we need forty gallons, minimum. Sucking it through that hose will take three hours, and furthermore, what you're doing is illegal." Some of the men started laughing and mumbling in

Spanish. Roca shouted out commands, and the man threw the jerrican and the hose into the scrub and climbed into the plane as the rest of the men were getting in and strapping on their belts. Roca sat in the front right seat and shut the door.

"As you wish, Capitán," he said. Matt quickly ran through the pre-flight checklist, pushed the mixture control levers to full rich, magnetos to both and called out "Clear," before pushing the start buttons. The big, two-bladed McCauley propellers came to life with a low frequency rumble. Matt donned his mint-green David Clark headset and taxied to the end of the runway. The wind was out of the east and Matt lined up with the center of the runway and slowly pushed the throttles up. The rumble turned to a roar as the Cessna accelerated. Matt pulled back on the control yoke at Vr (liftoff speed), retracted the gear and stayed down on the deck, building speed. For a second, he remembered the roof on the tiki bar. Some other time, he thought, easing the control yoke back and banking left as the plane climbed higher, heading for Nassau and the night.

Once leveled off, Matt started making plans. He looked over at Roca and raised his voice above the roar of the engines. "I need to see everyone's passports."

"I can assure you, Capitán, all these men have proper identification."

"I need to see them," Matt repeated. Roca reached into his lapel pocket and pulled out a passport of Colombian registry. The photo looked fairly recent. None of the other men had passports, just temporary resident alien cards that looked a shade this side of dust.

"I doubt Immigration's going to accept those, and if they don't, I'm the one who'll have to fly you jokers back out."

"Do you always treat your paying passengers with such lack of respect, Capitán?" Roca glared into Matt's eyes.

Matt imagined he was flying solo. For a minute, he allowed himself to dream of the future, when someday he'd be up at 37,000 feet, in command of a big Boeing jetliner for Eastern, Braniff, or Delta. He'd look out at the last rim of a brilliant orange sunset, just like the one before him now, and remember this trip with these ragtag bastards from

Barranquilla, and the memory, with all its hard edges made smooth over time, might actually bring a smile to his face.

The Nassau tower cleared Cessna N26ST to land on runway 15. Matt taxied to the general aviation ramp and shut down. Roca and his men stopped talking. A quiet unease replaced their previous bravado.

"You'll have to go inside while we refuel," Matt said. "This shouldn't take twenty minutes." Matt checked in at the Customs desk, then had the tip tanks topped off with 100-octane while Roca and his men went into the restroom to smoke cigarettes. Matt located a telephone, called the overseas operator, and gave her the number for the back bar at the Ramada. This ought to be fun, he thought. Matt strained to hear as Vince, the bartender, picked up.

"Vince, Matt Lavery. Is Wally there?"

"Yeah, hang on a second." A minute later, Wally grabbed the phone. "Matt, where are you?"

"Wally, listen, I'm in Nassau. I'm going to have to file an instrument flight plan to get home. I need you to call Customs and Immigration. We'll be coming in after hours."

"Yeah, okay," Wally said. "Just make sure you collect the late-fee first."

"And Wally," Matt said, "all but one of them has marginal identification."

Matt paid for the fuel and called the Flight Service Station to file a flight plan. When he walked out to the plane, Roca and his men were already in their seats with their belts fastened. Matt climbed in, latched the door, and prepared for the hour-long flight.

Nobody said a word en route until Matt shut down the engines on the Customs ramp. "Get your identification out and bring your luggage inside," Matt said.

"We've done this many times before, Capitán," Roca said.

The Immigration official looked up and frowned at the motley group, then with a tone of exaggerated irritation said, "Passports, please." Roca cleared without a problem. The official squinted at the wrinkled parchments the other men presented, gathered them in his hand, and went into another room. A few minutes later he appeared. "What's the purpose of your visit?"

"Pleasure," Roca said. "These men work for me. We're building a church in the islands. I promised them a little trip to the States as a reward for all their hard labor, a trip to Disney, perhaps."

The Immigration official glared at Matt, then perfunctorily stamped the men's papers and handed them back. "Through that door, place your bags up on the counter." As the men shuffled through the doorway, dragging their duffels, the official leaned over the counter.

"This is the last time. Tell Wally they've got to have clean paper, otherwise you'll be flying them back out. You may be looking at a suspension of your operating certificate and a heavy fine as well."

"It won't happen again," Matt said as he walked over to the Customs desk. The agent was rummaging through the other bags. He had a look on his face like he'd rather be back at the Copa Club. He stamped all the forms and waved the men toward the exit. "That'll be a hundred dollars for the late-fee," he said to Matt. Roca opened his wallet and took out two crisp hundred-dollar bills, placed the bills on the counter and said with a slight bow, "For your trouble."

The Customs official just shook his head and pushed the extra bill back at Roca. "That's the exit there," he said, pointing behind him. The Immigration official was turning out the lights in the back room while the men shuffled through the door, joking in Spanish and dragging their duffels. Matt opened the door to the ramp and started walking toward the plane when he noticed Roca following him.

"Your exit's out front," Matt said. Roca approached Matt, leaned into his ear and said in a muffled voice, "We left some things in the wing-lockers. Make sure Wally gets them."

"You smuggled something on my airplane?" Matt's heart was racing like he'd just come off a treadmill.

"I assure you this airplane is more mine than yours," Roca said.

"Don't you *ever*…I'm going right back inside to report you." Roca grabbed Matt's bicep and jerked him close. Matt tried to take his arm back, but Roca had him in a vice grip. Roca smelled like sweat and sweet cologne.

"Now you listen to me, *pendejo*," he said. "You do what I say, or I'll break this fucking arm of yours." He threw Matt's arm back at him, turned and walked into the building and out the front exit.

Matt felt feverish and his bicep stung like he'd been hit by the tip of a leather horsewhip. His heart wouldn't slow down as he climbed back into the Cessna and got clearance to taxi back to the Sunny South Air Terminal. Drugs, Matt thought. What else could it be? He kept hearing the words *guilt by association* echoing in his brain. The dream of an airline career would be over before it ever got off the ground. Matt parked the plane, shut down the engines, and climbed down off the wing. He made sure the ramp was deserted, then pushed the latch on the right wing-locker and opened the hatch cover. There was the usual cluster of red shop rags, a yellow plastic funnel and a can of engine oil. Matt moved the rags aside and reached up into the locker. His hand felt something cold and hard. He pulled a penlight from his shirt pocket and shined the narrow beam up into the locker, which was filled with bandoliers of machine gun bullets. For a second, Matt was relieved he hadn't found drugs. Then he wondered which was worse. Either had the power to destroy his dream if he was caught and found guilty by association.

He climbed the staircase by the side of the hangar, walked down the darkened corridor to the office, put the key in the door, and opened it. He hung the key to the plane on a hook behind Nadine's desk, closed and locked the office door, and walked down the steps and out the front door to where his Jeep was parked. He threw his flight bag in the back seat and climbed in. He sat in the Jeep for a few seconds and felt the quiet of the night wash over him. The canvas top was off, and above him a crescent silver moon shone through the swaying fronds of a palm tree. The gentle soughing of wind through the fronds, like brushes on the head of a snare drum, swept over him. Matt sat and listened to the rhythm. He was still seething from what just happened, and still seeing the white-hot image of what would have happened if that Customs inspector had decided to come out and search the plane.

Matt started to relax, his breath in sync with the swaying palms overhead. Then he turned the key and headed out of the parking lot, toward Federal Highway, and home.

He drove north, past the empty parking lot of the Cockpit Bar and Grill. He wondered how many beers it would take before he'd stop feeling Roca's grip on his arm. He didn't have much cash on him anyway, so he turned right on S.E. 17th Street, left on Cordova Road, then right on S.E. 15th Street and pulled into the parking spot beneath his apartment. He took the elevator up to the third floor, turned the key and walked in. It was dark, except for the fluorescent light over the aquarium on the kitchen counter. The lone angelfish seemed suspended, oblivious to Matt's arrival on the scene. Mrs. Yusko, his landlady, had placed a bowl of fresh grapefruit on the kitchen counter. Her son was Matt's age when he flew his last mission over North Vietnam ten years ago. Pieces of his F-4 Phantom jet were later found but not a trace of her son. Matt walked into the small bedroom and threw his flight bag on the floor. He took off his clothes, tossed them into a canvas hamper, turned the small night-light on in the bathroom, and stepped into the shower. The cold water felt soothing on his arm. He dried off, put on a thin white cotton robe, and went back to the kitchen. He kept a bottle of Jack Daniel's in the cabinet by the fridge. He opened the bottle, poured a dram over ice, and then carried the tumbler out through the sliding glass doors to the veranda overlooking the Intracoastal Waterway. Matt sat back in a white wicker chair, put his feet up on a small rattan table and shifted for comfort. He took a sip of the amber liquor and felt its radiating warmth. The lights from the oceanfront hotels shimmered in the black well of water. Sleek pearl-white yachts were moored along the seawall with their running lights on. I'll miss this, he thought. The tropical beauty, the tranquility. Matt thought of Wally and Nadine. They had been the two central people in his life for over a year, and after tomorrow, he'd probably never see them again.

Nadine was French Canadian; she met Wally when she and her girlfriends flew down from Montreal to charter a flight to the Green

Turtle Club on Abacos Island. It was a much needed vacation, the first since her husband's hang-gliding accident the year before left her widowed with a two-year-old son.

Wally was flying most of the trips back then, full of polish and pride in his new company. He was extremely cordial to the lovely young ladies with their French accents and long legs. Wally asked Nadine if she'd like to sit in the right seat. All the way across the Gulf Stream, he pointed out the islands of the Bahama Banks and how to tell the difference between a coral reef and a large school of bonefish. Over the roar of the engines, he told her stories of the Bermuda Triangle and tried to impress her with the instrument panel and his infinite knowledge. After the girls deplaned, Wally told Nadine he was looking for someone just like her to run the office, book the charters, and in short, be his assistant. Nadine was taken aback but told him she'd give the idea some thought.

When Wally flew back the following week, Nadine told him she would accept his offer. She needed a change, and aviation held a special place in her heart. She was business-like and kept her enthusiasm in check. She needed a new job and new surroundings, not a new man in her life.

Nadine quickly mastered the myriad details of running a small air taxi service. Wally entrusted her with every aspect of the business, everything except the finances. What Nadine didn't know then was that Wally's personal life was sinking, just as his little airline was taking off.

It was the year before, when Wally drove home after a trip and found the note from Donna. She said Wally cared more about his business than her, that the marriage was over and that their two young children would be better off in her care. Wally looked around his house and found half the furniture gone, his children's clothes, toys, and stuffed animals gone, all the artwork on the walls, most of the kitchen utensils, and the stereo all gone. Stunned, his blood flow freeze-framed. He collapsed on the bed in the guest room and cried himself to sleep.

Nadine's professionalism, gregarious way with customers, and quick wit were indispensable in the weeks that followed. The problem was that

Wally couldn't keep his mind in the cockpit. All he could think about were his two sweet little girls, and how much he missed them, even if that meant just watching them sleep or hearing their soft breaths on the pillows, their little stuffed animals clutched in their arms. At first, he was in denial that Donna was gone for good. Certainly, she'd come to her senses and change her mind. He was also in denial that he could still fly. He thought he could separate work from his private life, but the wake-up call came on final approach to runway 09 Right at Fort Lauderdale International one afternoon when the landing gear warning horn went off, startling Wally and scaring his passengers. He simply forgot to put the gear down.

Matt was teaching at a flight school down the hall from STA at the time. He always asked Wally for a job whenever he saw him. Wally was impressed by Matt's persistence but told him he needed more experience. When Donna left him, he called Matt over to the office after he finished with his last student of the day.

"How'd you like to fly a trip with me?" he asked.

"Just say when."

"Tomorrow morning. I've got to take some business associates over to Andros, thought you'd like to come along." The next morning, Matt met Wally on the ramp by the Cessna.

"Hop in," Wally said. Matt climbed up on the wing, opened the door and dropped into the right seat. Wally sat in the left seat and started going over the instrument panel and the cockpit setup. Soon the passengers arrived, and Wally and Matt flew them over to Andros. Matt was thrilled. Wally was a natural. He flew the plane with ease, instructing at the same time. On the trip back, Wally told Matt to sit in the left seat. Wally instructed and Matt absorbed it all like a dry sponge. After they'd parked the plane, while they were walking back to the office, Wally said, "How much multi-engine time have you got, Matt?"

"Counting today, only about twenty hours."

"Our insurance policy requires a minimum of two hundred hours. Tell you what, add an extra zero to your logbook and it'll be our secret. How'd you like to fly for South Tropic Airways?"

Matt could barely believe the words. It was the lucky break he'd been hoping for. He felt a quiet guilt about the lie in his logbook, but these were desperate times. There was always that Catch-22 in civilian aviation. No one would hire you without experience, but how could you get experience unless someone hired you? That night at the Cockpit Bar and Grill, Matt couldn't buy Wally enough shots of Dewar's, and Wally couldn't drink enough of them, knowing he'd be going home to an empty house.

Wally had been a prince in those early days, Matt had to give him that. At times he even seemed like a big brother, a mentor. Matt took another sip of Jack Daniel's and felt a pang of guilt. How could he just quit and run away? Was it really the smart thing to do? Was he just acting impulsively out of fear? In any case, Wally will feel betrayed, Matt thought. He did me a big favor, and this is gratitude? Matt could still feel the pain in his upper arm. He took another sip of the amber liquor, and the pain and guilt started to subside.

He woke early, as the eastern horizon beyond the beachfront hotels glowed scarlet with the dawn. He showered, dressed, and threw open his travel bag. He emptied the contents of the dresser drawers: two pairs of jeans, a few polo shirts, a pair of tropical beach shorts, dark blue slacks, and a herringbone tweed sport coat. He wrapped the photograph of his parents and the bottle of Jack Daniel's in between his jeans and a beach towel. He tossed in his camera and zipped up the bag. Then he called Mrs. Yusko and apologized for having to leave so suddenly.

Matt drove to the Sunny South Air Terminal on the north side of the airport. It was still early, but Nadine's red Fiat was already parked under the shade of a palm tree. Matt sat for a minute and felt the tension in his neck. He hated confrontation and still wasn't sure how he was going to tell Wally he was quitting, pulling the rug out from under him. He could feel the humidity in the air, already thick and heavy at 8:00 a.m. He felt clammy as he hopped down from the Jeep and walked through the front door. The air conditioning hit him like an arctic slap as he climbed the stairs. A thin trace of Nadine's lavender perfume lingered in the air. Matt could smell the aroma of freshly ground French Roast coffee as he entered the office. Nadine turned and broke into a smile, her blue eyes sparkling.

"Good morning. I saw the Cessna on the ramp when I drove in. I'm glad you made it back okay. It must have been long after sunset."

"It was," Matt said as he grabbed a cup from the table.

"I'll pour," Nadine said.

He sat down on the blue leather sofa across from Nadine's desk. For the first time, he didn't try to conceal his stare. She was wearing white strapless sandals with low, wooden heels and a pale-yellow cotton dress, open at the neck. Her legs were tanned and toned and reflected a soft sheen in the light. Matt felt a warm flush in his cheeks as Nadine sat down and crossed her legs. He turned his gaze and looked up at the clock on the wall.

"What?" she said.

"Nothing." Matt took a sip of coffee. Their eyes met.

"Why are you here so early? There's nothing in the book." Matt loved the way her French accent veiled her words.

"I need to talk to Wally."

"About last night?" she said. Matt wasn't sure how to answer. He didn't know how much Wally knew about the contraband in the wing-locker. Was he as innocent as Matt, or as guilty as Roca and the rest of them?

"What happened?" Nadine persisted.

"I'm leaving," Matt said. The words hung in the air and Matt chastened his impetuousness.

"What?"

"I'm resigning, Nadine. Today. Here are my keys." Matt set his office keys on Nadine's desk, a small tangible act that strengthened his resolve.

"I'll miss you," she said. She was staring at the framed watercolor painting on the wall. Two lone sailboats anchored in the blue water of a tropical lagoon.

"You, too. I hate to leave you and Wally in a bind. I know I should give more notice." Matt was fishing for her approval, needing her support to assuage his guilt.

"Something happened last night, didn't it?" She wasn't about to let him off the hook. "Wally called this morning. He said he wouldn't be in until noon."

Matt felt his resolve balancing on a wire. He had to focus, make a clean break. Part of him wanted to back down, be the dutiful employee, the consummate professional.

"Machine gun bullets." The words blurted from his mouth, too late to recant. Nadine got up and shut the door. She turned and sat down next to him on the sofa. Her eyes were all his.

Matt told her the story, filling in as much detail as he could remember. When he came to the part about Jorge Roca nearly ripping his arm from its socket, Nadine reached out and softly touched him there. She said nothing. She let Matt pause and collect his thoughts. When he was through, he said, "It's my inner voice, Nadine. It's telling me it's time to go."

"Then you must listen to it," she said. She was supporting everything about him, rubbing salve in his wounds and looking at him with those blue eyes. Their gaze alone had the power to heal. "The sooner the better," she said. "I'll explain everything to Wally for you."

"I hate to leave like this," Matt said.

"Wally's always reminding you of the hundreds of pilots out there with better résumés. Now he can hire them." They both laughed.

Nadine was making it too easy. She was supporting not just his decision to leave, but his very essence.

"I'll leave a forwarding address when I have one." Nadine was writing something on a piece of paper.

"Use my name and address for a reference, Matt. No doubt you'll need one soon." She was going above and beyond. Matt was afraid that if he kept talking, he'd allow himself to open up and reveal how he felt about her, how his face flushed when he saw her. It was quiet between them for a few seconds. Nadine gazed into her coffee cup. "I'll miss you," she said again. "Things won't be the same. Can I ask you one question?"

"Sure."

"How come you never asked me out? I mean, why didn't we ever—"

"I always wanted to," Matt interrupted.

"Was it because I have a child?"

"No, of course not." Matt felt exposed. Nadine had just picked the lock to his safe. He was cornered, with no way out except to leave. He took a deep breath. "I always wanted to," he said again. "It's not you, Nadine, it's me."

"The commitment thing? I'd never pressure you. I just thought we got along so well, like a team."

"Nadine, I'm not sure where I'm going, not sure whether I'll succeed or not. How could I take someone along on that kind of ride? It wouldn't be fair."

"It might have been fun," she said, looking into his eyes.

"Nadine, I think you're wonderful. You deserve better than this. I mean, this job, working for Wally."

"I know," she said, a smile returning to her face. "I'll let you go this time. Just promise me you'll write, at least once. I'll be thinking about you."

"I will," he said as he got up and reached for her. He pulled her close and she wrapped her arms around him and kissed him on the cheek. Matt felt weak; his knees were about to collapse. She smelled like fresh-cut flowers and her hair was soft against his face. Suddenly he was filled with confusion. Vertigo, that trick of the senses, seemed to be taking over. He was dizzy. He felt Nadine's soft breath on his neck as she held him. Matt responded the way he'd been trained in the cockpit, to disregard his senses and trust his instruments. He took a deep breath and gently pulled back. He let go of her waist and backed away. He looked Nadine straight in the eyes, glistening with the moisture of budding tears.

"Am I allowed one big mistake?" he said. She let out a soft laugh and nodded.

"Just one."

"I'd better be going," he said.

CHAPTER TWO

Matt held onto the banister as he walked downstairs. He felt light-headed and overwhelmed, still not sure he was making the right move. He hopped into the Jeep, pulled out of the parking lot, then caught the on-ramp to I-95 North. For years, Matt lived with a sense of purpose. He always had a plan, a way to get from A to B. But now he was at a crossroad. He knew his leaving would be a watershed event, but he had no idea where he was going next. The vertigo that set in when he was lost in Nadine's embrace was deepening, the insecurity filling him with doubt. Was he just scared, acting like an impetuous child? All he could do was drive.

The ragtop was off, and the wind blew through his hair, creating the kind of white noise his senses craved. As he crossed into Georgia, the western horizon became a rim of soft purple, the sun's rays bending and blending with the night. He reached into the glove box and pulled out John Coltrane's *Live at Birdland*, put it in the tape player and listened to the soulful jazz as the miles clicked by. The night air turned cool, and Matt pulled into a truck-stop. He bought a ham sandwich and a cup of coffee, pulled his windbreaker out of his travel bag, and headed back to the highway. He craved the hypnotic effect of the road and didn't want to stop.

The first hint of a loose plan was starting to formulate in his mind. He'd go back to Chicago, visit with his parents, and try to find a job. He wanted to drive through the night, but just before midnight, caught himself nodding off at the wheel. He woke to the sound of a horn blaring as he drifted into the other lane. He was just north of Atlanta when he pulled off the road and checked into a cheap motor-lodge.

He threw his clothes over a chair, collapsed onto the hard mattress, and turned on the TV news. Ted Koppel's *Nightline* was titled, "America Held Hostage—Day 187." The marking of time underscored the national vigil that gripped the nation. Images of hooded hostages filled the screen. Captured and held against their will, they were guilty of nothing but being in the wrong place at the wrong time. Matt thought of Ferguson, Jorge Roca, and Percy Watson—predators and their prey. Sleep was pulling him down like a lead weight in water. Thoughts of Nadine flooded in. He could still see her blue eyes, feel her touch. He remembered the trace of lavender in the air as he fell asleep in the dark and dingy room.

Matt woke to the sound of an eighteen-wheel tractor-trailer revving up its engine. He took a hot shower, pulled on a clean T-shirt and jeans, threw his bags in the Jeep, and got underway.

He drove straight through the morning, leaving the red Georgia clay behind as he wound through Tennessee, blue mist still blanketing the hills and hollers stretching out to the horizon. He took a bite of yesterday's ham sandwich and sipped cold coffee. The trucker music didn't match his mood, and all the news programs were broadcasts of the Iranian hostage crisis, the Russian war in Afghanistan, President Carter's appeal for an Olympic boycott in Moscow, the flood of Cuban exiles pouring into Miami and the crippling effects of stagflation, double-digit interest rates, rising unemployment and long lines at the gas pumps. America seemed weak on the world stage. Matt switched off the radio and drove on. He debated whether to call home and give his parents notice. He kept pushing back the thought that he was coming home with his tail between his legs, defeated at the start.

The highway rolled into Kentucky, the blue grass as green as Ireland. The bucolic panorama of horses calmed his mood. He stopped at a roadside café for fried chicken, mashed potatoes, fried okra, creamed corn and iced tea.

During the final hours of the trip, he tried to inject a shot of confidence into his mood, a feeling of new beginnings, but it wouldn't break through. It felt like an ending. The dim Chicago skyline came into view. Matt pulled off the highway at a convenience store and gassed up for the last time. He bought a bouquet of yellow tulips wrapped in cellophane for his mother and a six-pack of Heineken for his father, who mostly drank Hamm's. It'll be good to see them, he thought.

He decided to take the scenic route up Lake Shore Drive. He passed Northwestern University, the Grosse Point Lighthouse and the Bahai Temple, that incongruous Taj Mahal by the lake. He turned left and drove through Wilmette, then over the highway into Glenview. He looked down on the hill where he and his boyhood pals went sledding in winter. The hill looked so much smaller now. He turned left and saw the blue mailbox where he used to climb up and sit perched in the early evening, waiting for his father's old Buick to come around the bend. Sometimes he'd wait for hours, his gaze riveted to every approaching car, until finally he'd see it. He'd scamper down and run out along the road to greet his dad, who always had a big smile on his face as he opened the door, sat him on his lap and let him steer down the street and pull into the driveway in front of their small home.

Matt drove past the old, familiar houses, all cut from the same cookie-cutter mold. He passed his house and saw the hood raised on a red Cadillac, his father bent over the engine in blue mechanic's overalls. Matt parked along the curb, hopped out, and quietly walked up to his father's side.

"Hand you a wrench, Dad?"

"Matthew!" His father stood up, wiped his hands with a red shop rag, and shook Matt's hand. "What a surprise. What brings you home, son?"

"It's a long story. Care for a beer?" Matt held out the six-pack. His father smiled.

"Perfect timing. I just finished installing a new cruise-control for Big Lou. Let's go inside." Matt grabbed a duffel bag and the bouquet of flowers from the Jeep. They opened the beers in the small kitchen. Through the back window, Matt saw his mother kneeling in her garden, lost in a world of watering and weeding. She stood up when she heard the kitchen door slam shut.

"Matthew!" His mother wiped her hands on her apron, threw her arms around him, and smothered him with an embrace.

"I drove all the way up from Florida just to give you these."

"They're just beautiful," she said. "You look like you've lost weight, dear."

"I'll light the barbecue," his father said. "We'll have steaks tonight."

The same feeling came over Matt, just like when he was nine years old, sitting on his father's lap in the Buick. The memories of South Florida and all he'd left behind were temporarily forgotten. He'd come home, and it felt good.

During dinner, Matt told his parents, in limited detail, about flying for STA, how much experience he'd attained and how his logbook and résumé were filling up. He didn't mention the time the crankshaft failed on the right engine over the ocean, coming back from Freeport with a plane full of drunken passengers, their gaiety turning to fear and silence as they sat with their life jackets on, awaiting their fate. Or the time when the landing gear wouldn't go down, or the unwanted fuel transfer that forced another engine to quit. (A faulty check valve was found during a routine FAA inspection. Wally just hadn't gotten around to fixing it.) Or the time the cockpit filled with smoke due to an improper instrument installation.

"It all sounds wonderful, dear," his mother said. "The islands must look so pretty from the air."

"You're lucky to have a flying job at all, from the looks of this economy and all the airline layoffs I've been reading about," his father said. Matt nodded and took a sip of beer. "How long can you stay, son?"

"At least a few days. Things have been kind of slow lately."

"Why don't you both relax in the family room while I straighten up in here," his mother said.

"I taped the fights last night, son. Sugar Ray and that kid from Panama, Duran. Did I ever tell you I shook Joe Louis's hand once? In London during the war."

After the fights, they watched *Casablanca*. When Ingrid Bergman appeared through the doorway, when Bogart was boozy and bleary-eyed with that pained look, Matt said, "They don't make movies like this anymore, do they, Dad?" But his father was asleep on the couch. It was past midnight. Matt covered him with a blanket, turned off the TV and the lights, and climbed the staircase to his old bedroom. It was quiet except for the faint ticktock of his parents' anniversary clock in their bedroom down the darkened hallway.

Matt looked around and felt the old familiarity wrap itself around him. His old wooden desk with the model airplanes, the picture on the wall of his high school swim team, and the photograph of Karen that he swore he'd boxed up and put in storage before he left home; her brown eyes shining, a big smile on her face. She wore a white lab-coat, stethoscope around her neck. First year at Chicago Med., champion swimmer and good Catholic. They met at the university pool. She was in the lane next to him. He saw the blurred image of her lean legs and toned torso through his goggles. He had to quicken his pace to keep up. After a half-mile, it felt like his heart was about to burst when she finally stopped. He forced an introduction, gasping for breath. She wasn't even winded. She was a year ahead of him in school, taking organic chemistry and anatomy courses as a pre-med major. Matt was working in a cigar store, making money for flight school. She was on the fast-track to a successful career as a physician; Matt was on the fast-track to the uncertain. They were together for two years. She loved him, he knew that, but she was going to be a big success. Matt wasn't so sure about himself. And that was the wedge, the one drop of poison that soured what was beautiful between them. Matt picked up the photograph and held it in his hands. The memories tasted sweeter than the bitter reality they were based on. You could see the pure joy on her face. The sadness hadn't set in yet. Matt convinced himself it would never work. He could never keep up. He kept sending her vague signals, keeping a safe distance from commitment. His cool backstroking reached a climax at her graduation ceremony when he made a feeble excuse not to attend. He had to work.

They lasted one more year together. Then the phone rang in his apartment. Her voice sounded different. She called to say it was over. She'd met someone else. He was going to be a surgeon. It was meant to be. She wished him well. It was all for the best. Matt was stunned. He couldn't function. The landscape of his heart was a repository of raw emotion. No defenses had been erected, the pain was free to rush in and take over. He was shattered. All he could do was drive aimlessly to all the places they had been to together. During their two years together, it was he who said it wouldn't work. He was the one who wanted out. She was always arguing the opposite, optimistic and giving, caring until the end, when she could finally take no more. At that point she no longer found it difficult to reject him, like throwing a bag of garbage in the dumpster and slamming the lid with a loud bang for emphasis.

Matt took one more look at the photograph. For a moment he wished he could go back in time, see things differently and have more confidence. Maybe he could have been more positive, seen the good instead of the bad, thought of her more than him and things would have been different. He placed the photograph in the nightstand drawer and turned out the lights. In the dark, he thought of Nadine and the hurt look on her face when he said he was leaving. Maybe there was something missing from his blueprint, some vital component that never got installed from the start. A new fear started to germinate in the back of his mind. Maybe he would miss out on what is truly important. Maybe the whole parade would pass him by, and he'd be too old to do anything about it. He tossed and turned in fits of agitation, then finally fell asleep.

He woke to the smell of bacon and coffee and the sound of the radio in the kitchen. He took a hot shower, put on a clean pair of jeans and a blue T-shirt, and went downstairs. His mother greeted him with a smile, poured a cup of coffee, and placed a plate of steaming scrambled eggs on the table.

"Your father left at six. He said he'd try to come home early." Matt knew that early meant sometime before 9:00 p.m. After his job as a mechanic for the Cadillac agency, he worked for the school district doing maintenance and custodial work. He was like so many men of his generation. After growing up during the Depression and returning from World War II, he tried engineering school but knew what he really wanted to do was work with his hands. He married young, dropped out of school, and worked as a machinist before qualifying as an apprentice mechanic. He worked twelve hours a day, six days a week, hardly ever took a sick-day, and never complained. He was a simple man who had the gift of contentment.

"So, what are your plans, dear?" his mother said. She was doing the dishes and looking out at the garden, tilting her head to one side to see past a lock of graying hair.

"I've got to stay focused, keep building flight time."

"No, I meant today, dear. Why don't you just relax, go to the pool?" Matt shifted in his chair. He downed the rest of his coffee and stood up. "I've got a few errands to run first. I'll be home this afternoon." He gave her a kiss on the cheek and went upstairs. He changed into a pair of navy slacks and a white dress shirt, then picked up the manila folder of résumés.

He drove out to the county airport. The secretary at the flight school rolled her eyes when she grabbed his résumé and said they weren't hiring. Matt drove around to the corporate hangars at the far side of the field, but most of their doors were locked. He got back in the Jeep and drove to O'Hare and parked outside the Butler Air Terminal. Butler had a fleet of Lear jets in their charter operation. The chief pilot took his résumé. "I'll add this to the hundreds of others," he said. "Any jet-time?"

"No, I'm afraid not."

Matt got back in the Jeep. He felt like he had just asked where one might find a nice restaurant in Limerick during the potato famine. He tried to dismiss the rejections. The morning actually turned out just like he thought it would.

When Matt got home, his mother was busy working in the garden. She didn't hear the door squeak open.

"The garden looks beautiful, Mom," he said. His mother gasped, startled by his voice.

"I made a pitcher of iced tea," she said. "Care for a glass?" They sat on patio chairs, the late afternoon sun drawing a line of shadow on the ground between them.

"Have you heard from Karen?" The sun was sinking lower behind the roof of the house and the shadow line had moved to the far side of the patio.

"Lovely girl, Karen," his mother said. "I'm sure you'll find someone special soon."

Matt felt the weight of all his past decisions bearing down on him, fate in the shadows, laughing.

"I think I'll go for a drive. Why don't I bring back Chinese food from Nankin's?"

Matt drove to the beach and looked across the lake. A windsurfer was out on the waves, leaning against the breeze. The sun was setting behind the trees to the west, and the air felt cool. Matt looked over at the labyrinth of boulders surrounding the base of the observatory where he and Karen spent the night together after finals, wrapped in a wool blanket, their warm bodies entwined as they looked out across the lake and waited for the sun to appear on the horizon. He felt like a sentry keeping watch over a grave, like a part of him was transforming into a ghost, only capable of living in the past. For a moment, he wished he could have stayed under that blanket with Karen forever.

He got back in the Jeep and drove to Nankin's. It was dark inside, the only light coming from the glow of the blue paper-lanterns. Matt sat at the bar and drank a beer while he waited for the takeout order. He looked over at the table in the corner and remembered sitting there and breaking open fortune cookies with Karen just a few years ago. He could still hear her laughter as she told him to always add the words "in bed" to the end of every fortune. He took the cookie and broke it in half, pulled out the little piece of rice paper, and read, "A great abundance awaits you."

"See," she giggled, "It's true."

Matt picked up the heavy brown bag, steaming with the aroma of moo shu pork and pepper steak, and drove home. He opened the front door and set the bag on the kitchen counter. The house was quiet. He looked through the opening to the family room and saw his mother asleep on the couch.

Matt spent the next few days dropping off résumés at all the local airports. His father usually came home late, and the two of them would stay up watching old movies or *Honeymooners* reruns. The following weekend, Matt told his parents he wouldn't be going back to Florida. He'd gotten all he needed from his job there, and it was time to move on.

On Monday, his last chance was to drive out to a small airstrip on the western fringe of the metropolitan area called Sky Harbor. Off to the side of the county highway stood a billboard with a picture of a banana-yellow Piper Cub against the backdrop of blue sky with puffy white clouds. The sign said:

SKY HARBOR FLIGHT SCHOOL—GIVE YOUR DREAMS THE WINGS THEY DESERVE—NEXT LEFT.

There were a few hangars and a small office building. Matt pulled in and parked. He grabbed a résumé from the folder and hopped out of the Jeep. He walked toward the office just as a tall flight instructor with ruddy good looks was holding the door open for his student who was on the verge of tears. The flight instructor smiled as he placed his other hand on the woman's shoulder. He winked Matt's way and said, "Don't take it so hard, Mrs. Donovan. There's always powerboating." Matt walked in behind them. The instructor escorted his student to a small classroom and offered her a box of tissues. Matt walked up to the counter. The young woman seated at the desk saw the résumé in Matt's hand. "Looking for a job, are you?" Matt pursed his lips and nodded. "My name's Carol. I recognized the look. My husband flies for Delta. John!" she yelled. A portly man with thinning-gray hair and a quick smile leaned back in his chair and looked out from the doorway.

"This nice young man's lookin' for a job."

"Well, send him back."

"John Chambers," the man said, offering his hand. They shook hands with a firm grip. Then Matt sat down facing the small wooden desk, cluttered with papers and framed pictures of smiling children.

"Let's see what you've got." Matt handed over his résumé. "Twelve hundred hours total time, Commercial, Instrument, Certified Flight Instructor, BS degree. Looks like you're overqualified. All we teach here is primary, lots of first-timers. I just lost my senior instructor today. He's giving it up to go to law school. The job's yours if you want it. Pays ten bucks an hour." Matt was speechless. He wasn't expecting success. He shook his new boss's hand again and walked out of the office feeling faint.

Carol overheard the conversation and smiled at Matt as he walked out. "Sounds like it's your lucky day," she said as she handed him an application. John walked over to the vending machine and pulled some change out of his pocket.

"Care for a cup of coffee, Matt?"

"No, thank you, sir."

"Like to keep the quarter instead?" John chuckled to himself. Carol just shook her head. "He pulls that on someone every day," she smiled.

"Seems like a nice little flight school," Matt said. Just then, a loud bang came from behind the door to the adjacent hangar. The door opened, then slammed shut with full force. A short, wiry gray-haired man, whose face was red with broken blood vessels, stormed into the office.

"Dammit, John. Somebody stole my socket wrenches."

"Marty's in between students. I told him he could use them to change his plugs."

"That does it. I'm getting a lock," the man fumed as he went out to the parking lot and slammed the door behind him.

Carol leaned over and said in a soft whisper, "That's your other boss, Ray Baker. Most of the guys try to stay out of his way."

The weeks went by, and Matt started falling into a routine. He moved into a small apartment near the airport and enjoyed working with students again. He loved to see the shocked look on their faces when it came time for their first solo. After touch-and-go practice, Matt had them drop him off at the fuel pumps, make two touch-and-goes and a full stop landing, then taxi to the tie-down area and shut down. He'd be on the radio if they needed him. The apprehension on their faces was replaced with smiles of accomplishment as they taxied in. It wasn't a glamorous job, but it was honest work, a place to bide his time.

His mailbox was starting to fill with a steady stream of rejections. It was always the same: no openings. Matt tried to feel lucky about having any flying job at all, but it felt like his future was stuck in a holding pattern. Every day seemed the same. The replies in the mail were the same, and the nightly news was the same as well. It was now day 354 of the Iranian hostage crisis. Every attempt by President Carter to alleviate it had been a failure, and the election was just a few weeks away.

On Friday, Matt was just finishing up with his last student when John came up to him. "How'd you like to fly a charter this evening, Matt? Ronald Reagan is making a campaign stop in Peoria. All you have to do is fly this *Tribune* reporter down there, drop him off and fly home. Pays a hundred bucks."

The western horizon was turning as orange as a pumpkin as they leveled off at six thousand feet. The ground below was ablaze with the reds and yellows of fall. The farmland was quilted in squares of green and brown with patches of black earth from the recent harvest.

"What do you think his chances are?" Matt said over the roar of the engine. "I mean, he was a movie star. Are the voters really going to see him as a serious candidate?"

"I wouldn't underestimate him," the reporter said. "What Americans understand is wealth, power, and success. Right now, people aren't feeling like winners, and the voters will only put up with that for so long. Reagan understands that, just listen to him."

After landing, the ground controller instructed Matt to taxi to the far end of the general aviation ramp. Reagan's 727 sat parked on the tarmac in front of the main terminal building. Crowds of cheering supporters with signs saying *Reagan—The Time Is Now* were being kept behind barricades.

"I'll just get out here and walk over," the reporter said, shaking Matt's hand.

The night sky was filled with stars, and a big harvest-moon was rising in the east. Matt hadn't been alone in an airplane since he'd flown for Wally. It felt good to relax and enjoy the view without the distraction of passengers and students. He wished the flight was longer than an hour. After landing, Matt taxied to the tie-down area and secured the plane.

John gave him the key to the office and Matt noticed that all the lights were out except for a thin amber glow from under the door to the hangar. He put the key in the lock, opened the door and turned on the lights. The office was empty, but Matt thought he heard a muffled whimper coming from inside the hangar. He put his ear to the door but heard nothing. He turned the lights out, slowly turned the knob and pushed the door open a few inches. In the dark hangar stood a blue and white Cherokee up on jacks with its wheels and propeller removed. Dim yellow light shone from behind a curtained partition in the corner. Matt slowly moved behind the Cherokee and peered around the side of the curtain. His heart was thumping in his chest, and he could feel the sting of adrenaline rushing through his veins. It was Ray's room, where he kept a small twin-bed, a gray steel locker bought from an army-navy surplus store, and a small table and reading lamp with dust on its shade. On the floor by the bed was an empty bottle of Scotch whiskey. Backed against the corner, in the dark shadow on the bed, lay Carol. Tears streamed down her face as she kicked and clawed at Ray, who had her pinned down against the stained and moldy mattress. Ray was on top of her. Matt could see the sides of his lips pulled back into an angry smirk.

"You know you want it. Now shut up, you little tease," Ray growled. He had one hand over Carol's mouth and the other between her legs. Carol was screaming and kicking against the full force of a man who, through the booze, had nothing to lose. Ray was trying to hold her down with one hand and wrestle his jeans off at the same time. Matt could see scratch marks on Carol's arm, and her eyes were filled with terror and tears. Matt slowly moved back behind the nose of the plane and hid behind a red rollaway toolbox. He opened the toolbox, being careful not to make a sound. The darkness made it difficult to see what was inside. Matt reached in and felt a socket wrench, a pair of pliers, some safety wire, and a ball-peen hammer. Resting on the pull-out tray was a large chrome torque-wrench, not the ideal weapon to use against a man fortified by rage and Johnnie Walker. Matt looked around and saw a red fire extinguisher against the wall. He picked up the torque-wrench and tiptoed over and grabbed the fire extinguisher with his other hand. He crept around to the other side of the Cherokee, hidden by the half-closed curtain. Carol had a look of frantic desperation on her face, and Ray's voice sounded like he'd kill her if he didn't get his way. Matt slowly moved toward the curtain. He gently placed the torque-wrench on the hangar floor and pulled the safety pin from the trigger on the extinguisher bottle. He hoped the sound of his beating heart wouldn't betray him. Matt took a deep breath, grabbed the extinguisher with both hands and darted out from behind the curtain.

"Drop her, Ray!" he yelled as he aimed the nozzle and squeezed the trigger. Ray spun around just as a freezing blast of halon hit him in the face. He roared, let go of Carol and fell to the floor, gagging and shielding his bloodshot eyes with his hands. A look of wild terror shone on his face, like a caged animal gone berserk. He was coughing and wheezing as he recoiled and prepared to lunge at his attacker. Matt reached under the curtain and grabbed the waiting torque-wrench. Just as Ray was about to tackle him, Matt swung the wrench, with full force, in an arc that struck Ray in the ribs with the cracking sound of splintered wood. Ray roared out in pain as he collapsed on the floor and passed out, prostrate, like a tiger shot by a tranquilizer gun.

Matt leaned over the bed to help Carol. She clung to his shoulders as he held her and let her tears soak the front of his denim jacket. She was crying and coughing at the same time. Matt put his arm around Carol's waist and walked her to the office where he gently put her down on the brown leather sofa.

"Can you tell me your phone number?" he asked. "Is anyone home?" Matt handed her a cup of water from the cooler.

"My husband," she said. Matt dialed the number, and the voice on the line picked up after one ring. "I'll be right there," Carol's husband said when Matt told him what happened.

Matt dialed 911, then went back to see how Carol was doing. She was sitting against the end of the sofa with her legs together, waves of sobs overcoming her attempts to stop them. Soon, a rhythmic flash of red lights reflected off the office walls. Two police officers walked up the sidewalk. The officers came in and Matt told them where they could find Ray. They opened the door to the hangar with their sidearms drawn. Another officer came in and walked over.

"You just take it easy, ma'am," he said. "The paramedics will be here in a minute." Then the office door burst open, and Carol's husband ran over to her. Carol clung to him, her cries reduced to sniffles.

"Don't try to talk, honey. I'll kill that bastard; I swear I will."

"You let us take care of things, sir," the officer said. Then the paramedics came in. They dressed Carol's surface wounds, took her vital signs, then escorted Carol and her husband out to the waiting ambulance. Two police officers brought Ray in from the hangar. His hands were cuffed behind his back and the officers propped him up against the wall. He was moaning and mumbling and staring at the floor. One of the officers came over and started filling out his report. Matt recounted as much detail as he could remember. Then he was free to go.

It was after 10:00 p.m. when he arrived at his apartment. He opened the refrigerator and took out a cold beer. He sat in the dark bedroom, trying to blank his mind and erase the image of what just transpired. He turned on the small television opposite the bed. *Nightline* was reporting the hostage crisis in Iran. Matt flicked off the TV, downed the rest of his beer, and crawled into bed. Disturbing images of the hostages, Jorge Roca, Ferguson, Percy Watson, and now

Ray and Carol swirled in his mind. Life seemed like a grand conflict between predator and prey. The realization that tonight, at least, one bully lost the game gave Matt a moment of relief, and he rolled over and fell into a deep sleep.

He woke to the sound of knocking on the front door. John was standing outside. He looked like he'd been up all night.

"Our attorney called me at 5:00 a.m. He said you attacked Ray in the hangar last night."

"Come in," Matt said. John sat down in the small living room while Matt made a pot of coffee and told John everything that happened.

"Take the week off," John said. "We may have to close temporarily, possibly hire a new receptionist, sort things out. Don't worry about Ray. I'll take care of that. You rest up this week, and I'll be in touch."

Matt went for a swim at the Y then spent the rest of the day filling out more applications. At 5:00 p.m. the phone rang.

"Matt, it's Bruce Williams, Carol's husband."

"How is she, Bruce?"

"She's okay, physically, but emotionally she's still a bit shaky. We're going to see a therapist this week. She's still crying a lot."

"Let me know if there's anything I can do."

"Thanks. Listen, Matt, Carol told me what you did, as much as she could remember. I've called an attorney. He's going to need to take your deposition. You okay with that?"

"Sure."

"One more thing. I know how hard it is out there. Carol told me you're trying to get hired by a regional. Maybe I can help. Have you sent an application to Arkansas Airways?"

"I started alphabetically; they were one of my first rejections. Nobody's hiring."

"I used to fly for Arkansas Airways. They're based in Fayetteville. Carol worked in Customer Service. That's how we met. I'm still friends with George Harriet, the VP of Flight Operations. Let me send him a letter on your behalf. Can you read me your résumé over the phone?"

Bruce copied the details of Matt's résumé and told him he'd be in touch. Matt hung up the phone and felt a surge of relief. Maybe there was hope after all. He went over to his parents' house for dinner and told them everything that happened.

"Luck is the key," his father said. "You work hard, you do your best, then wait for Lady Luck to arrive. I've tried telling this to your mother many times."

"That poor girl," Matt's mom said. "I hope she's going to be alright. The police need to lock that bad man up, for a long time. What if he gets out and tries to hurt you, dear?"

"Don't worry, Mom. I don't think I'll be going back there, anyway."

The following week, Matt received a call from Janice Stevenson, George Harriet's personal secretary, inviting him down for a flight officer interview. His interview would be with Fred Blahdick, the chief pilot. A new anxiety welled up inside. Matt was hoping to see George Harriet for just a friendly conversation, a mere formality. Now, the possibility of rejection at the eleventh hour seemed real, almost expected.

He woke at 5:00 a.m. on Wednesday, showered, shaved, and put on a new shirt and tie. He placed the manila folder of résumés into a small attaché case and left for O'Hare.

He arrived at the boarding area where a bright green Braniff-727 was parked at the gate. Matt could see the array of colored annunciator lights on the flight engineer's panel. He felt flush with anticipation. When he boarded, he looked into the cockpit and saw the three crewmembers methodically going through their pre-flight setup and drinking coffee. Matt took a deep breath and smiled at the flight attendant as he went back and found his window-seat in coach. He closed his eyes and tried to relax. He tried to dismiss any thought that surfaced, to turn his mind into a blank sheet of paper, but it was a useless exercise. His mind was a static charge of worry. He wished the day was over and he was on his way home. When he opened his eyes, the big jet was throttling up and accelerating down the runway. With an imperceptible tug they were airborne, the miracle of flight revealed like a gift from God.

When they arrived in Kansas City, Matt made his way to the Arkansas Airways gate. "I have your boarding pass right here, Mr. Lavery," the young woman at the podium said.

Soon, he heard the snarling whine of the twin Garrett engines as the sleek red and white Metroliner came into view. The long fuselage pivoted in a 180-degree turn as the left engine was shut down and the plane came to a stop. The right engine shut down and the airstairs lowered as the first officer stepped out to unload the carry-on bags from the nose-compartment. An agent walked up to welcome the passengers and direct them into the terminal. Matt hoped he'd have a chance to talk with the pilots, to find out about Fred Blahdick and what to expect, but as soon as he boarded the plane, the first officer handed a copy of the weight and balance manifest to the agent and closed the door. The engines were winding up, and the cabin filled with a high-pitched roar.

On the hour-long flight, Matt looked down and saw the unfolding tapestry of the Ozarks, the bright sun shimmering on the lakes, the green-brown pastures, the hilltops with long rows of tin-roofed chicken houses, small towns, and country roads. A jolt of apprehension tightened in his chest as the plane started its descent. Everything was suspended up at cruise, like the hypnotic noise of an interstate road trip. But the spell was broken, and Matt realized he'd soon be under the gun.

The green hilltops rising up, the clunk of the landing gear dropping in place, and the drone of the propellers going to flat pitch all combined to challenge Matt's mood. The plane touched down with an abrupt thud, and the cabin filled with the snarling whine of the propellers reversing thrust. A strange quiet displaced the roar of decibels on speed as the engines shut down and the first officer climbed out of the cockpit and opened the door. Matt heard her warm, mellifluous drawl before he saw her.

"Welcome to Fayetteville, y'all. Watch yer step. Carry-ons by the nose, checked bags'll be inside in a minute, God willing. Watch yer head now." Matt was last to deplane. As he picked up his attaché case, he saw that the woman was wearing bib overalls and a pair of fluffy gray bedroom slippers. She had short red hair and pale blue eyes. In one hand she held a clipboard, in the other, a stick or riding crop. The first officer came down the airstairs, and Matt turned and introduced himself.

"Matt Lavery," he said, extending his hand.

"Buzz Ballard," the young man said with a grin.

"I'm here for a pilot interview with Fred Blahdick. Can you give me any pointers?"

Buzz leaned up toward the cockpit and yelled, "T-Ball, come on down." The captain appeared, carrying a black leather flight bag. He looked the same age as Buzz. His blond hair blew in the breeze and his smile spanned the full continent of his face. "Looks like we're hiring again," Buzz said. "This guy's got an interview with The Dick."

"Thomas Ball," the captain said, shaking Matt's hand. "Nice to meet you."

"I just came down from Chicago. Can you give me any pointers?"

"Let him do most of the talking, but don't let him trick you," T-Ball said.

"And don't kiss his ass," Buzz said. "We all let him think he's our boss." T-Ball and Buzz laughed and directed Matt down the far end of the ramp to a white barnlike hangar with red painted letters that said, "Drake Field, Fayetteville, Arkansas, Elevation 1251 Feet." Matt forced a smile and picked up his attaché case and travel bag. As he started walking toward the terminal, he saw the agent with the bib overalls walk over to a red pickup truck. In the truck were two young men wearing denim jackets and baseball caps. Their eyes were closed. The woman began beating her stick on the pickup as she yelled, "Waltay, Jimmy O, you git yer lazy butts out of that truck, this instant. The pit's still full on 501, and 445's due to land in five minutes. Now git!" The door opened, and one of the startled men clambered out and shuffled toward the back of the Metro as the other started up the truck and drove to the rear of the plane.

Matt followed the sidewalk that paralleled the flight line up to the hangar. As he opened the door, he heard the muffled sounds of angry shouts coming from behind an office window. Next to the doorframe was a sign that said, "Frederick C. Blahdick–Chief Pilot." Matt looked through the window and saw a pilot in uniform, sitting across the desk from a large man with short black hair and thick veins that protruded above the neckline of a red polo shirt.

"The hotel manager said their TV reception was down for two hours," he shouted. "One of the guests saw you do it. That's a two-week suspension without pay, Captain. What the hell possessed you to climb that fence and pull a prank like that?"

"I needed some time off."

"Two weeks!" Blahdick shouted. "I ought to fire you right now."

Matt felt the adrenaline race through his veins. His heart was pounding, and his face felt flushed. Just my luck, he thought. A lion's den. He walked across the reception area where a secretary sat behind a desk. "May I help you?" she asked.

"I'm here for a pilot interview with Captain Blahdick."

"Nice to meet you, Matt. I'm Janice Stevenson. We spoke on the phone. I'll just tell him you're here. How was the trip down?" she asked as she got up and walked over to Blahdick's door.

"Fine," Matt said, hoping his voice wouldn't crack.

"Now get out of my office, Winger. One more stunt and you're out of here, you hear me, mister?" Matt thought he saw the office window vibrate. The pilot came out of the office as Janice stood by the door.

"He's all yours, Janice," Captain Winger said with a big grin on his face. Janice just shook her head.

"Mark, this is Matt Lavery. He's just come down from Chicago to interview for a flight officer position."

"Didn't take him long to hire my replacement." Winger laughed as he shook Matt's hand. "You're in luck," Mark said. "Next to me, you're going to seem like Charles Lindbergh."

Mark Winger walked out the door, and Janice Stevenson went in to tell Captain Blahdick that Matt was waiting to see him.

"You can go in now," Janice said.

Matt took a deep breath, straightened his posture, and walked into Blahdick's office.

"Fred Blahdick. Have a seat." They shook hands, then Matt sat in the wooden chair opposite Blahdick's desk. The chair was still warm. "Let me just glance at your résumé." Matt handed over the single sheet of paper as Blahdick put on his reading glasses and leaned back in his chair. Matt looked around the office. On the walls hung photographs of Fred Blahdick: in the cockpit of a Metroliner; in a red Corvette; in full camouflage, holding a high-powered rifle and posing behind a dead deer, a trickle of blood streaming from its mouth; with his two young children on the beach by a palm tree with Mrs. Blahdick, Matt presumed. She looked tired.

"No turbine-time?" Blahdick asked.

"No, sir."

"How well do you know Bruce Williams?" Blahdick asked. Matt felt baited, like Blahdick was giving him the rope to hang himself. He had no idea what was in the letter from Bruce.

"I hardly know him at all," Matt said. Blahdick nodded slightly.

"Tell me," Blahdick said, "what is the role of a first officer?"

"To support the captain at all times," Matt volleyed back.

"Suppose you meet your captain, first flight of the day, and you smell alcohol on his breath. What would you do?" Matt wondered how many questions it would take before Blahdick had him cornered. Checkmate.

"I'd take him aside and ask if he'd been drinking," Matt replied, knowing his answer wouldn't suffice.

"Like I said, you smell alcohol on his breath, therefore he's been drinking." A frown was starting to form on Blahdick's face.

"I couldn't fly with him, period. I'd tell him to call in sick."

"And would you call me and tell me about it?" Blahdick asked.

"I'm not sure, sir. I think, if it was a first offense, I'd try to deal with it one-on-one, but I'd let him know if it happened again, I'd have no choice but to bring it to your attention."

"Are you running for Congress next?" Matt couldn't tell if it was a joke or an insult. Blahdick asked a few more general, get-acquainted questions. He appeared to be studying Matt's résumé, an artificial look of exaggerated contemplation on his face, enjoying the suspense he'd created. Then he looked over the top of his reading glasses and said, "I need four pilots to start after the first of January. Pays $10,000 a year. I'm prepared to offer you a job."

"I'll take it," Matt said, trying to contain himself.

"Arkansas's a nice place, sort of a best-kept secret. I think you'll like it here. Welcome aboard," Blahdick said as he reached over to shake Matt's hand. "Mrs. Stevenson will be sending you a confirmation letter with further details."

"Thank you, sir. I really appreciate this."

"Oh, one more thing," Blahdick said. "You have reason to suspect that any pilot's been drinking inside of the twelve-hour limit, or he's obviously impaired, I want to know about it immediately, understand?"

"Yes, sir," Matt said as he stood and walked out the doorway. Janice Stevenson came up to him with a smile on her face. "Congratulations, Matt. I checked your flight to Kansas City. It's running on time. Would you like me to give you a lift down to the terminal?"

"No, thank you. I'll just walk."

Matt picked up his attaché case and travel bag and walked out of the office and down the flight line to the terminal. He could barely feel his feet on the pavement. He gazed out at the green rolling hills, blue sky, and white clapboard hangar. He walked inside the terminal and approached the Arkansas Airways ticket counter where the young woman with bib overalls was standing.

"Well?" she asked.

"Excuse me?" Matt said.

"Didcha git the job?" Matt let the smile that was bubbling up inside him burst.

"Captain Blahdick hired me on the spot." The words tasted like chocolate in his mouth.

"Git out. Maggie, come out and meet the new meat," she yelled behind her. "It looks like it's yer lucky day. My name's Jackie Anderson."

"Matt Lavery," he said, shaking her hand.

The other agent came out from the back room. She was tall with long brown hair. She wore a dark blue suit with a white shirt and maroon silk cravat around her neck. "Maggie Pryor," she said, shaking Matt's hand. "Nice to meet cha. You have about thirty minutes before we start boarding. There's a coffee shop and magazine stand down yonder. Welcome aboard. Hope you enjoy it."

Matt picked up his attaché case and walked out the front door of the terminal. He gazed transfixed at the way the ground rose up like green ocean waves under the blue sky. The parking lot in the terminal was filled with cars with license plates that said, *Arkansas, Land of Opportunity*.

Destiny, with all its surprises, decided to deposit him on this land. It was as if the metabolism of fate required its own form of respiration, its own indiscriminate give-and-take with each breath. And if fate finally decided to blow some good fortune his way, he'd be packed and ready for the ride. Just like his father always said, "You work hard, you do your best, then wait for Lady Luck to arrive."

CHAPTER THREE

"Here's to you and your new job," Matt's father said as he raised his glass of Cold Duck. They all clinked their glasses together and sipped the pale pink effervescence.

"We all have so much to be thankful for," Matt's mother said as his father carved the turkey. The table was covered with a white linen cloth. Two silver candelabras with white candles flickered amber light off the cool beads on the water glasses. The table was crowded with serving bowls filled with steaming mashed potatoes, candied yams, green peas with a yellow pat of butter, warm spongelike stuffing with cut celery, a ceramic serving boat filled with brown gravy, green beans with slivered almonds, a wooden salad bowl filled with green spinach, bright red tomatoes, pungent onions, sliced cucumbers drenched in virgin olive oil, and a wicker basket with steaming dinner rolls tucked inside a red and white checked napkin.

"Everything looks delicious, Mom."

"Maybe things will start to turn around, what with the election behind us and all," Matt's father said. "If the Russians have any sense, they'll think twice about playing poker with Reagan. And those hostages, you mark my word, they'll all be coming home soon."

"I feel sorry for President Carter," Matt's mother said. "He tried so hard."

"Never fault a man for trying," Matt's father said, "but this country needs a change. Lot's going to be changing for you, son." Matt nodded and took a sip of wine.

"You're so quiet, dear. Is everything alright?"

"I'm fine, Mom, just thinking about Arkansas."

Matt had been thinking about his new job and new life ever since he got home from his interview. He kept the Braniff boarding pass on his nightstand as proof that it wasn't all just a dream. He felt pangs of anxiety when the phone rang, expecting a call from Janice Stevenson saying she was sorry, but their plans had changed. Bad luck was a hard habit to break. It seemed odd that he had so much time on his hands. No need to run résumés or work the phone, no job to go to. But what Matt was really thinking about at the table was Karen.

He remembered the Thanksgiving just a few years ago. They first celebrated with her parents and seven brothers and sisters, then the second time around with Matt's parents. After pumpkin pie and ice cream, they excused themselves and drove to Karen's apartment on Medille Street in the city. They parked under the streetlamp. A cold wind was blowing, and clusters of leaves skittered and swirled on the sidewalk as they walked up to Karen's building. The front door was made of heavy oak, and the foyer smelled musty, with a trace of varnish and mothballs. An old chandelier with small round bulbs hung from the ceiling, casting an amber glow. They climbed the creaking wooden staircase to the third floor. Karen took out the iron key from her purse and opened the two deadbolts and the door lock. It was cold inside. The lamplight from the street below made shadows of the tree branches that quivered and swayed across the ceiling. On the wall by Karen's desk hung a life-size poster of a human skeleton. Late one night, some months before, the clanking of the radiator woke Matt, and he saw the ghostly image suspended in the dark, its sinister skull smiling at him, as if it was saying, "Just wait buddy, your time is coming." With the intention of disarming the power the spook had over him, Matt decided to give it a name.

"How's it hanging, Johnson?" Matt said as Karen switched on the small reading lamp on the end-table and cranked up the knob on the radiator. "I'll start the teakettle," she said. "Want some?" Matt nodded and walked over to the stereo. Karen had a small collection of records: Carole King, Carly Simon, James Taylor, the Beatles, Seals and Crofts, and her favorite, Harry Chapin. They had seen him together in college at a sold-out concert. Matt used to sing Chapin's song "Taxi" to Karen—*You see, she was going to be an actress, and I was going to learn to fly, she took off to find the footlights, and I took off to find the sky*—except he'd substitute the word actress for doctor. Matt pulled out Stevie Wonder's *Inner Visions* album and placed it on the turntable. He looked toward the kitchen, still dark except for the blue glow from the gas flames under the kettle. The soft, warm light silhouetted Karen's high cheekbones, her long brown hair draped over her shoulders and down the back of her gray wool coat. Matt got up and walked into the kitchen as Karen reached for two teacups in the cabinet overhead. He stood behind her, reached around her waist and held her, resting his head on her shoulder.

"I like it in the dark," he said. Karen turned around, and they wrapped their arms around each other.

"I don't think I could eat another bite," she laughed. "Make yourself at home. I'll just slip into something more comfortable."

While Karen prepared herself in the bathroom, Matt looked around her apartment. He leaned down and tilted his head at the titles of the books on her shelves: *Clinically Oriented Anatomy* by Keith L. Moore, *The Pharmacological Basis of Therapeutics* by Goodman and Gilman, *Basic Pathology* by Robbins and Angell, *Anna Karenina* by Leo Tolstoy, *Jonathan Livingston Seagull* by Richard Bach, *The Little Prince* by Antoine de Saint-Exupéry (a gift from Matt), *The Joy of Sex* by Alex Comfort (another gift from Matt), and *The Bible*.

Matt felt small. He went into the bedroom, placed his teacup on the nightstand, took off his shoes and lit a candle. He pulled back the down comforter and propped himself up against the pillows. Stevie Wonder was singing "All in Love Is Fair" and Matt could hear Karen brushing her teeth from behind the closed bathroom door. He started running the numbers in his head, trying to figure out how much of a man's life would be spent waiting for his wife to finally appear. Twice a week, times forty-five minutes, times fifty-two weeks per year, times fifty years. Then the light went out in the bathroom and Karen appeared before him. She was barefoot and wore a short black silk negligee. Matt got up from the bed and reached for her.

"You're still dressed, Lavery," she giggled as she unfastened his belt buckle with one hand and pushed him back down onto the bed with the other. "I'm freezing," she shivered as she jumped in beside him and worked the buttons on his shirt. Matt pulled the comforter close around them and held her tight. "That feels nice," she said as Matt reached down and started caressing her…

"Breast or thigh, dear?" Matt's mother's voice startled him as he blinked the image of the flickering candle from his gaze and saw the platter of sumptuous turkey meat steaming before him.

"I really thought Carter was going to pull something out of his hat at the eleventh hour," his father said.

"The October surprise, you mean?"

"That's right. Do the Iranians really think they're going to get something from Reagan in return? It makes no sense."

"Let's think of something nice to talk about, shall we?" Matt's mother said.

After dinner, Matt and his father did the dishes while Matt's mother cut the apple pie and made a pot of coffee.

"Why don't we get up early and go over the Jeep together. I brought home some plugs and points, an air filter and fan belts. Let's check the brakes, too. It's got to be close to six hundred miles down there."

It was still dark when Matt came down to the kitchen and found his father frying bacon in a pan. Matt sat down and poured a cup of coffee. His father started frying eggs in another pan. Then he brought the food to the table, sat down, and Matt poured him a coffee. Then Matt's father took a piece of toast and started spreading a thick pat of butter over it. Matt looked at it and frowned.

"How's your cholesterol, Dad?" he said. His father just laughed.

"Don't you worry about me, son. I'm as spry as a cat. You mark my word. My cardiologist is probably just starting kindergarten." He patted Matt on the back.

Matt wished he could be as carefree as his father. There was always so much to worry about. How could you not take it seriously?

After Thanksgiving, Matt fell into an early morning routine. He'd wake at 5:30 a.m. to the news from the clock radio, then do fifty push-ups and sit-ups and a series of stretches. He'd pull on jeans and a blue sweatshirt, pick up his swim bag and drive to the Palladium for the 6:00 a.m. lap swim. It was the old routine from his swim team days. The hard, physical exercise, the hypnotic effect of stroking and breathing, of clicking off the laps, was a skill that kept him sane and fit. Sometimes, Matt would take a problem into the pool with him. The aquatic myopia and the hypnotic stroking allowed his focus to intensify, blocking out all distraction, and he'd emerge from the water with a clear solution. It was one of the few sure things.

It was December 9. Matt woke up on schedule and dropped to the floor to start his routine. Then he heard it: John Lennon was dead. The news entered his ears, hit his brain, and crashed into a brick wall. Shot right outside his home, for no apparent reason. There was always hope that the Beatles would get back together. Now that would never happen. Matt held his head in his hands and rubbed his temples. Lennon was an artist, a pacifist. JFK, RFK, MLK, now JWL. Blessed are the peacemakers, for they shall all die young, Matt thought. He sat on the side of the bed in the dark. Maybe if he went back to sleep, he'd wake up and realize it was just a bad dream. But the radio was loud and clear. Thousands of mourning fans were gathered outside the Dakota with flowers. There was no escaping it.

Matt didn't have the energy to swim, but he forced himself up. The routine would be a necessary flotation device. He put on his sweats, picked up the swim bag, left the quiet house and went out into the cold, dark morning.

It took fifty laps before he could bring himself to leave the water. Everyone in the locker room was talking about it. Matt drove home and opened the kitchen door. His mom was frying ham. There was a big pile of scrambled eggs in a serving bowl, fresh blueberry muffins and a pot of coffee.

"I don't know what this world is coming to," she said, shaking her head.

"It's such a shame," Matt said. "John Lennon was only forty years old. I planned on going downtown today but now I don't feel like it."

"Why don't you, dear. Maybe seeing the decorations will help get your mind off it."

Matt drove into Wilmette and parked the Jeep by the Linden Street train station. He walked into the old station and smelled the familiar scent of tar, oil-based paint, and newspapers. He bought a *Tribune* from Leo. Leo had always been there, as far back as Matt could remember. He walked with a stoop now, his tired eyes shadowed under bushy brows, the hair on his balding head turned to gray. He wore a faded navy-blue *Tribune* apron around his waist. Leo was just shaking his head, talking in his thick Eastern European accent. "So sad, so sad," he kept saying. "What with this world? I don't know." Matt knew that under the sleeve of Leo's jacket, tattooed into his forearm in dark blue dye, was an identification number from long ago. Leo knew what he was talking about.

The train went into a dark tunnel. The screeching of metal-on-metal and the blue flash of sparks reflecting off the window helped dull Matt's senses. He got out and climbed the steps into the light of State Street where he was met by the happy façade of Christmas. Parents brought their little bundles of joy to gaze at the elves and reindeer in the windows of Field's and Carson's. The children had smiles on their faces, and Santa Claus rang the Salvation Army bell on every corner. He walked into Field's and bought a white cashmere scarf with matching mittens for his mom. Then he walked east to Michigan Avenue, turned left, and crossed over the Chicago River. A cellophane layer of ice was forming around the pylons in the dark green water. Matt passed the white Wrigley Building and stopped where a group of people were huddled around a store window. A television was set up in the window, and the news was all about John Lennon. Someone had even committed suicide upon hearing the news. Matt felt sick inside. Death is not a solitary event, he thought. Grief rises up like a tsunami, drawing so many people into its undertow.

At the corner of Michigan and Erie, Matt looked to the west and saw the sign hanging from the corner of Chez Paul. It looked like a big black coach lantern with a bright white background and elegant black brushstroke letters. He saved for a whole year to be able to take Karen there for Christmas. The taxi dropped them off by the long white canopy that led from the curb of Rush Street, over the sidewalk and up the red carpeted steps to the heavy wooden door. Matt held the door open for Karen as they walked inside. The air was warm and filled with the aroma of garlic frying in a pan of butter, the faint sounds of a string quartet in the distance. Matt helped Karen with her coat and walked up to the wooden podium where they were greeted by the maître d' who was wearing a black tuxedo and starched white shirt. Matt felt like the ambassador to France as he announced that they had a seven o'clock dinner reservation.

"Very good, Mr. Lavery. Right this way, please."

Karen put her arm around Matt as they strolled into the dining room, past Impressionist oil paintings. As the maître d' pulled the chair out for Karen, she looked up and said, "Oh, that fireplace is just stunning."

"Yes," the maître d' said. "This building was constructed in 1885, seven years after the Great Chicago Fire. It was originally the Ambassador to Italy's private manor. That mantle was given to him by the king of Italy."

"I didn't know there was a king of Italy," Matt said.

"Neither did I," Karen said, covering for him.

In a few minutes, the sommelier brought out a silver bucket filled with ice and set it by the table. They ordered a 1974 Puligny-Montrachet, which the sommelier held in front of them before popping the cork with a few quick twists. He then poured a small amount of the pale, straw-colored wine into a glass and handed it to Matt. He took a sip, then handed the glass to Karen and she took a taste too. "It's very nice," she said.

They ordered Caesar salad for two, made right at the table. "You can have my anchovies," Karen said. After onion soup, served in hot ceramic bowls with melted Gruyère cheese baked brown on top and dripping over the rim, Karen ordered the Dover Sole with Béarnaise sauce and sautéed spinach, and Matt ordered the Shrimps Papa Paul with rice and baby carrots in an herbed butter sauce.

After dinner, the waiter wheeled out a cart with a silver tray full of chocolate mousse, profiteroles with vanilla ice cream inside a puff pastry with hot-chocolate sauce on top, Crêpes Suzette, cherries jubilee and crème caramel. Karen ordered the Crêpes Suzette. Matt ordered the cherries jubilee, soaked in brandy, which the waiter lit with the flick of a butane lighter. Blue flames shot up from the copper pan, and Matt felt the heat warm his face.

"Look, it's snowing outside," Karen said. There was a framed window with its drapes drawn to the side that looked out on Rush Street. A silhouette of white snowflakes flittered and danced against the black background. "Let's do this every Christmas," she said as she leaned over and kissed Matt on the lips. They got up to leave, and Matt helped Karen put on her gray wool coat and tied the scarf around her neck.

"I could get used to this," she said. He opened the heavy wooden door with the brass hardware. The snow was coming down harder, making the air dense and muffling out the sounds of the city. It was quiet, except for the clip-clopping of horses' hooves. Matt and Karen looked out from under the white canopy and saw the shiny ivory-colored carriage with spoke wheels. The coachman was in a black cape and top-hat perched above and behind the brown draft horse, which had a bright red bow tied around its mane. The carriage came to a stop as Matt signaled with a raised hand. The coachman stepped down and opened the carriage door, and Matt held Karen's hand as she climbed in. Matt gave the horse a gentle stroke on its muzzle, then climbed in. They sat huddled together under an old wool blanket. The driver made a clicking sound between his tongue and cheek and the horse started clip-clopping along. The carriage gently lurched forward, and Matt and

Karen felt the rhythmic rumble of the hard wheels on the pavement. They leaned to the side and gazed through the glass window. The snow was falling harder as they turned down Michigan Avenue. They craned their necks and saw the old Water Tower, candy-caned in a wide red ribbon, and the green and red lights at the top of the Hancock Building. Karen spread the blanket around them, and Matt could feel the heat radiating from the tangent of their bodies as he pulled her close and kissed her on the lips. Then he saw a tear about to lose its grip and fall down her cheek. "What's the matter?"

"Nothing," Karen said. "Let's just go back to my place."

You could have had her and you chose not to, now stop living in the past, he thought as he ghosted by the old Water Tower. Your mind's playing that cheap trick again, whitewashing over the bad times. Your little voice was whispering loud and clear for two years, and you finally did something about it, or rather she finally did something about it. It was for the best. Besides, would she have been willing to pack it all up right now and move to Fayetteville, Arkansas? Would you have been willing to give it all up to stay? You were right all along, so embrace your new deck of cards, he admonished himself.

On New Year's Eve his mother opened a bottle of Korbel Brut and they toasted the new year. On the stroke of midnight, Matt's father went out and blew the horn on the '79 Coupe de Ville he'd been driving for the last month. It wasn't unusual to see a different car in the driveway. The car belonged to Pinball Ray, one of his cronies down at Strum's Tavern. He was doing some work for Pinball; at least that's what he told Matt's mom when she asked about the Buick. It took another month before his father admitted that he bought the car from Pinball. Better to beg forgiveness than ask permission. "Another credit union loan?" his mother cried. "We'll never get out of debt." Matt's father slept on the couch in the family room for the next two weeks—but he kept the car.

On January 2, Matt held his breath as he dialed Janice Stevenson's phone number. "No, our plans haven't changed, Matt. Next Monday at 8:00 a.m. Tom Tomlinson will be your instructor. Did you receive the flight manual and other information I sent? Good, then we'll see you next week." He hung up the phone with relief.

On Friday, Matt finished packing the Jeep. He was amazed to see that the sum of his life's possessions could fit into the little CJ-5. Two suitcases of clothes, cassette player, camera with photo gear, the swim bag, and a box of books.

On Saturday, his parents got up early with him. After breakfast, Matt's father took him aside.

"Got any tools in the Jeep?"

"Just the jack and a lug wrench."

"I thought so." Matt's father handed him a cardboard box filled with the finest Snap-on sockets and Craftsman tools, a can of WD-40, duct tape, electrician's tape, wire strippers, a voltmeter, and a pair of jumper cables. Matt carried the last box outside. His mother came out, wrapped in her wool coat. "Well, this is it," Matt said. He hugged his mom, shook his father's hand, opened the canvas door, and climbed in. As he pulled away, he glanced in the big rear-view mirror and saw his father put his arm around his mother's waist as they walked back to the house. I wonder where he'll be sleeping tonight, Matt thought as he passed by the old mailbox, turned right by the hill, and rounded the bend, heading for I-94 South.

CHAPTER FOUR

A cold draft was coming through the gap in the canvas door as Matt headed south. The dark gray buildings of the Chicago skyline were barely visible. The overcast hung low and heavy, blanketing the city under a dirty sheet of clouds. Matt reached behind him and pulled the blue down sleeping bag from its nylon sack and spread it over his legs. He turned south on I-55 and opened a thermos of coffee. Steam swirled up and fogged the windshield. Matt drank the coffee and felt its warmth under the covers. He felt the rhythm of the highway lull him into a state of meditation. It was the Zen of the highway again.

The cornfields were frosted over, locked under a shiny porcelain glaze, and the ceiling was starting to lift, revealing patches of pale blue sky. Matt turned on the radio. The Marshall Tucker Band was singing, "Take the Highway." He wondered what force was behind that random ability of the radio to defy coincidence and target a single listener. After he and Karen broke up, the radio sang to him and him alone for days at a time.

He'd been on the road for ten hours as he headed south on Highway 71 and passed through Bentonville, Rogers, and Springdale. As Matt entered Fayetteville, the sky was thick with a low, dark overcast. By 4:30 p.m. it was completely dark. Highway 71 turned into College Avenue with rows of strip malls, restaurants, and motels. He turned right on Dickson Street and coasted past the post office and Collier's Drugstore. He was stiff and tired as he parked the Jeep outside a pool hall and climbed out. The air was cold and damp, and a mist of freezing rain formed a thin glaze on the street. Matt pulled the collar of his denim jacket close around his neck as he walked down the sidewalk. He looked in the window of the Whitewater Tavern and saw a long mahogany bar with large mirrors reflecting bottles of amber liquor and red wine. A young woman with short red hair and a long white apron around her waist was drawing frosty, foaming pints from the taps. Matt opened the door and felt the warm air, thick with the aroma of onions and cigarette smoke. The accent of the overlapping conversations confirmed that he was not in Chicago anymore. He pulled up to the bar, sat on a stool and looked up. Painted on the mirror behind the bar was a large red wild boar, charging, with a fierce look in its eyes, a snarl revealing white teeth with large, upturned tusks and the words "Hog Heaven" underneath. The bartender came over and said, "What can I getcha?"

"Just a draft," Matt said. "What do you recommend?"

"Hog's Breath lager," she said. "Make it right here." The woman smiled at Matt as she placed a frosted pint under the tap and drew the cold, foaming amber until it rose up and spilled over the sides. She placed the cold beer on a coaster in front of him and said, "So where're ya from?"

"Chicago."

"I knew a Yankee once," she smiled. "Ya just passin' through?"

"No, I'm here to stay, for a while at least. I'll be flying for Arkansas Airways."

"You a pilot?" she asked. Matt nodded. "For *Scareways?*" Matt nodded again, unsure of what he was acknowledging. "Then ya better drink up and let me buy ya the next one," she said, retreating to the far end of the bar to take another order.

A few minutes later, Matt's glass was empty, and the woman came back with another overflowing pint. "Name's Holly, Holly Branson," she said, wiping her hands on her apron and extending her hand.

"Matt Lavery. Nice to meet you," he said as they shook hands. "So, what can you tell me about Scareways?" he asked, trying to sound nonchalant.

"Well, they haven't killed anyone yet, not that I'm aware of. You must be very brave."

"Can you recommend a cheap motel?" he said. "I just need a place to crash for a few nights."

"The Thunderbird up on College Avenue is pretty cheap. Some people say it's a flea-bag, but I haven't stayed there since prom night," she winked.

"Thanks," Matt said. "We start ground-school on Monday. Maybe I'll see you around." He hopped off the bar-stool and waved goodbye.

"Well, you know where to find me," she said, and disappeared to the far end of the bar.

Matt felt the effects of the long drive and the beers weighing him down as he drove up to the front door of the Thunderbird and checked in. He parked outside his room and started unloading. He opened the door and pushed himself in against the warm, stale air, laced with the smell of carpet deodorant and disinfectant. He tore off his clothes, turned out the light, put a pillow over his head and slept for eight hours.

In the morning, a dim gray light was working its way into the room. Matt got up and opened the curtains. The Jeep was veiled in a thick, slate-colored fog. He showered, dressed, put on his denim jacket, grabbed his camera bag, and locked the door behind him.

He decided to drive around town to get his bearings. He drove down College Avenue, turned right on Dickson Street toward the university, then turned right on Arkansas Avenue past Old Main, the stately university building with its twin towers obscured by fog. He turned right on Maple Street and right on West Avenue, then left on Mountain Street and drove around the square. The Old Post Office, now a restaurant and night-club, sat in the middle of the square, surrounded by the First National Bank, Campbell Bell Department Store, Hugo's Underground Bar and Grill, and various office buildings. He ate a breakfast of country ham and eggs with grits and coffee at the Old Town Café, then drove south on Highway 71 past the outskirts of town. He passed the auto parts store, Big Al's Pawn Shop, the Trailways bus depot and Bypass Liquor as he came over the top of a gentle hill and saw the runway stretched out before him. The ceiling was ragged and the dark hills surrounding the airport were partially hidden by fog. Matt parked by the tall, girded steel tower supporting the rotating beacon. He could barely see the alternating green and white lights swirling in the mist.

Matt left the airport, confident of the morning route, and drove back to Dickson Street and parked. He walked down the sidewalk, past the Whitewater Tavern, the university bookstore, a laundromat, movie theater, old train depot and George's Bar and Grill.

The ceiling was starting to lift, and the gray of morning was filling in with color. Matt hopped back in the Jeep and drove east on Dickson Street. The street sloped upward as he crossed College Avenue and headed up to Mount Sequoyah He followed the curve of Skyline Drive and stopped near the summit, by a large white cross mounted on a stone foundation. The air was cold and damp as he grabbed his camera and hopped out. There was a clearing next to the cross that looked down on the town with the university and the low-lying hills beyond. Old Main was just visible through the mist. He climbed up on the front bumper of the Jeep, raised his camera, focused the lens, and heard the solid click of the shutter as he took the shot.

He got back in the Jeep and studied the map of northwest Arkansas. He drove down from the summit, headed west on Highway 16, and followed the S-turns out to Lake Wedington. The sides of the road were a mangled mass of gnarled kudzu, the vines strangling the trees and spreading out along the branches. Kudzu, indigenous to Japan, was used by the Civilian Conservation Corps back in the thirties to help control soil erosion. But now with over five million acres of the stuff, the trick was figuring out a way to get rid of it. The joke in the South was that you had to close your windows before going to bed otherwise you'd wake up with kudzu inside.

Off to the left, behind the trees, was Lake Wedington, its small beach and swimming area deserted. Picnic tables and campgrounds sat vacant, awaiting the thaw of spring.

Driving back to town, he crossed Leverett Avenue, turned right on Park Street, and saw the Olympic-size pool at Wilson Park, its water drained, clumps of soggy brown oak leaves gathered at the bottom.

Matt drove north on Highway 71 and followed the signs to Beaver Lake. He came to Horseshoe Bend, parked, and walked down to the water's edge. He stood on a limestone slab and looked across the lake to the opposite shoreline, dark with pine trees. A great blue heron flew past a few feet above the waves, head held resolute in front of its long black garden-hose neck, its graceful six-foot wingspan holding its blue-black plumage and trailing its long skinny legs behind. Matt grabbed the camera and tried to focus, but the bird was gone as quickly as it appeared.

He drove back to the highway and turned south toward Fayetteville. He ate a late lunch at Wyatt's Cafeteria then drove back to the Thunderbird, studied his flight manual, and went to bed.

From the depths of sleep, Matt dreamed he was still flying for Wally. It was just another routine charter, Wally assured him. He shouldn't worry about the abandoned dirt road he was to land on. He came in low, passed over the masts of the fishing smacks anchored in the clear blue water, dropped over the row of royal palms, and landed on the flat dirt road. He came to a stop, shut down the engines, looked around and saw the browns and greens of a lush island, awash in paradise. He climbed out onto the wing and saw distant headlights from an approaching car. As it got closer, Matt saw that it was a Jeep just like his. In fact, it was his very Jeep, with the same dent in the front right fender. The top was off, and a woman was in the driver's seat. Her skin was dark, and her long brown hair was blown back by the wind. She stopped in front of the wing and looked at him with tears in her eyes. As she held out her arms, Matt knew that it was Karen. Just then, the alarm clock blared and he woke up, dazed and disoriented.

CHAPTER FIVE

"Good morning, Matt. Help yourself to coffee," Janice said. Two other men were seated on the sofa. "This is Bob Grayson and Pete Sutherland." They all shook hands, then Matt poured a cup and sat down. "Where're you guys from?"

"Lafayette, Indiana," Bob said. "I've been flying canceled checks in a 402 for about a year."

"I'm from Macon," Pete said. "Been flyin' night-freight in a Twin Beech. How about you?"

"Chicago, just flight instructing. Before that, charters in a 310 down in South Florida."

"Did they go out of business?" Bob asked.

"No, they're still around. Things were just getting a bit too hot to handle."

"Tell me about it," Pete said. "I'm lucky to be alive. My boss bought all our equipment from the boneyards, real flying carcasses. He was too cheap to hire a licensed mechanic, tried to do all the maintenance himself. We had engine fires, electrical fires, gear problems, you name it. The Feds are going to nail him one of these days."

"Sounds pretty typical," Matt said, shaking his head.

Then the door opened, and a tall man with black hair, graying at the sides, walked in.

"Ah, the new victims," he said, shaking everyone's hand. "Tom Tomlinson. Nice to meet y'all. Morning, Janice."

"Morning, Tom. Everyone's here except Andy McShane. He called and said he couldn't get his car started. I'll just send him down to the terminal when he gets here."

"Everyone top off your coffees and follow me," Tom said. "We haven't had a class of new hires in over a year, so you'll have to bear with me. We're converting our old classroom into an office, so we'll have to move down to the main terminal. There's a room behind reservations we can use."

Everyone filed out of the building and followed Tom down the flight line. The sky was deep blue, and the morning sun glared over the green hills to the east. The three men simultaneously reached into their pockets and donned sunglasses. Tomlinson started laughing. "Don't y'all look like the Three Stooges," he said. The men laughed too, realizing they were all wearing identical dark green Aviator Ray-Bans.

Just then, a Metroliner taxied past, and the whining roar was deafening. "Make sure you carry plugs with you at all times," Tom said. "Or y'all'll be deaf by the time you're forty." In between the hangar and the main terminal stood a small brick building with long windows facing the runway and clusters of antennas on the roof. "We're lucky," Tom said. "We've got our own Flight Service Station right here. You can get an in-depth, face-to-face weather briefing any time of day." Tom opened the door, and the men followed him inside. "Hey, Bud," Tom said. "Got time to give our new pilots a tour?"

Bud Devry sat behind the wooden counter, ripping long sheets of paper from a teletype machine. His thick legs and wide girth hid the chair beneath him, making it look like he was balancing on a stick just a few feet above the ground. He was bald and had wrinkles in his cheeks that deepened as he looked up and smiled. "Sure thing." He stood up, raised the hinged portion of the counter, walked out, and shook the men's hands.

Bud explained the reams of weather faxes clamped to clipboards around the counter. "You sure picked the right place to get weather experience. We're the next stop down the line from Oklahoma. I've seen a lot of wicked storms in the last thirty-five years. We're hoping to get a new Doppler color-radar but government funding's the problem. Washington plans on closing many of the Flight Service Stations and consolidating them into one superstation per state. New technology to replace old men," he chuckled. "Won't affect me, though. I'm due to retire at the end of the year. I'll be watching the storms from a fishing boat on Bull Scholl's instead of a radar screen, but I'll be thinking of y'all. Feel free to stop by anytime. We're here twenty-four hours a day."

Tom walked the men down to the main terminal. He opened the door to a small room and turned on the lights. "Have a seat," he said. "Has everyone had a chance to go over the flight manual? We've got one week to get through aircraft systems, limitations, weight and balance, normal and emergency procedures, and regulations. Then we'll spend the following week in actual flight training. After everyone passes their check-ride, you'll fly your first real trip with an LCA, or line check airman, and then you'll be good to go. The learning curve's almost vertical, like trying to drink water from a fire hydrant. Do your homework, don't go catting around on Dickson Street, and you'll get through it just fine. Now I want y'all to realize one thing: There's no guarantee we won't ever have a crash. People could get killed. Look around, get a good look at each other's faces. Did everyone see *Fate Is the Hunter?*"

Just then the door opened and a young man with sandy brown hair wearing a leather jacket and khakis walked in, out of breath. He nodded at the other men and said, "Andy McShane. Sorry I'm late. My car is on its last legs, barely got it started." They shook hands all around. Then Tom said, "I've got to make a quick phone call. Let's all take a ten-minute break, then we'll begin."

During the break, Matt walked through a doorway that led from the classroom to the back of a large room full of cubicles. It was the reservation center or "rez." Each cubicle had its own phone and small green computer monitor. Matt walked, unnoticed, behind the beehive of activity and through a door that led from rez to the back of the ticket counter. There were stacks of checked bags in piles on the floor, sorted according to flight number and destination. One door led out to the tarmac, the other to the ticket counter. The two rampers Matt saw when he arrived for his interview were loading bags into a red pickup. Matt poked his head around the doorway to the ticket counter and saw Jackie Anderson checking in a passenger for the next flight to Little Rock. When she was finished, she turned around.

"You're back," she said. She was wearing a dark blue pantsuit with a white shirt and maroon silk cravat and the same gray slippers Matt noticed before. The name tag on her jacket said, "J. Anderson– Station Manager."

"Where's your uniform?" Matt said.

"Say what? Oh, *that* uniform. It was supposed to be my day off when you were here. I was just fixin' to take my son to preschool when the phone rang. One of my agents overslept and the place was falling apart, as usual. Had to come in and put out the fire."

"Like Smokey Bear."

"That's me, alright," she said. "So, how's it goin' so far?"

"We just started," Matt said, looking at his watch. "I'd better be getting back."

The men filed back into the classroom. Tom Tomlinson walked in smelling of pipe tobacco. He gave a general overview of aircraft systems, then covered some of the special systems like stall avoidance, which provided an aural warning and sixty pounds of forward control force in advance of an aerodynamic stall and the water injection system, which, in the event of an engine failure on takeoff, would augment the power available on the remaining engine, allowing the pilots time to raise the landing gear and climb away from the ground.

"Now, let's go back and review the electrical system in greater detail," Tom said. "DC power is supplied by two 24-volt batteries and two 200-ampere generators. The AC system receives power from two single-phase inverters." Matt could see Pete Sutherland's foot tapping the floor. The tedium was shattered when Jackie opened the classroom door with a frantic look on her face.

"Tom, we just heard from Flight Control that 442, our flight from Tulsa to Little Rock, is diverting into Fayetteville with an engine-fire. They're about five minutes out. The fire-and-rescue trucks are standing by."

"Who's the captain?" Tom asked, sliding his chair back.

"Randy Gillette."

"Good. Come on guys, follow me. Jackie, do we still have the binoculars and the portable VHF from the air show last summer?"

"They're in a drawer in the freight room. I'll get 'em," she said.

Tom got up and the men followed him out the door to the ramp where a small group of people were gathered. Jackie came out, handed Tom the VHF radio and the binoculars, and started pacing back and forth, smoking a cigarette.

"I thought you quit," Tom said.

"I did," Jackie shot back with a look that could cut through a KryptoLok. Tom raised the binoculars and looked out toward the northwest approach end of the runway. People were craning their necks and standing on tiptoes as the words came over the radio.

"Tower, AR 442, pig pen inbound." The pig pen was the university football stadium, home of the Arkansas Razorbacks, located six miles out on final approach to runway 16.

"AR 442, cleared to land one-six, wind one eight zero degrees at twelve knots, trucks are standing by."

The plane was five miles out. Tom gazed through the binoculars, scanning the approach path. "I see them," he said. A thin trail of black smoke streamed from the left engine, which was shut down, its propeller feathered with all three blades angled into the wind. Tom was staring through the binoculars and talking out loud.

"Come on Randy, you're looking good. Hold on to your gear, son. Don't drop it too soon. Keep it coming ... not yet ... not yet ... now!" Tom saw six small black dots fall into place under the fuselage, indicating the gear was down and locked. From that angle and distance, it seemed like a normal approach. The plane touched down and rolled to the end of the runway, using up all six thousand feet.

"Textbook," Tom said with a smile as the crowd clapped and cheered.

No sign of fire was visible. The onlookers filed back into the terminal as the plane taxied to the ramp. Tom was still smiling and saying "textbook," and that if the press called, the canned response was, "Just a precautionary divert, a possible engine overheat condition. No cause for alarm." It was standard procedure to shut down the left engine on taxi-in to save fuel and let the first officer open the entry door a minute sooner, so except for the fire trucks following a short distance behind, everything seemed normal. Don Bishop, the first officer, opened the door and climbed down the airstairs. He reached out his hand and helped steady the passengers as they came down. Some were ashen and shaking. Others smiled with relief, just glad to be on the ground.

Jackie was like a bottle of shaken champagne filled with Southern hospitality. As she approached the passengers, her cork popped, and her charm and charity erupted in a burst of bubbles and foam.

"Welcome to Fayetteville, y'all. Is everyone awlright? Who needs a hug?" Jackie helped Don steady an elderly woman whose legs were wobbling as she came down the steps. When she had both feet on the ground, Jackie wrapped her arms around her and gave her a hug. "Now don't you worry your purdy li'l head. You're safe and sound. We've got fresh coffee and doughnuts in the terminal. Now y'all just come with me and everything's going to be awlright."

When the last of the passengers deplaned, Randy came down the steps, smiling and holding his black leather flight bag. Two mechanics arrived from the hangar in a small red tug. Randy briefed them on the engine fire as they hooked the nose wheel to the tow-bar and prepared to tow the airplane up to the hangar. Tom walked up to Randy and Don with his arm outstretched.

"Congratulations, guys. Nice piece of stick and rudder work, Captain."

"Thanks, Tom," the men said, nodding at the others.

"Guys, I'd like you to meet our new hires." The men shook hands and more congratulations flowed.

"Beers are on me tonight at the Whitewater," Tom said.

"Thanks, Tom," Randy said. "But we're supposed to be in Memphis tonight. I'm not sure if we'll be flying or deadheading. We may not have a spare airplane."

"Don't forget to file a report with the FAA. Captain Blahdick'll need a copy, as well. And let me know if you're not feeling up to flying. We can try to find a reserve crew to cover for you."

"Thanks, Tom," Randy said. "I'm fine, just another day at the office. We'll take a raincheck on those beers, though."

"Nice to meet you, fellas," Don said. "See you on the line."

The two pilots picked up their flight bags and walked up to the hangar as the other men filed back into the classroom.

"That was a class act," Tom said as the men took their seats. "We've got some real talent here. Y'all'll be getting your on-the-job training from some of the best sticks in the business."

Tom passed out performance charts which showed available landing distance, stall speeds, accelerate-stop distances, maximum takeoff gross weight, and weight and balance computations.

"There's one last thing I have to discuss with you, gentlemen," Tom said. "This airline is an equal opportunity employer. When you get on the line, you'll have the distinct pleasure of flying with two outstanding captains, Jackson Gault, an African American, and Sandy Shyvers, a woman. If anyone thinks they may have a problem with that, please see me after class; I'll have something for you. Well, that's all I have for today. We'll start at 0930 tomorrow. I've got to give a check-ride to one of our captains before class. If y'all want to come along, you're more than welcome. We'll meet outside the hangar door at 0700. Now go let off some steam."

As the men filed out of the room, Bob Grayson lagged behind and went up to Tom. "Captain Tomlinson, I'm just curious, not that I have a problem flying with a black or a woman, I don't. I just wondered what it was you said you had to give us if we did?"

"A one-way ticket home, son."

"Oh. Well, like I said, I've got no problem with it."

CHAPTER SIX

Mark Winger woke up slowly, one eye at a time. His formidable girth bore down on the waterbed mattress, giving the impression that he was sleeping in a ditch. He lay motionless and looked out the cabin window across the frost-covered meadow to a row of four pine trees. Behind the trees was a steep limestone cliff that plummeted down to the riverbed below. In late summer, the White River slowed to a lazy trickle, but after the rains of spring and fall, the rapids would churn and rush like a wild ride at Water World. When the wind blew from the south, and when the sun heated the boulders, strong thermals would rise up the cliff wall in great shafts of invisible lift. Mark liked to go out to the precipice in autumn, lean against the trunk of a pine tree, and watch the leaves shoot upward, fluttering like swarms of monarch butterflies, at this secret spot where gravity sometimes worked in reverse. Mark watched as a red-tailed hawk rose above the treeline and banked its brown feathered wings, rising higher and higher in a tight spiral. He stared at the bird and followed the way it seemed to instinctively feel the wind, knowing just how to position its wings to maximize lift.

Mark Winger was one of the senior captains at Arkansas Airways. He not only demonstrated a deep understanding of the mechanical intricacies of the Metroliner but possessed an almost spiritual connection with the craft. The night before a check-ride, he would sit quietly in his tattered easy-chair and put himself into a state of meditation. He would visualize every type of maneuver he'd be tested on the following day: engine failure on takeoff (V1 cut), single engine approach and go-around, crosswind holding pattern, non-precision approach, ILS (instrument landing system) approach, steep turns, and stall recovery. He would also be tested on flight manual procedures: loss of electrical power, smoke in the cabin, rapid decompression, emergency landing gear operation, and engine-fire procedures. Mark saw his hands moving the control yoke and power levers, felt his feet moving the rudder pedals; he prioritized, refined, and reviewed his every move. This exercise in visualization enabled him to turn a high-stress roller coaster ride into a routine walk in the park, and after he finished, he downed a cold beer and went to bed.

All the first officers at Arkansas Airways liked to fly with Mark Winger. Aside from superior skills, he possessed a type of confidence and strength found in those rare individuals whose spirit is truly free. Mark had no fear of Fred Blahdick, no fear of the FAA, and no fear of thunderstorms or turbulence. He wasn't afraid to drink beer in the morning. He wasn't afraid of his weight, cholesterol, or blood pressure. He wasn't afraid to get old, and he wasn't afraid to die. The only thing he feared was the wrath of Maggie Pryor. Maggie knew this, and to her great credit, she tried not to use it to her advantage too often.

Maggie was still asleep, riding high on the opposite side of the mattress. Mark diverted his gaze from the window and slowly swung a leg over the side of the bed frame, trying to lift his great weight without swamping her. But the tidal surge couldn't be contained, and Maggie's long body bobbed up and down like a beachball in a hurricane.

"You're up," she moaned from under the pillow. Mark kicked an empty beer can out of the way and shuffled off to the bathroom.

"It's still early," he said. "Go back to sleep."

Maggie raised an arm and moaned as Mark disappeared into the swirling steam of a hot shower.

When he emerged, he could hear Maggie's soft, rhythmic breathing coming from under the pillow. The sunlight was pouring in over the ridgeline to the east. Mark stepped into a pair of jeans and put on a green flannel shirt and a pair of soft leather shoes. The only good thing about a check-ride was that you weren't wrapped up in polyester all day, he thought. He sat in the easy-chair and felt the calm and stillness of morning in the country, the reason he chose to live out here instead of in town. One last moment of peace before the screaming whirlwind. He listened to the clock ticking and stared at the shape of Maggie's ankles protruding from the covers. They had graceful lines and curves just like the rest of her body, and Mark had studied them from every conceivable angle in the two years they'd been together. He glanced at his Casio, got up, put on a dark blue down-vest and a pair of brown leather work gloves, picked up his black leather flight bag and gently closed the door behind him. He placed the flight bag in the truck-bed of his El Camino, climbed in, and started it up. He followed the dirt road that wound down from the grassy plateau over a cattle grate, past cows lazing on the cold ground, some shadowing their new-born calves, and over a planked bridge that spanned the White River near the town of West Fork. He passed the Piggly Wiggly market and pulled into the Stop & Go for a coffee and two plain doughnuts. He turned left onto Highway 71, passed the little town of Greenland and the main terminal building, and turned right by the hangar and parked by the chain-link fence. He climbed out, grabbed his flight bag and walked through the gate and around the side of the hangar. The sun was in full morning burn and Mark pulled out a pair of black wraparound Oakleys with amber lenses. A sleek red and white Metroliner was parked outside the open hangar door. Tom Tomlinson was going over the exterior inspection with Matt, Pete, and Bob.

"Morning, guys," Mark said. Everyone introduced themselves and shook hands.

"I remember you," Matt said.

"Yeah," Mark said with a laugh. "I had a feeling Blahdick would hire you."

"Anyone need to use the head before we blast off?" Tom asked.

Mark disappeared into the hangar for a minute while Tom and the three other men climbed aboard. Tom sat in the right seat while Bob

Grayson sat in the captain's seat. Matt and Pete crowded around the forward bulkhead as Tom explained the cockpit layout.

"I'm afraid, for takeoff and landing, y'all'll have to sit in the back rows for weight and balance purposes. I'll get on the PA and tell you when it's okay to come up." The men bent forward to clear the cabin top as they stepped back and strapped in.

"I guess Andy's not going to make it," Matt said. "He's probably having car trouble again."

"Or car trouble with his wife," Grayson said. Mark climbed up the airstairs and pulled on the chains that raised the door. He closed the door, dropped into the left seat, and placed his flight bag by his side. One of the mechanics stood on the ramp by a ground-power cart. The mechanic gave a thumbs-up sign and rotated his hand, indicating "clear for engine start."

Matt looked up and saw the men methodically flipping switches and reading checklists. The cabin filled with a roar, punctuated by two quick snarls as the propellers were released from their start locks and the plane began to move. The men reached into their pockets and inserted little sponge plugs into their ears. Soon they were accelerating down the runway. Matt looked up and saw Mark's pawlike hand placed on the power levers like a child clutching his favorite toy. As Mark gently applied back pressure to the yoke, the small round windows filled with the view of green and brown hills falling away as they gained altitude. They flew off-airways to a designated practice area. Tom took control of the plane while Mark put on the hood. The hood was a white plastic duck-billed headband that allowed the pilot to see the instrument panel but blocked out any forward view through the windshield. Tom put Mark through a series of steep turns, slow flight and stalls, all requiring different gear, flap, and power settings. Matt was surprised to feel a green queasiness come over him. He hoped he wouldn't have to use one of the comfort bags in the seat pocket. Then the plane climbed straight ahead, and Tom's voice came over the PA as he looked around the corner of the bulkhead. "Y'all doing alright back there?" The men nodded. "Why don't y'all come on up and we'll point out a few things."

Mark took off the hood, and Matt saw the same mischievous grin on his face that he'd seen during their first encounter outside Blahdick's office. As the men unbuckled and started filing forward, the plane suddenly dropped into a steep dive, plastering them against the ceiling. For a few seconds, the negative G-force had them pinned helpless, flapping and flailing like fish on hooks as their hands tried to find something to hold on to. Tom and Mark were laughing as Mark gently pulled back on the yoke, dropping the men over the seat backs and into the center aisle in a pile of arms and legs.

"Y'all okay?" Tomlinson said over the PA. Bob Grayson had an angry look on his face. Pete just shook his head, and Matt tried to put a smile on his face, accepting the price of initiation.

"Just trying to emphasize why we never, I repeat, *never* fly into a thunderstorm," Tom said, smiling. "We'll go down to Fort Smith and shoot a single-engine ILS approach with a go-around, then come back up and fly a non-precision approach to runway 34 with a circle-to-land on 16. Why don't y'all go on back, sit down and relax. You sure you're alright, Matt?" The men held on tight to the seat backs as they made their way back to the cabin.

Matt had never been so ready to get out of an airplane as the Metro taxied to the main terminal ramp and shut down. Tom got up and opened the cabin door. "Let's all meet back in the classroom in half an hour," he said.

T-Ball and Buzz were walking out to the plane, getting ready to take it on the run that went from Fayetteville to Little Rock–Memphis–Nashville–Knoxville–Nashville–Memphis–Little Rock–Fort Smith and then back to Fayetteville. Nine legs in twelve hours. "How'd he do, Tom?" T-Ball said.

"Textbook. Y'all always make me look good," he said, smiling.

"How's the airplane?" Buzz asked.

"Nose-wheel steering's inop," Mark said. "Otherwise, she's fine."

"There's a cold front moving in from Oklahoma," T-Ball said. "We may have to deal with it on our last two legs home tonight. If we're not too delayed, you guys wanna meet down at Hugo's at 9:00 p.m. for a debrief?"

"We'll be there."

"Anyone know a good place to go for a swim?" Matt asked.

"Check out the Boys' Club," Buzz said. "It's not fancy but it'll get you wet. It's just south of town, by the stadium." Buzz started performing the exterior inspection as T-Ball climbed up into the cockpit.

"Say, any of you guys like to play golf?" Buzz asked from under the left wing.

"I play a little," Pete said.

"T-Ball and I camp out at the links. We're usually the first ones in. T-Ball's obsessed with the game."

"Have a good trip," Matt said. "See you tonight."

Matt felt better after a mile swim. He left the Thunderbird at 7:30 p.m., drove to the square and parked opposite the Old Post Office. There was a red neon sign that said HUGO'S with a blue arrow pointing down. Steps led below the sidewalk level to a cavernous bar and grill with low ceilings and dim lights.

Pete Sutherland and Bob Grayson sat at a back corner table. They'd already started working on a pitcher of beer when Matt sat down.

"Check out your nine o'clock," Bob said.

Matt looked over his left shoulder and saw a young woman working behind the bar. She had a pretty face with a bright smile, long blond hair, and a low-cut, pleated blouse.

"Seems like a friendly little place," Matt said. Then Andy McShane showed up.

"Sorry I'm late again, guys," he said. "Sandy hasn't been feeling well lately. I was going to cancel, but she insisted I come out and join you." Matt picked up the pitcher and poured Andy a beer. "How does she like Fayetteville so far?"

"She likes it. She was born and raised in Boston so it's a bit of an adjustment. I told her it would just be temporary."

"Is she looking for a job?" Pete asked.

"Yeah, she's an ER nurse. She's already got an offer from Washington Regional."

"Must be nice to be in a profession where you're always in demand," Bob said.

"You got that right. Who knows if this flying gig's ever going to pay off. I told her, give me two years. If it doesn't work out, we'll go back home, and I'll re-invent myself. Sandy's the one with the brains in the family. She talks about going to med-school. I can't expect her to sacrifice her dream for mine; it wouldn't be fair."

"You mean you'd give it all up?" Matt said.

"Not without a good fight first, but you've got to be able to read the writing on the wall."

"I can't imagine this recession's going to last much longer," Pete said.

"Who knows," Andy said. "But you know a pilot's job security is like a candle in the wind. Get hit by a car or can't pass your physical, you're toast." Everyone nodded and took a sip of beer.

"My ex-girlfriend is in med-school," Matt said.

"You mean you actually let that meal-ticket go?" Bob said.

"A gambling man," Pete said with a smile.

"Not really," Matt said. "She met someone else, a surgeon."

"Tough competition," Pete said.

Bob Grayson looked over at the barmaid and gestured. "Look on the bright side, you're as free as a bird."

Matt forced a smile and took a gulp of beer. "It's all for the best, anyway. I couldn't expect her to pack up and follow me all around the country, living like gypsies."

"You got a point there," Andy said. Then the barmaid came over.

"Can I git you boys anything?"

"I thought you'd never ask," Bob said. Matt wanted to disappear. As the waitress walked away, Bob said, "One week. That's all I need."

"Get out of town," Pete said. "She's obviously got a boyfriend."

"Doesn't matter," Bob said. Pete and Matt looked at each other.

After a while, Andy looked at his watch and said, "I'd better take off. I don't want Sandy to get lonely. See you guys tomorrow." He got up to leave and threw a twenty-dollar bill on the table.

"That's too much," Matt said. Andy held up his hand. "It all evens out." As Andy opened the door and climbed the steps, a cold wind blew through the bar. Matt felt like leaving too, but he stayed.

"Andy and Sandy, cute," Bob said.

"What?" Matt said. He was staring at the bubbles at the bottom of his beer glass.

"That guy's too young to be tied down," Bob said. "That's *not* going to happen to me."

"I'm sure you're right," Pete said.

"He looks pretty happy to me," Matt said. Then the door opened, and T-Ball and Buzz walked in wearing jeans, flannel shirts and leather jackets. Pete waved a hand, and the men came over to the table.

"Hi, Ginger," T-Ball said to the barmaid.

"Hi, darlins. What can I gechy'all?"

"Six pitchers of your finest lager," Buzz said, grinning. "I'm celebrating."

"He just found out he's going to captain school," T-Ball said.

"Congratulations, ya big stud," Ginger said. "First one's on me."

"You guys better watch him when you get on the line. I couldn't teach him a thing in two years," T-Ball laughed.

"Pretty rough out there tonight?" Ginger asked.

"Windy as hell," T-Ball said. "Cells popping up all over the place. Strange for this time of year."

"So, how's it going so far?" T-Ball asked.

"Good," Pete said. "Tom really knows his stuff."

"Yeah, but you don't want to fly a line-trip with him," Buzz said.

"Why not?" Matt said.

"You know that expression, those who can't do, teach." Buzz grinned as he took a slug of beer. "Ahh, nectar of the gods."

"Help yourselves," Matt said, pushing forward a plate of chicken wings.

"Tomlinson's okay," T-Ball said. "It's Barry Dresden you have to watch out for."

"Yeah, that son of a bitch thinks he's the assistant chief pilot," Buzz said. "It's sickening the way he kisses Blahdick's ass." Kissing ass was a very big thing with Buzz.

"Have you guys found a place to stay yet?" T-Ball asked.

"I saw this ad in the *Gazette* for a house for rent," Bob said. "It's on Route 8, just north of the airport. Rent's $500 a month. You guys interested?"

"Won't hurt to take a look at it," Pete said. Then Ginger brought another pitcher to the table.

"So, how's Mike?" T-Ball asked.

"He's fine," Ginger said.

"You really gonna ride on his Fat Bob all the way down to Daytona and back?" Buzz asked.

"Nope," Ginger said. "Mike's giving me a '77 Super Glide as an engagement present. It's in mint condition." Mike Shield ran the service department at the Harley dealership down in Fort Smith.

"Instead of a ring?" Buzz asked.

"For now, at least," Ginger said. "I'm so excited. We're gonna ride all the way to Key West and get married on the beach. Mike said he'd go to the end of the world for me. I said I'd settle for the country, so that's how he got the idea. He's such a romantic."

Pete leaned over and said to Bob, "Maybe you should allow an extra week."

"We'll celebrate when you get back," T-Ball said.

"For sure," Ginger said as she picked up the plates and went back to the bar.

"Well, I'd better get going," Bob said, standing up and putting a five-dollar bill on the table. Pete looked at him. "What? I only had two beers," Bob said. "I'll set up an appointment to look at the house tomorrow."

On Wednesday afternoon, Tom said, "Well, that about wraps up systems. We're making good progress. One of our captains called in sick, and I got drafted to fly his trip tomorrow. Y'all take the day off and study the regs. We'll meet back here Friday morning."

After class, Bob, Pete, and Matt drove out to see the house. Route 8 was a winding dirt road north of the airport. A half-mile east of Highway 71 on the north side of the road stood a blue framed farmhouse with white trim and two stately white columns rising above a small porch that looked out across the road to an oval-shaped dirt racetrack. There was a detached garage to the left of the house in matching blue and white trim, and a backyard with two tall white oak trees. The men pulled into the gravel drive as the owner came out the side door to the kitchen. A quick tour of the house revealed three bedrooms on the second floor, two baths, and a living room and den, each with their own fireplace. The men got into a small huddle.

"It's perfect," Matt said.

"Ideal," Pete said.

"We'll take it," Bob said to the owner. "How soon can we move in?"

On Thursday morning, Matt paid his bill at the Thunderbird and packed up the Jeep. It felt good to be leaving something temporary and putting down roots. The sun was shining, and the forecast called for a high of fifty-five. Not bad for January, Matt thought as he pulled into the driveway and parked next to Bob Grayson's '76 Cutlass Convertible. It was 8:00 a.m. and Bob had already moved in.

The two smaller bedrooms faced the rear of the house. The other was the master-bedroom with a forward view of the racetrack and the green hills beyond. Bob had already unloaded his boxes and moved into the master.

Pete's pickup pulled into the drive a few minutes later, fire-engine red with big, bread-loaf fenders, the truck-bed full of boxes. Two toots on the horn announced his arrival. Matt walked out to the drive, and the men shook hands.

"This is going to be great," Pete said. "We'll have to host crash derby night when the track's in full swing, set up a keg on the front porch. Say, give me a hand with these speakers."

"Nice stereo," Matt said.

"Thanks. It's a Marantz 4100 Quad with Harman Kardon tuner and Mitsubishi belt-drive turntable. My ex-girlfriend once told me I should marry my Marantz instead of her."

"Why do they always think we never listen to them?"

"Right. Anyway, I kept hearing her words, *marry your Marantz, marry your Marantz,* like a mantra. That's why I named her Mary."

"You named your stereo Mary?" Matt laughed. What'd you name your pickup?"

"Well, it's a vintage '53 Studebaker. I thought Stud Bucket was the perfect sobriquet. Colleen, my girlfriend at the time, thought it was quite juvenile of me, like I'd watched too many Roy Rogers episodes as a kid. That was the first clue she might not have as much long-term potential as I thought," Pete laughed.

The two of them lifted the coveted boxes with all the veneration of pallbearers. They spent the rest of the morning moving in and hooking up phones and appliances, then stopped at noon for lunch.

"Have y'all discovered Drake's Café?" Pete said.

"Where's that?" Bob said.

"Follow me," Pete said. Matt climbed into the pickup, while Bob followed behind in his Cutlass.

They drove around the dirt road and turned left on Sixth Street. On the north side of the street stood a small pink cinder-block shack with matching outhouse. Drake's Café was a true mecca of Southern cooking, run by a group of silver-haired grandmothers. The plate-lunch special was either pan-fried chicken, meat loaf, beef tips or catfish stew with sweet corn, fried okra, black-eyed peas, collard greens, turnips, mashed potatoes with gravy, and cornbread fried in peanut oil, all for $2.75.

Peach cobbler or pecan pie with a flaky lattice crust was an additional fifty cents.

After lunch, the men went back to the house. Pete tied a hammock between the two white oaks in the backyard. "You can't be too comfortable after a meal like that," he said as he lay down and closed his eyes under the brim of a yellow John Deere cap.

Tom walked into class a few minutes late on Friday. He hadn't shaved and there were dark circles under his eyes. He'd flown the same nine-leg trip that T-Ball and Buzz flew earlier in the week.

"Sorry if I seem a bit shop-worn," he said. "We didn't get back till midnight. It turned into a fifteen-hour day after one of the ITT gauges quit when we got to Little Rock. By the time we had a new gauge installed, we were out of duty-time."

Fourteen hours was the maximum legal duty-time limit. Once a flight crew reached its limit, they could still stay on duty and fly indefinitely, as long as there wasn't any payload onboard. It wasn't uncommon to start a workday at 0600 and not get back until midnight.

"I know the regs can be about as boring as a tax return," Tom said. "I'll just cover the basics of Part 135 and try to orient them to line operations. We ought to be finished by noon." Matt looked over and saw Pete tapping his foot under the table again. Tom droned on, reading almost verbatim from the manual. Flight and duty-time limits, takeoff minimums, approach minimums, currency requirements, severe weather limitations, thunderstorm avoidance, and cold weather operations.

"The regs are incorporated in your flight-ops manual. If y'all don't have any questions, that'll wrap up ground school. Flight training starts tomorrow. Don't forget to go up to Penny's and buy your uniforms. See Janice for your epaulets and brass wings and take your suitcoat to Lori's on Dickson Street to have the stripes sewn on. Good luck guys. I'm sure y'all'll do just fine."

After class, Pete, Bob, and Andy walked out to the parking lot. Matt wanted to stop off at the ticket counter to say hi to Jackie, but when he looked toward the counter, it wasn't Jackie he saw. A flood of adrenaline set off an electric shock that held him all but paralyzed. Unable to think or speak, he ducked into the gift shop for cover and hid behind a rack of postcards. She was beautiful. He'd never seen her before. He started turning the rack of postcards around, feigning interest. He peered out through the rack of cards. She stood behind the ticket counter, wistfully staring out the front door of the terminal. She seemed lost in thought, and there was something about her that gave Matt the impression that she wasn't from Arkansas. The depth of her beauty was ineffable, stunning, beyond comprehension; a beauty that could turn the heads of both men and women in all the major beauty capitals of the world, Milan, Moscow, Miami where beauty is as ubiquitous as the sycamore trees in Paris. Matt stared out, protected by postcards that said, "Howdy from the Ozarks," and pictures of Old Main and the university in brilliant fall colors. Her eyes were bright and captivating, like deep ebony wells. Her hair was as black as the ocean on a moonless night and flowed in shiny waves, cascading down the sides of her face and curling off her shoulders. Matt couldn't help but stare. Every curve, every line, seemed sculpted from an artist's template. Matt knew she would be as off-limits as a goddess. Anxiety began to swirl; he knew he could never win her heart, yet he also knew he couldn't bear to be near her without trying to. Every impulse to act was countered by an opposite and equal paralysis. Everything was happening so fast. A minute ago, he was just walking through the terminal. Now, everything was spinning out of control.

"Forget about it, Ace, she doesn't date pilots." Matt almost fell into the rack of cards, his diffidence naked and exposed.

"Hi, Jackie," he said. "I was just looking for something to send my folks."

"Right. Well, come on. You've got nothing to lose, and I can assure you, nothing to gain, so you might as well let me introduce you."

"Thanks, Jackie, but some other time. I've got to get home. I've got some studying to do."

CHAPTER SEVEN

Olga Vargas was sound asleep, dreaming she was a little girl in her grandmother's kitchen in Old Havana. Although she had never been to Cuba, her parents' vivid stories imprinted so many images in her mind that she would sometimes adopt them as her own, especially in her dreams. She could smell the rich, dark aroma of coffee, boiling on the hot-plate stove. From a cast iron skillet on the other burner came the sweet smell of yuca fritters and plátano crackling in hot oil. Olga felt the soft breeze from her abuelita's pale yellow cotton dress as she moved about her small kitchen, repeating the same morning ritual as she had thousands of times before. From the open doorway, Olga's grandfather appeared, wearing a white guayabera shirt, his silver hair combed straight back, with thick, black-framed glasses and a pencil-thin mustache. Olga could smell the faint aroma of soap and cigar smoke as he smiled and came close to pat her hair.

"Buenos días, mi amor," her grandparents said, their words overlapping as they kissed the soft air between their cheeks. Abuelita handed her husband a demitasse of strong black coffee and the newspaper, which he took out onto the open terrace.

Olga rolled over in her sleep and placed her arm over the mound of pillows next to her head. The quiet stillness of the morning was shattered by the ringing of the telephone on the nightstand. Racked with sleep and confusion, she groped for the phone.

"Olga, it's Maggie. Where *are* you?" Olga squinted at the alarm clock: 8:30 a.m. "Oh, my God! I'm so sorry. I overslept again. I'll hurry as fast as I can. Is Jackie there yet?"

"No, I'm here alone. I'll cover for you, but it's about to get real busy."

"Thanks, Maggie, you're a dear. I'll be right there."

Olga wrapped her hair in a towel and stepped into the shower. Then she quickly dressed in her navy-blue uniform of pleated pants with matching jacket over a starched white cotton shirt with silk maroon cravat and London Fog raincoat. She tied a knit scarf around her neck and ran down the steps of her small apartment, which was located behind a stately white frame house on Washington Avenue. She unlocked the chain which held her little white Vespa to the porch, strapped on her white Piaggio crash helmet, threw a leg over the saddle, tucked her coattails beneath her, turned the key and kick-started the engine. She rolled down the drive and turned right on Washington Avenue, right on Dickson Street then left on Highway 71 toward the airport. She throttled up and felt the wind on her face before remembering the promise she made her parents not to drive over thirty miles an hour. She slowed a little and felt the cold air on her cheeks and hands. She reached the terminal parking lot in fifteen minutes, parked the Vespa, and ran into the terminal. A line of passengers had formed in front of the ticket counter, and Olga raced behind the counter and hung up her coat and helmet in the freight room. She straightened herself in the mirror, took a breath for composure and stepped up to the counter where Maggie was checking in two passengers at once. Businessmen were standing in line with nervous looks on their faces, glancing at their watches.

"I can help the next one in line. I'm sorry you had to wait so long," Olga said to a man with a large waistline, starched chinos and a red polyester sport coat.

"Absolutely no trouble at all," he said, smiling and staring into her eyes.

It wasn't just Olga's stunning beauty but her gracious manner as well. Jackie said Olga could charm the wool off a sheep. When she first started working for the airline, the other agents were jealous and resentful. Maggie would assign her tasks like opening boxes of quarterly timetables or sweeping out the freight room at the end of the day. Olga had been self-conscious about her beauty since she was a little girl and saw it as a curse as much as a blessing. Of course, it would attract people, mostly men, but it kept people at a distance as well. To prove she was more than just a pretty face, Olga always went the extra mile. She would see a need and tend to it, and she had a special way with passengers. Whenever Jackie or Maggie or the other agents had to deal with an irate passenger, Olga always volunteered to help. If there was a problem with no immediate solution, just her smile and empathy— and her eyes—had the power to diffuse, calm and cure. Little by little, she won over the other agents, and Jackie gave her credit for half the station's annual passenger revenue.

"You're just in time," Maggie whispered.

"I'm so sorry," Olga said.

"How's your mom doing?" Maggie asked.

"She's still in remission. We're just taking it day-by-day."

"We're all praying for her," Maggie said, giving Olga's hand a gentle squeeze.

"Thanks, you're a dear."

"I'll board 418 if you want to grab a coffee," Maggie said.

Maggie walked over to the boarding area and made a final announcement over the PA. She unlocked the door and escorted the passengers out onto the tarmac toward the plane bound for Memphis. Just then, a deafening roar was heard overhead, and everyone looked up to see the underbelly of a low-flying Metroliner on go-around, retracting its landing gear and making a climbing right turn. Some of the passengers had more than the usual look of worry on their faces.

"No cause for alarm, y'all," Maggie yelled behind her. "We're just doing some pilot training this mornin'."

Some of the passengers smiled, wanting to believe her.

Pete went first. He met Tom at 0700 for a quick briefing followed by two hours of flight training. Matt met them outside the hangar at 0930 after they taxied in and shut down.

"How'd it go?" Matt asked as Pete climbed down the airstairs.

"You're going to love it," Pete said, smiling. Then Tom came down the steps. "Who's the next victim? Matt, I'll be right with you." As Tom walked into the hangar, Pete said, "Did you see what Grayson taped to the refrigerator door this morning?"

"I didn't notice."

"It's a list of chores assigned by date, name and job description. He's got you cleaning the toilets on Tuesdays."

"Where does he get off?"

"Beats me," Pete said. "I don't plan on having a lick to do with it, though."

"Me neither; let's rip it down."

Matt was relieved to find that, after a series of stalls and steep turns, the airsickness he'd experienced before had been an isolated event. After an hour in the cockpit, he was starting to feel familiar with the plane.

Tom talked him through a visual approach to runway 16, followed by a missed approach, then an instrument approach wearing the hood. Tom took the hood off on final approach to simulate breaking out at minimums with the runway stretched out before them.

"Just follow me through on this first landing," Tom said, taking over the controls from the left seat. "Cross the threshold on a nice three-degree glide path. At about ten feet, start bleeding your power back as you apply a touch of back pressure to flair." Then the main wheels touched down with a gentle thud. Tom lifted the power levers with his fingers and pulled them back. The two propellers snarled as they went into reverse thrust. Matt made two takeoffs and landings, then Tom took control of the airplane and they taxied back to the hangar.

"You did fine for your first time out," Tom said. "How did it feel?"

Matt felt like he'd just kissed a girl for the first time as he got in the Jeep. He turned down the dirt road and wound around until the blue farmhouse came into view. Pete's pickup was nowhere to be seen. When he pulled into the drive, he saw Bob standing in the backyard, wrapped in a white terrycloth towel. He was shivering and swearing and covered in soap lather.

"What happened?" Matt said.

"The damn water-pump circuit breaker popped. I was right in the middle of a shower when the water stopped."

The water to the house was supplied by a well in the backyard. Once the electric pump stopped, the only way to restore it was to reset the circuit breaker, uncover the well, and reach down and start pumping with the manual pump handle to bleed the line of air.

Matt saw Bob lean into the well, lathered to the gills and foaming at the mouth, pumping and swearing for all he was worth.

"Good thing the landlord told us this could happen," Matt said. "We'd have been hard-pressed to figure it out for ourselves." Bob just grunted as he covered up the well and ran inside.

Matt followed behind. As he opened the side door to the kitchen, he looked over at the refrigerator door and saw that the list of chores was gone. All that remained was a torn fragment of yellow paper under a piece of tape. Matt smiled but had no way of knowing that, from that point on, he and Pete Sutherland would be friends for life.

The next week was spent in flight training. Pete and Matt had Tom as their instructor. Bob was assigned to Barry Dresden, a source of initial anxiety due to T-Ball's warning at Hugo's. But Bob found Barry to be amiable and professional.

By the end of the week, all the new hires had passed their flight checks and oral exams. Their new uniforms hung in the closet. All that was left was their initial trip with a line check airman. They would then be assigned trips to finish out the month. After that, they could bid for their flight schedules along with the rest of the pilots, every schedule being awarded according to seniority. Matt's number was fifty-nine out of sixty. Bob was last on the list.

On the day of Matt's initial operating trip, he shaved, showered, and put on his uniform. He stood before the full-length mirror that hung on the bathroom door. All his life he'd dreamt of this moment. At last, he was a real airline pilot (or would be when he got home that night).

He was assigned the easy, break-in trip from Fayetteville to Fort Smith–Little Rock–Memphis and back to Fayetteville. Three o'clock departure and back by nine. A piece of cake in good weather, and the forecast was calling for clear skies and unlimited visibility. Matt had never given a PA announcement before, so to preclude any gaffe, he wrote out the speech on a 4x5 card.

His line check would be with Wendell Steele. Wendell was an excellent pilot who possessed an intelligence that revealed itself without pretension. He held a master's degree in history and had spent two years in South America working for the Peace Corps. He had jet black hair, a black mustache, and could have passed for a young Omar Sharif.

Matt started to relax by the time they got to Memphis. They had an hour and a half before the nonstop to Fayetteville. The sun was blazing orange behind the Mississippi as the passengers boarded, and Matt handed a copy of the weight and balance manifest to the station agent.

After level off, when their duties were reduced to routine radio calls to Memphis Center, Wendell said, "Do you know much about labor unions, Matt?"

"Not really. My dad is in the International Association of Machinists. He's a Cadillac mechanic. I remember when they went out on strike. My father had to picket. He said they mostly just sat around on lawn chairs while the negotiators hammered out a contract. It got a bit tense, but then everyone shook hands, and they all went back to work. My mom didn't like it a bit. She was afraid he'd lose his job. My father told her not to worry, that the union would never let that happen."

"You may hear talk of it on the line," Wendell said. "The idea of us trying to organize surfaces from time to time, but so far nothing's come of it. I think it's pretty remote. Arkansas's a right-to-work state and the current Administration doesn't seem too fond of unions."

"Why would we even need one?"

"Well, right now you new guys are still honeymooning. A year from now you may see things differently, that's the problem. Pilots love what they do; it's more than just a job. There'll always be plenty of hungry applicants out there ready to take our place, so the law of supply and demand is inherently against any attempt to organize."

"Maybe that's the best rationale for a union in the first place."

"Maybe," Wendell said. "Just look at what Frank Lorenzo's doing, setting up Texas Air Corporation as a holding company, with New York Air as its non-union subsidiary. They're paying their pilots half as much. What's to stop him from acquiring a financially weak carrier and siphoning off assets and transferring capital, for no other reason but to put the squeeze on the unions and force their demise? And once that happens, the other airlines won't be able to compete. They'll be forced to do the same thing. Airline flying will cease being a coveted profession. Look what they're doing at People Express, turning it into some crude form of mass transit, Greyhounds of the sky. What we're seeing now may be just the tip of the iceberg. Deregulation's only two years old. The pendulum's going to swing from one extreme to the other, from tight route and fare regulations to a state of complete laissez-faire, a total free for all. The government should have figured out a way to free up markets incrementally. Some competition is healthy, but it can also be destructive. The consumer's going to have their cheap fares, but what about safety? Maintenance is expensive. Who's going to uphold the high standards that made this industry great? Who'll want to be a licensed mechanic with all that responsibility and get paid peanuts?"

"Just like us," Matt said.

"Exactly. I'm afraid we may be at the threshold of our careers but standing on a trapdoor. We'll not only be sent down the river, but first used as pawns to send the entire profession down the river. Lorenzo and his clones reap millions in their stock-swap deals. They call themselves airline builders, but we know that's just a façade of smoke and mirrors amassed on a mountain of junk bonds and busted union contracts. I'm afraid it's going to happen; the genie's out of the bottle."

It was quiet for a while. Matt felt hollow inside. Just when he was getting close to the prize, the whole thing seemed about to disappear. Matt was amazed that Wendell could spell things out so clearly without getting emotional about it.

"Reagan campaigned on the promise of ending this recession. I don't know how the unions are going to survive," Wendell said. "You're going to be hearing a lot from the guys you fly with. Just try to keep an open mind, that's all I'm saying. We all get together every few months to air our grievances, usually in some tavern. If someone has a safety issue, a problem with management, whatever, it's like a confessional. Whatever's happened to the other guy could easily happen to you. Sometimes it seems like we've already formed our own in-house union. Word of the next meeting gets around surreptitiously. It's informative and it's an excuse to drink beer."

Matt was feeling better. The sense of inclusion in a tight group of professionals renewed his confidence. Whatever happened, they would all be in it together. When the last of the passengers deplaned, Wendell and Matt shut down the cockpit and stepped down the airstairs onto the tarmac. A chill was in the air, and the Milky Way overhead pulsed with the twinkling of a trillion stars.

"Maintenance will be down to tow her up to the hangar; we might as well walk on up," Wendell said. "You did fine, considering it was your first trip. Just remember to keep your power on right across the threshold, bleed it back at about ten feet as you start to flair. The Metro's not very forgiving, as you're finding out." Matt's first landing in Little Rock had been firm to the point of embarrassment. He wanted to hide behind the cockpit curtain until the last of the passengers deplaned.

"We're having a pilot meeting in two weeks," Wendell said. "It's in your best interest to attend. I'll fill out your paperwork and you'll be all set. Congratulations, and welcome to the line."

Matt threw his flight bag in the back of the Jeep and climbed in. The ragtop was off, and he drove home with one arm wrapped around his chest to ward off the cold. When he pulled into the drive, he saw Pete getting into his pickup. He wore a white knit turtleneck shirt with blue Ultrasuede sport coat and a pair of soft faded jeans and black leather cowboy boots.

"Where're you off to, all slicked up?" Matt said.

"I was at Ozark Sports looking at canoes this afternoon. This nice little honey who works there, Rita, kind of the country type, very friendly. Anyway, we're meeting down at the Y'all Come Back Saloon. She's going to teach me how to two-step."

"Sounds like fun. Any more problems with the water pump?"

"Nope, as long as nobody pulls the circuit breaker." Pete smiled, closed the door to the pickup and started it up. He rolled down the window and waved as he backed onto the dirt road and drove away.

In the morning, Matt got up, put on a green flannel robe, and went downstairs. He put the kettle on the stove, ground some Colombian beans and waited for the water to boil. He looked through the kitchen window and saw that Pete's pickup was nowhere in sight.

Matt had the day off with no plans but to go for a long swim. Bob was on his initial trip with Barry Dresden and wasn't due back until 1:00 p.m. Matt took his coffee into the living room and was about to turn Mary on when he heard the crunching of gravel in the drive. He looked out and saw Pete open the door to the pickup. He stood and steadied himself against one of the big fenders before walking toward the house. Matt opened the door, and Pete limped into the kitchen.

"What happened to you?" Matt said. Pete grimaced, grabbed the door for support and sat down at the table. "Coffee?"

"Thanks. We were at the Y'all Come Back Saloon, knocking back a few shots of tequila, just having a nice conversation. Rita dragged me back to the mechanical bull. She was first to go. Apparently, she's quite accomplished on the thing. She was bucking and spinning and throwing her arm out for balance; everyone was whooping it up. She was going faster and faster with every yeehah from the crowd. All the guys were whistling, and her boobs were jiggling like a couple of paint cans in the shaker machine. Then she wound to a stop, climbed off with a big smile and said, 'Your turn.' Well, I was a good sport, fired up and all. Everything seemed fine. I was just starting to get into the rhythm of the thing when this good-old-boy jerks it into full throttle. I went flying through the air and landed with my leg twisted like a pretzel beneath me. Rita took me back to her place and rubbed me down with witch hazel. I didn't feel a thing after that; the girl should be a nurse. I fell asleep on her couch. When I woke up, it was throbbing like a son of a bitch."

"Are you gonna be alright today?" Pete was due to fly his initial line trip that afternoon.

"I'll be alright. I think I'll go upstairs, take some aspirin and go to bed. I'll tape my ankle if I have to."

CHAPTER EIGHT

Olga Vargas had the throttle wide open as she leaned forward, coaxing the Vespa up to the top of Markham Hill where her parents lived. She pulled into the driveway, shut off the engine and pulled the scooter up onto its kickstand, then walked around to the back door and went inside. "Hola Mami," she said, placing her backpack on the kitchen counter.

"I'm in here, Mija," her mother's voice came from her father's study. Olga went into the den and leaned down to kiss her on the cheek. Her mother was wearing a pair of black velvet house-pajamas with gold trim. She had the same olive complexion and dark eyes as her daughter. Her black hair, which had recently started growing back, was layered around the sides with streaks of gray. She was curled up in the double-wide brown leather chair with the family photo album in her lap.

"I have something for you," Olga said. "It'll just take a minute." Olga went into the kitchen and took down the juice blender from the cabinet. She tossed in handfuls of sliced organic carrots, beets, garlic, shiitake mushrooms, elderberry extract and blue-green algae. She turned on the blender and watched the frothing purple extract pour into a crystal glass. She garnished the brew with a stalk of fresh celery, wrapped the glass in a paper towel and brought it to her mother.

"Drink this," she said, handing the glass to her mom. Her mother closed her eyes and drank until it was gone.

"It could use a little sugar." She smiled, handing the glass back to her daughter.

"You can have sugar on your 100th birthday," Olga said as she took the glass back to the kitchen.

"Come and sit with me," her mother called out. "Did you see Papi today?"

"Yes, I checked him in for the one o'clock flight. He said he'd try to be home by nine."

Olga's father, Dr. Eduardo Vargas, was the Dean of the Department of Business Administration at the University of Arkansas. Once a week, Dr. Vargas boarded a flight to Little Rock to teach a graduate class in economics. He'd give a two-hour lecture and usually be home that same night.

Olga came back to her father's study, took off her shoes and curled up like a new-born kitten next to her mom. The chair always reminded her of when she was a little girl, sitting in her father's lap, listening to his stories, first in English, then in Spanish. She looked around her father's study and saw the floor-to-ceiling bookshelves, the framed photographs of Olga when she was a baby and through all her years, wedding photographs of her parents when they were barely twenty years old, her father's prized photograph of himself with Senator Fulbright (her father looked so young), and the recent photograph with Governor Clinton, who also looked so young.

Olga's mother opened the album to a black and white photograph of Olga's parents and grandparents at the Pan Am terminal in Miami. "Autumn 1960" was written in the margin.

"We had just arrived from Havana," her mother said. "There was so much confusion and excitement in the air. Your father and I were hopeful. We were just newlyweds. We saw it as an opportunity, a chance to start a new life together. But we were worried about our parents; they seemed so dazed and disoriented. We didn't know how my father would resume his medical practice. Here's a picture of Papi and your Uncle Leandro in the backyard, next to our mango tree. They were inseparable when we were young. Papi was always over at our house." Olga had heard these stories before but listened as if for the first time. She turned the page to a photo of her parents, standing in the boarding area at the airport in Havana just before leaving Cuba, a happy expression etched on their young faces.

"You are in this picture too, Mija. You see, I smuggled you out in my womb."

"In first class?"

"Of course," her mother laughed. "You were my secret stowaway. No one knew except your father." Olga's mother leaned to her side and gently pressed her cheek against Olga's hair. "We never thought of ourselves as immigrants, always exiles. It was hard in the beginning. There was so much talk of an invasion. We knew it would happen but just when, we weren't sure. Everyone was in a state of limbo. We didn't know if we'd be going back or not. And after the Bay of Pigs, we held out hope for another invasion attempt, at least until October of 1962." Olga's mother stared across the room, her eyes losing their focus. "We were so afraid, not just because the missiles were aimed at the U.S., and you were just a baby; we were afraid that U.S. missiles would be aimed at our dear friends and family who stayed behind. It was the worst form of double jeopardy imaginable. It felt like we took a deep breath in the morning and just held it in all day long. Then when President Kennedy promised Khrushchev there would not be another invasion attempt, we were devastated. For the first time, we had to face the reality that we would not be going home and that you would grow up as an American. That's when your father got the scholarship. We didn't want your life to be defined by the stigma of exile. Your father and I always wanted you to be free to create your own unique identity. We thought we could move to Arkansas, just give it a try. It wouldn't be too far away, not cold like New York. We would start a new life, and if we didn't like it, we could always move back to Miami, or perhaps the Dominican Republic or Puerto Rico. It was hard leaving our families behind. We felt twice exiled in the beginning. All our lives we'd been surrounded by cousins, aunts, uncles, grandparents, and friends. Suddenly, it was just the three of us. We wanted to have another baby, to give you a brother or sister, but I lost so much blood when you were born that the doctors told me it would be too dangerous to try again. I wanted to anyway, but your father insisted. He said he couldn't live if anything should happen to me. To dwell outside the arms of a large family is not the Cuban way, and I have missed that embrace and felt the ache of separation ever since." Olga noticed a tear running down her mother's cheek. She reached over and gave her mother's hand a gentle squeeze. "Don't misunderstand me," her mother said. "We have a very comfortable life here. It has been good for your father, and for me too, I suppose. I have made many dear friends. But it's strange in a way; the older I get, and the more distant my memories of Cuba seem, the more Cuban I feel. You live in a place and then it lives in you. Nothing can change that. I have no regrets that we left. My only regret is that things have not gotten better for the people over there, and that your Uncle Leandro chose to stay behind. But I still have hope. I know these last few months have been hard on you and Papi. I've been worried about you. You're not getting enough sleep. But I have the most amazing story to tell you."

"It happened the week after you and Papi brought me home from the hospital. One day, I was alone in the house. Suddenly, I felt this presence, but it wasn't like seeing a wraith or a spirit. It was a presence, like the feeling you get when you know someone is behind you, but you can't see or hear them; you just know they're there. I don't know how else to describe it. But it was not a vague feeling. It was powerful and present. A feeling came over me, a flood of emotion so strong I burst into tears. A sense of peace and tranquility washed over me like a wave. I'll never be able to describe it with words, Mija. It just felt like *love*. I was filled with such resignation, a trust and certainty that relieved me of the heavy weight I'd been carrying. I'd never felt anything like it before. I felt so liberated. I knew, without a doubt, that it didn't matter what happened to me because we were all destined to be together forever. You, Papi, me, your Uncle Leandro, your grandparents and cousins, all of us, our whole family. We will always be together, if not in this physical world, then someday in heaven. I was filled with certainty, so overwhelmed that I knew, right then and there, that I was going to be alright. And when your father took me back to the hospital a few months later and they ran those tests, the doctors said they'd never seen anything like it before; it was miraculous. I just smiled but wasn't surprised. I had been expecting it, but your father broke down and wept. The only time he ever cried for joy was the day you were born. So, Mija, this I can tell you with certainty: God *is* real, and we are all put here for a reason. There's no need to live in fear."

"I love you, Mami," Olga said as she leaned in to kiss her mother. "I've been so afraid."

"Come, let's go into the kitchen and cook together. How does arroz con pollo sound?"

Dr. Vargas opened the back door and saw his daughter's blue backpack on the kitchen counter. He went into the study and set his leather briefcase down on the desk. He walked down the darkened hallway and opened the bedroom door. Curled up with their eyes closed, their arms wrapped around each other as if they were together in the same dream, were the two loves of his life. He leaned down, kissed them both, covered them with a blanket, and backed out of the room. He went back to his study, turned the reading light on, and noticed the photo album on the end-table next to the reading chair. He opened the cabinet door to the mahogany bar by his desk and poured a dram of Bermúdez into a crystal glass over ice. Then he sat down in the soft leather chair, took a sip of rum, picked up the album, and started turning through the pages of his life.

CHAPTER NINE

It was Tuesday, January 20, 1981. Matt and Pete were down at the Whitewater Tavern playing pool. After their game, they sat down at the bar where Holly Branson was working the taps.

"Hey," Matt said. "How've you been?"

"Haven't won the lotto yet," Holly said with a smile. "Who's yer friend?"

"Pete Sutherland. Nice to meet you." He reached over the bar to shake her hand.

"You a pilot, too?"

"Sure am," Pete smiled.

"Well, you can have it," Holly said. "These feet stay right on the ground where they belong."

"How 'bout a pitcher of Hog's Breath?" Matt said.

"Don't blame y'all a bit. Comin' right up."

There was a TV set in the corner behind the bar. The news broadcast was showing a replay of Reagan's inaugural address from the west front of the Capitol Building. Scenes of jubilation as the featured story shifted to the release of the hostages from Iran after 444 days in captivity. Finally, they were coming home. Holly brought over the frosted pitcher.

"Now there's something to drink to," Pete said.

"To freedom," they said, clinking their glasses together.

"Just a few hours after the inauguration, and poof, they're released," Pete said.

"How's that for a coincidence?" Matt said.

"A highly premeditated coincidence."

"Since before the election, you think?"

"Who knows? Hey, nothing wrong with a little cloak-and-dagger, but a deal that kept them locked up till inauguration day?"

"Doesn't seem right. At least they invited Carter to welcome them home," Matt said.

"Right," Pete said, just as everything went dark before his eyes.

"I thought you were going to call me," a familiar voice said.

"Rita!" Pete said as he swung around on the barstool. "How've ya been, darlin'?"

She was of medium height and wore a pair of faded denim hip-huggers and brown suede boots. Her black hair was thick with tight, shiny curls that hung down to her shoulders. She had a purple mohair cardigan on, and Matt could see a teasing glimpse of pink lace framing her cleavage.

"I've been meaning to call you. We've just been kind of busy flying and all."

"That's okay," Rita said. "I've been busy, too. Who's your friend?"

"Matt Lavery," Matt said, reaching out to shake her hand.

"The Yankee. Now I remember. How's your ankle, Pete?"

"Good as new; you had the magic touch."

"You haven't seen anything yet."

"Whoa, take me back to the bull, no net needed."

"Care for a beer?" Matt said. Holly brought another frosted glass over and Matt poured.

"So, you gonna come back and buy that canoe, or what?"

"I'll bring my business manager over tomorrow and we'll make a decision. What do you say, Matt?"

"Sounds good to me."

"Matt drives a Jeep. Maybe we could all go on a camping trip this spring."

"Three's a crowd, though," Matt said.

"That's not a problem," Rita said as she wrapped her arms around Pete's waist. "I've got lots of friends."

"I think I'll go on back to the barn," Matt said. "I've got the Knoxville turn tomorrow. Can you find a ride home, bud?"

"Don't worry about him," Rita said. "He'll be just fine."

The alarm went off at 0400, and Matt resisted the urge to remain inert for another five minutes. He got up, showered, shaved, and put on his uniform. The seat to the Jeep felt like ice through his thin polyester slacks. The stars hid behind the dark ragged mist of a low overcast ceiling. Matt was scheduled to fly the Knoxville turn with Barry Dresden. Despite Bob's insistence that Barry was easy to fly with, Matt kept hearing T-Ball's warning that he was someone to watch out for. To make matters worse, the weather was down. Fayetteville to Fort Smith–Little Rock–Memphis–Jackson–Nashville–Knoxville–Nashville–Jackson–Memphis–Little Rock–Fort Smith and back to Fayetteville; twelve legs in fourteen hours, all without an autopilot, all in bad weather and all with Barry Dresden. Matt parked beneath the glow of the green and white rotating beacon, swirling in the mist. He tied his navy-blue raincoat belt around his waist and walked into Flight Control. Tony DeMarco, the Flight Controller, sat before a green computer monitor. Flight Control acted in a dispatch/crew scheduling capacity, passing along information regarding weather, maintenance, and miscellaneous issues.

"Morning, Tony," Matt said.

"Hey," Tony said. "Here's your weather."

Tony handed Matt a long ream of facsimiles that contained the current weather reports for all their destinations, forecasts, SIGMETs (significant meteorological reports), NOTAMs (notices to airmen) containing information about changes to approach minimums, NAVAID outages, runway closures, and airport construction. All that information made it hard to discern what was important from what was not. Tom mentioned in ground school that a good first officer arrives early and highlights the information of significance to make the captain's job easier.

Matt studied the weather reports and noted, with some concern, that many of their destinations were forecast to be right at landing minimums, a 200-foot ceiling with a half-mile visibility, and that few of the airports along their route offered suitable weather to qualify as legal alternates. Matt was highlighting the forecasts and writing in the margins when he heard the door slam shut behind him.

"Morning, Barry," Tony said without turning around. Matt smelled stale cigarette smoke in the air.

"What are you doing?" Barry said.

"Just highlighting the paperwork," Matt said, reaching out to shake Barry's hand.

"Don't do that again. How do you know what's relevant to your captain?"

"I was just trying to—" Barry grabbed the ream of paper and started perusing the data.

"If I miss something crucial because you didn't highlight it, it's my ass that's on the line."

"I won't do it again," Matt said, wishing he could just get back in the Jeep and go home.

"Maintenance is towing 501 down to the terminal," Tony said. "They had to do a gear inspection last night." Barry picked up his flight bag. "We'll stop off at Flight Service on the way down."

"Bye, Tony," Matt said, as they walked out into the cold morning mist.

Barry put his bags down, lit a cigarette, then picked up his bags and walked with the cigarette dangling out of the side of his mouth.

"Looks like it's going to be a long day," Matt said.

"Why is that?" Barry mumbled.

"Twelve legs in fourteen hours in bad weather," Matt said, feeling like an idiot for having to state the obvious.

"Just routine. You'll get used to it, or maybe you won't," Barry said as they set their flight bags down outside the door to Flight Service. Barry took a deep drag on his cigarette and flicked the butt into the frozen weeds. A flash of orange sparks scattered as it hit the ground.

It was warm inside, and Bud Devry was tearing reams of paper from the teletype machine and placing them under clipboards around the counter.

"Morning, fellas," he said with a mug of coffee in his hand. "I'm afraid we're under the influence of a stationary front extending down from a low in southern Missouri. The front's stalled out completely. It's going to be like pea soup around here."

"What are we down to?" Barry asked.

"Ceiling's ragged at 200 feet," Bud said. "Half a mile with ground fog. We'll be going down to a quarter of a mile soon."

"We'll have to depart empty," Barry said. "We're below takeoff minimums." Without a payload of passengers and bags, the flight could legally depart under Part 91, the less restrictive rules governing general aviation. They'd forfeit the revenue for the first leg but at least they could get out of town.

"Where're you boys off to today?"

"Knoxville turn," Barry said. "We can use Little Rock as the alternate for Fort Smith, and Fort Smith as the alternate for Little Rock, but we may have a problem finding a suitable alternate east of Memphis." Bud put on a pair of reading glasses and studied the forecasts.

"Meridian's forecasting 800 and 2 with light drizzle. That'd probably work."

"I hate to carry all that extra fuel," Barry said. "We'll have to bump revenue out of Memphis."

"I don't see anything closer that'll work," Bud said. "You might have to use Meridian for everything east of Memphis today."

It hardly paid to operate the Metro on a day like this. The operating margin was paper thin, and pilots were often reprimanded for carrying extra fuel.

"Thanks, Bud, we'll send you a pilot report," Barry said as the men waved a hand and walked out into the cold, dark morning.

Barry lit another cigarette and Matt got on the upwind side for the walk down the flight line to the terminal.

The inside of the Metro was dark and cold-soaked when they climbed up and stowed their bags. Matt got out his Maglite and went through the exterior inspection while Barry sat down in the left seat, turned on the battery switch and began setting up the cockpit. Matt was just finishing when Barry came down the airstairs.

"I just called Tony on the radio and told him we'd have to depart under Part 91. We've got about ten minutes if you want to grab a coffee."

"Okay," Matt said, following Barry across the ramp to the freight room door. Matt heard the commotion from the queue of passengers in front of the ticket counter. Jackie was trying her best to explain the situation to an irate passenger who spoke with a New York accent.

"Let me get this straight. You're telling us that, due to the weather, the plane *will* be allowed to depart, only we can't be onboard. Is that right, Miss?"

"I'm afraid so," Jackie said. She was trying, in vain, to explain the difference between FARs 135 and 91.

"So, Part 135 applies to revenue-carrying flights?" the man said.

"That's right."

"So that means if you don't charge us anything, we can go."

Jackie was waiting to see a sign of humor on the man's face but there was none.

"I'm afraid we can't do that, sir."

"But you just told us the airline will be refunding our money, and that plane is going to take off anyway, so what's the difference to you if we're on it or not?" The man was getting red in the face.

"It doesn't make a damn bit of difference to me," Jackie said. "Here's the FAA's number in Little Rock. Why don't you call them and ask them to explain it?" The man snatched the number from Jackie's hand.

"See if I won't," he said. "And while I'm at it, I'll be sure to tell them just what kind of *hick* airline you're running down here." Then Olga walked up next to Jackie.

"I think those regulations are for your safety, sir," she said. "You probably have a family, is that right?" The man stared, captivated by Olga's eyes, and nodded.

"We have a 12:00 p.m. flight I can try to rebook you on, Mr. Chambers. With any luck, we'll get a break in the weather by then, or I can direct you to the rental car counter and give you this voucher."

"You know, there is some work I can catch up on right here in the boarding area. I think I'll take a chance on the twelve o'clock."

"Fine," Olga said. "You're all checked in. We should have a weather update in about two hours."

"You're very kind," the man said, picking up his boarding pass and backing away from the counter. "Thank you again for your help."

"My pleasure," she said. "And thank you for flying Arkansas Airways."

Matt was behind the counter in the freight room and heard the complete exchange. He peered around the doorway, stealing glances at her until Barry came back with a coffee in his hand. Anxious passengers were trying to get him to tell them about the weather and their chances of getting out of town, but he just held up a hand and shook his head. He walked back to the freight room and said to Matt, "I'm going out to smoke a cigarette."

"I'll just grab a coffee and meet you onboard," Matt said.

Jackie was coming in from the ramp, her arms wrapped around her chest to ward off the cold.

"Care for a cigarette, Jackie?" Barry said.

"Shut up, Barry. You know I quit," she said.

Matt took a few sips of coffee and steadied the cup in his hand as he walked back to the ticket counter. He was hoping for a final glance at Olga before he'd be trapped three feet apart from Barry Dresden all day, just a wisp of her floral scent to hold against the hard nicotine reality. But Olga wasn't there. She was in the freight room stacking checked bags on the pile bound for Little Rock. She turned and quickly made her way back toward the doorway to the counter. It happened in a heartbeat. Just as Matt came through the doorway, Olga's trajectory darted into his peripheral view, but it was too late. Olga let out a breathless cry, not only startled by Matt's sudden presence but shocked by the scalding splash of black coffee all over the front of her starched white uniform shirt.

"Oh my God, I'm so sorry." Matt's heart was in his throat. He had yet to work out an initial introduction. He was hoping that somehow, subliminally, his body and soul would send out their own unique vibration. Her radar would pick up the signal, a few atoms would whisper his secret, and a seed would be planted in her subconscious, something that would germinate enough to blossom into a budding attraction. Maybe then he'd be brave enough to introduce himself, to try to make her acquaintance with actual words. But now it was too late. The grace and aplomb he was counting on was turned into a clumsy assault.

"Let me get a towel," Matt said.

"No, it's alright, really."

"Did it burn you?"

"No, I'm okay. It was my mistake." The stain on her shirt was no affront to Olga's vanity, just her professionalism.

"It wasn't your fault," she said. "I should have been looking where I was going."

"No, I should have," Matt said, still stunned and embarrassed. "Please let me pay to have it cleaned."

"No, it's alright. Please don't think any more of it. My name's Olga, by the way."

"I know. I'm Matt Lavery. Nice to meet you."

"Nice to meet you, too. Have a safe flight." Then she turned, walked through the doorway, and disappeared.

Matt stood motionless. He took a deep breath and tried to compose himself. He was still flustered as he opened the door to the ramp. The black of early morning was brightening to a dull gray, and Barry was back in the cockpit waiting for him. Two rampers stood by the external power cart, waiting to give the signal for engine start. Matt climbed up the airstairs, pulled the door up and locked it in place. He hung up his coat, sat down and strapped on his shoulder harness as Barry called for the pre-start checklist with a perturbed look on his face. Soon the propellers were spinning, and the digital engine-instruments were coming to life. Dresden released the props from the start locks as the cockpit filled with a piercing snarl and roar. He turned on the generators and signaled the ground crew to disconnect external power. They were set free by a salute, acknowledged with the flash of the taxi light as Matt called ground control for taxi clearance. Barry steered the nose-wheel with the tiller knob mounted on the side panel and Matt read the before-takeoff checklist. Then the tower cleared them for takeoff on runway 34. Dresden made the takeoff, and Matt called out the speeds as they accelerated down the runway.

"V1…Vr." At 120 knots, Dresden pulled back on the control yoke. "V2, positive climb," Matt called out.

"Gear up," Dresden commanded. They climbed straight ahead to two thousand feet, then started a climbing left turn to intercept Victor 13, the airway that would take them south to Fort Smith.

Matt tried to focus on the myriad tasks at hand, the job not only made difficult by Dresden's lack of charm but by the distraction in his mind, the vision of Olga Vargas.

He chastised himself, though he couldn't have precluded the mishap. And what was the loss? Jackie insisted that Olga didn't date pilots. What made him think he had a chance in the first place? But deep down, he held on to the ray of hope that she just might make an exception. He was in the right seat of an airplane that burned jet fuel. Why would one date with Olga represent greater odds?

"That was for us," Dresden snapped. "Fort Smith approach on 120.9."

"Twenty-point-niner, AR 421. Good day," Matt said into the mic. He missed the handoff from Memphis Center, just the kind of distraction he was hoping to avoid.

"You better listen up," Dresden said as he dialed in the frequency for the ILS approach to runway 25. Barry intercepted the localizer which lined them up with the runway centerline. He slowed to 160 knots and called for quarter flaps. As they intercepted the glide slope, Matt lowered the landing gear on command and gave Dresden half flaps. Matt called the tower over the outer marker and Dresden called for three-quarter flaps, then full flaps as they slowed to their target approach speed of

120 knots. At 400 feet above the runway, the approach lights came into view. "Approaching minimums, runway in sight," Matt called out.

They touched down, turned off the runway and taxied to the ramp. Dresden set the parking brake and shut down the engines. Then he went into operations and Matt filled out the weight and balance form.

The station agent walked the passengers out to the plane, and Matt took their carry-on items and stowed them in the nose. He handed the agent a copy of the weight and balance form as Barry came out and climbed into the cockpit. Matt climbed up and waved a hand. The agent waved back, and Matt could see her mouthing the words "Good luck" as he pulled the door closed.

"I'll fly this one, too," Dresden said. "If the Memphis weather lifts a bit, you can have the next one."

Matt was disappointed, unsure whether Barry's lack of confidence was due to Matt's performance or just Dresden's own insecurity.

They went through the same pre-departure procedures and disappeared into the thick gray overcast shortly after takeoff. On the approach to runway 15 at Adams Field, they broke out just above minimums, landed and taxied to the gate. Dresden flew the next leg and finally let Matt fly the short hop over to Jackson, Tennessee where the ceiling had lifted to 600 feet with 2 miles of visibility. It was almost noon; they were twenty minutes behind schedule. There was no time to stop and eat. They flew on to Nashville and Knoxville. Matt felt fatigued. The constant state of alertness, the stress of bad weather and the Dresden factor were taking their toll. It seemed like the trip should be over in Knoxville, but they were just halfway through.

It was pitch-black when they left Fort Smith for the short hop up to Fayetteville. Unlike their previous approaches, which had been precision approaches with localizer and glide slope for guidance, the approach into Fayetteville was non-precision. A localizer would line them up with the runway 16 centerline. They would slow, with gear and flaps extended, until passing the final approach fix (six miles out), then descend to the minimum descent altitude and look for the approach lights. If they saw the lights, they could continue down to the runway threshold and land. The localizer approach required the utmost precision on those foggy nights when Fayetteville was down to minimums. The problem was compounded by the fatigue factor, with crews coming home after being on duty for the past twelve to fourteen hours. It was forbidden by the FARs to descend below the minimum altitude unless the runway or the approach lights were in sight. Pilots had to resist the temptation to duck under for a quick look. The common expression was, "Don't let get-home-itis over-excite us." If the missed approach point was reached and the runway wasn't in sight, a go-around was mandatory. There were times when some experienced pilots considered the bright blue and white neon sign at Bypass Liquor to be the first segment of the approach light system, but they would never admit to busting minimums, the rationale being that it was safer than a minimum fuel divert.

The ceiling was up to 900 feet and the visibility over 2 miles. They flew outbound, away from the field, then reversed course in a procedure turn that lined them up with the inbound localizer course. They lowered the gear and flaps, slowed to their target speed of 122 knots, descended to the minimum altitude, broke out at 900 feet, and landed.

Once clear of the runway, they taxied to the ramp and shut down the engines. Finally, the deafening roar was silenced. After completing the parking checklist, Dresden climbed out and started walking up the flight line to the hangar.

"It sure was a long day," Matt said when he caught up with him. Barry didn't say a word. They dropped their flight bags off at Flight Control, and Barry just turned and walked out the door. Jerk, Matt thought as he looked at his schedule and saw, to his relief, that he'd be flying his next trip with Mark Winger.

The Jeep was cold, and Matt pulled his coat collar close around his neck. Winding down the country road, he looked up and saw a small break in the overcast, a lone star framed by a luminous corona, twinkling in the black well of night. He pulled into the drive and heard the crunching of gravel under the tires as he parked next to Pete's pickup. He turned the key and opened the side door to the kitchen. The house was quiet, and Matt heard a faint ringing in his ears. He went to the fridge and opened a cold beer. He smelled woodsmoke and saw the orange embers glowing in the hearth as he walked into the living room. The stereo light was still on and Matt reached up and turned the power switch off. As he climbed the staircase in the dim light, he saw something hanging from the banister post. He took the penlight from his shirt pocket and shined its beam on a pink lace brassiere.

Matt woke to the smell of fresh coffee and bacon. He took a quick shower, pulled on a pair of jeans and a blue flannel shirt, and went downstairs.

"Morning, Matt," Rita said, facing the stove. She was draped in Pete's long white terrycloth robe, tied around the waist.

"Morning, Rita."

"Care for a coffee?" she said. "Sure is a nice place y'all have. I was just going upstairs to see if Pete needs anything. Help yourself to bacon and eggs."

Matt sat down at the kitchen table. The trace of Rita's femininity lingered in the air. Matt took a sip of coffee and fantasized that Olga was his guest for the night, and it was her lacy lingerie that was hanging from the banister post. He took another sip of coffee and cringed, remembering the clumsy coffee calamity from the day before, knowing that somehow, he'd have to atone for it.

Matt heard footsteps coming down the stairs. Pete had to duck to clear the transom. He was wearing sweatpants and an orange Clemson Tigers T-shirt which hung below his waist. He filled his cup with coffee and pulled up a chair.

"Hey, didn't hear you come in last night."

"It was after nine. I was pretty beat."

"How'd things go with Dresden?"

"It was no day at the beach. How about you?" He tilted his gaze upstairs.

"Great. Rita's a real honey. Grab your coffee, I've got something to show you. We'll be right back, darlin'," Pete called out before the kitchen door slammed shut behind them. Matt followed Pete across the driveway to the garage. Pete opened the door and turned on the light. On the floor, resting on an oiled canvas tarp was a gleaming white canoe with honey brown varnished trim.

"It's beautiful," Matt said.

"She's a Sassafras 16. The hull's made of lapstrake fiberglass, the thwarts and seats are made from ash, and all the brightwork's coated with five layers of spar varnish," Pete said, beaming like a teenager at his first car. "Rita helped me bring it over."

"Well done. Every man should have one really nice toy."

"Let's plan a float trip down the Buffalo River," Pete said.

"Absolutely," Matt said.

By the end of March, Matt was feeling at home in the right seat of the Metro, his skills honed by repetition in the challenging area known as Tornado Alley. Tom Tomlinson was right when he said they'd be flying with some of the best sticks in the business. Captains like T-Ball, Wendell and Mark performed the job with ease. The way they dealt with stress, the tactics they employed to tackle tough weather, and their free-flowing senses of humor made the long days seem short. Matt was treated with mutual respect, and his confidence grew. Confidence in the cockpit was one thing, confidence with women, another.

Olga had been on his mind constantly during the days and especially during the nights. The longer time passed without an opportunity to approach her, the less confident he was that it would ever happen.

It was Monday, March 30. Matt and T-Ball were on the last leg home from the Meridian layover when they heard the news over the radio that President Ronald Reagan had been shot.

"Holy shit," T-Ball said. "Not again." Matt remembered the day when Kennedy was gunned down in Dallas.

"Who'd want to shoot Reagan?" T-Ball said. "That'd be like shooting your grandfather."

"Who'd want to shoot John Lennon?" Matt said.

"Exactly."

"Think we should tell the passengers?" Matt said.

"Might as well. They'll never forget where they were when they heard the news."

As the passengers deplaned with serious looks of concern, they queried Matt and T-Ball about the details. Jackie set up a TV in the freight room, and a small group huddled around.

The news was grim. The bullet entered Reagan's chest, punctured his lung, and lodged one inch from his heart. Press Secretary James Brady was undergoing immediate brain surgery. A Secret Service agent and a D.C. policeman were also injured. Secretary of State, Alexander Haig, was briefing reporters at the White House. His voice trembled and his face perspired as he said, "I am in control here."

"Where's George Bush?" Jackie snapped. "Shouldn't *he* be the one in control? Something's going on that they're not telling us."

The vice president cut short a Texas speaking trip and was due to arrive at the White House at 6:59 p.m.

"Haig's just enjoying his fifteen minutes of fame," T-Ball said.

Maggie Pryor just shook her head. "Who in the world could ever shoot a seventy-year-old man?"

CHAPTER TEN

Spring in the Ozarks was a kaleidoscope of color, the grayish tint painted over by white dogwood and mountain-laurel blossoms. Pink and purple azaleas appeared as if by magic, and jonquils, tulips and bright blue hydrangeas filled the parks, yards and countryside as Mother Nature's perfume floated on the breeze.

The ragtop was off the Jeep, and Matt drove home from the airport surrounded by the sights and smells of spring. He pulled into the drive and parked next to Pete's pickup. Pete was in the side yard wearing jeans, work boots, a white T-shirt, and a red bandana, tied around his forehead. He was leaning on a shovel; beads of sweat covered his face. Bags of compost and topsoil were stacked on the ground.

"Looks like you're on a mission," Matt said. "What are you planting?"

"Pole beans, pumpkins, jalapeños and basil. There's already a nice asparagus bed in place." Matt picked up a shovel and started digging around the border Pete had outlined with a white string.

"Going to the meeting tonight?"

"Sure am," Pete said. "Blahdick said it's mandatory. Everyone not out flying has to attend."

"Why don't we go together?" Matt said. "Stop off at the Whitewater for a beer afterwards. T-Ball said there's going to be a pilot meeting tomorrow night at his place. You might spread the word."

"Been doing that already."

Matt and Pete worked until the house blocked out the sunlight, leaving them in a trapezoid of shadow. Then they climbed into Pete's pickup, drove up to the square and walked into the new Hilton hotel. The meeting room was down the hall to the right of the lobby. Wendell, Mark, T-Ball and Buzz were seated in the back row.

"We're positioned for rapid ejection," Buzz said as they filed in and sat down in the row ahead.

"What's this all about?" Matt said, turning around.

"Blahdick just wants to crack the whip," Wendell said. "He could just as easily write a memo and stick it on the board, but he'd miss the theatrics."

Barry Dresden walked in and sat down in the front row. He was carrying a small notebook and pen.

"Trying to compensate for his lack of college education," Mark said. Andy McShane walked in and sat next to Matt.

"Is Grayson coming?" Matt asked.

"He's supposed to get in at six," Pete said.

Then Fred Blahdick and Tom Tomlinson walked in. Blahdick went up to the podium and tested the mic while Tom sat down next to Dresden. Bob walked in, barely giving a nod as he went up to the front row and sat on the other side of Barry. In the next ten minutes the other pilots came in and took their seats.

"Can I get someone in the back to turn out the lights?" Blahdick said.

Wendell got up and turned off the lights while Blahdick turned on a slide projector which lit up the white screen on the wall behind him. The first slide was a graph showing net operating expenses for the last four quarters.

"As you can see from this slide, expenses for aircraft, fuel, maintenance and salaries have steadily been going up." The next graph showed the revenue for the last four quarters. It too was going up, but at a slower rate. Blahdick had more charts showing load factor and net operating cost per seat-mile. Mark Winger was leaning back in his chair with his eyes closed.

"The bottom line is, gentlemen, we're hemorrhaging money. Our investors are getting impatient. They're not sure whether their decision to grow the company out of debt was the right one. They're meeting this week to decide whether to stay the course and hope for the best or pull the plug on the whole operation. The reason I'm telling you this is so you'll fully appreciate the rationale for the policy changes we're implementing: The first one is called the variable wage plan. Within certain parameters, effective next week, your salary will be pegged to profits or losses for each month. For example, if losses continue at their current pace, as much as a ten percent pay cut will be applied." A collective groan filled the room. "Wait," Blahdick went on. "But if we all work together and the economy picks up, the potential exists for everyone to receive as much as a fifteen percent bonus."

"Who's doing the math?" Mark blurted out.

"Our accounting firm in Little Rock, same as always," Blahdick said. "I can assure you that accurate and legal accounting methods will be used. But, in order to minimize the pain and maximize the potential for bonuses, further policy initiatives will be implemented. Starting tomorrow, anyone called in to fly on their day off before noon who says they're unable because they just had a beer, is either a liar or an alcoholic; both are grounds for dismissal." Jack Truman, the most senior pilot on the seniority list spoke up. "I promise you, Captain Blahdick, on my days off, by 0900 I've got a fishing pole in one hand and a beer in the other. I'm not lying and I'm not an alcoholic."

"Here! Here!" Shouts of support filled the room from the other Members of Parliament.

"And second," Blahdick went on, ignoring the protest, "starting next week we dispense with the luxury of laying over in separate hotel rooms. One room will be shared by each crew."

"No way!" chorused the group.

"The only one who will still have her own room is Captain Shyvers," Blahdick said.

"That's preferential treatment," Buzz said.

"Discrimination," T-Ball said.

"I assure you the benefits of equal opportunity do not apply to any of you gentlemen," Blahdick said.

"We work three feet apart from each other for twelve hours, and now we have to sleep three feet apart as well?" Wendell chimed in.

"Winger farts in the cockpit. Imagine what he does alone in his room," Buzz said.

"Open a window," Blahdick said.

Then Barry Dresden turned around and addressed the group. "Why don't you all grow up and show some respect? Captain Blahdick has the floor."

"Obsequious little sycophant," Wendell said under his breath.

"Ass kisser," Buzz blurted out.

"Look," Blahdick said. "I'm not saying this is going to be easy, or permanent. But sacrifices are required by all of us, assuming you still want your jobs."

Blahdick rambled on for the next fifteen minutes, showing graphs comparing the competitive picture between Britt Airlines, Rio Air, Air Midwest, Tennessee Valley Airlines, Air Wisconsin, and other small regionals, but no one was paying attention. The lights came on and the men filed out, grumbling and complaining. When they were outside the hotel, T-Ball, Wendell, and Mark quickly spread the word about the upcoming pilot meeting.

"There'll be a small collection for pizza and beer, as always," Wendell said.

"Keep it close to the vest, and don't all park right out front. No doubt Dresden'll have his spies out in force," T-Ball admonished.

After the meeting, some of the men gathered down at Hugo's. Matt and Pete pulled two tables together in the back corner. Ginger was drawing beer from the taps.

"Don't let us run dry, darlin'," Buzz said as she set two pitchers down on the table.

"Do you think the situation's really as bleak as Blahdick let on?" Matt said.

"Hell no," Mark said.

"It's an obvious ploy, just another excuse to stick their hands in our pockets," Wendell said.

"We're almost at minimum wage as it is," Andy said.

"Their other ploy-du-jour is the carrot and stick approach," T-Ball said. "You watch, they'll hold out the promise of big equipment, like the new ATR-42. They'll dangle that carrot in front of us, the allure of being served coffee in the cockpit by some sexy flight attendant, all linked to further pay cuts. If they get their way, we'll all be eligible for food stamps."

"I've already started growing vegetables," Pete said.

"Maybe we should run a still, make some hooch and sell it up in the hills to supplement our income," Buzz said. "After all, this *is* Arkansas."

"Face it, guys, what we really need is a union," Mark said. "That would jerk their chain, if nothing else."

Wendell put up a hand.

"Not here, guys. We can talk about that tomorrow night, behind closed doors."

"I've got to get going," Andy said as he put some bills on the table. "Sandy's been sick every day this week."

"Everything alright?" Matt asked.

"Oh yeah, thanks. We'll find out soon." The rest of the guys finished their beer, filed out and went home. Matt and Pete climbed into the pickup.

"What do you make of Grayson sitting up there next to Dresden at the meeting?" Pete said.

"I don't know. Dresden was his flight instructor. They've flown a few line trips together. Maybe he's his new buddy."

"Ass kisser," Pete mumbled as they turned right onto College Avenue. "He just gets on my nerves, ever since that memo on the refrigerator. Lately he's been bragging about some hottie he's been going out with who works behind the ticket counter. It's that same old line of his, 'All I need is a week.' It makes me sick." Matt felt something drop in the pit of his stomach.

"What's her name?"

"I don't know. I couldn't listen to it anymore." Matt was quiet the rest of the way home. The wind was blowing from the west as they got out of the pickup. The house was dark, and the wooden wind chimes by the kitchen door softly clattered as they went inside.

"Nightcap?" Pete said, opening the fridge.

"No thanks, I'm tired." Matt waved a hand as he climbed the stairs and closed the door behind him.

Matt lay in the dark and felt the familiar current of anxiety coursing through his veins. The thought that this coveted job could be yanked out from under him was bad enough, but what intensified his turmoil was the thought that it would happen before he had a chance to be with Olga, to more than atone for the unfortunate coffee calamity. Paradoxically, he fell asleep bolstered by the words Jackie said: she doesn't date pilots.

The next night, Matt and Pete drove to T-Ball's. They passed by the apartment and parked two blocks away on Cleveland Street. When they got to T-Ball's, they saw Bob Grayson's Cutlass parked in front by the curb. They walked up the driveway and entered through the back door. A crowd of twenty pilots was already there. Boxes of pizza were open on the kitchen table and there was a keg of beer resting in a tub of ice.

"Help yourselves, guys," T-Ball said. He was wearing a pair of red plaid pants and a green polo shirt.

Matt looked around the room and saw framed posters of Pebble Beach, Augusta, and Saint Andrews. In the corner, resting on a square of green Astroturf, stood a leather golf bag filled with wooden drivers, shiny irons, a pair of green and white golf shoes and a soiled white leather glove. On the wall hung a black and white framed photograph with the date, April 1964, written in the margin. In the photo stood the towheaded T-Ball next to his father at the Masters tournament, just eight years old in a St. Louis Cardinals baseball cap. Clutching a model of a DC-3 in one hand, the other hand's being shaken by Arnold Palmer, the day he became the first player ever to win the Masters for the fourth time. T-Ball had stars in his youthful eyes, seeds of passion finding fertile ground at an early age. Matt and Pete helped Wendell carry extra folding chairs into the living room.

"Looks like standing room only," Wendell said as more pilots filed in. Bob Grayson sat at the end of the sofa, eating pizza and drinking beer. Andy McShane showed up, followed by Randy Gillette and Buzz. Mark Winger came in with two more boxes of pizza. Soon, the only place to sit was on the floor. Wendell took out a yellow legal pad and sat down on T-Ball's easy-chair.

"Okay, guys," he said. "Make yourselves comfortable. For anyone who didn't get a chance to attend Blahdick's dog-and-pony show, here's a handout of the minutes. Before we get into the details, let's start, as always, with safety issues. Does anyone have anything they'd like to impart?"

"I'm tired of flying fourteen-hour days, twelve legs a day, without an autopilot, with only nine days off a month," Buzz said.

"We'll get to that," Wendell said. "I mean safety from an operational standpoint."

"We need to refuse single-engine boardings," Mark said. "It was at some regional airline out west a few years ago. A Metro was doing a quick turn, with the left engine shut down and the right engine running at idle. A little girl was about to board when the rubber ball she was holding fell onto the ramp and rolled underneath the plane. She chased after it and lost an arm to the prop; luckily, she wasn't killed. It was an avoidable tragedy, and for what, to save two minutes of turn-time? I'm amazed the Feds allow it."

Everyone nodded in agreement. The party atmosphere that heretofore existed took on a somber tone.

"All in favor of ceasing and desisting from single-engine boardings, raise your hand," Wendell said. Everyone raised their hand.

"Duly noted," Wendell said, jotting down the resolution in the legal pad. "We've had an alarming increase in the number of altitude busts reported by Memphis Center, undoubtedly due to fatigue. I propose that, whenever a new altitude clearance is received, both pilots confirm the change verbally and point at the newly set altitude on the instrument panel. If there's any doubt about the clearance, always request a read-back from Center. All in favor?" Everyone raised their hand.

"Duly noted."

"What are we going to do about this single room layover bullshit?" Buzz asked.

"I'm afraid there's nothing we can do," Wendell said. "They've got us by the balls, and they know it. I'll write up a formal complaint, link it to a safety-of-flight issue, but you all know it's like barking at the moon. If no one has anything else to say, I'd like to read the summary of the investigation into the engine failure recently experienced by Randy and Don." The room was quiet as Wendell started to read:

"Inspection at low magnification found that fatigue cracking had initiated from the surface of the root section on the high-pressure side of one of the thirty-six, stage one turbine blades. At a higher resolution obtained from electron microscope scanning, the progression of stage two fatigue cracking from the base of the faceted area was clearly observed. The evidence obtained is consistent with ductile overload fracture. The turbine inlet guide vane assembly also sustained appreciable mechanical damage during the engine failure. Many of the guide vanes contained transverse cracking within the leading edge. Early inspection revealed that one of the eleven IGV segments had sustained complete burn-through failure.

"There's more if you guys want to read the full report. In short, they threw a failed, stage one T-wheel blade and could have easily bought the farm if not for the coolheaded handling by Captain Randy Gillette and First Officer Don Bishop." Everyone raised their beers and saluted Randy and Don who stood up and clowned and bowed for the crowd.

"The amazing thing is that this sort of failure doesn't occur more often," Wendell said. "Especially in our type of operation, where we're temp-cycling to the max, which brings me to the next point.

"Most of you are aware of the power degradation problem we've been experiencing. We've known something was wrong with our engines for some time. Now the cat's out of the bag. We were right all along. They even have a name for it; it's called hot gas erosion. And the Garrett TPE-331 engine is highly susceptible to it, especially in our type of operation—short stage lengths, never getting above 15,000 feet, numerous start cycles. The tips of the turbine blades are being corroded by carbon, causing loss of thrust. We set 880 degrees on takeoff. We're supposed to see X amount of torque, but we're getting much less. Maintenance is removing the spade doors from the landing gear to reduce drag. We've got water injection and JATO (jet-assist takeoff) rockets on the later models, all to augment thrust in the event of an engine failure. But it's not enough. You've all been there, taking off from Fayetteville in the summer with a full boat. You rotate and just hang there in ground effect, as if the airplane can't decide if it really wants to fly. Retracting the gear finally nudges things upward, and that's with two engines. Lose one right at rotation, and we're toast. The Feds are finally coming up with a response. All the engines will have to be recalibrated; their true power output measured on the Dyno. Any engine with more than 10 percent degradation will be taken out of service. We'll all be given a set of performance graphs. The idea is that we match the highest of the two engine's degradation with the actual temperature at each airport in the system. The new gross-weight represents how much payload must be offloaded. A logical response to a problem we've been complaining about for two years. But it's going to cost a fortune. Airplanes will be grounded until properly checked and calibrated, the cost of lost revenue, the replacement cost of an engine that specs out over 10 percent. The bottom line is, the Metro's just not the right airplane for the job. Brand new, right out of the box, maybe, but not in reality. Blahdick's about to issue a detailed memo on the subject. The Feds are going to require aborting the takeoff for any engine that doesn't make minimum torque by 80 knots. Blahdick's going to refute that on safety grounds, claiming that high-speed aborts are more dangerous than the remote possibility of an engine failure. Personally, I think they're scared shitless that we'll be aborting half our takeoffs and the airline will come to a screeching halt."

"Sounds like we're moving in that direction anyway," T-Ball said.

"That's another reason why we need to be cool about this union thing," Wendell said. "There's one last thing I have to say, then we'll call it a night."

"The thunderstorm season is fast approaching. As you all know, we're right in the heart of Tornado Alley. With our woefully inadequate X-band radars, we can't always be sure that what's on the scope is the real picture out in front of us."

"Attenuation, you mean?" T-Ball said.

"Exactly. You're in so much rain that the image of whatever's out in front of you gets blocked out. Without a clue, you could be led right into the jaws of a level-six monster cell. What we need is new C-band, digital Doppler, color-radar, but they cost a mint and the likelihood of that happening is like a snowball's chance."

"So, what's our recourse?" Don Bishop asked.

"Same as always," Wendell said. "Get a thorough weather briefing from Flight Service, don't hesitate to add fuel for a possible reroute. Deviate around weather and divert if there's no better option. Remember guys, it's your lives, your passengers' lives and your tickets that are on the line. Blahdick, George, Dresden, Tomlinson, they'll all be gone someday. The passengers think the FAA and management keep them safe. We know the truth. The buck stops with us. We won't accept acceptable risk. Fly safe. Take no chances. The night you inconvenience sixteen passengers by diverting to Memphis because of tornados in Meridian will all be forgotten a year later. But take a chance, one little drop of the ball, and kill a planeload of passengers? Their families, their loved ones, they'll never forget, and you'll be dead and gone. We know what's at stake. We know the truth. Our management gives lip service to safety, like politicians or used car salesmen. To them it's all a matter of acceptable risk and the bottom line. But we're the ones strapped to the can; there's no one else out there. The cockpit's no place to be on a dark night, surrounded by lightning, with your fuel gauges as low as the balance in your checking account."

"I've had enough of this horseshit," Mark Winger said. "It's BOHICA every time we turn around. We need a union." The other men nodded in agreement.

"They can't keep treating us like this," T-Ball said. "I say we vote to have real representation."

"Union! Union!" chanted the rest of the group. Wendell held up a hand.

"I know it's tempting, for no other reason than to stick it to them. But the chance of sixty pilots forming a union, with Reagan in the White House, in a right-to-work state, is about as remote as Buzz having a date with Cheryl Tiegs."

"You mean, right-to-work for less," Mark added.

"Right," Wendell continued. "I spoke with a labor lawyer who's a friend of my father's up in Pittsburgh. I told him what kind of conditions we're forced to work under. He said he supports our effort to organize, but we need to be fully aware of the risks involved. I'm more inclined to save it as a last option, a Hail Mary pass, if you will."

"But aren't we there already?" T-Ball asked.

"No, I don't think so. It just seems premature."

"I say we stick it to them, and then some," said Mike Ingles, one of the junior captains.

"Careful," Wendell said. "I want to caution everyone to keep a lid on this. The lawyer told me that, on average, five percent of the workforce can expect to be fired when the company gets wind of our intentions. That means at least three of us will be sent down the river and used as scapegoats. That's usually all it takes before the rest cave in."

"But don't we have a legal right to unionize?" Buzz asked.

"Technically, the Wagner Act of 1935 gives us that right. Anyone who gets fired can file charges. But the charges take over three years to resolve on average. First through the General Counsel, then to a full hearing before the Administrative Law Judge, then an appeal to the Board, then up to the U.S. Court of Appeals, then maybe a remand back to the Board, then back up to the Court of Appeals, and finally, a judgment enforcing the Board's order. You'll get reinstated, but when you come back, the union drive will most likely be over. There won't be any protection. The company will probably fire you again, for something else, of course. Eighty percent of those who win reinstatement are fired within a year. To organize successfully we need both economic and political clout; unfortunately we have neither. The most we can expect from the Wagner Act is the right to *attempt* to organize. Let's not lose sight of why we're here in the first place, guys. The big airlines, and management knows it. So, everyone stay cool. Do your jobs with the same level of professionalism, and absolutely no open talk about a union. Keep calm, sit back and let's see what they have in store for us next. We've got to choose our battles, or we'll all be hung out to dry. Now, does anyone have anything else to add?" The room was silent. "Alright then, be careful out there, keep alert. We'll be sure to pass on any developments through the normal channels. Good night, gentlemen, and thank you for your support."

On Sunday morning, Matt woke up to a quiet and empty house. He went downstairs, ground some oily black Colombian beans, and put the kettle on the stove. Pete was laying over in Meridian, and Bob was in Harrison. Matt had the morning to himself and the Meridian trip that afternoon. He took his coffee into the living room and turned on the stereo. The lights dimmed as the house system adjusted to Mary's heavy amperage draw. He took the black vinyl copy of *Rubber Soul* out of the album jacket and placed it on the turntable. He stared at the four young faces on the cover. His mind darted back to that dark day in December. He decided to see what Mary could do so he turned the volume up high, then higher. The Klipsch loud-horns delivered the decibels with ease, and the empty house came alive with "Nowhere Man" reverberating off the windowpanes.

The sun was rising above the treeline as Matt opened a window and smelled the fresh, humid country air breezing through the house. He put on a pair of shorts, laced up his old Adidas, went out through the kitchen door and took a deep breath of air, tinted with earthy traces of fresh cut hay and wildflowers. He jogged past the dirt racetrack and followed the road around to the east. Off in the distance he saw the dark hulking masses of Black Angus cows at rest on the ground. Birds sang in the tree branches overhead. He heard the rumbling sound of a pickup, a small cloud of dust kicked up in its wake. He kept his pace and slowed his breath, trying to obtain the benefits without depleting his reserves. It would be after 10:00 p.m. by the time they'd land in Meridian.

Matt arrived in Flight Control at 1:00 p.m. He was scheduled to fly with Buzz on the trip that went to Tulsa–Fort Smith–Memphis–Tupelo–Laurel Hattiesburg and Meridian. Buzz had only been a line-captain for three weeks and Matt was looking forward to flying with him. The weather looked good, just a few isolated thunderstorms over central Arkansas.

"Shouldn't be a factor," Buzz said, looking the forecasts over in Flight Control. "Say, thanks for highlighting the paperwork; I'm a slow reader."

They walked down to the terminal ramp and started their pre-flight set-up. Matt finished the exterior inspection, then went into the freight room. He could hear Olga's voice through the open doorway. It had been almost two months since their first encounter. Matt felt a halting stab of anxiety. He wasn't prepared. He didn't know what to say to her and was afraid of putting his foot in his mouth. He felt sheepish and exposed, as if anyone who passed by could read his mind. He turned, opened the door to the ramp, walked back out to the plane, stood by the open nose-compartment, and waited for the passengers. Soon the door to the boarding area opened and Olga escorted a group of passengers out to the plane next to his, bound for Little Rock. He saw the outline of Olga's figure, the gentle swaying rhythm of her confident stride, the way the sun glinted off her dark, flowing hair, the striking beauty of her ebony eyes. All the passengers followed behind except for one gentleman who walked close by her side. He was lithe inside a dark-blue Armani suit, his black hair graying at the sides. He seemed polished, urbane, and sophisticated, his aura exuding eminence and accomplishment. The two of them smiled as the man walked up and handed his brown leather attaché case to the first officer who placed it in the nose-compartment. Then the man turned, and he and Olga embraced. Matt watched through the corner of his eye, turning his head away to conceal his stare. He felt a wave of jealousy take over and was unable to think, the maelstrom weakening the support of his legs. He couldn't look at her. He felt like an Andy Frain usher inside his uniform. There was no point in trying to fake it, to somehow board the plane with such aplomb that she would take notice and think of him that night in her bed. Give up, he told himself. She's already gone. No wonder she doesn't date pilots.

Maggie brought his passengers out to the plane, and Matt placed their carry-on bags in the nose. He turned, climbed up the airstairs and closed the door. Matt looked out the windshield as he dropped into the right seat and reached behind him for his shoulder harness.

"Olga's a fox," Buzz said, grinning as he gazed down onto the tarmac and watched her walk back to the terminal. "You ready to rock and roll?"

CHAPTER ELEVEN

The next day was Saturday, April 11. After twelve days in the hospital, Ronald Reagan returned to the White House. His rapid recovery would be seen as an allegory for the country and the economy as well. Matt was off that weekend. After a morning swim and lunch at Drake's Café, he decided to drive out to the airport and stroll through the terminal. He didn't see Olga's Vespa in the parking lot but went in anyway. He opened the door and walked up to the ticket counter. It was in between the morning and afternoon banks, and Jackie was staring out at the distant hills.

"Hey Matt, whatcha doing in civies?" she said.

"I'm off this weekend. Can't kick the habit, I guess."

"Tell me about it," Jackie said. "Matt, I'd like you to meet my son, Justin." Jackie reached down behind the counter, picked up the little boy and held him in her arms. His hair was ruddy brown, just like Jackie's. He wore black and white high-top sneakers, a red Arkansas Airways cap and a pair of gold pilot-wings pinned to his blue T-shirt.

"Hi, Justin," Matt said. "Do you like airplanes?" The boy nodded, putting his face in the crook of Jackie's neck.

"He's my little hero," she said. "We're just a bit shy sometimes, aren't we, J?"

"Have you ever been inside the cockpit of a real airplane, Justin?" Matt said. The toddler shook his head.

"Do we have anything on the ramp, Jackie?"

"506's just sittin' out there," she said. "It's not due to depart for over an hour."

"If it's alright with your mom, how would you like to have a tour?"

"Why, that's a fine idea," Jackie said. "Go with Mr. Lavery, sweetheart. I'll be right here when y'all git back."

Matt walked around the side of the ticket counter and Justin reached up and took his hand. Matt felt a warm flush, a prelude to fatherhood. The sun was bright overhead as they walked out to the red and white plane that sat framed by the green hills surrounding the airport. The cockpit was hot, and Matt helped Justin into the left seat.

"This is where the captain sits. I'm a co-pilot so I sit in the right seat. The co-pilot helps the captain fly the plane."

Justin looked around with shy hesitation.

"Go ahead, put your hands on the wheel." Justin grabbed the control yoke with his little hands, and Matt showed him how the two wheels are interconnected.

"If you move this wheel, the other one moves too. Pull back and we go up; push forward and we go down," Matt said, helping Justin move the wheel. A smile appeared on Justin's face.

Maggie had just arrived to work the afternoon shift. She and Jackie were getting ready for the crowd of passengers that would soon be flooding in and out. Jackie looked out onto the ramp and saw Matt and Justin walking toward her. Justin was still holding Matt's hand, both with smiles on their faces.

"You know, Maggie," Jackie said, "I used to think all men are dogs. Now I'm not so sure."

CHAPTER TWELVE

On Sunday, April 12, Matt and Pete turned on the TV news to watch the launch of the first space shuttle, Columbia. Violent plumes of orange flame and billowing white exhaust blasted across the TV screen as the shuttle cleared launch pad 39A at the Kennedy Space Center. The crowd cheered as the shuttle roared upward. Eight minutes after lift-off, Commander John Young and pilot Robert Crippen jettisoned the shuttle's big fuel tank which broke up in the atmosphere. There was concern that some of the shuttle's heat-shield tiles had been damaged from the shock waves induced during blastoff.

"Man, what a ride," Pete said. "I'd give anything to fly that thing."

"I don't know," Matt said. "Who are you gonna call if you break down? The nearest mechanic's three G's and two hundred miles below, and that 3,000-degree re-entry seems a bit too hot to handle."

"You're a pessimist, Lavery. Where's your sense of daring? What about the science, the beauty, the sheer poetry of it all? Not to mention the view. That alone is worth lighting your balls on fire."

"You've got a point there."

That night, Matt called his parents. He hadn't spoken with them in over a week. "Matthew, what a nice surprise," his mother said. "How are you, dear?"

"How's the flying going, son?" his father said.

"Everything's just fine."

"That's wonderful, dear. When can you come home for a visit?"

"I'm not sure, Mom. I'll try to come home this fall."

"Son, did you hear the news about Joe Louis?"

"No, Dad, I didn't."

"He passed away today."

"Sorry to hear that. I know you had a lot of admiration for him."

"I'll never forget that fight back in '38, between Joe Louis and Max Schmeling. I was just a kid. It was the most famous boxing match of all time. Schmeling had beaten Louis before in '36, so this was a re-match. Schmeling was Hitler's golden boy. Nazi officials were touting that no black man could beat a man of Aryan superiority. Schmeling's prize money was going to go toward building tanks for Nazi Germany. The fight only lasted two minutes. Louis battered Schmeling, forced him against the ropes with paralyzing body blows. On the third knockdown, Schmeling's trainer threw in the towel and the fight was stopped. The crowd went wild. There wasn't a man of color who wasn't in the ring with Joe at that moment. The Brown Bomber struck a blow right to the heart of Hitler's master race theory, democracy triumphed over fascism, and racism took one hell of a beating, for a few hours, at least. Did I ever tell you I shook Joe Louis's hand in London, during the war?"

"I think you did."

"Well, it's a darn shame. The man was a prince, gave away just about every dime he ever made. I think he was only sixty-six years old, too. There's a lesson in that, son."

"What's that, Dad?"

"Nobody knows how much time they've got. You've got to live for today. I know you're focused on getting your career off the ground, just don't forget to enjoy your life along the way."

"I won't, Dad."

"Well, take care, son," his father said.

"You, too," Matt said as he hung up and felt the quiet of the house return.

The next afternoon, Matt showed up in Flight Control for the one-day trip to Fort Smith– Little Rock–Memphis and back to Fayetteville.

He was looking forward to flying with Wendell again. A small group of pilots was gathered around the bulletin board, reading a memo from George Harriet. Everyone was shaking their heads.

To all Line-Pilots

Captain Blahdick has accepted a position with an airline out west. Effective this Monday, Captain Barry Dresden will be the new Chief Pilot. Capt. Blahdick has been instrumental in helping to build this airline into what it is today.

I know you join me in wishing him well, and that you will afford Capt. Dresden the same respect.

George

"What the f—" Buzz said.

"Why in the world would George pick Dresden, of all people?" Don Bishop said.

"He knows, since we already can't stand him, there'll be no need for an initial break-in period," Buzz said.

"I don't see that it really matters," Wendell said. "He'll be flying a desk, mostly. The first-officers should be happy about that."

It was 3:30 p.m. and the temperature was hovering in the low nineties. Matt felt perspiration around the rim of his uniform hat as he stood by the nose-compartment and waited for Maggie to escort the passengers out. They had been operating under the new degraded-power program for the past month. Matt got out his performance chart and calculated that three passengers would have to be denied boarding.

Maggie waved goodbye as Matt pulled the door closed and dropped into his seat. On taxi-out Wendell briefed Matt about the takeoff:

"We'll set 880 degrees and arm the water. At 80 knots we should see 1700 pounds of torque. Try to set the temps as accurately as you can and make a mental note of both torque values. I'm compiling data to send to the Feds."

The tower cleared AR 412 for takeoff on runway 16. Matt set 880 degrees on both engines. At 80 knots he noted the left engine at 1720 pounds, the right at 1670.

"Eighty knots, thrust set," Matt called out. "V1 … Vr … V2."

At Vr, Wendell eased the control yoke back and the nose wheel lifted off the runway. Matt scanned the altimeter and vertical speed indicator to confirm a positive rate of climb. Both instruments showed little sign of life. Matt looked up and saw the end of the runway rapidly approaching. The airplane seemed to be stuck a few feet above the ground. The airspeed indicator crept up to 125kts and Wendell pulled back farther on the yoke. Finally, the vertical speed indicator and altimeter came to life.

"Positive climb," Matt called out.

"Gear up," Wendell commanded. A few seconds later the airspeed accelerated, and the airplane began to climb. Wendell banked left and turned to intercept the course that would take them to Little Rock.

"What a lead sled," Wendell said. "Did you copy those numbers?"

"Got 'em right here. You think we would have made it if we'd lost one?"

"I doubt it, even with the water injection."

"I guess we have no choice but to trust the numbers," Matt said.

"Yeah, I don't like it either."

On the last leg out of Memphis, the western horizon was backlit by a blazing rim of orange and magenta. Matt could see the dark hulks of the river barges ghosting southward on the Mississippi. Once they leveled off, Matt asked, "Are we moving in any direction on the union front, Wendell?"

"It's still preliminary. Personally, I don't want to see it come to that, but we have to be prepared in case we get hit with something out of left field. Most of the guys are being cool about it, although I'm a little concerned with Mike Ingles. He's a bit of a loose cannon."

Matt got up early the next morning and went into town to read the paper over a cup of coffee at the Caffeination Café. As he turned down Mountain Street, he saw the white Vespa parked outside of Ozark Health Foods. His father's advice to seize the day came to mind. As he parked along the curb he thought, if Reagan can take a bullet, I can do this. He felt his heart beating in his chest as a little bell over the door announced his arrival. Olga was standing at the front counter wearing khaki shorts, a pale orange blouse and a pair of leather sandals. She looked up and smiled.

"Hi, Matt."

"Oh, hi Olga. I just came in for a carrot juice," he said, regretting his need for pretense.

"That sounds good. I'll have one too."

"Coming right up," Hal Dunning, the proprietor, said.

"Hal, this is Matt Lavery, one of our pilots."

"Olga's my best customer," he said with a smile.

"What is all this?" Matt asked.

"Elderberry extract, plum vinegar, blue-green algae, shiitake mushrooms, brown rice, miso, alfalfa sprouts and Kukicha tea."

"Does it taste good?"

"For the most part," Olga laughed. "Some things take a little getting used to."

"It must be good for you."

"Oh, it truly is. My mom was sick and now she's well. This kind of food will help keep her that way. It was hard for her to give up sugar but she's getting used to it." Matt was trying to affect an air of nonchalance but feared he was running out of things to say.

"So how do you like riding your Vespa?"

"I love the feel of the wind in my face," she said.

"I do, too. I take the top off my Jeep when the weather is nice. Sometimes I'll even drop the windshield to the hood." He almost invited her to go for a ride but stopped short, not wanting to press his luck.

"Do you ever take it off-road?" Olga asked, taking a sip of juice.

"Sometimes. Pete and I are planning a camping trip to Richland Creek. He just bought a beautiful canoe."

"I love the outdoors," Olga said. "It's so peaceful."

They finished their drinks and Olga reached for her purse.

"Let me buy these," she said.

"No, it's my pleasure," Matt said.

"If you'd like, I can just put everything on your tab," Hal said.

"The next one's on me, then," Matt said.

"Deal," Olga said, placing her arms through the straps of her backpack.

"Thanks again, Hal," she said as she turned toward the door.

"My pleasure, as always. Give my best to your mom."

"Nice to meet you," Matt said. As he opened the door for Olga, the bell chimed overhead again.

They walked over to the Vespa. Olga gracefully swung a leg over the saddle and pushed the scooter off its kick-stand.

"It was nice talking with you," Matt said.

"You too," she said, turning the key and kick-starting the engine. She waved a hand as she pulled out into the street.

Matt climbed into the Jeep and hit the steering wheel for joy. It was an innocent encounter. It may have meant nothing to her, as she was always polite, but at least it was an opener.

By June, Fayetteville had blossomed into a true botanical paradise. The temperature was in the 90s by noon. The line-pilots were feeling the heat in the cockpits and in their pay-checks as well. The engines on the Metros were struggling to make takeoff power, and the company was struggling to make a profit.

On Friday, June 12, for only the second time in history during the regular season, the Major League Baseball players went out on strike. It was Sunday morning, and Matt was in the kitchen reading the paper when Pete came downstairs.

"Got any aspirin, bud?"

"In the cabinet by the fridge," Matt said. "What happened to you?"

"I was attacked by Jose Cuervo last night at the Whitewater. A bunch of the guys were shootin' pool."

"I'm going to the Wilson Park pool. Wanna come?"

"Not a bad idea," Pete said, pouring a cup of coffee.

"Did you hear the baseball players went out on strike?"

"Hell, those guys make more in one season then we'll make in fifty years," Pete said.

"Nobody's life is in their hands, either."

"Well, more power to them if they can get it," Pete said. "It doesn't seem fair to the fans, though."

The Razorback football fans were the most fanatic (hence the word), loyal, obsessed, and zealous group of people in the state of Arkansas, due partly to the fact that there were no professional teams. Nothing could quite compare with the sheer insanity of an autumn weekend in Fayetteville when the Hogs were playing at home. Cars, trucks, and busses were decorated to resemble every form of swine, and parties raged up and down Dickson Street until late into the night. The leader of the team was Coach Lou Holtz, or Coach, as he was known about town and at the airport where he was a frequent flyer. He became something of a national figure after the Razorbacks' stunning win over Oklahoma at the Orange Bowl in 1978. And he was well on his way to compiling one of the best win/loss records in University of Arkansas history. He was the closest thing the town had to a celebrity, so when it was announced that Coach would be on *The Tonight Show* with Johnny Carson on Friday, June 19, everyone made plans to watch.

Matt and Pete went down to the Whitewater Tavern where a few extra TVs were set up around the bar. There was a crowd of airline people at a table in the corner, and they sat down with Jackie, Mark, Maggie, and Andy.

When Lou Holtz walked onstage, the crowd in the tavern went quiet. People were glued to the tube. Coach started a jovial banter with Johnny Carson about golf courses, his goals in life, being skinny and his upcoming summer schedule. Then he started joking about what it was like in Arkansas. He said, "Back in Fayetteville, we have our own little hometown airline, where you don't just buy a ticket, you buy a chance!" Johnny started laughing, followed by the studio audience, and then some in the Whitewater joined in. But those at the table in the corner were quiet, except for Jackie.

"Why, that son of a bitch! Did you hear what he just said about us? The nerve. We're just as professional as Delta or American. Who does he think he is, pandering to everyone's perception, or misperception, of Arkansas? He'd probably tell 'em we don't even wear shoes if he thought it'd get a laugh." She was turning red in the face. Then she flung a leg up on the table and said, "See my shoes, you skinny little whistle-blower? Well, you can just kiss my shoes the next time you show up at the ticket counter to take your big chance to Little Rock." Maggie tried to jump in and calm her down, but Jackie was on a roll. "What's everyone got against Arkansas anyway? Hell, we're home to Walmart, Tyson Foods, JB Hunt, the Daisy BB Gun factory and some of the most drop-dead gorgeous scenery in the whole damn country."

Pete looked over at Mark, incredulous. He whispered, "Daisy BB Gun factory?"

"Just let her go," Mark said with a grin. "Come on, Jackie, don't get your undies in a bunch. So what if he blew his big chance to increase his property value? It was just a little tease, no real harm done."

"Yeah, well, we'll see about that," Jackie said.

A few weeks later, Coach showed up at the ticket counter for the afternoon flight to Little Rock. Jackie happened to be working that day. She was just as sweet as Southern molasses as she gave him his boarding pass and checked his leather suitcase and golf clubs.

"I can't tell you how proud we all were the other night when we saw you on the TV," she said. "Imagine, little ol' Fayetteville, Arkansas, finally on the map. Now you have a nice, safe flight and we'll see ya when ya get back." Coach Holtz proceeded to the boarding area and Jackie lugged his bag of golf clubs and suitcase back to the freight room. Walter was loading bags, putting them on the cart to take out to the plane.

"Walter, take these two and put them on 507," she whispered.

"But, Miss Jackie, them bags is tagged to Little Rock, and 507's going to Dallas."

"Excellent reading, Waltay. Now, you do as I say, ya hear?"

"Yes, ma'am," Walter said, as he loaded the bags onto the other cart.

"And don't worry," Jackie said. "He'll get 'em back—someday."

On Monday, Matt met Mark Winger in Flight Control at 0700. They were flight planning the first day of a two-day trip that went to Memphis–Tupelo–Meridian–Laurel-Hattiesburg–Meridian–Tupelo and back to Memphis for a short layover. Severe thunderstorms were in the forecast east of the Mississippi later in the afternoon. On the walk down the flight line to the terminal ramp, Mark said, "Matt, don't make any plans for the last weekend in September. That's when I host the annual end-of-summer blowout party. Last year almost everyone came. I put a blue tarp in the back of my El Camino starting in July. That's your signal. The guys buy cases of beer and put them under the tarp. By party time we usually have a couple hundred. I live in a cabin just south of West Fork. It's up on the plateau just west of the river. The farmer I rent from mows the field for us. We build a bandstand, a bonfire, and a big barbecue pit. I'm hoping to get Sashay to come up from Macon. They're one of the best bands around."

When they got to the plane, they stowed their bags in the cockpit. Then Matt began the exterior inspection. "I'm going to grab a coffee," Mark said. "Want a cup?" Matt went back up to the cockpit, put his flashlight in his flight bag and took out the charts he'd need to start the day. He looked out through the windshield and saw Olga walking across the tarmac toward his plane. He'd only seen her a few times from a distance since their encounter at Ozark Health Foods. His heart was racing as he came down the airstairs. Olga wasn't escorting any passengers and there wasn't another plane on the ramp. It appeared that she was walking out to talk to him. His mind raced. Olga smiled as she walked up to Matt.

"Good morning, Olga."

"Hi, Matt. Captain Dresden just called. He said he needs to speak with you on the phone, right away."

"Did he say why?"

"No, he didn't." They started walking back toward the terminal together. Matt felt embarrassed in front of her. The possibility that he was guilty of something hung in the air. Distant memories of a visit to the principal's office to explain why he'd been absent on the Cub's opening day flashed in his mind.

"I'll dial the number for you," Olga said as they entered the freight room.

"This is Matt Lavery," he said when Dresden picked up.

"Matt, your mother just called. She asked that you call her as soon as possible." Matt held his breath as he dialed the number.

"Matthew," his mother's weak voice came on the line. "Honey, I don't know how to tell you. Your father had a heart attack this morning. He's in intensive care at Evanston Hospital. I just came home to pack some things, then I'm going right back. Barbara's been with me the whole time." Matt felt a surge of adrenaline spike through his veins.

"Is it serious?"

"They don't know yet, dear. He's still unconscious. You may want to come home."

"I'm on my way," Matt said. "Are you alright?"

"I'm just a bit scared," she said. "Here's the number at the hospital. You can reach me there."

The receiver felt heavy in his hand as he hung up and felt fear coursing through him like molten lead, numbing his senses until all that was left were a few brain cells to work the words out of his mouth. He called Barry Dresden and told him what happened.

"Don't worry, Matt. I'll get a reserve to sub for you. Let us know if there's anything we can do."

Janice Stevenson made his travel reservations. He would go to Memphis on the same flight he was supposed to fly, then catch a

Republic flight up to Chicago, arriving at noon. His flight was running forty minutes late, not departing until Andy McShane could show up to take his place.

Jackie heard the news from Flight Control. She hung up the phone, walked back to the freight room and saw Matt in a daze, staring out the window at the distant hills.

"Matt, I'm so sorry," she said. He heard his name, and when he turned around, Jackie put her arms around him. He felt the sting of tears welling up behind his eyes. Olga came back, too.

"We're all praying for your father," she said. "I'm so sorry to hear the news."

"You can board early if you want time to be alone," Jackie said.

He stowed his bag in the nose and climbed aboard. It seemed strange to be making a right turn to the aft cabin instead of a left to the cockpit. This was supposed to be his trip, his normal life. In just a few minutes everything was knocked off balance, like a gyro from its gimbal; nothing as it should be. He sat in the back of the plane, his mind flooding with fear. What if his father should die? What would happen to his mom? What would happen to him? His father had always been there for him with so much strength and support. Then his mind darted back to Olga, and how he wished she had hugged him the way Jackie had.

Matt's thoughts were interrupted by the sound of footsteps coming up the airstairs. Andy McShane threw his flight bag up in the cockpit and turned and saw Matt sitting alone in the back of the plane.

"Hey, Matt," he said as he leaned forward and made his way to the rear of the cabin. "Sorry to hear about your dad."

"Thanks. We don't know how serious it is. Sorry they had to call you out on such short notice."

"No problem."

"How's Sandy?"

"She's great. It's official. We're expecting our first baby in November."

"Congratulations, that's great news. I'm happy for you both. We'll have to celebrate when I get back."

"You just call us if there's anything we can do." Matt nodded as Andy turned to go out and greet the passengers.

Matt felt the aperture of his senses closing in, like the way the old black and white TV-screen looked late at night when the stations signed off. After the Air Force fly-by and the National Anthem, the image would shrink to the center of the screen, chased by the darkness until all that remained was a little white dot.

The roar of the engines helped dull his senses as the plane gained altitude. Matt felt small looking out over the sprawling Arkansas landscape, blue haze draped over the dark green waves of the Boston Mountains, rice fields along the river delta, the long, tin roofs of the chicken houses. His mind was racing above its red-line limit, about to shut down. The landing in Memphis jolted him back. Andy handed Matt a small piece of paper after the last passenger deplaned.

"Call us if there's anything you need."

"I will," Matt said. "And tell Sandy congratulations for me." Then Mark Winger came down the airstairs.

"Hang in there, Matt," he said before walking into the operations room.

The Republic DC-9 departed on schedule and Matt closed his eyes. He thought about the circular irony of life he'd just encountered: a new life being brought to Andy and Sandy, his father's life possibly being taken away.

Please God, let me wake up and realize it was all a bad dream, he prayed. His father was just fifty-seven. He sounded like his same old self the other night on the phone, as spry as a cat. Maybe it was all a mistake, a misdiagnosis. Maybe he'd walk into the ER and his father would be up and ready to go home, having befriended half the nurses and doctors on his floor.

Matt picked up the keys to a compact rental car and drove to the Evanston Hospital. A sick feeling came over him as he walked into intensive care and smelled the sterile air and saw orderlies pushing wheelchairs and gurneys. He opened the door to the waiting area and saw his mother and her friend, Barbara, sitting on chairs in the corner. His mother's eyes were swollen, her face a chalky pallor.

"Hi, Mom. Hi, Mrs. Detman," he said. They stood up and everyone exchanged hugs.

"I'm so glad you're here, dear."

"How is he?" Matt said, afraid to hear the answer.

"They're not giving us much information. It happened this morning. You know your father always leaves the house at 6:30 a.m. I heard the door close like always. Then when I got up fifteen minutes later, I noticed his car was still in the driveway. I thought that was strange. Maybe he was driving someone else's car and I just didn't remember. Then I opened the door and saw him lying on the pavement. He was still trying to breathe."

"I was picking up the paper from the front lawn when I heard your mother scream," Barbara said. "Then I ran inside and dialed 911."

"Did anyone try CPR?"

"Oh, honey, we didn't. I couldn't think at the time." She was on the verge of tears.

"Fifteen minutes," Matt said. "You found him fifteen minutes after he left the house?"

"About," his mother said.

"And when did the ambulance arrive?"

"About fifteen minutes after I called 911," Barbara said.

"That's thirty minutes," Matt said, feeling sick.

"We followed them to the hospital in my car," Barbara said.

"What did the paramedics do in the ambulance?"

"We don't know, dear. We've been in to see him twice. The rest of the time we've just been sitting here waiting."

"I want to see him," Matt said.

"Dear, I should warn you. Dad doesn't look so good." Martha Wahlund, the attending nurse, opened the door to intensive care.

"It's nice to meet you," she said to Matt as the three of them walked in.

"Your father is heavily sedated," Martha said. "His vital signs are stable but he's still unconscious." Martha pulled the curtain back in the first room on the right, while Matt held his breath and braced against a flood of tears as he followed the women in. Before him lay the man he idolized and admired with a pride that never waned, even when he grew to realize that his father was human after all. His father was a simple man who lived by two simple rules: treat others the way you would want to be treated and do everything in moderation. He was uncomplicated and saw the inherent good in everyone.

Matt froze when he saw his father lying before him. It was worse than he thought. His eyes were closed, his breath forced by a respirator, his skin ashen and deathlike. It's going to take a miracle, Matt thought.

"Hi, Dad," he said in a weak voice. There was no response. Matt placed his hand on his father's arm. It felt cold.

"It's me, Dad. It's Matt. Hang in there and everything's going to be alright." His words were meant to convince them both. The sting of tears welled up, becoming harder to hold back.

"Dear," his mother said as she picked up her husband's limp hand. "We're both here; take all the time you need." There was no response. Matt glanced up at the monitor and saw his father's heartbeats displayed in a steady stream. They looked so normal to his untrained eye. Then Martha appeared from behind the curtain.

"His heart rate just went up a bit. He must know you're here."

"Do you really think so?" Matt's mother said.

"Absolutely. Keep communicating with him. There's great healing power in that. I've seen it many times before."

Matt wondered how far out on a limb this nurse was going, wanting to comfort and encourage, without dispensing false hope. He thought about articles he'd read about patients who were pronounced clinically dead but later revived. How they recounted similar out-of-body experiences, looking down from the ceiling at their lifeless bodies as the medical team worked on them, seeing the brilliant white light at the end of the tunnel, the disorientation of being reincarnated because it just wasn't their time; they had children to raise, important work to finish. Matt looked up at the ceiling and scanned the four corners above his head, thinking, are you there, Dad? Suddenly, a wave of pain and sadness crashed over him. He put his hands over his face as bursts of tears came pouring out. His mom was crying too as they held onto each other, trying to find some balance, something to grip against the grim reality before them. Matt regained his composure and noticed that Martha had left the room.

"Why don't you go home, have something to eat, and try to relax? I want to stay with him a bit longer," Matt said.

"That's a good idea, Louise," Barbara said. "Matt can call us if there's any change and we can come right back." Matt's mom nodded and Matt escorted the two women out to the waiting room. He hugged his mom again.

"Thank you for all your help, Mrs. Detman." Matt hugged her, too, before the women walked out through the main door. Then he went back to the ICU and walked into his father's room. He pulled up a chair by the bed. He couldn't believe it. His father looked so helpless, wired to life-support, a tube in his mouth, being kept alive by a respirator. He knew his father never wanted to go like this; he'd said so many times before.

Matt felt the quiet closing in around him, the shrinking dot on the TV screen. He was tired, emotionally drained. He folded his hands and bowed his head. He had spent a good portion of his life making touch-and-goes with Christianity, but never a full-stop landing. Hedging his bets, he began to pray.

He was halfway through his prayer, and half asleep, when something stirred his senses. It was an old feeling, familiar, an intense awareness, a comfort and closeness he'd known intimately. He heard the soft swish of the curtain being drawn open. He turned, and his mouth dropped open.

"I'm so sorry, Matt. I saw your father's name in Admissions." He stood up and felt his legs buckle, straining to carry the weight. In a heartbeat she was in his arms, and his arms had never felt so good.

It was Karen.

CHAPTER THIRTEEN

He held onto her, his embrace tightening against the whirlwind of emotions that sent his world spinning out of control. In the two years that he and Karen were together, she had become a part of the family, the daughter his parents were never able to have. At times Matt thought their breakup was harder on his father than it was on him. Matt always admired the ease at which Karen showed affection for his parents, so when she gently let go of him and pulled away, he could see tears in her eyes.

"Don't be frightened by the way he looks," she said. "The respirator and trach tube are helping him breathe."

"You made it, you're really a doctor."

"Are you still flying?"

"I'm flying for Arkansas Airways, a small airline based in Fayetteville."

"Then you made it, too," she said, making everything seem so easy. The root cause of all his insecurities summed up nice and simple, as if she were really saying, "I told you so."

"They're just nineteen-passenger turboprops," he said. Her hair was cut shorter than he remembered. "You look great."

"Thanks. I'm working in pediatrics. The hours are long, but I love every minute of it."

"I'm still in a daze," Matt said. "I was supposed to fly a trip this morning, then I got the call. I should be in Memphis right now but instead, I'm here with you."

"Life is strange sometimes," Karen said.

"I don't know what to do for him," Matt said, looking down at his father's chest, rising and falling to the respirator's commands.

"Why don't you go home and get some sleep. I'll speak with Dr. Patel and find out all I can. If there's any change, I'll call you right away. I'll give you my pager number; you can reach me anytime. I'll be here at the hospital all night."

Matt knew her advice made sense, but he didn't want to leave. He was here in this small room with two of the most important people in his life, both perhaps destined to leave him forever. All he wanted to do was wrap himself in Karen's arms. She looked at her watch, then jotted down her pager number on a piece of paper.

"Tomorrow will be a long day," she said. "Go home and get some sleep. And say hi to your mom for me. I'll come by tomorrow." Matt held on to that promise as he took the paper from her.

"I'm so glad you're here," he said, looking down at the ring finger on her left hand.

"You know I always loved your dad." Matt felt a ripple of relief: no diamond to dash his far-flung fantasy. Even if the worst should happen, she'd be there for him. They still had a bond between them, a mutual connection, and for now that connection was all that was sustaining him.

Matt woke in the middle of the night, confused and disoriented. The ticktock of his parents' anniversary clock down the hall brought him back to the sad reality. It was too late to be rescued by a dream. He would have to face it head on, no matter what. Then he heard the muffled sounds of sobs coming from his parents' bedroom. He thought about going to her to ask if she needed anything, a glass of water or something stronger, but instead, he reached up and pulled the pillow down over his head and tried to blank his mind.

Soon the dull light of dawn invaded his senses, and the dark hole he'd been hiding in vanished. He wished he could deny the reality that awaited him, but he had no choice but to get up and face it.

He woke to the smell of bacon and coffee. After a shower, he went down to the kitchen. His mom was gone. He poured a cup of coffee and opened the kitchen door.

"I thought I'd find you here," he said. His mother was kneeling on the ground, her eyes swollen and red, a pair of pruning shears in her hand.

"Your father helped me plant these," she said, pointing to a bed of burgundy red peonies. "They always herald the beginning of summer with such beauty and fragrance, but by the end of June, they're all gone."

"Your garden looks beautiful, Mom." He reached down, offered his arm, and gently pulled her up. She leaned against him as they walked back to the house.

"I saw Karen last night," he said. "She's a resident at the hospital."

"What a surprise. You always made such a nice couple." Matt wasn't sure he should have mentioned it. He thought it would cheer her up, but now he wished he'd kept it to himself, like hiding his own piece of buried treasure.

"I didn't bring any clothes with me, just what I packed for my layover."

"Your father probably has a few shirts that will fit you."

Matt went up to his parents' room, opened his father's dresser drawers and saw all the familiar colors and patterns. He felt an eerie sense that his father's clothes might never be worn again. Matt found a new blue polo-shirt, pulled it on and went downstairs.

"I'll drive," he said, holding the door open for her. They drove in silence for a few minutes.

"Maybe today will be a good day. I prayed all night; now it's up to God," his mother said. When is it not? Matt thought. If there was any fairness left in life, they would do their part, visit, and pray like dutiful soldiers, and their efforts would be rewarded. Miracles were happening 'round the clock in the maternity ward. Why couldn't God just throw out one more?

Martha Wahlund opened the door when they got to the ICU.

"Good morning," she said cheerfully, as if this were just a bed-and-breakfast she was running. "There hasn't been much change, although he did move his hands this morning."

"That's wonderful," Matt's mother said. Matt refused to take the bait. Martha pulled back the curtain.

"Dr. Patel said he'd stop by this morning. He can answer any questions you might have. I'll be nearby if you need me." She disappeared behind the curtain.

"Hi, Dad," Matt said, but there was no response. Matt put his hand on his father's arm. It still felt cold and inert. The miracle might have to be bigger than he thought.

"He knows we're here," Matt's mother said. Matt nodded. They pulled up chairs and sat down by the headboard, the monitor displaying a steady stream of blipping heartbeats, his chest rising and falling to the respirator's commands. Soon the sad stillness of the room was interrupted by the swish of the curtain.

"Good morning," he said in a distinct Indian accent. "I'm Dr. Patel. I was the attending physician who treated Mr. Lavery when he was admitted."

"Is he going to be alright?" Matt's mother asked.

"We don't know yet. He's suffered a serious myocardial infarction. The paramedics attempted to defibrillate him thirty times in the ambulance."

"They shocked him thirty times?" Matt said.

"Three coronary arteries were completely blocked. Right now, he's unable to breathe on his own. It is unclear how much brain damage he has sustained."

"Brain damage," Matt mouthed the words and put a hand on the bed frame for support.

"I'm consulting with Dr. Slavin, the pulmonologist. We just have to be patient. If there's improvement, then we'll see if he can breathe on his own. I'm afraid, at this point, there's not much more I can tell you."

"What do you think his chances are, Doctor?" Matt said.

"For a full recovery? I can't say. Just be assured that we're doing everything we can. It's a good thing you're both here. The presence of family has been known to elicit a powerful healing response. Please feel free to call me if you have any questions." Dr. Patel handed them each a card with his phone numbers on it and walked out of the room. That wasn't much to go on, Matt thought, as a deeper sense of hopelessness set in.

The day dragged on with more of the same. The hands of the clock barely seemed to move. They took turns standing, placing a hand on his forehead, whispering in his ear. It seemed so long ago when Matt prayed for a miracle, yet it was just this morning. Options, luck, and hope were falling away like grains of sand through an hourglass. Matt's thoughts were like green flashes from fireflies on a hot summer's night, glowing and then quickly fading to black. Maybe the miracle was the very fact that his father was dying, the miracle of death, of being born in reverse, or in a straight continuum; just moving into and out of different planes of existence, like passing through a revolving door. This earthly life might be just a prison compared to the next, a chance to suffer and grow, to learn lessons and fulfill a contract. Maybe his father was the lucky one. Matt felt overwhelmed by the mystery of it all, like trying to comprehend infinity. He felt weak. He looked over and saw his mother's head nod forward then jerk back slightly as she took a quick breath of air. Then the swish of the curtain. Turning, he felt the warmth of her hand resting on his shoulder.

"Hi, Matt. Hi, Mrs. Lavery." Matt's mother opened her eyes and stood up, a reflexive smile spread across her face.

"Karen, what a nice surprise." They hugged and kissed each other on the cheek. "And call me Louise," she said. "Look at you, a real doctor. Congratulations, dear. We're so proud of you."

Matt felt the geometry of his family strengthened by Karen's arrival; the sad reality of his father's condition replaced by Karen's aura of optimism. She was still a part of the family, in some confusing capacity.

"How are you holding up? Can I get you anything?"

"We're just fine, considering the circumstances," Matt's mother said. "You must have such a busy schedule. Thank you for stopping by."

Karen drifted over to the headboard and placed a hand on Matt's father's forehead. Matt felt flushed with love for her, as strong as he'd ever felt before. It only made him feel more the fool for ever wanting to leave. Maybe it wasn't too late after all. Maybe his father's heart attack was all part of a greater plan to reunite them. Maybe that was the miracle God had in mind. Matt glanced at Karen's left hand again. When she was about to leave, he followed her out behind the curtain and down the hallway.

"There's so much I have to tell you," he whispered.

"Me too," she said.

"Are you free for dinner tomorrow?" he asked. "How does six o'clock sound?"

"I'll meet you at 6:30 p.m. at the Blind Faith Café," she said. "It's on Dempster Street, a few blocks in from the beach. If anything changes, you can page me, and I'll call you right back." They hugged each other, then she turned and walked away. Matt felt a familiar rush, the same feeling he felt years ago on their first date, something to cling to against all that was crumbling around him. He had a smile on his face as he drew back the curtain to his father's room, emboldened by a renewed sense of strength, a strength he couldn't keep to himself. He put his arms around his mom and hugged her. "Everything's going to be alright, Mom. One way or the other, it's going to be alright."

The next day unfolded much the same as the day before. There was no change to his father's condition. How long could this go on, Matt wondered. Where would they draw the line? And who would draw it? Hadn't he read about patients who were in a coma for years and then simply woke up, as if from a five-year nap?

After lunch, Matt's mother went back to the hospital while Matt drove his father's car to Field's to buy a pair of khakis and a dark green polo shirt. Then he went to Mangle's and bought two bouquets of yellow roses. He stopped off at home, changed into his new clothes, and put one of the bouquets in a vase on his mother's nightstand. Then he got back in the car and drove to the hospital.

"How is he, Mom?" His mother just shook her head.

"The same, I'm afraid." When they finished their ritual of mutual encouragement, Matt said, "I'm meeting Karen for dinner tonight."

"That's wonderful, dear."

"If you think you'll be alright."

"I'll be just fine," she said. "Don't worry about me. You two go out and have a nice time."

"It's just as friends," he said.

Matt arrived five minutes early. He looked at the bouquet of yellow roses on the right seat of the rental car. He picked them up and placed them on the floor behind him. Too presumptuous, he thought. He didn't see Karen's car anywhere.

He scanned the dining room, sat down in a booth along the wall, and started reading the menu. Seitan stir-fry, vegan burritos, pumpkin purée, miso soup, twig tea and an assortment of fresh-squeezed juices. The memory of Olga at Ozark Health Foods raised the bar of surrealism. What was he doing here, about to have dinner with Karen while his father lay in a coma just a few miles away? He ordered a cup of coffee and tried to convince himself that this was just an innocent dinner with an old friend. They broke up, lost touch, got on with their lives. What's over is over, Matt thought. There's no going back. Swirls of steam rose up from the black surface of his coffee. Matt looked at his watch: quarter to seven. Then he looked up and saw her walking past the front window. He stood and waved as she entered the room. She wore a pair of faded denim jeans, a white cotton shirt and leather sandals. They kissed on the cheek, then she sat down and slid in across from him.

"Sorry I'm late, I've been on the phone for the past hour. Have you looked at the menu?" The waitress came over and Karen ordered the seitan stir-fry. Matt ordered the macrobiotic plate.

"Do you still eat pizza?"

"Sometimes," she laughed. "I was at Gino's with a friend a few months ago. It made me think of you." Karen took a sip of water, then reached out and placed a hand on his arm.

"I'm so sorry about your father."

"How long do you think he can go on like this?"

"Nobody knows for sure."

"I think they know," Matt said. "They just won't admit it." He admonished himself for sounding cynical. God knows she'd heard enough of that from him in the past. "I don't mean to sound like a pessimist," he said. "It just doesn't look good."

"I know it's always been hard for you to have faith," she said.

Matt felt the familiar barb of condescension. Careful, he cautioned himself, don't fall into the old pattern. There's nothing at stake anymore; we're just good friends.

"I guess you still know me pretty well," he said. "I'm a realist." When their food arrived, Matt looked down at the plate, overflowing with brown rice, bright green kale, alfalfa sprouts, ivory-colored cubes of tofu smothered in a mushroom sauce, and bright orange squash.

"It's very colorful," Karen said with a laugh.

They ate for a few minutes, and Matt was drawn to Karen's left hand again. He couldn't contain the question any longer.

"I thought you were married," he said. Karen looked past him, as if speaking to someone in the next booth.

"We were engaged."

"I'm sorry. It's none of my business."

"No, it's okay. I believe everything turns out for the best."

"The eternal optimist," he said, hoping he hadn't revealed a certain tone she was certain to pick up.

"You should try it."

"I have. Then I turn on the five o'clock news and give it up. All that pain and suffering in the world, how can that all be for the best?"

"I believe it can be," she said without a trace of defensiveness. "There's so much we can't see, just beyond our sight."

"You mean faith," Matt said.

"Yes. As a pediatrician, how could I possibly come to terms with the reality of adult diseases that stalk and kill innocent children? I couldn't have a normal life without faith. You've told me how miraculous it is that you can land a plane in the fog, barely even seeing the ground. You couldn't fly without some form of faith. You put your faith in technology, trust it with your life. It's not much different." Matt nodded. He was looking into her brown eyes, remembering the way she used to look when she had had faith in him, when she trusted him with her mind, body, and soul, and how he let her down. The tears, the pleading, the clinging sadness, like shattered glass. It was quiet for a few minutes, the act of eating giving relief to the fragility between them. When it was almost too quiet, Matt said, "So, what made you want to become a doctor?" He instantly regretted it. This was Karen, his Karen. Had he forgotten everything about her? Was he not paying attention to her at all during their two years together? That familiar look of disappointment spread across her face.

"You asked me that same question on our first date."

"I'm sorry," he said. "I really do remember. I just didn't—"

"Know what to say?" she filled in the blank. Matt nodded.

"Aside from the science, which I love, if a child is suffering, I want to be there, to heal and comfort and be truly needed."

"I envy your patients."

"Well, you had your chance, mister," she said with a smile. The word *had* struck a blow. Any hope that was well-springing to the surface, like tiny bubbles, was quickly dashed. "And how about you?" she said.

"Why did I want to become a pilot?"

"No, silly, I remember why. Are you seeing someone special? You can't tell me the women in Arkansas have been able to resist you." Matt laughed.

"Actually, they have. I can't tell you how it felt to see you the other day. You were like a life preserver, just your presence."

"It was nice to see you, too," she interrupted. "I'm just sorry about the circumstances." A shy quiet fell over them again. Matt felt himself falling over the edge of something. A feeling he thought had been relegated to old memories and photographs. Could it be possible? She said everything happens for a reason. Could something as horrible as his father's heart attack really be a cosmic invitation to go back, to have a second chance to correct a terrible mistake? Just when he was about to cast his net out farther, to ask if she'd like to go for a walk on the beach, she opened her purse and took out some bills. "I really have to go," she said. "My treat." She slid out toward the end of the booth. Matt felt panic take over. He slid out, paralleling her movements. They stood together. "Say hi to your mom for me."

"I'll walk you out," he said. He almost put his arm around her, then checked it. Opening the door, he felt lost and defeated. His hopes had been nothing but fantasy. Why should she, why would she feel the same feelings that came over him as he sat across from her? They had gone down a long, painful road together. She had come to terms with it, moved on, and turned herself into a physician, a healer. And he left. How selfish, how egocentric to think she could just wipe all that away over a bowl of miso soup, let him back into her life and pick up where they left off. When she said everything happens for the best, she was telling him that their breakup had been for the best, not this little surreal encounter. He wanted to usher her over to his car and give her the bouquet of yellow roses.

"I just live a few blocks from here. I'll be in touch soon." She was dismissing him, and he had no choice but to accept it. He thought of walking her home but decided against it. They hugged each other and kissed on the cheek.

"Thank you again, Karen," he said as she let go and turned away.

He sat in the car and watched as she turned right on Hinman Avenue, her sway and stride as unique as a fingerprint, so familiar yet gone again. His emotions were racing out of control. He couldn't go home to the stillness and sadness. He got out of the car and walked east, away from the sun which was setting behind him, casting a soft glow over the beach and the water beyond. He walked across the grass, past an oak tree and a playground, then took his shoes and socks off and walked across the warm sand to the water's edge. The white triangular sail of a boat, ghosting along the dim horizon, gave his mind something to latch onto. He lay down and felt the warm sand conform to his shape. Why was this happening? He couldn't push the question out of his mind. His father, Karen, was there any point in even trying to understand it? Maybe there would never be an answer. Everything just happened because it did. Everything was arbitrary, coincidental, random. Maybe Karen was right, maybe he was a cynic, unable to believe in anything intangible. They just sat across from each other in a place called the Blind Faith Café, a place she had chosen. Matt shook his head. He didn't have a clue about what would happen next. All he could do was try to make it through the night.

The house was dark except for a rim of fluorescent light glowing under the kitchen cabinets, illuminating the note his mother had written:

Dear, your friend, Pete, called. He said to give you his best regards and to call him tomorrow. I hope you and Karen had a nice time. Love, Mom.

Matt smiled. He'd hardly thought of the life he'd left behind just a few days ago. It'll be good to talk to him, Matt thought as he walked up the darkened staircase and groped down the hall to his room.

He woke early, showered, shaved, and got ready for the somber vigil that lay ahead. When they arrived at the ICU, Martha Wahlund was there to greet them.

"He moved his hands again this morning."

"That's wonderful," Matt's mother said.

"The good news is that he was doing it in response to my commands." Matt tried to remain stoic, digesting the information with an analytical detachment. "We're going to start bringing the morphine level down. We'll see if he can breathe on his own tomorrow. Dr. Slavin, the pulmonologist, will be dropping by this morning."

Matt's mother went up to her husband and stroked his forehead. "Can you hear me, dear? Squeeze my hand if you can hear me." Matt's heart sank when he saw no response, the look of hope on his mother's face dashed.

"I think he's asleep, Mom." They sat in their chairs and watched the revolving second-hand on the clock. Reverend Robinson, from the Presbyterian Church, stopped by and said a prayer. At eleven o'clock Dr. Slavin arrived. He told them the same thing that Martha had said, that they'd remove the trach tube tomorrow and that he'd be slowly taken off the morphine in preparation.

"Can we be present, Doctor?" Matt's mother said.

"Yes, although it's important that he stay calm with limited interaction."

"Just so he knows we're here," Matt said.

When Dr. Slavin left, Matt and his mom went home for a quick lunch. Matt tried to keep from getting overly optimistic but caught himself entertaining the renewed possibility of a miracle. They were half through with their turkey sandwiches when Matt's mother said, "Have you called your friend, Pete, dear?"

Matt dialed the number. On the third ring he heard Pete's slow, Southern drawl come through the line.

"Hey, old man, how are you?" Matt said.

"Hey," Pete said. "How's your daddy doing?"

"Not too well. He's been unconscious the whole time. They're going to see if he can breathe on his own tomorrow."

"Sorry to hear that."

"But I saw Karen, my old girlfriend."

"Doctor Karen?"

"Yeah, she's doing her residency in pediatrics at the hospital."

"How was that, seeing her again?"

"It was nice, kind of strange, though. I'll tell you when I get back. Say, Pete, do me a favor, will you? Call Dresden and tell him I'm still not sure when I'm coming back. I'll call him in a few days myself. Open my closet and take out my navy-blue suit and a shirt and tie and send them up here?"

"No problem, I'll take care of everything. Say, get a load of this: The day after you left, Grayson came back from a trip with Mike Ingles. They had a layover in Memphis together. After they checked in at the Airport Sheraton, they went down to the bar for a beer. Well, there was this hottie sitting alone at the bar. She came over and said she noticed them at the front desk. Grayson said she was really putting the move on Ingles, so Bob excused himself and went back to their room. He read a *Flying* magazine for half an hour, then turned out the lights and went to bed. At 1:30 a.m., he woke up and Ingles and this babe were going at it like a couple of hamsters on speed."

"What did he do?"

"He said he just rolled over and put a pillow over his head."

"Yeah, right."

"Wait, there's more. Bob said they were still in bed together when he woke up at 0500. He took a shower, suited up and went down to the coffee shop. When he got back to the room, she was gone, and Ingles was packed and ready to go."

"What did he say?"

"Bob said Ingles just laughed, shook his head and said, 'Now that's what I call a layover.' He was so cocky, not a lick of embarrassment."

"Unbelievable."

"Yeah, well get this. Somehow Dresden found out about it. He called the hotel and asked if Ingles paid for the additional, third-person occupancy. Of course, he hadn't paid a dime. Dresden said it was no different than theft, that it gave the company a bad name. He called Ingles into his office this morning and fired him on the spot."

"You're kidding? He ought to get a lawyer and sue."

"It won't be that easy. Dresden also accused him of drinking inside of the twelve-hour limit. He said he had witnesses. He told Ingles that if he resigned, he'd drop the drinking charge and there'd be nothing about it on his employment record. If not, he'd be fired, and both charges would follow him around like his shadow. Try getting hired by Delta with that on your record."

"Man, that's just what Wendell warned would happen."

"Exactly."

"So, what did he do?"

"He quit. What else could he do? Dresden had him by the balls. Then Ingles just went apeshit, started screaming at him, calling him an asshole and a son of a bitch, and threatened to get even. Dresden just sat there with a grin on his face. Wendell thinks the whole thing was a setup, that the girl was a plant."

"My God."

"I'll tell you what I think. Only two people know what happened that night besides Ingles and the girl. It wouldn't surprise me in the least to find out that Dresden was using Bob as a mole."

"Did you tell Wendell?"

"Not yet, but I'm going to. There hasn't been a dull moment since you left. Oh yeah, Rita says hi. She says she's got someone she wants you to meet. I told her you could use something like that."

"Well, thanks, I guess. I'll call you in a couple of days."

"Hang in there, bud."

Later that afternoon, Matt went out to the patio and filled the barbecue with charcoal. His mother was working in the garden.

"I'll make dinner tonight," he said.

"That'll be nice, dear."

"Chicken or steak?"

"Chicken," she said. "Maybe you should start watching your cholesterol." Matt lit the grill, went into the kitchen, and filled the wooden salad bowl with fresh green arugula. He added some sliced heirloom tomatoes, cucumbers, and onions, and tossed in oregano, salt, and pepper. He drizzled on a liberal amount of olive oil and fresh lemon juice, then seasoned the chicken.

"I've got some fresh-cut basil," his mom said, opening the kitchen door. Then the doorbell rang. She wiped her hands on her apron and went to answer it.

"Hello, Louise," came the familiar, gravelly voice.

"Hello, Lou, come on in." Big Lou came into the kitchen carrying a five-pound Krakus ham and a case of Old Milwaukee.

"Hiya, kid," he said to Matt as he walked into the kitchen and set the gifts on the counter. He shook Matt's hand with his massive paw and gave Matt's mom a bear-hug.

Big Lou, his father's best friend, was six-foot-four, two hundred and sixty pounds, with thinning silver hair combed straight back, and broken blood vessels which gave his face a sunny rosacea behind a two-day growth of white whiskers. He wore dark blue, oil-stained work pants and steel-toe shoes speckled with little drops of white latex paint. He gave off the same distinctive blue-collar scent as Matt's father, a blend of sweat, gasoline, cigar smoke, Old Spice, and beer. Matt thought Lou must have come as the official envoy from Strum's Tavern.

"Thank you for the ham, Lou," Matt's mother said. Lou waved a hand.

"How're you two holding up?"

"Just taking it day by day, I guess," she said.

"They may try to see if he can breathe on his own tomorrow," Matt said.

"Everybody's praying for your dad," Lou said.

"Can you stay for dinner, Lou?"

"No thanks, Louise. I've only got fifteen minutes."

"How 'bout a beer?" Matt said.

They took their beers out onto the patio while Matt's mom went upstairs to change. As Matt put the chicken on the grill, Lou took a gulp of beer, then said in a strained, gravelly voice, "Your old man's the finest person I've ever known. And he's so damn proud of you."

"Thanks, Lou," Matt said.

"I can't tell you how many times I've seen him go out of his way to help someone, do 'em a favor. He's the salt of the earth, I tell ya." Lou's eyes were red and glassy. "You just call me if there's anything I can do."

"I will."

"And don't give up hope."

"I won't."

"I'd better get going. Nice to see ya, kid." Lou turned and waved a paw as he walked away.

The next morning, Matt and his mom were up early. They barely spoke over coffee and toast for breakfast. Matt looked at his watch: 0700.

"I guess we'd better go," he said.

Another nurse, whom they didn't recognize, opened the door to the ICU.

"Good morning, I'm Jan Spencer. Martha's with Mr. Lavery," she whispered. Matt and his mother slowly pulled the curtain back and stepped inside. A jolt spiked through Matt's senses as he saw his father sitting upright in the reclining bed, the trach tube replaced by a small oxygen mask. He was turning his head back and forth like a blind man, trying in vain to move his arms which were strapped to the bed frame. A gurgling sound came from behind the fog-filled mask. Matt was terrified. As bad as he'd seen his father look, he never seemed in pain. Matt had been comforted by the thought that his father was unconscious and heavily sedated throughout the whole ordeal. Without the drugs, his father looked racked with pain, confusion, and distress. A hunter's prey, mortally wounded but still alive. His father was in agony and there was nothing Matt could do but watch. Martha seemed different too, nervous, edgy.

"I'm afraid he's not doing too well on his own," she said.

Without thinking, Matt blurted out, "Hang in there, Dad, you're going to make it. Just don't give up." His father was shaking his head back and forth, his forehead wet with perspiration. He was trying to focus on Matt and utter a sound.

"He's trying to talk," Matt's mother said. They strained to understand the words, but the sounds were barely discernible. Matt felt dizzy, like he was falling into a dark hole.

"I think he's saying let me go," Matt said. His father seemed like he'd reached his limit. He gazed right through Matt with a wild, crazed look in his eyes, as if Matt were some grotesque being. Matt felt full of fear.

This wasn't his father; it was someone else. Matt felt like his presence was only making things worse. He grabbed his mother's arm.

"Maybe we should come back later." His mother was ashen, tears streaming down her face.

"We'll be outside in the waiting room," Matt said to Martha.

Two hours went by, drinking coffee and trying to read. Then Martha came out and knelt beside them.

"We've put him back on the respirator and started a morphine drip. He's sound asleep now." Matt breathed a sigh of relief. "There's really nothing more you can do here. Why don't you go home and try to relax? Dr. Slavin said he'd call you this afternoon."

"Maybe he'll do better in a couple of days when he's a bit stronger," Matt's mom said.

"Maybe," Martha said. Matt was quiet.

When they arrived home, Matt said, "I think I'll go for a drive. I won't be too long." Without consciously intending it, he found himself outside the Blind Faith Café. He parked the car and walked toward the beach. Like so many times when life was closing in, he'd retreat from land and seek out water. To be on it, in it, or just to gaze upon it, was the best therapy. He sat in the grass, just a few feet from the sand, and leaned against the trunk of an oak tree. A few catamarans and windsurfers in tropical colors darted back and forth over the wavelets. Matt sat back and tried to blank the image of his father from his mind. He wished Karen were there with him. He felt a wellspring of affection for her, a sad regret that he hadn't seen things more clearly when they were a couple, hadn't had the confidence, hadn't given her what she needed. He wished she felt the same spark he did, thought the same thoughts, that maybe it wasn't too late to try again. The crisis of his father's heart attack reminded them both that they still shared a common bond, were still linked together in some way. But even if she felt a hint of those same things, it would be quite a leap to think she could think of him in a romantic way, as a couple, allowing herself to risk her heart and take a chance again. How could he tell her how he felt? She wouldn't believe it. She'd think it was just due to the trauma and stress, that he was reaching out to her in a time of grief, like a drowning man grabbing at a life preserver. He was suddenly back in her world. Maybe it was too much for her to handle. Maybe she appeared out of a sense of obligation, and it might be taking a toll on her, too? Not what she needed, especially after breaking off her engagement. And what about Olga? She had occupied his heart and mind to the point of obsession since the first day he saw her. But how realistic was that? The longest of odds kept his chances at bay, like planning, scheming, and hoping to win the lottery. For now, all he could think about was how much he wished Karen were there by his side. He wanted to tell her how horrible it was to see his father in agony. He wanted to let go and feel her arms around him, feel her holding him and telling him to have faith. And he wanted to hear her whisper his name and tell him that he'd never be alone, that she'd be there for him always.

Matt jerked his head back and opened his eyes. The light was casting shadows on the sand. He looked at his watch. It was 6:30 p.m. He picked himself up, brushed the grass and sand from his pants, and walked back to the car.

His mother was seated on a patio chair. A bottle of red wine and two glasses stood on the black wrought-iron table. She didn't seem to notice when he came through the kitchen door. She was staring out across the lawn.

"Sorry I'm late, Mom. I lost all track of time."

"That's okay, dear. Care for some wine? I wish you'd been here when Dr. Slavin called."

"What did he say?"

"He said we need to be prepared for the end," she said with a dazed look. "I asked him if they could try again in a few days when he's stronger. He said maybe, but we should be prepared for the same response."

They sat, staring out across the lawn, each in their own world of grief. The stillness was interrupted by the buzzing of cicadas, the wind whispering through the cottonwood trees. Matt took a sip of wine. He remembered the time when his father said he never wanted to be hooked up to a machine. "Just turn out the lights and let me go. And don't let my tools go cheap," he joked. Matt recalled the morning's image like a nightmare, heard his father's desperate plea echoing in his mind, stabbing at his heart. He took another sip of wine and a deep breath. "You know, Dad never wanted to go like this."

"I know, dear."

"It would be cruel and selfish to keep him like this, if it's just not meant to be."

"I know," she said, reaching for the bottle and pouring some wine into his glass and then into hers.

CHAPTER FOURTEEN

Reverend Robinson said he'd never seen so many people attend a funeral service in all his life. All the mechanics from the shop were there, dressed in sport coats and ties. The superintendent, principal, and teachers from the school where his father worked were there. Neighbors, friends, his sister Betty from San Francisco, Harvey (the bartender at Strum's), Pin-Ball Ray, Little Raymond (the tax assessor's chauffeur) were all there—and Big Lou.

Big Lou, who jumped with the 82nd Airborne on D-Day, liberator of Europe, iron-worker, loyal member of Local One, south side. Big Lou, tough as nails, hard as steel, crying like a baby, reminding Matt of the words of Rubén Dario: *Nothing is more sad than a Titan weeping.*

A framed photograph of his father stood on a small wooden table, the confident smile, the tweed sport coat. A single red rose and a small votive candle lit next to the elegy by Edna St. Vincent Millay, his mother's favorite poet: *Where you used to be, there is a hole in the world, which I find myself constantly walking around in the daytime, and falling in at night…*

Matt never shook so many hands. It was comforting to have them all there, but their combined palliative effect paled in comparison to the way he felt when the door opened, and Karen walked in. She wore a navy-blue dress with pleated hem, stockings, and black high-heeled shoes. In her hands she carried a vase of white long-stem roses, his mother's favorite. Matt walked up and took the flowers and set them on the table with the others. Karen placed an open-faced sympathy card in front of the roses. On it she had written the words of Aeschylus: *He who learns must suffer. And even in our sleep pain that cannot forget falls drop-by-drop upon the heart, and in our own despair, against our will, comes wisdom to us by the awful grace of God.*

Matt leaned down and read the words. "I think I'm about to lose it," he said.

She reached out with open arms and pulled him tight against her. "Don't say anything," Karen said. "I'm so, so, sorry."

"I know. He'd be happy knowing you're here." Karen nodded. "I told him I loved him, but I'll never know if he heard me."

"He heard you," Karen said.

"I wish we had a chance to talk," Matt said. "After the other night at the café, I've been thinking about you, the way we were, how things have changed." Karen looked away. "There's so much I want to tell you. Do you think we could get together before I have to leave?"

"Tomorrow night," she said. "After Friday, I'll be pressed for time."

"Why don't we go to the Sybaris Lounge? I'll pick you up."

"No, I'll just meet you there," she said. "There's something I have to do first."

Matt was still wearing his blue suit, white shirt, and dark blue pinstriped tie as he drove down Lake Shore Drive. The lakefront was full of people bicycling and jogging under the clear blue sky. The cool lake water caught the warm rays like shimmering shards of mirror glass, the shallow aqua dropping off to cobalt in the distance. A bright rim of orange flooded over and around the buildings to the west as he passed by Lakeview and Lincoln Park. The tall skyscrapers rose before him like sentinels to the American dream.

The Sybaris Lounge was one of Matt's favorite places. The ninety-sixth floor of the John Hancock building; the top of the cock. They had been there in happier times. Maybe the memories might stir something within her, he thought, but in any case, the view will be sensational. On a clear day you could look out and see the other side of the lake, Navy

Pier, Grant Park, Meigs Field, Evanston, and the gleaming Bahai Temple. To the west, the sunset, suburbs, and jet traffic at O'Hare.

Matt was half an hour early. He took the high-speed elevator, swallowing to equalize the pressure. It only took forty-five seconds to reach the ninety-sixth floor. When he stepped out and saw the view, he felt like he'd reached the summit of the earth and found it turned into a cocktail lounge. He sat down at a small table facing the west windows. He didn't bring flowers this time; there had been too many lately. His words would have to suffice. He would take his time with her, be kind and gentle, a payback for all she had done, and for so much more. He would listen to her, really listen to what was on her mind and in her heart. And he would try to accept whichever way the winds of fate decided to blow, a new skill that losing his father had forced upon him. The sun was sinking lower, painting streaks of orange and violet over the Fox River Valley and the farm fields beyond. It was Friday night, and the city beneath his feet was getting ready for gaiety. He leaned forward and gazed down on Michigan Avenue where horse-drawn carriages were giving rides to other people's dreams. Then he felt her hand on his shoulder. He relished her touch for a conscious second, then stood and turned around, and they embraced.

"What a gorgeous view," Karen said as Matt pulled the chair out for her.

"Look, you can see the horse-drawn carriages," he said.

She had changed into an olive-green silk dress with Persian pattern fringed with fine, ruby-colored tassels and an exquisite pair of diamond earrings. Matt knew she wouldn't have bought them for herself. The waitress came by and Matt ordered two glasses of Cabernet. When the wine arrived, Matt lifted his glass. "To you," he said.

"To your father," she said, their glasses clinking. They sipped their wine for a few minutes, then Matt reached over and gave Karen's hand a gentle squeeze.

"I never could have gone through it without you," he said. She stared straight ahead. Matt could see the sun setting in her watery eyes. She kept staring out into the distance. Then she turned and faced him.

"The hardest thing I've ever had to do was let you go. But I knew in my heart that I had become nothing but a habit to you, and I had to break the stalemate, for my future as well as yours. But when we broke up, I thought my life was over. I thought about us all the time. I couldn't get you out of my mind. I'd hear a song or see something that reminded me of us. I could barely study. But as time went by, I started accepting the fact that I couldn't have you back, that you were gone for good, and I had a choice. I could let it destroy me or I could persevere and get stronger. Fortunately, I chose the latter. And when I started getting my life back, started regaining that part of me which was lost, I realized that what happened between us was all for the best, that there was a reason we came together, and a reason we came apart. It was our destiny, and I've been able to see other experiences, other parts of my life, through that same perspective."

Matt was looking into her eyes, listening to every word. "I believe it wasn't just a coincidence that you were working in the same hospital where they brought my father, and it wasn't just a coincidence that we came together again."

"Me too," she said. "I've been thinking about that and trying to understand it. I mean, besides the obvious, that I should help you through such a sad time." Matt was on high alert, listening with all his senses. Was she about to confirm that she, too, felt there was a hidden meaning behind their reunion? That maybe they should try again?

"Then it came to me. I finally understood." She stopped to wipe something from her eye. Just say it, Matt thought. Say it or I will.

"I realized that we never had a chance for closure. We had that fight, and you left, and that was it, over. All the good times we had, all the love we made, all the things we shared were over, with all that energy just hanging in the air. I can see it so clearly now. We've been given a second chance, a sweet, second chance to say goodbye. To close what we had with dignity and respect."

Matt felt the bottom drop out. He had been a fool for thinking all those thoughts, for allowing himself to have hope. He had to give her up, right then and there. Accept it, no matter what. Pick up the pain and try to go on.

"Like a funeral."

"Yes," she said as she looked straight into his eyes, a look of relief on her face, glad that he understood.

"I don't think I can take two funerals at once."

"Closure can be a wonderful thing," she went on, as if she hadn't heard him. "A graceful letting go, a total acceptance. Seeing things for what they are and not for what we want them to be. And remembering all the good times."

Matt nodded, straining to keep composed. He looked out the window and saw a red balloon floating upward on the wind. The western sky was a faint thread-line of magenta, the darkness flooding in from all directions with the brilliant city lights below. A band was setting up instruments and testing the microphone. Matt took a deep breath, then reached out and took Karen's hand.

"I'm sorry," he said. "I'm sorry I didn't have more confidence, that I doubted us so much, that I doubted myself. You deserved better."

"No," she said. "It was all perfect, even the pain was perfect. And Matt, I want you to know that I'll always love you. Just because we both had to move on, to follow our destinies, doesn't change that."

"I love you too," he said as the band started playing a slow song. "Would you like to dance?"

She stood, and Matt guided her around a few chairs to the small dance floor in the northwest corner of the lounge. They wrapped their arms around each other, knowing that it was for the last time. Matt gently pressed the side of his face against her hair. As they slowly revolved around, he looked up and saw the long rows of amber streetlights stretching out to the western horizon, like approach lights to the future. He breathed in her warm scent, stroked her back, and slowly said, "In the winter of my life, when I'm old and gray and sitting by the fire, my heart will reach above the hearth, and take down the photo album of you and me, of us. And I will linger on the last page, before closing the book for the final time … and I will always remember you, just as you are tonight."

Lying in bed in his parents' house, his mother's house now, the sadness and emptiness that had been stalking him finally had him pinned against the ropes. He'd braced against it for days, been strong and stoic, done his job. But it was all over now, and Matt could hold back no longer. The sobs burst from deep within, the tears drenching, like he'd been left out in the rain. Finally, exhausted and depleted and unable to take it anymore, he fell into a deep sleep.

In the middle of the night, he dreamed he was back at the Sybaris Lounge, about to take the elevator down to the ground floor. When the doors opened, he stepped in, but just as he was about to transfer his weight, the elevator disappeared and he plunged down the deep, dark shaft, arms and legs splayed, spinning out of control as he fell into the abyss.

CHAPTER FIFTEEN

The flight to Memphis was over in a heartbeat. Matt hadn't really been present in the moment. He was concerned that he'd return to the cockpit dazed and disoriented. How could he fly if his mind was darting helter-skelter, trying to comprehend and adjust to the loss in his life?

Returning to Arkansas took on a different tone compared to the first time when everything was new. No longer was he leaving home and going to a strange new place. He was leaving a life he had once known, a life evaporating away like morning fog, and going home, home to Arkansas.

He checked in at the Arkansas Airways ticket counter and acknowledged the thoughtful remarks by the customer service agents. In a way, this little airline was like a family, everyone pulling together, everyone in the same boat. Flight 437 to Fayetteville was scheduled to depart on time. Captain Jackson Gault and First Officer Don Bishop would be the crew. There were scattered thunderstorms in the forecast for their arrival, but Matt felt relaxed, knowing he'd be in good hands. He shook hands with the crew and took his seat. Soon the familiar whine of the engines filled the cabin as they climbed above the barges on the Mississippi, leveling off above the fertile fields of Arkansas. The white glare on the horizon softened to streaks of purple and pink. Scattered gray masses of towering thunderheads flashed strobes of lightning, creating a certain non-threatening neon aura. It was as though the entire atmosphere had transformed into a vast summer carnival.

Matt felt a new comfort, a welcomed ease, like returning to a tropical island. He couldn't get over all that had happened in such a short time, how Karen appeared out of the past, and how wonderful and painful it was to see her again. He kept hearing the words she spoke, the thoughts she imparted. They were given the gift of closure, and he was given the time to experience its grace with his father as well. What if his father had just died on the spot without Matt's presence on the scene? He would have been deprived of the time to touch him, to say goodbye, and tell him that it was okay for him to go. Closure. Karen seemed to understand it so well, but what was it really? An emotional housecleaning? Putting things in their proper place? A neat way of containing the pain, for a while at least?

Matt gazed out the window and saw the dark green rolling hills and the last glimmer of amber sunlight reflecting off the waters of Table Rock and Beaver Lake to the north. Then the high-pitched roar of the engines dropped an octave; they were throttling back, starting down. It would all be over in a few minutes, and it would all be beginning as well.

The Jeep had been in the parking lot with the ragtop off for ten days, leaving it exposed to the torrential downpours of summer storms. Matt wondered if the seats would be soaked as he walked down the footpath from the main terminal. But when he looked up and saw it, the top was on. He threw his bag in the back seat and hopped in. There was a warm can of Budweiser by the gear shifter with a note that just said *Welcome home, bud.*

The light was on in the kitchen when he pulled into the driveway and heard the familiar sound of gravel crunching beneath the tires. A lone firefly flashed its green glow in the dark backyard as he walked across the driveway. The note on the table said, **Down at the WW, shooting pool. P**

Matt wasn't ready to socialize. He still had thoughts to think, feelings to feel. But the house had the same stillness and quiet as his parents' house, giving it a sadness that he'd had too much of lately. He changed into soft jeans and a white cotton shirt and headed into town.

He walked into the Whitewater Tavern and smelled the familiar cigarette smoke and onions, the white noise of hundreds of overlapping conversations draped in sweet Southern drawl, the clanking of beer bottles, the revolving ceiling-fans, and the big red Razorback in the mirror behind the bar. It seemed like a different world; a welcomed world compared to what he left behind.

Matt made his way through the crowd, turned left into the pool room, and saw Pete leaning over a green felt table, his cue cocked and ready, one eye closed, concentrating like a marksman looking through the scope of a gun. Matt stopped and waited until the shot was fired and the red three-ball ricocheted off the green rim and rolled into the corner pocket.

"Nice one," Matt said.

"Lavery, you're back, son," Pete said with a smile.

"Hi Matt," Rita said as she got up from her chair along the wall, came over and gave him a big hug.

"Steady," Pete said, putting a cold bottle of beer in Matt's hand and giving him a firm slap on the back.

"How're ya doing, bud?"

"Hanging in there. It's good to be home."

"Wanna play?"

"You finish this one first," Matt said. Pete was playing against some good-ol'-boy in a jean jacket with the sleeves cut off.

"Matt, I'd like you to meet a friend of mine. This is Brenda Covington," Rita said.

"Nice to meet you," Matt said, reaching out to shake her hand. Brenda was wearing a pair of blue denim shorts and a red, low-cut cotton blouse. She had the look of a Bavarian, beer garden beauty with long blond hair and deep blue eyes.

"My pleasure," she said, leaning forward to shake Matt's hand. "I've heard a lot about you."

"Oh? Do you live here in town?"

"In Bentonville."

"What do you do there?"

"I'm a massage therapist. I'm also going to nursing school."

"I'm so sorry about your father," Rita said.

"That's so sad," Brenda said, affecting an exaggerated look of sympathy.

"I'm still in a daze from it all," Matt said. "It happened so fast; it just came out of nowhere."

"But life goes on," Brenda said, and everyone nodded in agreement.

"You're up next, son," Pete said. Matt saw Pete racking up the balls. As they leaned over the table, just before shooting the lag for opening break, Pete whispered to Matt, "Not bad, heh?"

They were halfway through their game when Matt looked up and noticed that Rita and Brenda were gone.

"Probably taking a powder," Pete said as he pulled a couple of cold longnecks from a galvanized bucket of ice.

"So how are you two doing?" Matt said, taking a bottle.

"Pretty good. Rita's so easy, she just blows with the breeze."

They shot a few more balls and were almost through when Rita and Brenda came back to the table. Rita slid her arm around Pete and whispered something in his ear. Then Pete grabbed his pool cue and hung it up on the wall.

"Well, that about wraps it up for me, sport. I just got in from the Knoxville turn this afternoon and I'm beat. I'll see ya around the ranch." Rita gave Matt a kiss on the cheek, put her arm around Pete, and they left the room.

Matt felt spotlighted. He didn't know what to say to Brenda, wasn't sure what to do. He started moving the rack of billiard balls on the table, trying to mask his anxiety with some form of activity. Then he grabbed his cue and said, "Would you like to play?" She kept her eyes on his and slowly shook her head. She was drinking from a longneck beer bottle, her wet lips lingering longer than necessary around the rim of the bottle, looking up at Matt with her blue eyes. She walked up to him and placed her hands on his shoulders and started kneading the muscles in his neck, relieving ten tons of tension in an instant.

"You're so tight," she said. Matt felt weak.

"Just one game?" he said.

"No," she said. "Why don't you come with me. I've got a different game we can play." Helpless, he let her take him by the hand and guide him out the front door.

It wasn't unusual for Matt to wake up and not know if he was in Memphis, Dallas, Knoxville, or home in his own bed. What was unusual was the sound of singing coming from the bathroom. He lay nestled in the white down comforter and let the pieces of last night's jigsaw puzzle fall into place. He had been in a similar situation once before, and his first recollection was accompanied by panic and regret, a head-holding hangover, and the words, what have I done, repeating over and over. But this was different, a needed therapy. His only real concern was how to get home. She had taken him by the hand, driven him to her place, poured him a beer, then quickly stepped out of every stitch of clothing, and signaled for Matt to do the same. She led him through it all like a paint-by-numbers exercise, placing his hands precisely where she wanted them, moving in accordance with her wishes. She massaged his aching muscles and released tension from places he wasn't even aware of. She made it effortless, made it seem like she was submitting to him instead of the other way around. He needed everything she gave him, and when he was spent and had nothing more to give, he fell asleep and slept deeper than he had in years. He woke with the same sense of release and lay still, lingering in the moment. When she emerged from the shower, she had on a short lavender silk robe and was towel-drying her hair.

"You're awake," she said, sitting down on the corner of the bed.

"Thank you for last night," he said. "I really needed that."

"You mean *me*," she corrected.

"Right," Matt said, a yellow caution flag waved. "I needed you."

"You're welcome. How would you like to go down to Devil's Den today? We could pack a picnic lunch."

"Thanks, but I should be getting home. I've got a lot to catch up on. Some other time, perhaps."

"Alright, I'll drop you back in town when you're ready. There's a clean towel in the bath." He got up and stepped into the shower, relieved that she hadn't pressed him any further.

Matt got out of her yellow Pinto on West Avenue, a few blocks from where the Jeep was parked. He kissed her, out of an uncertain sense of obligation.

"Call me," she said, handing him her number.

"Take care," he said, waving a hand and walking away. He turned right on Watson as she passed him and waved again. Matt waved back and kept walking. When the Pinto was gone from sight, he doubled back and turned left on Rollston where his Jeep was waiting patiently for him. It felt good to put his left hand on the steering wheel, his right hand on the shifter, to feel in control again, to be heading home.

Matt picked up his swim bag, grabbed a blue beach towel, and drove to the Wilson Park pool. The pool was crowded with people enjoying the cool crystal water on this hot, sunny Sunday in late June. One lane was dedicated to lap swimming, and Matt dove in and swam in slow, rhythmic strokes. He tried the old trick of blanking his mind, self-hypnosis, his stroke like a mental metronome, but it wouldn't work. Too many thoughts were crying for attention, like little children. He thought about his mother and father and Karen. He still hadn't let go of the life he left behind and still hadn't figured out what to do about Olga. All he knew for sure was that he was here to do a job, to fly the Metro, to move closer to his dream. He'd have to focus, bring his full attention to the job at hand and be alert for any sign of attention deficit. After forty laps, he got out of the pool, dried off, then went to see Captain Dresden to tell him he was ready to go back to work.

Even though it was Sunday, Matt found Dresden at his desk.

"Are you sure you're ready?" Barry said.

"I'll be fine."

"Alright. You missed the July bid, so I'll have to put you on reserve. Just jot down your preferences for days off. Take tomorrow off and be ready to sit reserve at 0500 on Tuesday. And Matt, if you're having trouble concentrating, call me and we'll work something out."

When he walked out onto the ramp, the sun shone like a white-hot orb overhead, and a vaporous mirage blurred the surface of the runway. A Metro was parked outside the open hangar, its entry door and over-wing hatches opened for ventilation. Matt walked over, climbed up into the cockpit, sat down in the right seat and studied the instrument panel to bring his mind back to the job.

On his way back to the Jeep he ran into Mark Winger who was just returning from the two-day Meridian trip. His El Camino was parked a few spots down from the Jeep.

"Hey Matt," Mark said. "Glad you're back in one piece."

"Thanks. So, what's been happening? I heard about Mike Ingles from Pete."

"Dresden set him up, no doubt about it. Ingles came down to my cabin and we had a few beers. He said he might get a lawyer and sue. I told him to call me before doing something stupid."

"Like what?"

"Like burning down Dresden's house or something; he was full of rage and revenge."

Then Mark loosened the bungee cord that held the blue tarp in place and threw his flight bag into the truck-bed. Under the tarp were a dozen cases of beer. A reflexive grin appeared on Mark's face. "So, when are you going back on the line?"

"Dresden put me on reserve, starting Tuesday."

"Well, hopefully they won't call you very much."

"Say hi to Maggie for me."

"Will do," Mark said as he climbed in and pulled out of the lot.

Driving home, Matt thought about Barry Dresden. He'd seen first-hand what kind of person he could be. The disdain he engendered among the line-pilots was well deserved, yet he gave Matt his full support when Matt needed it most. Maybe it's too soon to tell, he thought as he pulled into the drive.

CHAPTER SIXTEEN

Summer in Arkansas had a lazy, languid feel about it that seemed to slow the speed of time. All the windows in the house were left open. Fans circulated the soft, honeysuckle breezes, and the sheer white curtains hung limp in the morning, then rustled in the afternoon, heralding the early onset of the thunderstorms that rolled in from Oklahoma.

Matt spent his days waiting for the phone to ring (Flight Control calling with an assignment) or going to the pool. On days off, he'd drive up to Horseshoe Bend and swim across the cool waters of Beaver Lake, or go out past Gentry to Old Blue, where an ice-cold branch of river water made for an ideal workout. He spent most of his time with Pete or alone, the salve of solitude allowing him to transition from his old life to the new. He told himself it was just temporary, but a part of him feared he was retreating into some far corner, and if he kept going in that direction, he might never fully return.

On Wednesday, July 29, Pete and Matt joined a worldwide audience of over 700 million people to watch Prince Charles and Lady Diana Spencer get married. They were sitting in the den watching the news.

"How much do you think this wedding cost?" Pete said. "Certainly, the father of the bride can't be expected to fork it up."

"More than both of us will ever make in a lifetime."

"The tax-payers'll probably have to pony up and pay."

"I think I'd rather keep the cash and elope."

"Me too," Pete said. "I read in the paper that the unemployment rate in England is over eleven percent, highest it's been in fifty years, and Margaret Thatcher's predicting it to go higher."

"All those workers should have lots of time on their hands to watch the wedding."

"Yeah, well I hope it's an open bar. The least the Royal Family can do is invite them all over for a pint," Pete said.

On Monday, August 3, Matt was in Flight Control at 0500 for the long, one-day Knoxville turn with Wendell Steele. There was a letter from Barry Dresden on the bulletin board.

ATTENTION ALL LINE-PILOTS

Members of the Professional Air Traffic Controllers Organization (PATCO) have announced their intention to walk off the job this morning if negotiations with the FAA fail to meet their demands for higher wages, a shorter work week and better retirement benefits. The FAA has assured us that we can expect the same level of safety, and that their contingency plan of utilizing three thousand supervisors, joining two thousand non-striking controllers and nine hundred military controllers, combined with a flight schedule reduction at the major airlines by up to fifty percent during peak hours, will result in the same efficient flow of traffic. I urge you all to conduct yourselves with the same level of professionalism. Be alert for any non-standard clearances and be patient if you encounter any delays. Please report any safety issues to me personally. Thank you and fly safe.

Barry Dresden

"This should be a fun day," Matt said when Wendell walked in.

"We'll just keep alert," Wendell said. "It's ironic. PATCO was about the only labor union to support Reagan in the election, and here it is, less than a year later, and he's pointing a gun at their heads, giving them forty-eight hours to report for work or they'll all be fired, all that skill and experience gone."

"But they're federal employees," Matt said. "Didn't they have to sign a no-strike agreement?"

"Yeah, otherwise you could have the military or the fire department or the police go out on strike, like what happened in Boston in 1919 when Calvin Coolidge was the governor of Massachusetts. Reagan's a big admirer of Coolidge. Those controllers better read their history or they're gonna get hung out to dry."

"They're not going to get much sympathy from the public," Matt said.

"This is a real litmus-test for labor. The key thing to watch for is the response from the other unions. Reagan's got no choice but to play tough, show his resolve. If it turns into a show-down between Robert Poli and Ronald Reagan, the controllers are screwed. I wouldn't want to be in their shoes this morning."

Wendell and Matt took off on schedule and flew to Fort Smith–Little Rock–Memphis–Jackson–Nashville–Knoxville–Nashville–Jackson–Memphis–Little Rock–Fort Smith, and back to Fayetteville. Twelve legs in fourteen hours. No major work stoppage from the 33,000 members of the Air Line Pilots Association took place. As they were walking up the flight line, Wendell's shoulders were slightly hunched forward under the weight of his flight bags.

"You wouldn't have known there was a controller strike unless you'd heard about it beforehand," Matt said. Wendell just shook his head.

"Matt, can you imagine flying this kind of schedule when we're fifty years old?"

"But hopefully this is just a stepping-stone to the major leagues."

"There may not be much difference between leagues in the future," Wendell said. "Not after today."

The next Friday, Matt returned from a Dallas trip with T-Ball. Pete had just finished the Kansas City turn with Buzz. It was hot and humid inside the house. Pete was changing out of his uniform and putting on khaki shorts and a T-shirt.

"I think I'll take the canoe out to Lake Wedington," Pete said. "Wanna come?"

They piled some blankets into the pickup bed, gingerly lifted the canoe, tucked it in, and tied it off with half-inch nylon braid. Pete drove like an old man on Sunday as they wound around the curves of Highway 16, the kudzu tangled around tree limbs like lengths of last year's Christmas lights. Soon they came to the campgrounds on the east side of the lake.

"Let's launch from here where it's less crowded," Pete said. They walked the canoe to the grassy shoreline and placed it in the shallow water. Matt climbed in, sat in front, and held the canoe steady with his paddle while Pete dropped into the stern. They shoved off and started paddling, their reach and pull in perfect sync, as if connected by an invisible timing belt, both putting in a quarter-turn on the upstroke, feathering the blade to the wind. The glare of the sun reflected off the shimmering surface of the water as they glided along, trickling water-drops falling from their paddle blades, soft gurgling sounds around the hull, small spinning whirlpools trailing in their wake.

"Let's keep to the shoreline and see where all these coves and crannies take us," Pete said. The sun was just starting its slow summer sink, and the rays felt warm on Matt's face. He closed his eyes and kept stroking, in perfect harmony with the surroundings.

"She's a nice boat."

"She sure is. Say, Rita and I are going up to Tontitown for the Grape Festival tomorrow night. Why don't you come along? Call Brenda and we'll double, have a nice spaghetti dinner, drink some good red wine."

Matt opened his eyes just as a great blue heron swooped down and glided low over the water, beating its long gray wings, banking left and disappearing into the shadows of the laurel and rhododendron thickets.

"I saw a great blue heron out at Beaver Lake the first day I arrived. They're kind of prehistoric looking, don't you think?"

"You're changing the subject, son. I just asked you a simple question." Matt felt cornered, like being called to conjugate a verb in Latin class. He and Pete shared many a conversation, felt the comfort of comradeship. They confided in each other, and Pete had been a great support when Matt's father was dying. But Matt never told him how he felt about Olga, how she occupied his thoughts and how consumed he'd become over his inability to approach her.

"Listen," Pete said. "It may be none of my business. I mean, it's obvious you're not light in your socks or anything. I'm just curious why you haven't even tried to align yourself with the ladies? You've had plenty of opportunities. I know Brenda'd be over in a heartbeat if you'd just call her. When we go out, you don't even notice women smiling at you. You never make a move. I'm just wondering why? I mean, life is short. You gotta live a little, you know?"

"I guess I just don't want to lock myself into something I can't get out of, be out of circulation, so to speak, and miss a greater opportunity."

"A greater opportunity?"

"Yeah, like my destiny."

"I see. You're taking the passive approach. You're just waiting for the right person to fall into your lap, like standing under an apple tree with your pockets open, since that'd be your destiny." Matt wished he'd change the subject.

"From where I stand, the right ones never just fall into your lap. You've got to go out and make it happen. Destiny's just a novel way of explaining the way things turn out, a way of rationalizing the irrational. I think of destiny as something we're all born with, like a wet hunk of clay. You have that clay, and that's your destiny. But it's up to you to mold it and shape it. That's your burden. Sure, if you hang around long enough, a few ladies will come your way, but if there's a real treasure out there, I wouldn't take a chance on your definition of destiny. She could be gone as fast as fog lifts. I'd just go right out and take my chances, see if I couldn't make some magic."

"I suppose you're right."

"In the meantime, why don't you call Brenda, and we'll double date tomorrow night? It'll be fun."

"I'm just afraid if I start something that isn't meant to be, I'll have a hard time breaking up, and I don't want to hurt anyone's feelings. I did that once before."

"Suit yourself."

"What about you and Rita? Is she that special someone or are you just biding your time?"

"Don't know yet, but I do know one thing. I'm sure as hell not *wasting* my time."

That night, Matt thought about what Pete had said. He heard his father's words: *Life is short, you've got to seize the day.* Matt wanted to seize it, to muster the courage the moment required, but it seemed as hard as lighting a wet match in the wind. Maybe he should just forget about launching some grand scheme, putting his faith in a plan, and just take a deep breath, walk right up to Olga, and ask her out on a date like any normal person. But he was paralyzed, straitjacketed, unable to face the almost certain rejection. Then what would he do? Knowing someone as beautiful as Olga really existed would pale anyone else in comparison. It wasn't just her physical beauty, it was all the little things he'd noticed about her, the intangible things, like her kindness and empathy, her softness with children, and the graceful way she held herself. It was the way she looked when she thought no one was looking, like the time he saw her from a distance, standing alone behind the ticket counter, a tired look on her face, gazing out the front door, reaching up to pull back a lock of fallen hair, that far-off look as if she were lost in a dream. It was much more than beauty; it was more like chemistry, and right now the chemistry was killing him.

CHAPTER SEVENTEEN

September came and the summer heat softened. The cool night air hinted of falling leaves, pumpkins, scarecrows, and sweaters. The blue tarp in Mark Winger's El Camino bulged with beer as the line-pilots made their contributions in earnest. The Wilson Park pool closed for the season, the water drained, clumps of brown oak leaves clustered in the corner of the deep end. The thunderstorm season waned, but Tornado Alley had a history of not throwing in the towel without a fight. Late season thunderstorms could be some of the most severe, as the tug-of-war played out in the atmosphere.

The Monday before the party, Matt was paired to fly a two-day trip with Mark Winger. The first day began with a Kansas City turn, then on to Little Rock and Memphis. The weather was turning cool and blustery when Matt showed up in Flight Control and saw Mark perusing the paperwork. Mark looked up when Matt walked in.

"We may have our hands full with this one," he said. "Look at all these SIGMETs. We'll make it up to Kansas City alright, but there's a line of severe weather east of Tulsa, moving this way. It's forecast to get here right at our arrival time." Matt leaned over the counter next to Mark and began reading SIGMET 27 Charlie and the latest severe weather-watch bulletin.

SIGMET 27C 09211800z–From 20nm SW of ICT to 40E of TUL to 30 SE of SLR. A line of severe thunderstorms 30 miles

wide with tops to FL550 moving 26020kts wind gusts up to 60kts and damaging hail possible.

BULLETIN – IMMEDIATE BROADCAST REQUESTED

TORNADO WATCH NUMBER 369

STORM PREDICTION CENTER – NORMAN, OK

1300PM CDT MON SEP 21, 1981

The Storm Prediction Center has issued a tornado watch for portions of eastern Oklahoma, northeast Texas and northwest Arkansas.

Effective Monday night and Tuesday morning from 6:30 p.m. until midnight CDT.

Tornados—hail to 1 inch in diameter—thunderstorm wind gusts to 60 knots and dangerous lightning are possible in this area.

The tornado watch area is along and 60 statute miles east and west of a line from 20 miles southwest of Wichita, Kansas, to 40 miles east of McAlester, Oklahoma, to 10 miles southwest of Sulphur Springs, Texas.

Remember, a tornado watch means conditions are favorable for tornadoes and severe thunderstorms in and close to the watch area. Persons in these areas should be on the lookout for threatening weather conditions and listen for later statements and possible warnings.

"Figures, my last trip before vacation," Mark said. "When we get back, I'm going to spend the rest of the week getting ready for the party. I still have to set up the bandstand, dig the barbecue pits, and pick up the ice maker and fifty folding chairs from AZ Rentals."

"I'll give you a hand," Matt said.

"Thanks. Twelve hundred pounds should be enough fuel to get us up there. We'll plan on adding some extra on the return. We won't be able to fuel in Fayetteville if there's lightning around the airport. Let's stop off at Flight Service on the way down."

They walked into the Flight Service Station as Bud Devry was ripping reams of paper from the teletype machine, which was clicking and spitting out words like some crazed stenographer gone berserk. He waved a hand.

"Be right with you, fellas." Bud collected the papers and stepped through the hinged opening in the counter. "Where're y'all headed?"

"Kansas City turn, then Little Rock–Memphis," Mark said.

"We're looking at a serious frontal convergence to really stir things up tonight," Bud said. "Remnants of Hurricane Gladys, the one that hit Brownsville yesterday morning. She's been working her way up Texas all day, decreasing in intensity but still a force to reckon with. There's also a cold front extending from a low over Garden City, Kansas. The two systems are forecast to meet over northwest Arkansas this evening. It's going to get nasty with squalls in advance of the front. Your flight should be impacted mostly by Gladys as she passes through. After midnight the cold front will dominate. We'll see a wind shift and a 30-degree temperature drop with frontal passage. What's your ETA back here?"

"1730 local," Mark said. Bud grabbed the terminal forecast.

"After 2200z we're looking at 800 broken and 2 miles with moderate rain and a 40% probability of 300 overcast and ¾ mile with heavy thunderstorms and rain showers, peak winds 180 at 24 gusting 40 knots. After 0200z…200 overcast, ½ mile with heavy thunderstorms, rain showers with hail and wind gusts in excess of 40 knots."

"What's the long-range forecast for the weekend?" Mark said.

"Should be clear and cool."

"Perfect for the bonfires," Mark said. "We've been collecting wood all year. You're invited, same as always."

"Thanks, I'll be there. You boys be careful out there tonight."

The flight departed on time. When they leveled off, they looked out to the west and saw frequent flashes of lightning inside the dark cloud build-ups.

When they shut down on the ramp in Kansas City, Mark checked the latest weather reports while Matt went up to the terminal to buy coffees.

Mark was back in the cockpit when Matt climbed in and handed him a steaming cup.

"Fayetteville's still good, but a funnel cloud was just sighted fifty miles west of Siloam Springs. There's a pilot report from a King Air south of Joplin getting moderate turbulence in heavy rain showers. With any luck, we'll get in just before the shit hits the fan."

It was Matt's turn to fly. Mark would work the radios. After level off, they looked out to the southwest and saw the sky darkening, an approaching wall of dark olive-green punctuated by massive cloud build-ups, like some atmospheric eruption spewing out great roiling plumes of ash and smoke. They were abeam of the northern boundary of the weather and saw the billowing thunderheads fused together in a solid mass of impenetrable force. The sun was setting low on the horizon, and bright streaks of orange, indigo and magenta silhouetted the shafts. It was ironic that weather so hazardous could be so beautiful. Many a night, Matt had traversed long weather systems and seen the mountains of clouds, backlit with brilliant internal strobes, like some cosmic coming-out party, flash photographed by a million paparazzi.

They were just north of Joplin when Mark said, "Monitor ATC on number one, Matt. I'm going to call Flight Service and get an update." Mark dialed up 122.0 and called Fayetteville Flight Watch. Bud Devry's cheerful inflection modulated back over the radio-waves.

"AR 417, Fayetteville Flight Watch, go ahead."

"AR 417's requesting the current weather for Fayetteville–Fort Smith–Harrison and Little Rock, as well as a convective update for northwest Arkansas."

Bud read back the weather reports, then added, "A funnel cloud's been reported west of Siloam Springs and an Ozark DC-9 climbing out of Tulsa reported continuous moderate chop from flight level one eight zero through flight level two seven zero. Need anything else?"

"No thanks, Bud. We're southbound on Victor 13, twenty north of Joplin at 15,000 in continuous light chop."

"Back on number one," Mark said. "Fayetteville's down to 800 broken and 2, with isolated thunderstorms and rain showers, winds 190 at 18 gusting 30, an Ozark 9's getting the shit beat out of it climbing out of Tulsa, and a funnel cloud's been reported west of Siloam Springs."

"We should still be able to get in on the localizer approach," Matt said.

"I'm just thinking about the next leg. If that funnel cloud gets much closer, I'm going to cancel it myself. Dresden can fly it if he wants to."

The sky darkened, and flashes of lightning appeared off to the right as they began their descent. Mark was making fine adjustments to the radar.

"This radar's worthless," he said. "It won't paint a thing until it's almost too late to do anything about it." Then he made a PA announcement while Matt tuned the nav-radios for the approach. Rain hit the windshield in sheets of angry spit, and the turbulence increased at the lower altitudes. The airspeed oscillated plus or minus 10 knots as they intercepted the localizer, and Matt had to apply aggressive control inputs to keep the airplane on course and altitude. They descended to 2,800 feet, extended the flaps, dropped the landing gear, slowed to their final approach speed, and reported their position. The tower cleared AR 417 to land on runway one-six. They broke out at 800 feet and Matt focused past the rain-covered windshield as they touched down, and the snarling reverse thrust forced the standing water to rise up in swirls of mist. Mark took control at the end of the rollout. Matt raised the flaps while they taxied to the tarmac and shut down next to four other Metros.

"Looks like we're canceling already," Mark said. "We may get lucky, yet."

The freight room was a beehive of activity as they walked in out of the rain. A long line of passengers had formed at the counter, and piles of bags were stacked everywhere. Jackie, Maggie, and Olga had their hands full. The 6:00 p.m. flight to Tulsa and the 6:20 p.m. flight to Dallas had just canceled, and passengers were being directed to the rental car counter. Maggie came back to the freight room lugging two heavy suitcases.

"Allow me," Mark said as he took one of the bags.

"Just set it down with those others in the corner," Maggie said.

"How 'bout a kiss?" Mark said.

"Not a top priority right now," she snapped as she darted back to the counter.

"Ah, rejection, I know it well," Buzz said. He'd just come down from Flight Control. Raindrops covered his navy London Fog.

"Buzzard, where're you off to?" Mark said.

"Memphis. I figure if we can board in five and be off no later than fifteen, we'll be able to turn away and beat it. Any delay and we'll be forced to cancel."

"We'll be right behind you," Mark said. "If you cancel, I'll do the same. We can go see Barry together. Don't forget the party this weekend."

"Are you kidding? I'm in hock up to my shorts from all the beer I've been putting in your truck. Now it's payback time. Well, better get this over with. I'll call you on fingers." Fingers, or 123.45, was a frequency dedicated to air-to-air communication. Buzz opened the door, pulled his collar tight around his neck, and leaned against the rain that was blowing sideways across the tarmac.

Then Maggie came back to the freight room.

"What are y'all doing just standing around? Buzz told me if you don't get off in the next fifteen minutes, we'll have to cancel. That's the last thing we need, now git!" She was shooing them out the door.

Matt started for the door when Mark said, "How do you expect me to concentrate with you flirting like that, playing hard to get and all? Now how 'bout that kiss?"

"Winger, I swear, if your ass isn't out that door this instant, you're never going to taste these lips again."

"Fielding threats, that's all I do. No respect. I swear, I've seen every stitch of clothes in that woman's closet but never a single sleeve with four gold stripes," he mumbled under his breath as he opened the door and leaned against the gale.

Matt was back in the cockpit, looking through the windshield at Mark walking toward the plane, head bent down, the brim of his hat shielding his face from the rain that was drenching the tarmac.

Buzz's flight was parked next to theirs, and Matt saw Jackie escorting the passengers out to the plane. She wore a red Arkansas Airways raincoat and held a red and white umbrella over her head. The sky was darkening to a thick, misty charcoal, backlit with frequent flashes of lightning. Matt could feel the plane being buffeted by the wind. Then he looked out and saw Olga leading a short queue of passengers out to his plane. Mark climbed up and took off his wet raincoat while Matt put on his hat and bent forward.

"It's now or never," Mark said as they traded places. "I can think of a hundred things I'd rather be doing right now."

"Someone's got to do it," Matt said as he felt the rain pinpricking his face. He looked up and saw Olga's graceful sway, her beauty shadowed under an umbrella. She looked poised to the point where Matt thought she could walk through a storm like this and still stay dry. Next to Olga was the same Armani man Matt had seen months before. His hair was shiny black with gray streaks combed straight back. He wore a light beige trench-coat and held a brown leather attaché case close to his chest. Behind him were three other passengers. Matt couldn't help but stare at Olga and the man. Then Jackie walked up to Olga and said something to her. Olga and the man embraced before Olga turned and started back toward the terminal. Olga was always so proper. Matt wondered how she could engage in such a public display of affection. He diverted his stare and looked up at the nose baggage compartment. Jackie brought the passengers to the airstairs and collected their umbrellas while Matt put their carry-on bags in the nose. Matt climbed the airstairs, and just before pulling the chains to raise the door, he heard Jackie say, "He's her father, Matt. Have a safe flight." He tried not to smile as he waved a hand and shut the door, but the words were just what he needed. He hung up his drenched London Fog and slid into his seat. Walter was out on the ramp by the external power cart, giving the engine-start signal by rotating a raised orange-wand. After start, Mark turned on both generators and gave the disconnect signal. Walter unplugged the power cart, saluted with the wand, and walked away while Matt called ground control for taxi clearance. As they made their way out to runway one-six, Buzz's flight was lining up on the runway, the nav and strobe lights lit up like a Christmas tree in a waterfall. The rain was beading up and running off the windshield, blurring their vision like a wet shower-door. The tower cleared AR 416 for takeoff, and Matt saw the Metro roaring down the runway, spray gushing back from the prop blast. Then the strobe lights rose above the runway and banked away to the east, and a bolt of lightning flashed less than a mile to the west.

"I wonder what's taking so long?" Matt said.

"AR 426, Drake Tower, hold short for company traffic on a three-mile final."

"Sounded like Bob Grayson on the radio," Matt said. "He's doing the St. Louis–Dallas trip with T-Ball tonight."

"Lucky bastards'll be dead in the water after they block in. They'll be all warm and snug down at Hugo's," Mark said. Matt looked out through the rain-spattered windshield and saw the bright glow of the landing lights and the blinking strobes flashing off the rain as the approaching Metro broke out of the overcast and descended to the runway threshold. The plane touched down and the propellers went into reverse, kicking up a cloud of spray and mist.

"Nice piece of edgework," Mark said. "We must be close to minimums." Then another lightning bolt flashed on the other side of Highway 71 and the rain showers intensified.

"AR 426, Drake Tower, it shouldn't be much longer. We're just waiting for Center release."

"Two more minutes and I'm going to shit-can this thing," Mark said.

T-Ball and Bob shut the plane down on the ramp, and Jackie greeted the passengers with umbrellas, then escorted them to the terminal. When the last passenger was inside, Jackie turned and walked with the umbrellas in her arms to the freight room door.

The tower finally cleared AR 426 to taxi into position and hold on runway one-six.

"We'll set 880 degrees, arm the water, and plan on an immediate left turn on course for weather avoidance," Mark said.

"Sounds good," Matt said before reading the final items on the checklist and adjusting the radar while Mark turned on the landing lights and lined up with the runway centerline.

"AR 426, left turn on course is approved, cleared for takeoff, one-six, wind one eight zero degrees at two zero, gusting two eight."

"Cleared for takeoff, one-six, AR 426," Matt replied. Mark gently pushed the power levers up and Matt set them at an inter-stage turbine temperature of 880 degrees, calling out "80 knots, thrust set" as the airspeed increased. The rain showers streamed off the sides of the windshield in crazed rivulets, and the runway lights diffused.

"V1 … Vr," Matt called out as Mark pulled back on the control yoke. "V2."

Just as Jackie was about to reach for the freight room door, she heard the deafening sound of intense thunder, like cannon fire, exploding right behind her, and saw a flash of lightning that lit up the entire face of the brick freight room wall. In reflex, she turned, and in horror, saw the departing Metro behind a curtain of spray and mist, engulfed in a huge ball of fire.

"Oh my God!" she cried out as her legs gave way and she fell onto the ramp, covered with umbrellas. The right wing banked low to the runway and the airplane seemed to be hanging at a crazed angle, like some air-show stunt. The door to the freight room opened and Walter appeared.

"Miss Jackie, are you alright? What was that sound? Sounded like an explosion."

Jackie was on her knees, crying, the tears flowing into the rain on her face. She looked up at Walter with fear and desperation and yelled,

"Don't just stand there … pray, goddammit!" Then Maggie and Olga came back and saw Jackie through the open door and ran over to her. The orange fireball was glowing behind the blowing rain and mist down at the far end of the runway.

"My God! Is that 426?" Maggie said.

Jackie nodded. "Maggie, Olga, they're going to be alright, ya hear me? Everything's going to be alright, I just know it."

Olga held on tight to the door-frame. "Papi," she cried, in uncontrollable spasms.

"Engine fire, number two, positive climb," Matt called out as the cockpit flooded with bright orange light.

"Gear up," Mark commanded. His eyes squinted like two knife-cuts to his face, his body braced, his mind in concentration overdrive. He pressed hard on the left rudder pedal and turned the control yoke to the left to level the wings. "Set 944 degrees on number one," he called out. Matt set the power, then scanned the instrument panel. The vertical speed indicator was pointing toward zero.

"We're not climbing," he said, as the end of the runway was fast approaching. Mark applied more left rudder and took out a touch of aileron to lessen the drag.

"Feather number two," Mark called out. Matt put his hand on the right stop-and-feather knob.

"Check me on two," Matt said. Mark glanced down at the power quadrant.

"Two's checked." As soon as Matt pulled the stop-and-feather knob, the airplane regained directional control.

"We're right at V2, vertical speed's a hundred up, we've got to come right," Matt said. "We're still below the hills south of Greenland." Neither pilot could see the terrain through the rain-covered windshield, but they knew instinctively what the topography looked like. Mark let the airplane drift slightly to the right, through the gap where the highway bends through the hills.

"We're almost out of water," Mark said. "When she runs dry, set 923 on number one, or 2363 pounds of torque, whatever comes first. Careful not to over-temp her."

A brief let-up in the rain allowed Matt to look out and see the sickening sight of treetops and hilly terrain rush by just a few feet beneath them. Then Mark and Matt went through the engine-fire checklist.

Maggie knelt down, wrapped her arms around Jackie and helped her to her feet.

"I know," she said. "They're going to be alright." They both put their arms around Olga and closed the freight room door. There was nothing more to see outside but darkness and rain. The phones were ringing. Jackie took off her raincoat and picked up. It was Tony in Flight Control.

"Jackie, we just heard what happened from the tower. They've lost radio contact. I just spoke with George. Everything for the rest of the night is canceled. I'll call you if we hear anything."

Jackie hung up the phone. Her heart was racing as she forced back the flood of tears that was about to breach like a broken levee. She ripped the side off a cardboard box, took a black felt-tipped marker, wrote the words CLOSED – SORRY, and went out and taped it over the edge of the counter. A group of irate passengers started interrogating her, wanting answers and demanding service. All Jackie could do was look up and say, "I'm sorry, y'all, tonight is just not a good night to fly." She went back to the freight room where Olga and Maggie were holding onto each other, Olga still heaving with sobs, and Maggie about to break down again. Jackie knew from experience that the best way to keep from falling apart was to have a plan. She knew she'd go stir-crazy sitting by the phone all night long. She was a survivor, and she would survive this, too.

"Olga, honey, why don't you go home and be with your mom? Maggie and I will drive you. There's no way they can send up a search helicopter in this weather. Maggie, let's get in my car. They took off to the south, so that's where we'll go. We'll search all night. Olga, if we find out anything, we'll go straight to a pay-phone and call you. I promise."

Olga nodded and blew her nose in a white tissue. Jackie called Tony and told him that she and Maggie were going south to search for the plane.

"We still haven't heard anything," Tony said. "We've contacted Scott Air Force Base and the Washington County Search and Rescue team. If they did go down somewhere, they should be able to pick up the plane's emergency locator transmitter. So far, they haven't shown up on Memphis Center's or Fort Smith's radar. T-Ball said they'd probably turn east, away from the weather, and maybe head for Harrison, but they haven't shown up there either." Jackie hung up the phone and felt sick.

Olga and Maggie climbed into Jackie's ivory white VW hatchback. When they reached Olga's parents' house, Jackie and Maggie got out, hugged Olga, and promised to stay in touch. When Olga was inside, Jackie said, "Maggie, let's stop off at my place real quick. We'll pick up some flashlights and fill the back seat with blankets and sweaters and a first-aid kit. Go into the kitchen and fill a bag with whatever food you can find. There's a gallon jug under the sink. Fill it up with water. There's a bottle of brandy in the pantry; throw that in too."

Jackie lived in a small white clapboard bungalow, south of town on Putnam Street. They parked in the drive and went inside. Mrs. Fuller, the next-door neighbor, was sitting in an armchair next to Justin, reading a bedtime story. He was dressed in a pair of blue pinstriped baseball pajamas with bright red felt slippers. "Mommy," he said, breaking into a smile and scampering down off the chair, "I'm reading a story." Jackie scooped him up and gave him a big hug and a kiss and told him to be a big boy because Mommy had something she had to do this evening, and Mrs. Fuller would put him to bed and stay right there with him until she got home.

Jackie and Maggie loaded up the car, and Jackie gave Justin a kiss goodnight. She made a quick call to Tony in Flight Control—still no word. Then she grabbed a box of tissues and headed out the door. They climbed back into the hatchback and headed toward Highway 71. Flashes of lightning were all around the airport. The runway lights and rotating beacon lit up behind the blowing rain. As they passed the main terminal, they noticed that all the amber floodlights in the parking lot were out, and it was dark inside the terminal. As they continued south, Maggie started crying and shaking her head. Jackie reached over and put a hand on her knee.

"You just hold tight, honey." The consolation seemed to have the opposite effect, as Maggie's crying intensified, the tears streamed down her cheeks like the rain on the windshield.

"Mark came back." She struggled to get the words out. "He was just teasing me, being his same old self, and asked me for a kiss." She sniffled hard, then took a proffered tissue from Jackie and blew her nose. "I was trying to get the flight out before it was too late, and I just shooed him away like a fly at a picnic, and now I'll never see him again and I'm so sorry and I swear if God will just let them live, I'll never—"

Jackie cut her off. "You couldn't have known. You did nothing wrong. Mark loves you; he knows how you feel about him, how we all get from time to time."

"I know, Jackie, but if I had just stopped and let him kiss me, and they got delayed and the flight canceled, they'd still be alive. I don't know how I'll ever live with myself."

"Now you hush with that kind of talk, ya hear?"

"I swear, if they're alive, I'll never let him go without a kiss goodbye. If … oh, Jackie, what are we going to do?"

"We're going to do just what we're doing right now. Roll down your window. You look off to the right and I'll look off to the left."

They could see nothing but blackness and streaks of raindrops falling through the headlight beams. Maggie tried to compose herself.

"Jackie, what if we find them and they're all—"

Jackie cut her off again. "Don't you say it. I won't hear it. Honey, if you don't want to do this, I'll just take you home. I know this is a long shot, but it's all we can do so we have to do it."

Maggie nodded. "I'm sorry," she said.

"We'll go as far as Winslow," Jackie said. "Take every side road between here and there. Past Winslow there's nothing but mountain peaks and gorge. We can't get down there. Then we'll go off to the east. Tony said they probably turned east to avoid the weather." Then Jackie reached into her purse, took out a cigarette and a lighter, and lit the cigarette.

Maggie reached over, plucked the cigarette from Jackie's lips, and threw it out her window. "You quit, remember?"

"We're still not climbing," Matt called out. "Drifting right." Mark was concentrating, scanning the instrument panel, eyes darting, hands and feet reacting with the reflex of a tightrope walker.

"Look back, Matt. Can you see the prop?"

"The blades are only partially feathered, there's no rotation. Looks like it's seized up." Then a flash of lightning appeared just off to the right. "Cell at one o'clock," Matt called out.

"Can't avoid it," Mark said. "See if you can pull the stop-and-feather control out farther." Matt pulled the number two stop-and-feather control, but it wouldn't budge.

"She's all the way out," he said.

"Hold on," Mark said as they entered the cell. Lightning lit up their faces and rain showers sprayed the windshield.

"Positive climb," Matt said. "Two hundred up." They were in an updraft, the cell giving a momentary boost. "V2 plus ten, positive climb," Matt said. Mark pulled back a touch on the control yoke and they gained a hundred feet of altitude, then they popped out of the back side of the cell. "Descending," Matt said. "V2, hundred down, drifting right."

"Matt, get on the PA and say something to the folks. Don't sugar-coat it. Tell them how to brace when we give the signal."

Matt wondered if the passengers would even be able to hear his words. It was like last winter, when he and T-Ball flew up to St. Louis in a winter storm with ice-fog that closed down Lambert Field enroute. They were forced to turn back. Matt got on the PA and explained what was happening. Drake Field had gone down to minimums. By the time they descended on the localizer approach, the visibility was nil. They never saw the approach lights, not even the neon sign of Bypass Liquor. They went around, retracted the gear and flaps, and headed for Tulsa.

Again, Matt got on the PA and explained what was happening. When they got on the ground in Tulsa, the passengers deplaned in a state of confusion, thinking, all the while, that they were in St. Louis. None of the announcements had gotten through, just a garbled, static-filled screech each time.

Matt took a deep breath. His heart was in his mouth. He didn't know if he could utter a word, let alone a coherent sentence.

"Matt, she's just not climbing. Give us twenty degrees more on number one. Twenty degrees, no more. We'll over-temp just a touch." Matt barely moved the power lever and the ITT shot up fifty degrees. "Too much," Mark said. Matt pulled it back with needle-threading precision until the digital readout showed 945.

"Set." The airplane kept drifting right. Mark had to turn the control wheel to the left, but their speed started dropping off due to the increased drag from the ailerons.

"No good," Mark said. "Set it back at 923."

"We need more left rudder," Matt said as he looked over at Mark. Sweat was beading up on his forehead and he looked like he was suffering from severe abdominal cramps.

"There is no more left rudder," Mark said. "She's all the way to the stops." The words sounded like a death sentence. They needed more power, and more left rudder to counteract it. Otherwise, they were trapped, flying in a slow, descending right turn, and up ahead and off to the right were the cliffs along the west bank of the White River.

In the past, on long road trips when his mind was just treading water, Matt wondered what a bug must feel when it hits the windshield at seventy miles an hour. How it could be alive and conscious, and then in a millisecond, be squashed out of existence.

There was a gap in the rain showers, and in the shadow of evening, up ahead and off to the right, Matt saw the running rapids of the White River. The riverbed was strewn with the jagged edges of boulders, boulders that could rip through aluminum like the teeth of a tiger shark through seal blubber. The sickening specter of the solid limestone cliff wall on the far bank was inexorably drawing them to their death like a sadistic Siren.

"V2 minus five, sinking a hundred," Matt called out, as if there was something Mark could do about it. The cliff was getting closer, and mist was rising up from the riverbed below. Matt swallowed, dry in the mouth. He could imagine the exact point of impact straight ahead, a black circular scorch mark against the white cliff wall, like a period at the end of the final sentence of his life. Death, with its greedy smirk, loomed in the windshield and stared them right in the face.

Mark was flying with every ounce of skill gleaned from over seven thousand hours in the air, rudder to the stops, holding the control yoke in his hands, coaxing and caressing the stricken ship, like a lover he refused to let go.

Up ahead, above their hopeless altitude, were four pine trees by the edge of the cliff. They were south of West Fork, close to the plateau by Mark's cabin. It was the spot where Mark would come to watch the red-tailed hawks spiraling upward on the currents, the spot where autumn leaves would shoot straight up like embers from a hot chimney flue, the spot where gravity sometimes worked in reverse.

"Airspeed's increasing, hundred up," Matt called out. The pine trees and the edge of the cliff were coming closer. They were still too low, stuck in a right turn below the rim of the cliff. Whatever orographic boost they were getting wasn't going to be enough to save them.

"We're not going to make it," Matt thought. For an instant, he thought of his poor mom. How could she take losing her husband and only son, just three months apart? Then he thought of Olga. He saw her beauty and held on tight to the image, a final photo. He wished he hadn't lacked the confidence. He should have asked her out, taken his chances. Then maybe she and Maggie would come every year on September 21, and lay three flowers at the base of the pines by the edge of the cliff where they met their end.

Matt looked up and saw the windshield fill with limestone, the pine trees above them. He closed his eyes, and just before the impact, heard

Mark's words loud and clear, a final command from his captain, the last task he'd ever perform in this life.

"Full flaps!" Mark called out. It was a last-ditch move. There was no precedent for it; such an unorthodox maneuver would never be found in the flight manual. Full flaps in a single-engine configuration would overwhelm them with drag. But first, for an instant, it would allow the wing to produce a single shot of lift. Matt reached up and threw the flap handle all the way down. Mark pushed the left power lever straight forward, firewalling what was left of number one. Then he pulled back hard on the yoke, and the airplane shot up and to the right as he commanded, "Signal to brace." Matt pushed the PA button on his audio panel and transmitted, "Brace…Brace … Brace!" Then Mark pulled the left power lever back almost to idle and, with his pawlike hands, rammed the control wheel full left, leveling the wing. The gear warning horn was blaring and the stall warning horn beeping as they brushed through the tops of the pine trees, and there, stretched out in front of them in the rain-soaked shadows, was the meadow behind Mark's cabin. They had no depth perception and the ground rose up. "Feather number one," Mark commanded as he and Matt both pulled the yoke hard aft to try to raise the falling nose. But there was nothing left, no response; the airplane was spent. They hit the ground, hard but in control. Then they bounced back up into the air. The second impact was shattering, like dropping a television set from a third story window. It forced them hard against their harnesses, with the sound of metal screeching and ripping as the fuselage cracked open behind the wing. Mark and Matt braced against the brake pedals, even though the landing gear was still up. They were skidding at a diagonal to the furrows. Up ahead lay a narrow rock-strewn creek and a wooden fence. The Metro skidded over the rocks that peeled through the aluminum underbody like a can opener. The nose dropped down and impacted slightly below the lip of the creek, then leaped up and charged through the fence like a rodeo bull, finally coming to a stop on the other side. In an instant, the screeching and scraping, the roar of the engine, and the sound of the wind was replaced by an incongruous calm. Matt and Mark took off their headsets, unfastened their harnesses and heard whimpering and moaning coming from the dark cabin behind them. Mark turned off the left generator and battery switch.

"Go back and pull the over-wing hatches. I'll get the airstairs. There's a tree-lined ravine just off to the left. We'll run everyone over there. Let's move," Mark said.

Matt grabbed his Maglite and ran back to the cabin. The beam of light shone through a noxious haze of kerosene fumes. The young couple from Little Rock were in the back of the plane, unbuckling their belts and beginning to move forward. Matt reached for the over-wing escape hatch and yanked it out of its frame. He called to the passengers to come forward so he could help them through the small egress.

"Run straight for those trees, get down in that ravine, and stay low to the ground," he shouted.

Mark rotated the door handle and pushed, but the door wouldn't budge. Then, with full line-backer force, he lunged at the door. It sprang open and he went flying out. He landed on the ground on his right side and felt something snap in his shoulder. He got up and climbed back into the plane. An elderly woman was sitting just ahead of the wing on the left side. She was sobbing and holding her head in her hands. "Ma'am, can you just take my hand?" Mark said. The woman reached up and Mark unbuckled her seatbelt, led her to the airstairs, helped her down, and carried her to the ravine, his right shoulder throbbing with each pounding step.

Matt heard a deep moan coming from the cabin. He shined his light through the haze and saw Olga's father seated just aft of the wing, where the fuselage had cracked in half.

"I can't move my leg," he said.

"Which one?" Matt said.

"The right one."

"We've got to evacuate right now, sir. I'm sorry if this hurts but I'm going to have to pull you free." Mr. Vargas nodded as Matt reached under his armpits and pulled with a steady force, aft and to the left, toward the center aisle. Mr. Vargas let out a tortured cry and his face grimaced as if his leg had been ripped from its socket. Matt pulled him up and steadied him. "Hold onto this seat while I get in front of you," Matt said. Mr. Vargas stood on his left leg and leaned against the seat. The air was full of kerosene fumes and they were both coughing and covering their mouths with sleeves and handkerchiefs, to no avail. Matt climbed over the seat, faced forward in the aisle, and leaned over.

"Just drop your full weight onto my back, sir."

"My briefcase," Mr. Vargas said. Matt turned, reached behind the seat, found the leather attaché case, and held it in one hand while Mr. Vargas draped over Matt's back, and they started moving toward the open door. An orange glow flickered through the starboard windows and lit up the smoke-filled cabin. Matt reached up with one hand to steady himself by the doorframe as he gingerly stepped down to the ground. The smell of kerosene, acrid smoke, pine trees and fresh mowed grass flooded Matt's senses as he started to run, bent over, carrying Mr. Vargas like a rucksack. Cries of excruciating pain couldn't be contained as they made their way toward the ravine.

Mark was just climbing up, about to run back to the plane, when he saw Matt drop down into the ravine and place Mr. Vargas on the ground. The rain started falling in drenching sheets, followed by the deafening roar of an explosion as the right fuel tank blew and the airplane became engulfed in flames. They watched in horror, mesmerized in a trance, like lifeboat passengers on the Titanic. Everyone was silent, detached, as if they were in some dark movie theater, complete with special effects. Then the young woman from Little Rock cried, Mr. Vargas moaned, and it became all too real. It started getting cold as the flames died down.

"Matt, my cabin is just on the far side of this field. We've got to get these people inside and call for help."

The young couple said they could walk. Mark helped the elderly woman up. She was still holding her neck, which seemed skewed from its normal alignment. Matt turned toward Mr. Vargas. "Sir, can you let me carry you like before? Or we could come back with a blanket and use it as a stretcher." Mr. Vargas shook his head.

"I'll be alright," he said, clutching his briefcase. Matt lifted him up onto his good leg, then reached behind and hoisted him onto his back. They climbed out from the ravine and away from the smoldering carcass of the once-noble flying machine, the flames still licking their prey. The grass was soggy and squished beneath their feet as they followed Mark with blind faith, away from the glow of the dying inferno and into the darkness. The overcast layer hung low and full and flashed with the diffused brilliance of lightning that illuminated a small, dark cabin up ahead. Matt was overcome by a feeling of surrealism as Mark reached into his pocket, took out the key, opened the door and reached for the light switch.

"Power's out. I've got a candle on the fireplace mantle," he said as he disappeared into the dark. Matt and the other passengers huddled by the doorway. Mark lit a match, and the amber glow of the candle lit up his face and started filling the room with dim amber light. Mark turned toward the others and saw the same look of astonishment on each of their faces as they gazed around the room and saw hundreds of cases of beer, stacked from floor to ceiling, like a warehouse for some backwoods brewery.

"Anyone like a beer?" Mark said as he went into the kitchen and picked up the phone. There was no dial-tone. "Shit," he said under his breath. "Phone's dead, too."

Matt came into the kitchen as Mark took a candle from the drawer and lit it. "What's wrong with your arm?" he said.

"I must have torn something when I fell out of the plane. I'll be alright. Here, pass these around." He handed Matt some beers which he took out to the passengers. Matt was about to offer one to the elderly woman when she said, "Actually, I'm not much of a beer drinker. You wouldn't happen to have some Scotch whiskey, would you? A little Macallan, perhaps? If not, then some Johnnie Walker Black. If not, then whatever you have will be fine."

"I'll ask the host," Matt said as he turned and went back into the kitchen where Mark was taking down a bottle of Glenlivet from the cabinet over the sink.

"Can't say I blame her, really," he said with a grin. "It's freezing in here. I'll pass out some blankets and make a fire."

"Sit down and have a beer," Matt said. "I'll do all that. Where's your wood?"

"Out back under the lean-to. Oak is on the right, hickory's on the left. I usually save the hickory for special occasions like Christmas or Maggie's birthday. We might as well bring in a full load of it."

"Right," Matt said as he opened the fridge and his heart almost stopped. Before him lay a pink suckling pig, hairless, snout facing out, eyes closed behind dark purple slits.

"Should have warned you," Mark said. "It's the roasting pig for the party."

"Of course," Matt said as he grabbed two beers and sat down at the table. He looked over and saw Mark's left leg shaking, the effect of prolonged pressure to the rudder pedal.

"Can't stop it," Mark said before taking a long pull of cold beer. Matt took a sip of beer, a deep breath, and let out a long sigh.

"I can't believe we made it."

"Yeah, we'll never get so lucky again, that's for sure," Mark said.

"I'm worried about Mr. Vargas," Matt said. They got up and walked back into the living room.

"We're going to try to move you onto the bed, sir," Matt said. "Do you think you can do that?" Mark and Matt carried him in a sitting posture into the dark bedroom and set him on the edge of the bed frame.

"This is a waterbed, sir," Mark said. "It'll feel a bit unsteady at first, but then you'll get used to it." Mr. Vargas's leg was throbbing, his body racked with pain. He clutched his fists tight by his side and tried to replace the grimace on his face with a smile as they carefully placed his legs across the mattress and propped two pillows behind his head.

"Would you have any aspirin?" Mr. Vargas said.

"I think so," Mark said. "We'd better take a look at your leg, first." Mr. Vargas unbuckled his belt and unfastened his pants. Mark and Matt gently pulled the pant legs down. Matt tried to control the reaction on his face when he saw the right tibia, halfway between the knee and ankle, protruding from bloodstained skin.

Mark went to find some aspirin and rubbing alcohol while Matt went into the kitchen and soaked a towel in cool water. He came back and gently draped it over Mr. Vargas's forehead. Mark came back with three tablets of ibuprofen and some rubbing alcohol. They cleaned the wound and covered it with a bag of ice, then covered Mr. Vargas with a wool blanket. "See if you can get some sleep," Matt said.

Mark went out to the living room to tend to the others while Matt went out to the woodshed with a canvas bag and brought in the split oak, hickory, and pine kindling. Mark brought some cots out from the back storage closet and set them up by the fireplace. The elderly woman was sitting upright in a chair sipping whiskey. Her upper body was rigid, and she moved her eyes instead of her head. "Ma'am, we're going to get some help for you real soon. Would you like to lie down?" Mark said.

"I will directly," she said. "Right now, I'm as cozy as a kitten."

Matt built a stack of wood, then threw a stick-match at the base of the pine kindling. Soon the little cabin was aglow with warm amber light. Mark changed into jeans, a wool sweater, and a rain jacket. "You hold down the fort," he said to Matt. "I'm going to go find help."

Mark and Matt went outside. Mark went into the shed and wheeled out a classic 1969 Triumph Bonneville in traditional English racing green and chrome.

"You're in no shape to ride that thing," Matt said.

"Got much time on a bike?" Mark said.

"Not really."

"My Bonnie's kind of temperamental. I've got to coax and kick her just to get her started, kind of like Maggie," he said, grinning at the afterthought. "But once she's warmed up, there's no stopping her. I'll be okay. Stay here and keep trying the phone."

Matt nodded. "Don't you have a helmet?"

"Oh yeah, I forgot." Mark went inside and came back with a white Bell crash-helmet, crazed over in scratch marks with one deep fissure down the middle.

"How'd that happen?"

"Long story," Mark said as he straddled the bike and jumped down on the kick-starter. There was no response. "Haven't ridden her in a month," he said. "Maggie wants me to sell her. I told her I'd think about it, but you know, if Maggie and I should break up, then I'd have nothing." Matt nodded.

Mark dropped down on the kick-starter again. This time the engine sputtered to life and belched blue smoke out the tail-pipe. "Keep the home fires burning," he said as he waved, throttled up, and wobbled down the dirt driveway.

"Wait!" Matt said, but Mark couldn't hear him. He was fishtailing behind a veil of blue smoke, careening down the drive, collecting his right shoulder in tight as he bumped over the cattle grate and felt the pain, like falling on a rail spike. Matt watched him go until he disappeared around the bend. "Nice piece of edgework," Matt said under his breath.

There was no point in knocking on his landlord's door. Mark knew he'd be visiting his brother in Pine Bluff. He turned left onto Highway 170 and wound down the road until he came into West Fork and was met by the eerie specter of a whole town awash in darkness and shadow, as if he'd entered a scene from an Orson Welles Mercury Theatre broadcast, a science fiction movie, the power grid taken over by extra-terrestrials. It was almost midnight, and Mark imagined being met by the barrel of a twelve-gauge shotgun as he pulled the bike into a stranger's driveway and knocked on the door. He thought he might be better off heading straight for Highway 71 where he could open the bike up, easily do 70, and make it back to the airport in fifteen minutes. He turned left on Main Street, crossed the railroad tracks and passed the dark Piggly Wiggly and the Stop & Go Market, then wound down toward Highway 71.

The wind was clocking around to the north and the temperature was falling. The rain, which had diminished to a fine mist, cast a sheen on the highway before him. There was no traffic and Mark opened the throttle up and felt the bike accelerate between his legs. He was feeling confident, the reality of what they'd been through still raw in his nerves, giving him a new lease on life. They had survived the ordeal. Everyone was going to be okay. Help would soon be on the way. Then, in a flash, a darting shadow appeared from the right. A skunk skittered onto the pavement in front of him. Mark leaned to the right to go around it. The pavement was slippery, and the bike started to swerve. He wrestled to regain control as the bike left the highway and careened off the shoulder onto the grass and down into a shallow ditch. The front tire struck an old tree-stump and Mark somersaulted over the handlebars and fell against the base of an old gray planked fence. The last thing he felt was the searing pain in his upper arm, like he'd been nailed to the boards.

Mark woke up slowly, one eye at a time. At first, he had no idea where he was. He was curled up in a fetal position against the base of the fence, helmet cocked at an angle across his face. He looked up through the poplar branches and saw the low clouds racing across the sky. Through gaps in the overcast, bright white moonlight shone down on the wet grass around him. It was cold. The air held a thin trace of skunk. The recollection was gathering in his mind. The night before, the nightmare before, was coming back. He opened his other eye and tried to move. The pain was waking up, too, and starting to burn into his nerve endings like an acid drip. He groaned, placed his good hand over the fence, and pulled himself up. He leaned against the fence and paused until his body adjusted to vertical. The bike lay in a heap, its front fork and wheel bent like junkyard scrap. Mark looked at his watch. It was 2:30 a.m. He was cold and wet, and his arm was throbbing. He gathered a few fallen poplar branches and draped them over the bike, placed his helmet under the blind, then limped back to the shoulder of the road and started walking north. A few stars were shining through gaps in the overcast. Mark picked up his pace and felt the pain reach a certain level, then stabilize. He was making progress again.

He'd try to hitch a ride with any approaching vehicle. At worst, it was just a two-hour hike to the airport. The clouds overhead were thickening, and darkness closed in around him. Drops of rain fell on his cheeks. Then headlights appeared on the highway. Mark turned and walked backwards. He tried to hold out his right arm and raise his thumb, but his shoulder was locked, and he could only bend his elbow a little. The pickup didn't even slow down. It roared past him doing 70, and the cold blast of mist hit him on the cheeks like a slap in the face. "Jerk," he said out loud, then turned around and kept walking.

Jackie and Maggie were at the end of their collective rope. They had driven all through the night, searching down every dirt road, field, and pathway, looking down into ditches and up into trees, to no avail. They stopped at a roadside pay-phone to try to call Tony in Flight Control, but the phones were dead. They cried together and consoled each other as the hopelessness of their endeavor took hold. They made it as far as Winslow, then moved their search down Route 74 to the east. At 3:30 a.m. Jackie said, "Maggie, honey, let's go home. We're going to need to pull ourselves together just to face the day. We'll go home and try to figure out what to do next." Maggie just nodded. There was nothing more to say.

The rain was falling against the windshield, and Jackie switched on the wipers. The two women were physically drained, emotionally shattered. Jackie's eyes flooded over, and tears poured from her swollen lids.

Another pair of headlights appeared on the highway. Mark turned around again and stepped to the edge of the pavement. He cocked his arm up as best he could and held up his thumb.

"Look out!" Maggie shouted as the hatchback veered off the highway, its right front tire briefly dropping onto the shoulder.

Mark jumped back from the pavement as Jackie swerved left and straightened out the wheel. In a flash, like the shutter-action of a camera at 1/500th of a second, Maggie thought she saw the blurred image of a man, a spark of familiarity, fleeting, its clarity just a shade above pure imagination.

"Sorry," Jackie said. They drove on and were almost back at the airport when Jackie said, "Look, lights. The power's back on." The parking lot was flooded with amber light, and Jackie pulled in and parked in her spot.

"I'm going to go in and see if the phones are up," Jackie said.

Maggie didn't want to leave her alone, and she didn't want to be left alone either. "I'll go with you," she said. They walked in and went behind the counter to the freight room.

Jackie picked up the phone. There was a dial tone. "It's working," she said. She dialed the number, and Tony picked up on the first ring.

"Tony, it's Jackie. We're back, have you heard anything?"

"No, Jackie, we haven't. An Air Force C-130 picked up a weak ELT signal south of Fayetteville, then the signal went dead. They picked up another strong signal coming from Harrison but traced it to a small plane in a hangar. We've alerted the Civil Air Patrol up in Rogers. They'll be taking off at first light. The phones just came back up twenty minutes ago. We got a call from the *Gazette* and the *Times*, that's all."

Jackie didn't even react. No news was both good and bad. "Tony, Maggie and I are going home. Will you please call the second you hear anything?"

"I'm going home too," Tony said. "I'll leave a message with Chris."

Jackie let the phone drop into its cradle. Then she said, "Maggie, I just need to be alone to collect myself for a few minutes. Why don't you go on home and get some rest? I'll be okay. One way or the other we'll get through this."

Maggie gave Jackie a hug, then turned and left the freight room. As she was stepping around the side of the ticket counter, the door to the terminal opened. Startled, she looked up and saw a man in a dark, soiled jacket. He was wet, with dirt on his face and hands. At first, she was confused. Blankness, like a brief paralysis, came over her. But then, like Mary Magdalene, called to bear first witness to a miracle, she saw it, that grin, that unmistakable grin that spread from cheek to cheek, as Mark raised his good arm and half his bad arm and came straight toward her.

"We made it, Mags! We made it! Everyone's going to be okay." They threw their arms around each other, and both started to cry as Maggie shouted, "Jackie!"

CHAPTER EIGHTEEN

Matt was asleep on a wooden chair in the kitchen, giving what little privacy the cabin afforded to the passengers who were asleep by the fire. The ringing of the phone startled him, and he almost fell to the floor. He picked up and fumbled to place the receiver to his ear.

"Matt, it's Mark. Is everyone alright?"

"Yeah, they're all asleep, at least they were."

"I'm back at the airport. We just sent for an ambulance. It should be there in a few minutes. How're you making out?"

"I'm okay, glad to be alive. How's the arm?"

"It'll be alright. Listen, the parking lot is starting to fill up with news crews. Maggie and I are going to slip out onto the ramp and walk up to my car. I think I'll just crash at her place in town for a while. I don't know about you, but I don't feel like talking to anyone. If the media asks us any questions, let's just refer them to George or Dresden. Let Barry bask in the limelight. We'll have enough paperwork to fill out between the company, the FAA, and the NTSB. They'll be swarming all over the scene like an open bar on Saint Patrick's Day. I just hope they'll be done dismantling the airplane by Friday. A scorched empennage rising up out of the grass like a tombstone is the last thing we need as a party decoration."

"I know what you mean. I'll call you at Maggie's if something comes up."

In a minute, Matt heard the low-frequency rotor-beat of a helicopter descending behind the cabin, and the wailing of an ambulance coming up the dirt road added to the invasion of the dawn.

Because of the crash, Mark decided to postpone the party until the following weekend. The days were spent filling out reports and answering questions. Mark started his vacation, and Matt was given two weeks off to recover. They both referred the media to Captain Dresden and spent as much time as possible in seclusion.

Matt couldn't stop reliving the ordeal in his mind. He kept a clean, dry T-shirt by his bed and a glass of water on the nightstand. On cue, the same part of the nightmare would wake him, drenched in sweat, heart jackhammering, dry in the mouth. In the afternoon, he'd call Mark to see how he was doing. It felt like he'd been to Hades and back, and the only one who could understand was Mark.

On Wednesday, Pete and Matt drove down to Mark's cabin to drop off some food, loudspeakers, a couple of galvanized buckets and an icemaker. They looked out across the field and saw a crane suspended over what was left of the charred wreckage. The accident investigators were tagging the remains of the fuselage, which was scorched the color of cigar ash, with traces of ghostly Arkansas Airways lettering on the sides.

"You sure are one lucky son of a bitch," Pete said.

"I still can't believe we made it. I thought it was all over."

"You guys deserve a medal."

"Mark does, that's for sure. I'll never get over the way he flew that stricken ship. We had nothing left to work with. I can't stop seeing it in my mind."

"And damn, of all the places to stick it on, right in Mark's own backyard."

"I know. It was like God was showing us the way home."

"How do you explain a thing like that?"

"You can't," Matt said. "You just can't."

Mark hooked his big, fifteen-inch woofers to pad-eyes mounted on the roof-shakes and ran the speaker wire down through the bedroom window to his Harman Kardon amp. The Rolling Stones' *Tattoo You* album had just been released in August, and as the first of the party guests arrived on Friday, they were greeted by one hundred watts of "Start Me Up."

Hundreds of bottles of beer were submerged in tubs of ice and placed all over the yard. Long tables were set with platters of spicy chicken wings, coleslaw, potato salad, herbed cheese, and chips.

Behind the cabin stood clusters of kettle barbecues and a long, rectangular barbecue pit with hand-operated rotisseries spanning its width. Racks of ribs and hundreds of chicken wings, legs, and thighs were marinating in spicy red barbecue sauce in coolers on the porch.

In the freshly cut meadow stood the huge bonfire mound that had grown to the size of an Indian tepee, layered full of oak, hickory, pine, and birch logs. A single stick-match would set the inferno ablaze, and it would burn from Friday night through Sunday.

Off in the distance, just this side of the pine ridge, ran the long skid mark that ended where the grass was charred black, and shiny remnants of aluminum covered the rocks in the creek bed. That was all that remained of AR 426. The tail section had been dismantled and hauled off just that morning, the work crew and crane abandoning the scene just in time for the festivities.

Mark was in grand form in jeans, flip-flops, and a Hawaiian shirt, a beer in one hand, his other arm resting in a sling. He'd been diagnosed with a dislocated shoulder and had to be put under anesthesia while an orthopedic surgeon pulled his arm back into place.

Matt parked the Jeep along the side of the dirt road, and he and Pete walked up to the cabin carrying stacks of white cardboard boxes filled with barbecued spareribs from Coy's Place up on College Avenue. Mark met them at the door like he was ready for a day at the beach. Matt and Pete shook Mark's left hand.

"How's the arm?" Matt said.

"Almost good as new. I'm just wearing this for show," Mark said with a grin. "Maggie told me, no way could I drink and take the Demerol

I've been on, so I said fine, I'll go off the drugs for the weekend and promise not to drink too much. Then I told her, hey, you may not have to drink to have a good time, but why take the chance? Then she punched me in my good arm and gave me one of her looks. Other than that, she's been real nice to me lately and I've been taking full advantage of it."

The band was setting up in the field, and Mark went back to help. People were arriving in waves. Everyone was in a festive mood, especially this year. Coming so close to losing two of their own, but then having them back from the brink, caused everyone to count their blessings, and the joy and laughter flowed like cold beer from the tap.

Maggie and Jackie were in the kitchen helping start the massive barbecue marathon that would run for the next forty-eight hours, filling the air with the aroma of mesquite-roasted pork, chicken, and ribs. Mark lit all twelve barbecues and the long pit, in preparation for the pig. The band started to play, which ramped up the volume of laughter and conversation. Wispy blue smoke perfumed the air with hickory as it drifted up and hung among the branches of the white oak and pine.

Matt felt a close connection with almost everyone there. But even though this airline was like a second family, he always felt more comfortable alone or in one-on-one situations. He busied himself with menial tasks, pouring drinks, tending the ice buckets. He didn't want to talk about the crash. After an obligatory attempt at socializing, he grabbed a beer and went out on the back porch. The band was playing "Sweet Melissa" when Matt looked through the window and saw Olga walk in. He felt his next heartbeat high up in his throat. Olga was wearing a pair of white denim slacks with matching jacket and an olive-green silk blouse. She wore brown leather shoes with short wooden heels and decorative stitching that looked handmade in Milan. Her hair was held in place by a brown suede barrette, and the only makeup she wore was clear lip-gloss. Matt tried not to stare when he saw her walk up to Mark and give him a kiss and a gentle hug, being careful of his right arm. Mark poured her a Perrier and lime as Matt turned away and walked out onto the grass toward the band.

He took a sip of beer and heard the laughter radiating out from the crowded cabin yard. He kept walking, away from the laughter and out toward the long, dark skid mark at the far side of the meadow. The air was clear, and the sun was turning the western rim of the meadow into a fiery orange. A chill was in the air as he walked to the end of the plateau and stood at the base of the four pine trees. He looked out past the rim of the cliff wall and out over the river basin. He could almost reach out and touch the exact spot where he nearly lost his life just a few days before. He replayed the nightmare and thanked God once more for letting them all live. It was still hard to believe, the incongruity of hearing laughter off in the distance at a place that could have flooded with tears if things had gone just a split-hair differently. Matt turned and walked back along the skid mark until it ended by the rock-strewn creek and the broken fence. Shiny traces of aluminum etched into the rocks reflected the sunlight in shimmering silver sparkles. He looked down, lost in thought, and remembered the smell of kerosene, the cries of agony, the explosion, and the fire. Then he looked up and saw the silhouette of a figure in white moving toward him in the low light of the setting sun. He recognized the graceful stride. She walked up and stood next to him.

"Hi," Matt said.

"Hi." They were quiet together, then Olga said, "I just wanted to tell you how grateful I am to you and Mark."

"It was mostly Mark. I've never seen anyone fly like that before."

"My father told me you pulled him from the plane and carried him to safety."

Matt looked into her radiant eyes. "How is he doing?"

"Much better, thanks. He's home, working and resting. The doctor said after three months his leg should be almost good as new."

"I'm glad to hear that."

"My father's life means a great deal to many people. I want you to know I'll always be grateful to you and Mark for saving him." Then she opened her arms and hugged him and kissed him on the cheek. Matt was at a loss to think or speak. He had seen her do the same thing with Mark, so he tried not to attach anything to it.

"When my mother was sick, I thought it was impossible for a person to pray any harder than I did. I was so afraid of losing her. But again, I found myself praying and praying and promising God anything and everything if He would just work a miracle and save my father—save everyone."

"I know what you mean. I prayed that way before my father died."

"I feel like I've been given a precious gift, twice over. I'll never take anything for granted again."

"Me neither," he said. "So much can be taken away in a heartbeat."

It was quiet for a few moments. Matt almost put his hands in his pockets. He took a deep breath.

"Olga, I have to tell you something. I was sure I was going to die. We couldn't hold altitude. I stared out and saw the cliff wall right in front of us, coming closer and closer."

"You must have been terrified."

"I knew we were about to crash, and my life would be over. I thought of my poor mom and how hard it would be for her to lose her husband and son, almost back-to-back. And then I thought of you. I saw your face, and I thought of how beautiful you are and how much I've wanted to get to know you, really know you, who you are, what your passions are. But because I hesitated, wasn't confident enough to approach you, I would never get that chance, and it filled me with regret."

"You thought of me?"

"Yes. Olga, I feel like I've been given a precious gift, too, a deeper appreciation for life, an awareness of how we need to live in the moment and cherish each day. Losing my father was a tragedy, and almost losing my life was … well, I feel changed, like nothing will ever be the same. The fall colors are just starting to turn. It's my favorite time of year. Would you like to come with me to Eureka Springs next weekend? We could pack a picnic lunch." She stared away, then back at him. Then she reached out and took his hand. Her hand felt soft and warm and sure of itself.

"I'd love to," she said.

They turned and walked back to the party. The sun was casting a bright magenta glow behind the western treeline, and the band was playing "Tupelo Honey" by Van Morrison. Matt's legs felt as light as the wisps of smoke that hung among the branches as they walked side by side, away from the spot where he almost lost his life and out toward the open meadow.

PART TWO

"Man is a marvel of nature. To torture him, destroy him, ban him from his ideas is, more than a violation of human rights, a crime against all humanity."

Armando Valladares

CHAPTER NINETEEN

The week was spent in preparation for Saturday. Matt washed and waxed the Jeep, took his tweed sport coat to the cleaners, and put fresh film in the camera. He went to bed early Friday night, unencumbered by any semblance of anxiety. He was going to enjoy the day with a beautiful young lady and not let his mind make any more or less of it.

He woke early, showered and shaved, and put on a clean white cotton shirt, his best pair of jeans, a pair of leather walking shoes, and his tweed sport coat. He packed some fruit, bread, cheese, and a bottle of Bordeaux in a wicker picnic basket, then placed the basket and a wool blanket in the back seat of the Jeep.

The sun was glowing behind the hills to the east as he reached the end of the dirt road by the airport. The whine of a Metro taxiing down the flight line reminded him that he'd be back in the cockpit on Monday for the first time since the crash. He drove into town and parked across from the stately white framed Victorian. Matt walked up the side driveway under a canopy of sugar maples, their bright leaves like flames of red and orange. He reached the back of the house and saw Olga's white Vespa parked by the porch. The sense of serenity that had enveloped him all week vanished, and he felt his nagging anxiety return. He climbed the steps, took a breath of fresh air, and rang the bell.

"Coming," Olga said as she walked through the kitchen and opened the back door.

"Come on in, I'll be ready in a few minutes." Matt followed Olga down a narrow hallway into a small living room. "Make yourself comfortable," she said as she ducked into the bedroom off the hall. "There's juice and water in the fridge."

"It looks like it's going to be a nice day, highs in the mid-seventies."

"That's wonderful," Olga said. Matt looked around the living room. A framed poster from the National Gallery of Art hung on the wall: *Children Playing on the Beach* by Mary Cassatt. There was a small wooden desk by the window with bookshelves to either side. Matt read some of the titles: *Wuthering Heights* by Emily Brontë, *Veinte Poemas de Amor* by Pablo Neruda, *Gone with the Wind* by Margaret Mitchell, *How to See Your Health: Book of Oriental Diagnosis* by Michio Kushi, and *The Selected Poems of Federico García Lorca*. A photograph of Olga's parents stood on her desk next to another photo of young people at the beach. His eyes locked onto a gold framed photo of Olga and a young man, smiling, with their arms around each other.

"Almost ready," Olga called out from the bedroom.

"Take your time," Matt said. There was a small stereo on a wooden table with albums and cassette tapes underneath. Matt looked through some of the albums: Joni Mitchell, Carly Simon, Celia Cruz, Beny Moré, Christopher Cross, and Sérgio Mendes.

Olga came out wearing a brown leather jacket over a white cotton blouse, tapered jeans, and the same leather shoes with decorative stitching that Matt noticed at the party.

"You look nice," he said.

"Thank you. I packed a little snack for us to eat along the way." She picked up a red paisley carpetbag from the kitchen counter and they walked out onto the back porch.

"Nice house," Matt said.

"The owner is the Dean of the law school. He's a friend of my father's."

"How's your father doing?"

"He's gradually getting better, although I think he's going a bit stir-crazy being confined to the house all day. He said to say hi to you, by the way." They walked down the driveway to the Jeep. Matt took the carpetbag and placed it on the rear seat, then offered his hand as she stepped up and sat down.

The sun was rising, and Olga put on a pair of tortoise-shell Calvin Klein sunglasses.

"I see why you like this," she said. "It's so open and free."

"It gets a bit drafty in winter, but I don't mind," he said. They drove through Springdale and Rogers, then turned right on Highway 62 in Bentonville. Every other vehicle was a Walmart tractor-trailer going to and from the huge new storage facility like honeybees working a hive.

"I don't see you at the airport very often," Matt said.

"I just work part-time. I'm still taking classes at the university. I changed my major last year from business administration to holistic nutrition, so I'm making up for some lost credit-hours."

"Were you going to follow in your father's footsteps?"

"I'm not sure. I was undecided, and things just evolved. I actually had to take one of his classes in macroeconomics."

"How was that? Having your father as your teacher, I mean."

"It was hard, a bit uncomfortable, for him as well. He couldn't show any favoritism, and no slack was cut for my benefit. I never studied so hard in my life. We were both aware of the nepotism aspect, how it would look if he should give me an A."

"And did he?"

"Of course," Olga laughed. "But I've gravitated away from business. Right now, I'm more interested in the health sciences."

"Would you ever want to be a doctor?"

"No. Maybe a nutritionist or a therapist. I'd like to keep people from needing doctors in the first place."

Soon the highway was surrounded by rolling hills and trees with leaves turning golden yellow, orange and red. They passed a sign for the Pea Ridge National Military Park. "Let's stop for a few minutes," Olga said. "The grounds are just beautiful. I came here once in high school. We were studying the Civil War in history class, and I wrote a paper on Pea Ridge. It's one of the best-preserved battlefields in the country." They pulled off to the left, parked in the lot, and walked into the Visitor Center.

They toured the exhibit that explained that the Battle of Pea Ridge was one of the deciding battles of the Civil War. It was a bitter two-day fight on March 7-8, 1862, where the Union Army succeeded in ending the Confederate threat to the trans-Missouri region and the city of St. Louis.

After touring the exhibit, Matt and Olga went outside and strolled along the perimeter path. They sat down on a wooden bench that faced the gentle rolling expanse of green. Split rail fencing and historically placed canons outlined sections of the battlefield.

"This is such a beautiful spot. It's hard to imagine the bloodshed that took place," Olga said.

"I hear Vietnam is beautiful too," Matt said.

"I wish we could learn from the past."

"It seems so simple. The way to avoid war is to refuse to wage it, find some other solution," Matt said.

"I remember reading about a war in Central America that was fought over a soccer game," Olga said. "It was between El Salvador and Honduras when they were in the playoffs for the 1970 World Cup in Mexico. Honduras won the first game 1-0 in Tegucigalpa, after the Salvadoran team had been kept awake the night before by fans shouting, throwing stones, and blowing horns. A teenage girl was watching the match on television in San Salvador. When Honduras scored the winning goal in the final minute, she got up, took her father's pistol from the desk drawer, and shot herself."

"My God."

"The entire capital took part in the televised funeral. A military honor-guard, the president, and the entire Salvadoran soccer team marched behind the flag-draped coffin. The next match took place in San Salvador. This time it was the Honduran team that was kept awake all night. The players were taken to the stadium in armored cars. El Salvador won 3—0. Scores of Honduran fans were kicked and beaten as they fled toward the border. Two fans died and many were taken to the hospital. The border between the two countries was closed."

"All over a soccer game?"

"My father says, in Latin America, the line between politics and soccer can be very thin. Many governments have been overthrown after the defeat of the national team. Losing players are seen as traitors. When Brazil won the World Cup in Mexico, an exiled Brazilian journalist was distraught because it all but assured the military right-wing to five more years in power. Anyway, a few days later at dusk, a plane flew over Tegucigalpa and dropped a bomb. Panic swept the city. Both armies amassed at the border. There was a cease-fire after a hundred hours because other Latin American states intervened, but six thousand people were killed, and thousands more were wounded."

Matt was looking at her eyes as she spoke. He had a feeling in his stomach, like dropping over a dip in the highway at high speed. She spoke with such sincerity, like things really mattered to her. He looked out at the rolling green field, felt the crisp morning air, and heard a cluster of crows cawing in a nearby tree.

"I remember thinking about how tragic the Civil War was, especially since it not only split apart the nation but families as well, cousin against cousin, friend against friend," Olga said. "It was just like that during the Cuban revolution, too. Those loyal to Fidel went off to the Sierra Maestra mountains to fight against the Batista loyalists. In many cases, family members and classmates were at war against one another. My family left Cuba in October of 1960, but my uncle stayed behind. He supported Fidel Castro and the new regime and thought it unpatriotic to leave. My father and uncle would get into many heated discussions. My uncle said that even if the revolution failed, it was their duty to stay and come up with a better solution."

"Wasn't Castro confiscating homes and property and nationalizing all the private businesses?"

"Yes, that's mostly why my family left. In the beginning, most of the small businesses were allowed to operate, but things really fell apart in 1968 when Fidel outlawed all private enterprise. After that, just having a pair of shoes repaired became a matter of the state. People lost all incentive to succeed. Fidel forces them to sacrifice everything for the revolution."

"And what is your uncle doing now?"

"He's in prison. After it became obvious that Fidel had no intention of using the revolution to build a new democratic society, to hold free and open elections, my uncle completely changed his mind. He went from being a champion of the revolution to an overt dissenter, something Fidel cannot tolerate. He began writing articles in support of the counterrevolutionary rebels, many of whom had fought alongside Fidel but later turned against him and were banding together up in the Escambray Mountains. My uncle was arrested by G-2, Fidel's secret police. My grandparents and parents were so afraid when they found out. My father contacted some friends and found out he was being held at La Cabaña, the old colonial fortress in east Havana. Every day, my uncle witnessed men being escorted down into the moat around the fortress. They were executed by firing squad just for saying they thought communism was wrong. Then my uncle was transferred to the Presidio Modelo, the prison on the Isle of Pines, south of mainland Cuba. He spent two years there, where he was beaten and tortured for attempting to escape. Then he was transferred again. My parents try to get information about his whereabouts, but it's next to impossible. My father keeps in touch with Amnesty International and Americas Watch and receives regular updates on many political prisoners. He writes countless letters to the State Department, the International Red Cross, the United Nations, and other human rights organizations. He even wrote a letter to François and Danielle Mitterrand, appealing for help."

"But didn't Castro recently release everyone from jail, right before the Mariel boat-lift? Aren't many of those refugees down at Fort Chaffee ex-prisoners?"

"Yes, my father got word that my uncle had been released, and that Mariel was going to be a reality. My mother was ecstatic. She hadn't seen her brother in almost twenty years. We saw it as the answer to our prayers. My father went to Key West and chartered a boat along with four other Cuban businessmen from Miami. It was a rough crossing. Everyone got seasick. When they arrived in Mariel there was chaos everywhere. They were confined to the port for days. My father gave my uncle's name to the authorities, along with the name of their vessel. He couldn't understand what was taking so long. Then he found out that my uncle was being held at El Mosquito, an exit-processing camp nearby. Dozens of military tents were set up in the compound which was surrounded by barbed wire. Men in military fatigues patrolled the perimeter with bayonets and barking dogs. The heat was unbearable, and there was stench and flies. The refugees were tired, hungry, and confused. They sat for days, waiting for their names to be announced over a loudspeaker. Then they would board a bus that would take them to the docks. Finally, my uncle heard his name being called. He boarded the bus and waited. Nothing happened. The bus had broken down, and everyone had to wait in the broiling sun until another bus could be located. My uncle was losing his patience. When a member of the military police came by, my uncle just snapped. He started shouting, 'Death to Fidel! Down with the revolution!' and spat on the ground. He was arrested on the spot. An agent from G-2 came to tell my father to go home, that my uncle would not be allowed to leave. My father was furious. He found out through other refugees what had happened, but no one knew where my uncle was being held. My father was forced to come home and face my mother empty-handed. Instead of the joyous celebration we had planned, my mother just broke down and wept. She was distraught for days, almost unreachable, and it was two months later when she found a lump in her breast."

"Do you think all the anguish and stress could have caused it?"

"We'll never know. But the mind and body are much more interconnected than we realize. Emotions have a powerful effect on physiology. Why don't we go? It's too beautiful a day to talk about such sad things."

They followed the highway up and down hills and switchbacks, the valley of northwest Arkansas stretching off to the right in a tapestry of autumnal splendor, the rise of the Ozark Mountains veiled in a thin purple haze. They crossed over the White River, passed the Thorncrown Chapel and a log cabin lodge, and came into the little town of Eureka Springs. Matt parked the Jeep on Main Street, strapped the camera around his neck as they got out, and walked across a decorative black wrought-iron foot-bridge. The sky was deep blue, and the sun warmed the crisp morning air. Two banjo players with beards and bib overalls were seated on a bench playing a bluegrass tune. Matt and Olga listened for a minute, then Olga placed a dollar in the open banjo case. They passed the stately Basin-Park Hotel and looked in the windows of an art gallery, a Tiffany lamp and stained-glass store, an art supply store, jewelry shop, and hat emporium.

"Let's go inside," Olga said. Matt opened the door for her under the sign that said, Heads Up Hat Shop. Inside, hundreds of hats adorned mannequin heads. Olga picked up a white Panama fedora with black silk trim and placed it on Matt's head.

"Quite dapper," she said as Matt turned, looked in the mirror, and laughed. Then Matt saw a bright red felt down-brim hat, reminiscent of the ones worn by flappers in the Roaring Twenties.

"This one's for you," he said. Olga placed the hat on her head, faced the mirror, and pulled it down slightly over her forehead. She put a hand on her hip and turned and faced Matt with a coquettish expression. The flash from the camera went off, taking her by surprise.

They left the hat shop, walked back to the Jeep, and drove up Spring Street to Crescent Drive. They passed by glazed granite walls where cool spring water poured from spouts and overflowed into ornate pools surrounded by purple and yellow wildflowers and green ferns. Magnolia trees and manicured lawns lined the street. Many of the old Victorian homes were undergoing phases of restoration, and the air held the scent of fresh cut lumber. Off to the right, across the expanse, they could see the white stone statue of Christ from the Passion Play amphitheater, arms outstretched to form a cross, like a miniature version of the statue atop Corcovado Mountain overlooking Rio de Janeiro. They reached the Crescent Hotel and parked. Matt picked up the picnic basket as they walked past a bronze crescent moon-shaped fountain with water pouring down its sides. The lobby was adorned with antiques, pine wood paneling, tapestries, a black grand-piano, and a stone fireplace. They ordered a pot of jasmine tea from the Crystal Dining Room restaurant, then took the picnic basket out onto the back porch where wicker chairs and tables were set up behind bronze telescopes. Matt pulled a small table in between two chairs and they sat down. Olga set the teacups on the table. As she was pouring, she began to smile.

"What's so funny?" Matt said.

"I was just remembering the look on your face when we first met."

"I wanted to die."

"Maybe I'll just pour you half a cup," she said with a smile.

They ate lunch and sipped tea, taking turns looking down the sloping green terrain through the telescope, the leaves on the trees ablaze with autumn shades of red, yellow, and orange.

After a while they packed up the basket and drove along the back side of Crescent Drive. Matt turned left on Main Street and drove for a mile before coming to the Eureka Springs Railway, a stretch of track that held an old black steam-locomotive and a bright green passenger car converted into a dining room. They got out and looked at the collection of steam tractors and rail-cars.

"Climb up on the caboose," Olga said. "I want to take your picture." Matt handed her the camera and climbed up the black iron steps. He put his hands on the rail and smiled down at her as she snapped the shot.

"Your turn," Matt said. As he was climbing down, an elderly couple who had just left the dining car walked past.

"Would you like me to take one of the two of you?" the gentleman said with an English accent.

"Yes, thank you," Olga said, handing him the camera. Olga and Matt climbed up the steps, stood next to each other, and faced the camera.

"Just a spot closer," the gentleman said from behind the viewfinder. Matt and Olga stood with their hips touching. Matt felt a warm wave pass through him. He reached out and gently placed his arm around Olga's waist.

"That's the ticket," the man said. Matt felt the ethereal touch of Olga's arm wrap around him and gently pull him closer. The shutter clicked and they climbed down.

As the man and woman walked away, Matt heard the woman say, "What a lovely couple." Matt and Olga stood silent for a few seconds before walking back to the Jeep.

"Do your parents miss Cuba?" Matt asked on the way home.

"Yes, very much, but they don't regret their decision to leave. Things are very bad there. There's little opportunity and incentive. There's nothing to motivate the people except Fidel's interminable speeches, appealing for more and more sacrifices for the revolution. 'Patria o Muerte' is his mantra. If my parents had stayed, I would have been forced to join the Young Communist Pioneers at five years old. And if my parents had objected, they would have faced constant harassment from the regime, especially since my uncle is considered an enemy of the state. I could have been expelled from school. My mother says the loss of parenthood is one of the worst human rights abuses. Parents are forced to surrender the passing down of their thoughts, values, and religious convictions to the total control of a police state. Fidel tries to steal the minds and souls of Cuban youth at a very early age. I would have been forced to repeat things like, 'Fidel es mi papa y Cuba es mi mama.' The regime dictates every aspect of society. My Aunt Miriam was telling us about her friend's daughter, Magalis, who lives in Havana. She had a baby boy last year. The state mandates that every mother breastfeed their baby for the first seven months. The problem was that Magalis didn't produce enough milk. She was forced to see a doctor to obtain a ration coupon for baby formula. Instead of just going to a store to pick up formula, she had to go to seven buildings all over the city and wait in long lines in the sweltering heat before the paperwork could be approved. The bureaucracy is a nightmare."

"I can't imagine living under so much oppression," Matt said.

"My father says Fidel has created the most sophisticated form of oppression in the world. Cuba receives over five billion dollars in annual Soviet subsidies, but food is still rationed. There isn't enough. The average salary is 160 pesos, about eight dollars a month. A brain surgeon receives twenty dollars a month, four times what a dockworker makes. People stand in line for hours waiting with their *libretas,* their ration coupons, only to find that there is no cooking oil, very few vegetables, almost no pork. Cubans joke that socialism has only two fundamental problems: lunch and dinner."

"Why do the people put up with it? Why don't they rebel?"

"They can't. Every neighborhood is monitored by the local Committee for the Defense of the Revolution, the CDR. Neighbors spy on each other. Any hint of counterrevolutionary talk or activity is reported to the secret police. People could lose their jobs or be sent to prison. They have to spend almost all their time trying to feed their families. They don't have the time or resources to attempt a coup. But my uncle rebelled. He spoke out against the revolution and was arrested. He never knows if each day will be his last. My father thinks things are going to get worse, that the Soviet Union won't be able to continue subsidizing the Cuban economy. But anyway, yes, my parents miss Cuba very much."

"We always went to visit our relatives in Miami twice a year when I was growing up. My parents just seemed to come alive in their presence. Everyone would dance and sing and cook and eat. And when we came back to Arkansas, everything seemed so quiet. It was as if my parents were forced to wear clothes that were too tight. It just took a few days for them to adjust. As a young girl, I think I interpreted that as sadness, the same sadness they felt about my uncle's imprisonment, and that somehow, I would have to be this perfect daughter in order to keep any additional burden from their lives. I thought I could absorb their pain by being good and making them proud."

"That must have been so stressful," Matt said.

"More than I realized at the time. When I was in high school, we had a foreign exchange student from Argentina whose name was

Manuel. Manuel must have assumed that since we were both Latin, I was to be his girlfriend. One Saturday night, we went to the movies together. I was mortified when I felt his hands groping me all over in the darkened theater. I got up and walked home. When my mother opened the door, tears were pouring from my eyes. She pulled me into her arms and let me cry. I'm sure she could smell his cigarette smoke in my hair. When my sobs were reduced to sniffles, she asked me if I went out with Manuel because I thought it would please her and my father. I never thought about it that way before, but I knew she was right. I was doing it to please them, and she had suspected it all along. She said that my father's and her love for me was infinite, since before I was born, and nothing I could do, one way or the other, could ever change that, and what they wanted, more than anything, was for me to follow my heart's desires."

"So, what did you tell Manuel?"

"Hah, well I tried to let him down gently, so I wrote him a letter. I just told him, in no uncertain terms, that the one thing he had to learn about American women is that we're nobody's property."

The sun was heavy in the western sky, and a chill was in the air. Olga buttoned her jacket collar. Matt turned the heat up, reached back, and handed her the wool blanket. She took the blanket and spread it over her legs, then tried to cover Matt with it too. They drove on, and Matt felt overcome with joy. Countless times he'd dreamt of looking over and seeing Olga by his side, and here she was. The day had been a rare gift. She was as much an angel as he imagined, possessing a natural grace that went hand in hand with her profound beauty. As they wound around the country highway, he glanced over and saw her looking at him. He smiled, but quickly turned and faced the road again. Olga yawned, and Matt slid a John Coltrane tape into the stereo. "That's nice," she said.

"Are you warm enough?"

"I'm fine." After a few minutes of silence, she said, "Will you be alright on Monday? I mean, back flying."

"I think so. I'm flying with T-Ball."

Dusk was brush-stroking the western sky with pink and purple streaks. A jolt of anxiety came over Matt as he turned right on Washington and parked along the curb. How to end the perfect date? He wanted her to invite him to come in with the bottle of wine, to sit next to her on the sofa, to feel her arms around him.

"I'll walk you to the door," he said. Matt got out, went around, and offered his hand as she climbed down from the seat.

"I had a nice time," she said as they walked up the driveway under the orange and red canopy of maple leaves. They reached the back porch and climbed up the wooden steps. "I have to work early tomorrow," she said. "I'll be thinking of you on Monday."

"You too," Matt said as he leaned in, and they kissed each other on the cheek.

"Good night," she said, unlocking the door.

"Good night."

As he walked down the steps, he turned his head and saw her watching him through the back-door window. He waved a hand and saw her smile before closing the blinds.

The day had been perfect. He wasn't ready to go home, to lie in bed in a quiet room, to miss her and worry about his chances for another date. He drove into town and saw Pete's pickup outside Hugo's. He parked, descended the staircase below the sidewalk, and opened the door. The place was filled with the comforting sounds of beer glasses clinking and people laughing and talking. Pete and Rita were seated at the end of the bar.

"Son, where've you been?" Pete said. "I've been trying to reach you all day. Looks like it's open season. Dresden's just suspended Mark Winger, pending further investigation."

"What? You've got to be kidding. On what grounds?"

"Violation of FAR 91.13: operating an aircraft in a careless and reckless manner so as to endanger life and property, or some such bullshit."

"That's absurd, totally unfounded. Mark's the best pilot on the property and everyone knows it."

"Don't you see? The son of a bitch is jealous, and he knows Mark's pro-union."

"What did Wendell say?"

"Wendell's called a mandatory meeting at the Hofbräu this Thursday night. It looks like we're heading for a showdown. I'll tell you what I think," Pete said, looking over his shoulder and lowering his voice. "Remember when we were new to the line, back in February? Grayson had just come back from his first trip with Mark. They were empty on their last leg up from Fort Smith, and it was Mark's turn to fly. The weather was clear as glass. Right after takeoff, Mark told Bob to cancel their instrument flight plan; they would just fly home visually. Right after they canceled, Mark pushed it over and dove down, almost to the treeline. They dropped deep into the valley south of Winslow, followed the contour of the terrain and scared the shit out of Grayson. Mark was just grinning and laughing. When they landed and shut down on the ramp, Mark shook Bob's hand and said, 'Welcome to the line,' like it was some sort of initiation. Now, I'm not saying I condone what he did. The weather was clear, and he knows that terrain like the back of his hand. Maybe it *was* a stupid stunt, but Grayson flew his next trip with Dresden. I'll bet you anything he told him all about it. And when you guys pancaked it on in Mark's own backyard, I'm sure Dresden saw it as just another stunt."

"That's absurd. We were about to hit the cliff. There were no other options. Without Mark's skill and knowledge of the terrain, I wouldn't be here right now."

"Yeah, I know, but without a flight data and voice recorder, it's just your word against his. Dresden'll believe what he wants, especially if it'll help him fire a union man. It seems we don't stand much of a chance going against him, one-on-one. Our only hope is to put our links together and form a chain."

"Unionize?"

"That's what I think Wendell's thinking. Thursday night ought to be interesting."

Olga locked the door, closed the blinds, and put the teakettle on the stove. She placed a peppermint tea bag in a cup of hot water, walked into the bathroom, and started filling the tub. The mirror was misting over, and Olga lit a cluster of white candles, set the cup down, and started to unbutton her blouse. Modest to a fault, she uncharacteristically stepped out of her clothes and stood before the mirror. She took a white washcloth, wiped the steam from the mirror and saw her image, natural and unadorned. A feeling came over her that made her shiver. She had grown up with the luxury of confidence and security, supported by loving family and friends. She felt she could do anything she put her mind to, that she was in charge of her own destiny. That sense of sureness was shattered by how close she came to losing her mother, first, then her father. For the first time she became aware of external forces having the upper hand. She wiped the mirror and tried to see something more than the shape and contour of her body. She tried to look beyond the steamy surface, to penetrate deeper, to look inside herself for clues, clues that would reveal which path to take, which choice to make—clues to divine the future. Then something unnerved her, and she switched the lights off and stepped into the warm bath. Amber light from the candles flickered against the white tiled walls, and Olga reached for the teacup and slid down into the water.

It had been a beautiful day. She felt comfortable and relaxed, free, and unguarded. She took a sip of tea and stared into the candlelight. He had been a gentleman. He seemed to truly listen to her, with more than a sense of hearing. She felt he was listening to her very essence as well as her words. His eyes were kind, something that could not be affected. There was a mix between the vulnerable and the strong, something that attracted her, like the confident way he looked while driving, when he hadn't noticed her staring at him. Then for a second, she caught herself wishing he was there with her, sharing the warm water together. Unnerved again, she pulled the stopper and stepped out of the tub. She wrapped herself in a white terrycloth towel as the water swirled down the drain in a dizzying vortex.

CHAPTER TWENTY

"I'm not flying," T-Ball said when Matt met him in Flight Control Monday morning. "They're all yours today."

"Thanks," Matt said as he stood next to T-Ball at the counter and perused the ream of flight papers.

"Looks like we've got a winner. High pressure's dominating and the closest thunderstorm's way down in Florida," T-Ball said. It was the long Knoxville turn, and the whole route would be flown over terrain awash with the brilliant colors of fall.

"You okay with the fuel?" T-Ball asked.

"Eight hundred pounds to Little Rock should be enough," Matt said while T-Ball signed the release. They walked down the flight line as the slanting glow of early sunlight appeared above the hills to the east.

"Coffee shop's just opening up. I'll get us a cup," T-Ball said.

Jackie came back and wished Matt a safe trip, and then T-Ball came back with two cups of coffee. They walked out to the plane and stood by the airstairs.

"Going to the meeting on Thursday?" T-Ball asked.

"Wouldn't miss it."

"Just between you and me, I think the union's a go. Dresden's stepped way over the line. If they want a war, they're going to get one."

"You think we can really pull it off?" Matt said.

"I don't know, but it'll be quite a show, something to tell your kids about someday." Jackie came toward them, escorting a small group of passengers. Then T-Ball took Matt's coffee up to the cockpit and strapped in.

The long day went like clockwork. T-Ball was his jovial self, telling a few more jokes than usual for Matt's benefit. The Great Smoky Mountains around Knoxville were a bright palette of autumnal color. The sun was setting as they departed Memphis, the dark hulks of the barges on the Mississippi inexorably ghosting toward New Orleans. Matt was relieved to feel at home in the cockpit, glad to be back in the saddle again.

CHAPTER TWENTY-ONE

Ben Weinberg grew up in Washington, D.C., in the fifties. His grandfather had been a staff attorney for the Department of Labor during the Roosevelt Administration. Ben would later recall, with warm memory, the many stories told around the dinner table about his grandfather's boss, Frances Perkins, Secretary of Labor and the first female cabinet member in U.S. history. Ben's grandfather often spoke with great admiration for Madam Secretary's (she was the first to coin the title) deep commitment to social progress and workers' rights. Back in the 1930s, during the depths of the Great Depression, when the unemployment rate reached twenty-five percent, Frances Perkins, through her great courage and commitment, supported sound labor policies, encouraged workers to unionize, and promoted the first Social Security system in U.S. history. Her deep empathy for the plight of workers was largely a result of witnessing, first-hand, the tragic Triangle Shirtwaist Company fire in Manhattan in 1911, where 147 young women and girls were killed when a fire broke out on the ninth floor of the Asch building east of Washington Square. Fifty women jumped to their deaths, most of them immigrants, some as young as twelve years old. They worked fourteen-hour shifts during a 60 to 72-hour work week, sewing for $7.00 a week. Two years before, the women had tried to form a union but lost. One of the two doors was kept locked, in reprisal.

Ben grew up following in his grandfather's footsteps, graduating from Columbia Law in 1968, that apocalyptic year when napalm and mayhem had a grip abroad and at home, the collective agony of the assassinations of Martin and Bobby, the fight for civil rights, the protests to end the Vietnam War, the Russian invasion of Czechoslovakia—the year when peace was not given a chance.

Ben joined the protesters before and after classes, always aligning himself with justice and siding with the underdogs. So, when his classmates were being hired at six-figure salaries for big name firms like Sidley & Austin, Latham & Watkins, and Cravath, Swaine & Moore, Ben decided to find fulfillment in the trenches as a labor lawyer, defending the American dream in coal mines, auto assembly plants, and steel mills.

It was rewarding work in the beginning, helping to enhance workers' rights, boost their pay, and protect their pensions. The rich could always take care of themselves, but the little guy needed a helping hand, intellectual and political power to level the playing field. But by the late seventies, Ben was frustrated and tired of always butting heads, trying to explain labor law to people who, in some cases, lacked even a high school education. So, when the opportunity arose to work full-time for the Air Line Pilots Association back in Washington, D.C., he jumped at the chance. These were professionals he could relate to. Some were even lawyers and doctors themselves. And with the ink of deregulation barely dry, every ounce of expertise, every new technology, and every political strategy would be needed to fight back against management forces more determined than ever to break labor's back.

Ben stood in front of the mirror in his hotel room and looked at his face. His hair was thinning with streaks of gray. Wrinkles appeared that weren't there a few months before. Lately he'd been wondering if he wasn't deluding himself—the apostasy of a priest who shudders from the rogue agnostic thought, a single doubt that could undermine his whole raison d'être. After all, wasn't the labor movement just a grand cabal, a noble conspiracy? America was founded on individualism and opportunity. What could be more opportunistic than being a scab? Everyone free to cut their own deal, sink or swim by one's own cunning and skill. Maybe he should join his classmates, go over to the other side, make his fortune, retire early, and do some *pro-bono* work to assuage the guilt. But then he thought of that young man, Mike Ingles, who called him from Arkansas asking for help. He'd been fired from his low-paying job as a pilot for Arkansas Airways, solely because he was suspected of trying to form a union. On their own, those pilots wouldn't stand a chance. But with Ben's help, they could at least put up a fight.

Ben shaved, put on dark brown slacks, a white shirt, and a camel-hair sport coat, picked up his attaché case, and walked one block from the Hilton to the Hofbräu.

The Hofbräuhaus in Munich, that famous beer palace off the Platz, was celebrating over four hundred years of serving some of the finest beer known to man. Due largely to the *Reinheitsgebot*, or beer purity law of 1516, where the only ingredients allowed were barley, hops, and water—yeast being added some two hundred years later—the quality was second to none. The Weissbier was thought to be a beauty treatment, and the court ladies of Munich would drink as much as seven liters a day. With its high, frescoed ceilings, Oompah bands, and crispy pork with dumplings, one could spend a delightful afternoon.

Just about the only things the new Hofbräu Bar and Grill had in common with its namesake were wooden tables and beer, and even that was a stretch. The one thing it did afford on that Thursday night in October was a separate room in the back that could be cordoned off for private parties and meetings. Pitchers of beer were placed on the tables, and waitresses were instructed to leave the door closed. Wendell was seated at the front table with Mark Winger on his right and Mike Ingles on his left. Everyone who wasn't out flying the line was there. The air was filled with anticipation. Being all together in close confines allowed them to feel their solidarity, trying it on for size, knowing it was going to be their greatest asset. No one could keep still, like boxers in the ring before a fight. The volume of conversation was ramping up as Wendell looked at his watch, stood up, and addressed the crowd.

"Gentlemen, I don't need to tell you about the conditions we've been forced to tolerate, the lack of adequate rest, the variable wage plan, the long hours, the lack of vital safety equipment, the performance degradation. We live it, day in and day out. You've heard me say I didn't think it was time to seek relief by unionizing. But attempting to appeal to the common sense of our management," boos erupted from the crowd, "and trying to show them that their penny-pinching approach is counterproductive, has all been in vain. Even after coming so close to a fatal crash, and only through the exemplary skill of our fellow airmen, was a tragedy averted. Management not only fails to heed that as a wake-up call, but instead continues to ramp up the harassment and intimidation by indiscriminately firing whomever they please. Without some strong response from our side, we will be interminably abused and treated as cheap, disposable assets. I think we've reached a point where we have no choice but to draw a line. On our own, we're weak; together, we can be a force to reckon with. So, I ask you, what recourse do we have?" Cheers erupted, and "*Union, union, union!*" chorused through the crowd. "Please keep it down, these walls are thin. It now gives me great pleasure to introduce Ben Weinberg from the Air Line Pilots Association." More applause filled the room as Ben stood up and walked forward to address the group.

"Thank you, Wendell, gentlemen. It's an honor to be with you today. I first became aware of your situation when Mike and Wendell contacted me a few months ago. What you've been forced to tolerate falls right in line with the standard management playbook. These same oppressive working conditions were what caused David Behnke and other courageous pilots to form the Air Line Pilots Association back in 1931.

"If you elect ALPA to represent you, you will have at your disposal all the legal, political, and financial support that ALPA can provide. You will not be just a group of sixty-some pilots fighting your battles alone, you will become equal members of a global fraternity. What ALPA can do for you is provide expertise in the area of contract negotiations, legal representation in the event of an accident, incident or unlawful dismissal, safety expertise, and retirement planning. There are no guarantees of a successful outcome. The history of organized labor in the U.S. is the bloodiest in the world. But without banding together, your chances are slim."

"If our vote for ALPA is successful, does that mean Mike gets his job back?" T-Ball asked.

"We're working on a separate lawsuit regarding his case, but it will enhance our chances of success if the vote goes through."

"As soon as management finds out, they're going to make life a living hell for us," Buzz said.

"We have to be prepared for that," Ben said. "Document everything and funnel it to me through Wendell. Do your job with the utmost professionalism, same as always. No sick-outs, no job actions. We'll try to expedite the process as much as possible. I have a complete copy of your seniority list. The authorization cards will go out in the morning mail. That's all I have for now. Good luck, and I hope to be back soon with good news." Everyone clapped as Ben and Wendell walked out of the room.

Matt drank a beer with the others after the meeting. From the general conversation, it seemed like the vote would be a landslide victory. A group of pilots clustered around Mark Winger and Mike Ingles, offering encouragement. When Matt could get a word in, he said to Mark, "How are you holding up?"

"Couldn't be better. Dresden doesn't realize he was actually doing me a favor. Even the best trip can't beat a day off. Besides, I've been thinking about hanging it up anyway."

"You're kidding, before the vote?"

"Naw, I wouldn't give Dresden the pleasure. Maggie's father needs someone to run his horse ranch in Ocala. We've been talking about moving down there."

"What about flying?"

"I've had the course. I might miss it from time to time, but there's other things."

"Well, I hope you stay," Matt said.

Then Pete put a hand on Matt's shoulder. "I'm going over to Rita's place. I'll see you tomorrow."

After Pete left, Matt got in the Jeep and drove to Olga's house. He knew she would still be at the airport. He reached under the seat and pulled out the small paperback book of poems by Kahlil Gibran. Since their first date, he'd reached for the phone numerous times, only to hesitate and retreat. He didn't know what to say. He thought he'd found a new confidence in the days following the crash, but now that he'd been with her, seen up-close just how wonderful she was, the thought of saying something clumsy, ruining such a perfect beginning, caused his old insecurities to return. Emboldened by de Bergerac, and not wanting to leave anything to chance, he decided to let the poet speak for him. He hoped she would think of him, as he thought of her when he read the words from "A Lover's Call:"

Remember you the trails and forest we walked with hands joined,

And our heads leaning against each other,

As if we were hiding ourselves within ourselves?

He scribbled a short note and inserted it before page one.

Dear Olga,

I just wanted to tell you again what a nice time I had at Eureka Springs.

I hope you like this little book.

Best regards,

Matt

He walked under the canopy of maples and felt his heart beating in his chest as he climbed the porch steps, propped the book by the back door, quickly walked back to the Jeep, and drove home.

The house was dark and empty. The living-room window was open, and a cool breeze blew through the house. Matt knew he couldn't sleep. He was too filled with thoughts of Olga and the union vote. He walked out the kitchen door and crossed the dirt road. A heavy harvest-moon was rising in the east, full and orange. Dry leaves crunched under his feet as he walked over to the old plank fence around the racetrack. He turned and leaned against the fence and saw the image of the house, bathed in soft moonlight, the two white columns illuminated like sentinels. He looked up at the night sky and tried to find the North Star. He gazed at the shadow of the abandoned track and thought of the futility of racing around in circles, risking your life only to end up back where you started. He thought of the pending union vote. Sure, they'd band together like brothers in solidarity, they'd put up a good fight, show management. But what if the company really was up against the ropes, like Blahdick said? What if their response to a unionized workforce would be to shut the whole place down, liquidate? The pilots would win the battle, alright, but it might just prove to be a Pyrrhic victory. *You boys think you're so smart? Well here, take your pink slips and turn off the lights on your way out.* Matt would lose his job *and* Olga. Would he be willing to give it all up for her? How could he let management or fate turn their budding relationship into just an ephemeral fluke? A sick sense of déjà vu pressed down on him as he walked back to the empty house and climbed the staircase in the dark.

No one seemed to notice the news. On that very day, October 22, 1981, the U.S. Federal Labor Relations Authority voted to decertify the Professional Air Traffic Controllers Organization as bargaining representative for the nation's air traffic controllers.

That night, Matt had a dream. He was standing by the side of Highway 71, just north of the airport, with all his earthly possessions in a bundled heap, using his thumb to hitch a ride north. The clouds hung low and heavy with rain. He looked south toward the terminal and saw the little white Vespa coming his way. A smile came to his face, a feeling of relief flooded over him, but the Vespa went by in a blur. She hadn't even noticed he was there.

CHAPTER TWENTY-TWO

It was Saturday afternoon. Matt and Buzz were flying the last leg of the two-day Meridian trip. The weather was crisp and clear, high-pressure air, soft autumn breezes, not a cloud in the indigo sky over a quilt of bright red, orange, and gold.

After the union meeting on Thursday, everyone braced for reprisal. Management had to know the cat was out of the bag, but so far, everything was quiet. There was even good news. George intervened and overrode Dresden's suspension of Mark Winger. He was to be reinstated immediately.

At the end of the trip, Matt started planning the phone call he would make to Olga that evening. It had been a week since their date, two days since the book-drop. He flung his flight bag into the back seat of the Jeep and climbed in. His eyes fell to a white envelope sealed in a plastic bag and taped to the base of the gear shifter. He reached down and carefully ripped it open.

Dear Matt,

I thought of you on Monday and hoped you had a smooth return to the skies. I just wanted to tell you what a nice time I had last weekend. I'll be at the Café Alto this evening, working on a paper. It would be my pleasure if you could join me.

Olga

PS I loved the book.

Matt read the note again and felt a Christmas morning joy fill his senses. Elated, he drove home and took a deep breath of cool autumn air. It felt good to still be alive.

The Café Alto was tucked in among a few specialty shops off Mountain Street, south of the square. Matt parked a block away and walked. He was wearing a charcoal gray turtleneck sweater and a pair of jeans. A large bronze sculpture of an alto sax cantilevered out from over the doorway. Approaching the entrance, he heard the soulful sound of tenor sax, accompanied by bass, drums and piano. The band was playing the Dexter Gordon tune "Where Are You?" The place was crowded but quiet, except for the music. There was no cover charge, just little wooden boxes affixed to the tabletops for tips. There was an espresso and wine bar along the wall, and the band was set up in the rear corner. Little green shaded lanterns on each table cast a soft, warm glow around the room. The walls were plastered with brilliant black and white photos of the jazz greats, taken by gifted photographers like Herman Leonard and Francis Wolff, soulful shots of Louis Armstrong, Art Blakey, Duke Ellington, Miles Davis, and others.

Olga was seated on a red leather chair in the corner, opposite the band. A notebook and pen lay on a small wooden table next to a cup of tea. Matt stopped for a moment to take in her candid beauty.

"Hi Matt," she said as he leaned down, and they kissed each other on the cheek. "It's nice to see you." Their words overlapped as Matt pulled up a chair.

"The band sounds great," he said. "What are you working on?"

"It's a paper for my class in nutritional therapies, about the effects of soy-based foods on estrogen levels. The Japanese have less cancer and greater longevity than we do, and their diet is rich in soy. That doesn't necessarily imply a direct link, but it could be a clue. It's just something I'm interested in."

"It was nice to get your note," Matt said.

"I didn't know you liked poetry," she said.

"That was mostly my mom's doing. She made me memorize every line of *Renascence* by Edna St. Vincent Millay when I was a kid. She's her favorite poet."

"I like her too. She was quite avant-garde."

"I noticed you have a lot of poetry on your shelves."

"I adore it," she said. "When I was a little girl, my parents used to read Pablo Neruda, Gabriela Mistral, Federico García Lorca, and José Martí to me in Spanish, then Robert Frost, W.B. Yeats, and Walt Whitman in English."

"Didn't that make learning a new language more difficult? I mean, the lyrical aesthetic of the words, as opposed to their literal translation?"

"I don't know. I was exposed to Spanish and English at the same time. I suppose I was confused for a while, but then I think it allowed me to appreciate the unique artistry of each language. My mom teaches Spanish and French at Fayetteville High School. She also teaches an advanced course in Spanish poetry, so it's something that's ever-present in our home."

Just then the waiter came over. "What are you drinking?" Matt said to Olga.

"I'm fine with tea."

"Just an espresso, please," Matt said.

"I thought about you on Monday. How did it feel to be back flying?"

"It was fantastic. The weather was perfect, and the fall colors were just brilliant. Plus, T-Ball sets the perfect tone in the cockpit; he's a joy to fly with."

"I'd like to fly with you sometime."

"You wouldn't be scared?"

"Of course not." The waiter came and brought a small cup of espresso to the table. Olga picked up her tea.

"Salud," she said.

"Salud. I've always wanted to learn Spanish. I was trying to study it when I lived in Florida."

"It's easy. I could teach you."

"I'd like that," he said. The band was playing the Horace Silver tune, "Song for My Father," and Matt and Olga were quiet as they listened.

When the music stopped, Olga said, "Maggie told me the pilots are trying to form a union."

"We're trying to keep it a secret."

"Well, your secret's safe with me."

They listened to another set, then Olga looked at her watch.

"I shouldn't stay out too late. I promised my parents I'd make breakfast for them in the morning." They got up and Matt put some bills in the wooden box on the table. He held Olga's leather jacket while she put her arms through the sleeves, then they walked outside into the chill of the autumn night.

"Did you drive your Vespa?"

"No, I just walked. It's only fifteen minutes."

"Let me drive you home."

"I'll walk you to the door," he said after they parked. As they walked up the driveway, a cluster of dried maple leaves swished and crunched under their feet.

"I love the fall," Olga said as they walked up the wooden steps to the back porch. She reached into her purse and took out the key.

"I had a nice time," Matt said.

"Would you like to come in for a cup of tea?" she said. They walked in and Olga turned on the lights. "Make yourself at home. Put some music on the stereo if you like."

Matt walked into the living room and turned on the lamp. He went over to the collection of albums, took out *Getz/Gilberto* and placed it on the turntable. Soon the room was filled with the soft, tropical sounds of bossa nova; Stan Getz on tenor sax, Antonio Carlos Jobim on piano, João Gilberto on guitar, and his wife, Astrud, singing the lyrics to "The Girl from Ipanema."

Matt sat down on the little sofa against the wall and waited. His heart was beating with anticipation, still amazed that he could be in this cozy little apartment with Olga. The teakettle whistled for a second, then Olga came in with two steaming cups on a little wooden tray.

"It's peppermint green tea," she said as she set the tray down on the end table and handed Matt a cup. Olga sat down on the sofa and took off her shoes. She softly blew the steam from her cup, sat back, and sighed.

"I love Brazilian music," she said. "You can just feel the passion. I'd love to go there someday."

"I would too," Matt said. "Do you speak Portuguese?"

"No, but I understand it a bit. It's similar to Spanish."

"I was serious about learning Spanish. What would be the best way to begin?"

"Books and tapes are a good start. You need to train your ear and your tongue. The correct pronunciation is very important. You have to practice your Rs. Rs are always problematic."

Matt was looking at her as she spoke. The lamplight cast a satin sheen on her lips. He wanted to reach out and pull her toward him, put his arms around her and feel the warmth of her body next to his.

"You have to know the difference between a short R, like *caro*, which means expensive, and *carro*, which means car, where you twirl the double R off your tongue." Matt repeated the two words, stumbling a bit with the double R. It sounded like one of the Rs was still stuck in his mouth.

"Good," Olga said. "Now try this word—*ferrocarril*. It means railroad. You have two sets of double Rs in the same word, so it's a bit of a challenge."

Matt tried it again and Olga let out a little laugh.

"Again," she said. Matt tried it again, trying not to sound like he was gargling in the bathroom.

"Better," Olga said. "Again."

Matt tried to twirl his tongue like his life depended on it.

"Almost perfect," she said, repeating the word as Matt gazed at her moist lips.

"Again," she said, and Matt slowly pronounced the word.

"Perfect," she said. Matt couldn't take his eyes off the sheen on her lips. Then, without hesitation, he leaned in and kissed her. Time stood still. He was afraid he might have stepped over a line too soon and ruined everything. Then, after a few breathless seconds, she said with a soft exhale, "Again."

CHAPTER TWENTY-THREE

After that night, there wasn't a day that went by when Matt wasn't in touch with Olga. He carried a pouch full of coins in his flight bag so he could call her from phones all throughout the Mid-South. He'd leave notes and letters on her back porch, and she would do the same, using the glovebox in the Jeep to drop off cards, letters, and homemade cookies. When they couldn't be together, they would each lie in bed and talk on the phone until late into the night. It was from these conversations that Matt learned that Olga had always wanted a brother or sister, that she sometimes felt lonely, even among friends, and that she, too, loved the water, imagining herself living by the ocean someday. She loved animals, especially horses. She loved cooking, music, poetry, and books. She loved photography and was passionate about painting. It was also through these late-night conversations that Matt knew, without a doubt, that he was falling in love with her. But it was still a guarded secret. Not even Pete knew. There was something special between them that they weren't ready to share with the world. It was a treasure, something that had a raw essence about it, something that could turn into heaven or heartbreak. Matt was intensely aware of this, another fear he tried to suppress.

It was mid-November, and the preliminary union vote passed by a safe margin. It was now official. Management was formally notified that the pilots of Arkansas Airways wished to conduct an election for representation by the Air Line Pilots Association. Matt and Pete were in Flight Control with Wendell and T-Ball when they saw the memo on the bulletin board.

Management had just announced their intention to purchase two Metroliners from Air Wisconsin and hire an additional twelve pilots. The ten percent pay cut was being replaced by a two percent bonus in accordance with the terms of the variable wage plan. The fiscal quarter was shaping up to show a profit.

"I don't get it," Pete said. "I would have thought they'd be threatening to sell two Metros and furlough twelve pilots." Wendell was silent, his mind shifting gears, adjusting to the change in stratagem.

"It might make sense after all," he said. "A modified version of the carrot-and-stick. Ben told me that, with the holidays approaching, the soonest we can expect to have our votes counted will be after the first of the year. That gives management roughly six weeks to bring in twelve new pawns, paint a rosy picture, a wine-and-dine con job by Dresden. It's possible we could lose the vote by a thin margin. It's time to fight fire with fire, educate and enlighten every new pilot on the property. I'll write up a list of reasons why management can't be trusted, try to spell out what life is really like around here. We'll all be like missionaries out to save the souls of the heathen."

When Matt got in the Jeep, he threw his suitcase in the back seat and opened the glove box. He smiled to himself when he saw the powder blue envelope.

Hi Matt,

I hope you had a nice trip. I saw you through the corner of my eye when you passed through from Tulsa. I wanted to run across the ramp and throw my arms around you but that wouldn't have been very professional, would it? I miss you.

Olga

PS. My mother's invited you over for Thanksgiving dinner. I didn't know if you already had plans.

CHAPTER TWENTY-FOUR

It was Thursday, November 26, Thanksgiving Day. Matt woke up with a profound sense of gratitude, again for surviving the crash and for having Olga in his life. He put on a pair of dress slacks, his finest white cotton shirt and herringbone tweed jacket, and then carried a terra-cotta pot of yellow chrysanthemums out to the Jeep. Pete and Bob had both gone home for the holidays and he had the house to himself. He was relieved, two weeks ago, when his mom called and asked if he would mind if she went to California to spend Thanksgiving with his aunt. Neither of them were ready to endure that first Thanksgiving without his father. His absence would cast a latent pall of sadness on the surface celebration of the day.

At noon, he got in the Jeep and drove down the dirt road. The trees stood bare and a slight chill was in the air. He turned toward the stadium, then left up Markham Hill to Garvin Drive, found Olga's parents' house, and parked.

It was a well-kept ranch-style home with a white ash tree in the center of the front yard. Sculpted gardens outlined the front of the house, their flower beds empty, awaiting the spring. Matt walked up the stone path and rang the bell. A minute passed. He wasn't sure if he should ring again or knock. Maybe the bell wasn't working. He waited another minute. Just before reaching up to knock, the door opened, and Olga stood before him. She was wearing a pair of leather boots and a denim skirt with a brown suede vest over a light blue cotton blouse.

"Hi, Matt. Sorry it took so long. We were just basting the turkey. It's almost ready."

"You look fantastic. These are for your mom," he said, handing her the mums.

"They're just beautiful. Come on in." Matt walked in behind her. Crossing the threshold, his senses were filled with a wave of tranquility, a tangible sense of serenity, an energy pulsing to a different law of physics. The air was also thick with garlic, onions, and some spices that Matt didn't recognize. They went into the kitchen where Olga's mother was wiping her hands on her apron. "Matt, this is my mom."

"It's nice to meet you, Mrs. Vargas," Matt said, extending his hand.

"It's a pleasure to meet you too, Matt. You can call me María if you'd like. The flowers are just beautiful. I'll set them on the dining room table."

"Come with me," Olga said. "My father's working in his office." They walked down the hallway; its walls lined with framed photographs. The sound of classical piano at low volume came through hidden speakers.

"Papi, Matt's here," Olga said as they walked into the room. Dr. Vargas was seated behind his mahogany desk, which was cluttered with books and magazines, file folders, writing tablets, a calculator, reading lamp, an old mahogany humidor, and a crystal cigar ashtray. There was an IBM typewriter on a little pull-out shelf to his left. On his right stood a small wooden wine rack, giving the impression that Dr. Vargas was surrounded in his own sort of cockpit, with everything he needed within arm's reach. Matt noticed the pair of crutches leaning against the bookshelves. Dr. Vargas's face lit up, as it always did, when Olga was before him. He started to get up. Matt extended his arm.

"Please don't stand for me, sir," Matt said as they shook hands. Dr. Vargas sat back down, the smile still on his face.

"I like your office," Matt said.

"Thank you. I believe every man needs a little sanctuary, a place to crawl into. If I didn't have that clock on the wall, I would lose all track of time."

"How's the leg, sir?"

"It's coming along fine, thank you. Fortunately, I wasn't planning on running a marathon this year."

"What are you working on, Papi?" Olga said.

"These are just some economic policy papers for Bill Clinton's gubernatorial campaign."

"Didn't he just leave office last January?" Matt asked.

"That's right."

"Why was he defeated in the election?"

"His license-plate tax increase was not well received, and people blamed him, as well as Jimmy Carter, for the riots of the Cuban inmates down at Fort Chaffee. He was only thirty-two when he became the youngest governor in the nation. Perhaps the voters thought he needed to learn a lesson. Maybe he'll get a second chance."

"Matt's been asking me about Cuba," Olga said.

"Oh, really?"

"When I lived in Florida, Cuba was in the news every day."

"Yes, they say Florida is the only state in the nation with its own separate foreign policy," Dr. Vargas laughed.

"But throughout the rest of the country, Cuba seems like an enigma. It's so close geographically but so closed off. It seems like it barely exists," Matt said.

"Ask me whatever you wish about Cuba," Dr. Vargas said. "I'll be happy to tell you, for I assure you, Cuba very much exists." Just then, Maria called them to the table.

Olga and Matt helped Dr. Vargas to his crutches. Then they walked into the dining room and took their seats at the long, dark wooden table, the scene of a host of dinner parties for university dignitaries and state politicians. The table was covered with a white linen cloth, the pot of mums flanked by two crystal candelabras crowned by soft ivory flames. Dr. Vargas took his seat at the end of the table, and Mrs. Vargas sat at the other end, facing her husband. The table was a veritable feast of culinary delight, the air wafting with exotic scents and spices. The golden-brown turkey had marinated overnight in olive oil, garlic, sea salt, and pepper, and the cornbread was baked with anise. A trace of licorice filled the air. There was a bowl full of fluffy long-grain white rice, and in lieu of gravy, a large ceramic bowl full of chopped onions, garlic, and tomatoes sautéed in olive oil with cilantro, salt, and thin slices of jalapeño peppers. There was a platter of sliced papaya drenched in lime juice, a fresh spinach salad adorned with sliced pineapple and avocado, and a china bowl filled with glazed sweet potatoes baked with brown sugar, cinnamon, and white wine.

"Matt, I thought you might like to try a different kind of Thanksgiving meal. It's the one day when Olga lets me eat whatever I want," María laughed.

"It all looks and smells divine," Matt said.

"Eduardo, would you please do the honors?" María said. Dr. Vargas picked up the large carving knife and fork while platters and bowls were passed around.

"I love the whole idea of Thanksgiving," María said. "It's my favorite adopted holiday." After the turkey and the rest of the food had been served, María bowed her head and succinctly said, "May God make us truly thankful."

"Amen," whispered the others. No words were spoken for a minute. Only the sounds of scraping silverware on china could be heard.

"The one thing I've wanted to say, Matt, is how truly grateful I am that everyone survived that horrible ordeal, and how thankful we are for the role you played. I would have thanked you sooner, but I've had a hard time talking about it. Just the act of verbalizing it seems to replay the horror all over again," María said.

"I told Olga it was mostly due to Mark Winger, my captain."

"Will you please give me his telephone number?"

"Of course," Matt said. "It's funny, as horrible as it was, something good actually came from it." Matt looked across the table. His eyes met Olga's and she smiled. "I've been filled with this awareness of how important it is to seize the day, to not waste time and opportunity."

"I'm familiar with that expression, *carpe diem*," María said, "and yes, I understand the wisdom behind it, but it sounds like it implies such a stressful pace, a race to amass achievement, an endless treadmill of attainment. I, too, had a near-death experience recently. The message I was given was that we must learn to simply receive the day, to relish the divine generosity of each day, to receive it as a perfect gift, and I've been completely at peace ever since."

"I like that," Matt said. Olga was looking at her mom and smiling.

"So Matt, what exactly has Olga been telling you about Cuba?" Dr. Vargas said.

"About the oppression, the lack of opportunity, the scarcity, and she told me about her uncle." María looked down, and the smile vanished from her face. Matt felt horrible. Where was his tact, his sensitivity?

"I should be pleased that this new decade has not turned out so well for Fidel," Dr. Vargas said. "Starting in January of 1980, with the death of Celia Sánchez, but I must admit, in spite of everything, and for just a moment, I actually felt sorry for him. No man should lose the love of his life to cancer."

"I don't know how she could have been so close to Fidel and not seen what was truly happening," María said.

"She was Castro's wife?" Matt asked.

"No," María said. "After Mirta, I don't think he remarried. There were always women but with Celia it was different. They were extremely close, like revolutionary soulmates. She was the one person who could disagree with Fidel. That's why I can't understand it. She must have known."

"It was a shock to Fidel when she died," Dr. Vargas said. "One of the few things he couldn't control. He lost his anchor and was sent adrift. Then on April 1, just three months later, he lost control again when six Cubans seeking asylum crashed a bus through the gate of the Peruvian embassy, killing a Cuban guard. Fidel was outraged, but instead of closing the embassy, he withdrew the other Cuban guards that were protecting it. That blunder unleashed a tidal wave of asylum seekers. Within the next three days, over ten thousand Cubans were packed desperately on the embassy grounds. It was the incident that led to the Mariel boatlift, an example of one of Fidel's favorite strategies, exporting dissension.

Over 125,000 Cubans fled to Miami. Then, three months later, on July 26, the sacred anniversary of the Moncada attack, which launched the revolution, tragedy struck again. Haydée Santamaría, one of the most revered heroines, shot herself to death. Haydée had been with Fidel since the beginning, from the early days when he planned and organized the Moncada attack with Haydée's brother, Abel. When the attack failed, the *Fidelistas* that hadn't been shot were rounded up and thrown in prison. Haydée, along with Melba Hernández, another revolutionary heroine, were forced to hear, from their cell, the bloodcurdling screams of agony coming from their comrades who were being tortured to death. One of them was Haydée's fiancé. The utter barbarity of Batista's henchmen was revealed when a sergeant nicknamed *El Tigre* came to Haydée's cell, opened his bloodstained hand, and showed her the eye of her beloved brother."

"Eduardo, please. It's Thanksgiving. Can't we talk of more pleasant things?" María said.

"Forgive me," Dr. Vargas said. "I just thought Matt might be interested in learning why the revolution was fought and why we all had so much hope in the beginning. We thought Fidel was fighting for a free and democratic Cuba, the fulfillment of the dream of José Martí, the martyred apostle of Cuban independence. But our parents did not share our youthful idealism; they had seen too much."

After dinner, Mrs. Vargas said, "Olgita, help me bring out the flan."

"Matt, may I interest you in an after-dinner cigar?" Dr. Vargas said.

"Papi, don't corrupt him," Olga called out from the kitchen in a teasing voice.

"I'm afraid it's too late," Matt said. "I used to work in a store called Dwight's Pipes when I was in college. It was my job to stock the humidor. In the dead of winter, we'd host a pipe-smoking contest. Everyone was given the same amount of pipe tobacco and two stick-matches. Whoever kept their pipe lit the longest was the winner. It wasn't like watching Wimbledon, but it was a reason to get out of the cold."

"As worthy an entertainment as any," Dr. Vargas said as Olga came into the dining room carrying a bright yellow ceramic plate with a coconut flan, covered in a caramel-rum glaze. Mrs. Vargas followed with a pot of dark black coffee. After dessert, Dr. Vargas said, "Matt, come join me on the terrace." The terrace was a cedar deck supported by wooden pillars sunk into the downward-sloping hill behind the house. The center of the deck was framed around a cedar elm which provided a natural canopy of leaves in summer and fall. Through the branches, the university and the town could be seen in the distance. Two steamer chairs with dark green padding were placed on both sides of a teak liquor cabinet with glass tabletop. A crystal cigar ashtray was placed on top. A chill was in the air, and Dr. Vargas wore a black wool cardigan sweater. Matt wore his tweed sport coat.

"Have a seat," Dr. Vargas said as he propped his crutches against the tree, sat down, and stretched his legs out along the length of the chair. Olga opened the French doors and brought out her father's humidor. She opened the box, and her father chose two cigars and handed one to Matt. "Romeo y Julieta–Double Robustos," he said with a look of reverence.

Olga disappeared, then came back with a silver serving tray with two demitasses and a thermos of strong black coffee.

"Call me if you need anything," she said as she went inside and closed the door. Dr. Vargas took out a small guillotine cutter and butane lighter from his pocket. He clipped the ends of the cigars and handed Matt the lighter. Matt used the flame to char the end of the cigar before lighting it.

"I'm always reminded of the story of President Kennedy. Just before he signed the trade embargo against Cuba, he sent his press secretary, Pierre Salinger, out to procure 1,000 Cuban Petit-Upmanns. As soon as Salinger came back and proudly told the president that he had 1,200 cigars in his possession, Kennedy took out his pen and the embargo became law."

"These aren't Cubans, are they?"

"No, they're Dominican," Dr. Vargas said. "However, I do have a substantial cache of Cohiba–Esplendidos in safe storage, but I refuse to smoke them until Leandro is set free."

"Where did you get them from?" Matt asked.

"Like Kennedy, I too have friends," Dr. Vargas said, smiling. "María's father, Alberto, loves cigars. He was a doctor in Havana. When our families got ready to leave, he went to see a cigar-roller friend of his, Héctor Ramírez. Héctor worked at the Partagás Factory in Havana. Alberto had delivered all four of Héctor's children and had been their family physician for years. To show his appreciation, Héctor would often give him boxes of the finest cigars. Alberto knew that Fidel decreed that all professional diplomas, licenses, and certificates were to be confiscated from anyone leaving Cuba and abandoning the revolution. Héctor carefully placed Alberto's medical-school diploma on a sheet of wax paper, then rolled it inside a fine Churchill Maduro. He did the same with María's mother's wedding ring. Then he dipped the ends of the cigars in cane juice just in case Alberto should forget and try to smoke them.

"If you really want to understand what's going on in Cuba today, you have to understand a bit of Cuban history," Dr. Vargas said. "I promise not to talk longer than our cigars last. I've learned to recognize a certain look on my students' faces when I've become a bit long-winded," he laughed.

"The history of Cuba is one of colonialism and imperialism, replete with dictatorship, brutality, and revolution. Four hundred years of Spanish rule began when Christopher Columbus arrived in October of 1492 and called Cuba the most beautiful land he'd ever seen. The agrarian economy was based on sugar, tobacco, and cattle, all requiring an unprecedented amount of slave labor. Life was brutal for those who toiled in the fields, and Spanish officials feared an uprising. By the 1860s, a mounting call for independence ushered in the Ten Years' War, but independence remained an elusive goal.

"Another war for independence began in 1895, when José Martí landed on the southeast coast and joined other rebel leaders. Martí was a writer, poet, diplomat, and journalist. In addition to Spanish rule in Cuba, Martí was vehemently opposed to slavery. In 1880, Martí moved to New York where he mobilized the Cuban exile community.

"In April 1895, just one month after Martí landed back in Cuba, dressed in black and riding a white horse, he was shot dead by the Spanish Army. But the war continued, with the guerrillas gaining ground.

"America was already heavily invested in Cuba's sugar industry, and the U.S. government was under pressure to intervene on behalf of the rebels. In a show of support, President McKinley sent the USS *Maine* to Havana. On a February evening in 1898, an explosion ripped apart the forward third of the ship. Two hundred men lost their lives. A naval board of inquiry hastily concluded that a mine had detonated under the ship. The American public reacted with outrage. The common cry was, *Remember the Maine, to Hell with Spain.*"

"I remember that from high school," Matt said. "The attack that led to the Spanish–American War."

"Not directly," Dr. Vargas said, "but it did result in the end of diplomacy. In April 1898, the U.S. Congress declared war with Spain. After a key battle in July, when Theodore Roosevelt led a charge up the San Juan Hill in Santiago de Cuba, the war was almost over. In December 1898, at the end of the Spanish–American War, Spain renounced its hold over Cuba, and the U.S. gained Puerto Rico, Guam, and the Philippines. But what truly incensed the Cuban people was when U.S. army generals raised the American flag, not the Cuban flag, over the governor's palace in Santiago, and maintained a presence in Cuba for the next three years. Cubans had fought for their own independence only to have it snatched from their hands."

"Who could blame them?" Matt said.

"Then in 1924, a successful businessman, Gerardo Machado, took over. His reign was marked by terror and torture. He took over the military and the political parties and pilfered ten million dollars a year from the national treasury. Students at the university rebelled. Their goal was to overthrow Machado and reclaim the independence that was denied them by the United States. Under mounting pressure from the U.S., Machado was forced to leave the country.

"In 1940, self-appointed chief of the armed forces, Fulgencio Batista, was elected president and served until 1944. In 1952 he led a military coup that brought him back to power with the infamous proclamation: *The people and I are the dictators.* He soon tore up the Constitution, denying the people basic political liberties and the right to strike.

"In 1945, a young Fidel Castro began law school at the University of Havana. At that time, a Cuban politician named Eduardo Chibás was gaining popularity by invoking the spirit of José Martí and calling for an end to American imperialism. In August 1951, after giving a radio address, in a bizarre gesture meant to shock the Cuban people into taking action, he took a pistol and fatally shot himself in the stomach. Fidel would later equate his own 26th of July Movement with Eddy Chibás's. More coffee, Matt?"

"Just a bit, thanks."

"Soon, Batista was basking in support from the U.S. as the Cuban economy prospered. Luxury hotels went up in Havana, and glamorous nightclubs and casinos run by mob bosses like Meyer Lansky, Santo Trafficante, and Lucky Luciano raked in millions, with Batista always getting his share of the take. Crime and corruption were growing at an alarming rate, and outside Havana, serious problems with education, health care, and housing remained.

"This was the climate that existed when Fidel organized the attack on the Moncada Garrison. Many of Fidel's supporters were killed, and Fidel was forced to flee before being arrested by Batista's army. After Fidel and his brother Raúl were released from prison, as part of a general amnesty, they fled to Mexico City, where they met Ernesto Che Guevara. Guevara became one of the eighty-two rebels who received training in the art of guerrilla warfare, in preparation for the rebels' return to Cuba.

"In November 1956, they boarded the sixty-foot cabin cruiser, *Granma*, which Fidel had purchased from some Americans for $15,000. The overloaded yacht was designed to hold just twelve people, and it nearly sank on the harrowing voyage. Just as José Martí had done some sixty years earlier, they landed in Oriente Province on the southeast coast. But the boat had been spotted from the air, and the element of surprise was lost. Many of the men were gunned down in the swamps. Fidel, Raúl, Che, and Camilo Cienfuegos, the main leaders of the movement, were among the twelve survivors. They made their way up into the Sierra Maestra and joined forces with Celia Sánchez, who had already done much to organize the fledgling rebel army.

"Captivated by the romance of revolution, Herbert Matthews, a reporter for the *New York Times*, would visit Fidel and the rebels in the Sierra and bring the story of the courageous freedom fighters back to the supporting American public.

"By December of 1958, the U.S. was withdrawing its support for Batista with an arms embargo. When the city of Santa Clara fell, the end of Batista's reign was in sight. Before dawn, on New Year's Day 1959, Batista and his entourage fled for the Dominican Republic with some three hundred million dollars safely deposited in foreign accounts.

"On January 8, Fidel, along with Camilo Cienfuegos, Huber Matos, and other rebel leaders, were given a hero's welcome as they rode triumphantly into Havana on a tank. And when Fidel addressed the adoring masses for the first time, from the Plaza de la Revolución, white doves, which had been released to symbolize peace, flew over the crowd. One landed on Fidel's shoulder, which mesmerized the crowd. From that moment on, the people belonged to Fidel.

"Then the circus-trials and summary-executions began. Freedom of the press and speech were obliterated, and political liberties disappeared. Almost as soon as the dream was achieved, it turned into a nightmare. But Fidel held the masses under his spell.

"When Fidel said there would be no need for elections, María's brother, Leandro, became furious. All those who fought with Fidel and believed that the revolution was about democratic restoration had been duped. Small bands of counterrevolutionaries, many of whom had fought valiantly with Fidel, fled up into the Escambray Mountains and tried to launch a counterattack.

"When Fidel imprisoned Huber Matos, a loyal comandante with moderate views, it became obvious that Fidel had no intention of creating a democratic state. The revolution was moving inexorably toward Marxism.

"Fidel branded Matos a traitor. Raúl and Che Guevara wanted him executed, but Fidel feared turning him into a martyr. The trial resembled a circus court-martial. Huber Matos was sent to prison for twenty years. The last voice of moderation, silenced. He endured hunger-strikes and abject cruelty, spending sixteen years in solitary confinement. He was tortured on several occasions, his genitals punctured, his stomach crushed by the boot of a guard. He never expected to get out alive. But he was finally set free two years ago and was reunited with his wife and four children in Miami.

"This was the last straw for Leandro. He was becoming suspicious of a pattern. Anyone with charisma and daring, anyone who represented competition to Fidel, was executed, imprisoned, or allowed to stay dangerously in harm's way. Leandro wrote articles, he protested, he hurled harangues at Fidel in the Plaza de la Revolución. That's when he was first arrested. He was imprisoned at La Cabaña, the colonial fortress in east Havana. Every day, he was beaten by the guards. Every day, he witnessed the executions down in the moat, not knowing if he would be next. I hope I'm not boring you, Matt? Would you care for more coffee? Some rum, perhaps?"

"No, thank you. Please go on." Just then, Olga opened the door. She batted the air with her hands and coughed in mock disapproval.

"I just came to see if you needed anything. Matt, are you cold? I could bring you a blanket."

"I'm fine," he said. "Your father is giving me a history lesson."

"Well, don't stay out too long. We're starting to feel neglected in here."

Olga went inside and closed the door.

"So, tell me, Matt," Dr. Vargas said, "are you just here temporarily? I imagine most of the pilots aspire to go on to the major airlines, is that right?"

"That's right. It's a stepping-stone."

"I see," Dr. Vargas said. Then it dawned on Matt, the reason Olga didn't date pilots: pilots were transients. One might leave and break her heart, or she would leave and break her father's heart.

"But many pilots at the major airlines commute to work. If I flew for American and was based in Dallas, I could easily live here and just catch a flight to work the way most people take the bus. It's very common."

"I see," Dr. Vargas said. "Now, where was I?"

"You were talking about Leandro."

"Ah yes, Leandro. I've never known anyone like him. He is in my earliest memories. God has never put a gentler man on the face of the earth. He would move out of the way to avoid stepping on an ant. He has a profound sense of justice and morality, a childlike innocence, until he witnesses an act of cruelty. Then he becomes like a lion, fierce to the point of recklessness. It is his greatest gift and his greatest curse. It is the root of all his troubles, and many of my own.

"I remember once when we were young, we were playing in our neighborhood when we saw two boys, both older than us, shooting at a defenseless little totí bird with a slingshot. Leandro ran up and told the boys to stop. They just laughed at him. He went on about the protection of God's creatures, but still they wouldn't stop. Then Leandro tried to snatch the slingshot away from them. They punched and kicked him and threw him into a thorny acacia thicket. I had no choice but to come to his aid. We both went home badly bruised, but we never saw those boys again. There isn't a day that goes by when I don't think about him. He loved to quote the words of Dante: *The hottest places in hell are reserved for those who, in times of great moral crisis, maintain their neutrality*. I met María because of him, and from María came Olga. His only crime, just like Huber Matos, was speaking the truth. He never hurt anyone, yet he's wasting away in prison, deprived of the simplest pleasures. I must admit, it's hard for me to enjoy things like that delicious meal we just ate, knowing the agony and suffering he's forced to endure. Leandro, of course, is not the only one; there are hundreds of decent, honest people, locked away in dungeons and tortured, just for disagreeing with Fidel. I'm reminded of the words of William Fulbright: *The citizen who criticizes his country is paying it an implied tribute.* Did you know he used to be the president of the University of Arkansas?

"Just this past year, I attended a conference on human rights in Toronto, sponsored by Amnesty International and a host of Canadian intellectuals. One of the committees had compiled a list of political prisoners in Cuba. There was a debate taking place about whether to sign a general petition on behalf of all of them, which probably had very little chance of success, or to concentrate our efforts on singling out just one prisoner. The prisoner chosen was Armando Valladares, because of how young he was when he was imprisoned, and how long he'd been held captive. Naturally, I proposed a compromise to include Leandro's name on that short list, for similar reasons. Unfortunately, the position advocating for the freedom of all the named prisoners won out and nothing came of it."

"It sounds like you're still coming to Leandro's defense, just like when you were young."

"It's the very least I can do," Dr. Vargas said. "Let's see how the ladies are doing, shall we? Did you enjoy the cigar?"

"Very much so," Matt said.

Dr. Vargas took a deep breath of night air before reaching for his crutches. "I love to come out here on a hot summer night," he said. "With the aroma of the cigar and the whisper of sugar-cane in the rum, if the wind is out of the south, I close my eyes and I can smell the tobacco fields of Pinar del Río."

Matt couldn't sleep. He lay in bed and thought back to Jorge Roca, the hostages in Iran, Ray Baker assaulting Carol, the murder of John Lennon, the assassination attempt against President Reagan. Even Pope John Paul II had been shot by a Turkish gunman just last May. Matt thought of Leandro, and of Huber Matos. Valiant, decent people, trying to do good in the world but victimized, oppressed, held hostage, imprisoned, tortured, killed. What gave a human being the right to plunder the life of another?

Then he thought of Olga's father. Matt had witnessed first-hand the courage he displayed under intense physical pain, and he was beginning to understand the deep, underlying pain which permeated Dr. Vargas's life. He felt respect and empathy for this erudite gentleman who held himself with such dignity and grace, who felt so much love for his family, and concern for his students and for the state of humanity. Matt felt an undercurrent of connection with him. Of course, they shared the trauma of the crash landing, of a near-death experience, but it was more than that. They both, in their own way, feared losing the same woman.

CHAPTER TWENTY-FIVE

The weeks before Christmas were spent decorating and shopping. Matt hated the fact that on their first Christmas together, Olga and Matt would be apart. He promised his mom he'd fly home on Wednesday, December 23. He'd catch an afternoon flight back to Fayetteville on Saturday, and Olga and he would celebrate together then. For the first time in his life, he wasn't looking forward to the holidays.

The house had turned into a veritable museum of the past. His father's tools were still in the garage, his dirty work shoes still by the back door. Matt stood before the open closet door and stared at his father's clothes. He ran his hand over his father's favorite silk sport coat. He picked up his father's electric razor and some of his father's whiskers fell into the sink. He opened the cologne bottles, each eliciting its own torrent of memories. Everywhere he went, he could see and feel his father, his profound presence made manifest by his agonizing absence.

The next day, Matt took his mom to the Drake Hotel for high tea. The dining room was adorned in fine holiday splendor. What was the fascination with tea? he wondered. It always seemed too watery to hold such appeal. But he was relieved to be around a crowd of people. Even his mom seemed to cheer up.

The next morning, Matt woke to the smell of coffee and cinnamon. He showered, dressed, and came into the kitchen as his mom was frying Canadian bacon and scrambling eggs. After breakfast, they went into the living room. All the old familiar ornaments hung on a small tree. Matt gave his mom a pair of pearl earrings and a set of gardening tools. She gave him a navy-blue swimsuit and a pocket-size 35mm camera. Matt tried to relax for the rest of the day. He was anxious and impatient. He couldn't wait to be with Olga again.

The day after Christmas, he caught a flight to Tulsa, then made a quick connection to Fayetteville. Pete and Bob wouldn't be home until the next evening. He walked into the empty house, turned up the heat, put hickory and pine logs in the fireplace, and a bottle of champagne in the fridge. He changed out of his travel clothes, put on a hooded sweatshirt, and laced up his old Adidas. He'd been on edge for the past three days, unable to take it out in the pool.

It was cold and cloudy, and the hint of snow was in the air as he jogged down the dirt road to Highway 71 and back. He showered, put on a pair of soft jeans and a green wool sweater, then went into the kitchen and chopped onions, garlic, and green peppers. He melted butter in a pan and added sliced mushrooms, salt, and vermouth. Then he fried Italian sausage and put everything into a pot of thick marinara sauce. He spread a red cloth over the kitchen table and placed a gold candle in the center. He tossed a garden salad in a wooden bowl, then emptied the box of spaghetti into a pot of boiling water. It was 5:30 p.m. Olga would be there soon. At five to six, he heard the crunching of gravel in the drive. Olga was driving her mother's blue Monte Carlo. Matt watched her through the window as she opened the trunk and took out a decorative Christmas bag. As she walked in, a thin trace of perfume followed on the air.

"For you," she said, handing Matt the bag.

"Merry Christmas," they said as Olga unbuttoned her coat and they kissed. Olga was wearing a black suede skirt with white tights, a bright red cashmere sweater, and a delicate white pearl necklace.

"You look beautiful," he said.

"I missed you. How's your mom? Did you have a good trip?"

"She's fine, but I could feel my dad's absence every second. It just wasn't the same." Olga wrapped her arms around him and gave him a hug.

"Something smells divine," she said. "My parents said to say hi, by the way."

"Did you have a nice Christmas?"

"Yes, just a quiet family-celebration. Ever since 1969 when Fidel outlawed Christmas, my parents have never felt comfortable with a lavish celebration."

"Castro outlawed Christmas?"

"Yes, but of course, New Year's Eve and New Year's Day are still celebrated. New Year's Eve for the end of the Batista dictatorship, New Year's Day for the first day Fidel took over."

"It sounds like Castro just didn't want to compete with Jesus Christ," Matt said as he walked over to the stereo and set Nat King Cole's Christmas album on the turntable. Through the windows, a flurry of soft white snowflakes danced in the black of night. Matt lit the candle and they sat down to eat.

"These mushrooms are delicious," she said.

"They're sautéed in butter and vermouth."

"I see. Trying to get me tipsy, mister?"

"Maybe." After dinner, Matt lit the fire and the row of candles on the mantle. He put on a Johnny Mathis Christmas album, and Olga handed him a present. Matt unwrapped the red foil paper, revealing a set of Spanish language tapes.

"These are fantastic."

"I hear they're pretty good," she said. "They're the tapes used by the U.S. Foreign Service. Of course, you're still going to need your private tutor," she laughed.

"This is for you," Matt said, handing Olga a square box wrapped in green paper with gold ribbon. She carefully peeled back the paper and opened the box. A smile flashed across her face. It was the first framed photograph of the two of them, arms around each other, standing on the back of the caboose at Eureka Springs.

"I love it," she said. Matt placed a pine log on the fire and adjusted the geometry with an iron poker, making the hearth fill with flames and crackling embers. Olga moved back a few feet and sat down on the rug. Matt went into the kitchen and brought out the bottle of champagne in a bucket of ice with two crystal flutes. He extracted the cork with a loud pop, poured the rush of bubbles into the flutes, and sat down beside her.

"To you," he said, raising his glass.

"To you," she said. They sipped the ice-cold champagne and stared into the fire. He took two pillows from the sofa and placed them on the rug. They lay close to one another, and Matt could smell a trace of the wine on Olga's soft breath. They took another sip of champagne and Matt kissed the moisture from Olga's lips.

"I can taste the champagne."

"Take another sip," Olga said. Matt took another sip of the crisp champagne and Olga pressed her lips to his and tasted with her tongue.

"You're intoxicating me," she said. They both laughed, lying side by side, watching the flames dance and swirl, sparks shooting up the chimney with an occasional pop from the exploding ember. Olga had a far-off look in her eyes as she stared into the fire.

"Matt, how long do you think you'll be here?" she asked. Her question knocked him out of his ethereal state, and a touch of sadness now hung in the air. The implication that something so precious could be perishable, replete with an expiration date like a milk carton, filled him with angst. The thought that she might be resigned to the ephemeral nature of their relationship, even expecting it to end, unnerved him.

"Olga, I never planned on meeting you. I never knew anyone like you existed. Before I met you, the only things I was sure of were my doubts. Now that I've found you, I know I could never leave you." She kept staring into the fire, her expression unchanged. Maybe this was not the response she wanted to hear. Maybe she just didn't believe him. Maybe it was too soon for his words to carry any weight. He didn't press it further, but the magic of the moment seemed somewhat diminished. They softly kissed each other by the fire and Matt moved his hand along the hourglass curve of her body.

"Have you ever wanted to just freeze the passage of time, to stop the tape and just stay right in that one single moment, forever?" Olga said.

"I know exactly what you mean."

"But of course, that's impossible."

"Not really," Matt said. "If you're truly living in the moment, using all your senses, then you imprint it into your memory, and it never leaves."

Matt got up and put another log on the fire. He put Miles Davis's *Kind of Blue* on the stereo and reached down and helped Olga to her feet. They wrapped their arms around each other and slowly moved to the soulful jazz. Matt saw the flames reflecting off Olga's lips. They took a few more sips of champagne, then lay down on the rug and fell asleep with their arms entwined.

"What time is it?" Olga said when she woke up. Matt squinted at his watch.

"It's just midnight."

"I should be going; I have to get up early." Matt helped her on with her coat and walked her out to the car. White snowflakes were coming down against the black of night, and the air was cold and smelled of woodsmoke. They wrapped their arms around each other and kissed one last time before Olga got in the car and waved a gloved hand as she backed out of the drive. Matt stood in the cold night air and watched until the red taillights disappeared around the bend.

CHAPTER TWENTY-SIX

It was Wednesday, January 13, 1982, a date that would live up to its numerical infamy. Earlier in the week, a ferocious, arctic air mass blanketed the east coast. Record freezing temperatures were recorded in Atlanta, and the citrus crop in Florida was at risk.

Matt met Buzz in Flight Control at 0500 for the long one-day trip that went from Fayetteville to Little Rock–Memphis–Birmingham–Mobile–Pensacola and back along the same route. It was bitter cold in the cockpit when Matt arrived to perform his pre-flight duties. The low overcast clouds were dark and gray, and snow was in the forecast.

They departed on schedule and broke out above the cloud tops at seven thousand feet. The intense morning sun lasered into them and they both donned their Ray-Bans. It wasn't until they were halfway to Little Rock that the chill in their bones subsided. Matt made sure the cockpit curtain was completely closed when he saw Buzz wrestling off his uniform pants and shedding his long johns.

The legs to Memphis and Birmingham were routine. Light rain was falling in Mobile as they flew an instrument approach and broke out at five hundred feet. Due to an upper-level inversion, as the water droplets met the twenty-five-degree surface temperature, they froze. When the last of the passengers had deplaned, Matt saw that the Metro had begun to resemble a glazed pastry. Soon the airplane was encased in clear ice. Matt and Buzz scoured the airport in search of adequate de-icing equipment. If they were up in St. Louis, they'd be sprayed with warm glycol from a de-icing truck, but in Mobile, Alabama, icing conditions like this were almost unheard of, and Matt and Buzz searched in vain. The only solution was to have the airplane towed into a heated hangar and wait for the freezing rain to subside.

Six hours passed before they could depart. Flight Control canceled their remaining stops, and they fueled for an empty, three-hour ferry-flight home. It snowed all day in Fayetteville, and when they broke out on the localizer approach, their eyes were met by a winter wonderland blanketing the hilly terrain.

Matt brushed the snow off the Jeep and drove home in four-wheel drive. It was 10:00 p.m. when he dragged himself into the warm kitchen and saw the light on in the den, where Pete was stretched out on the sofa watching the news.

"Hey, you made it. Helluva long day, huh?"

"I'll say. We got stuck in a wicked ice storm in Mobile with no de-icing equipment."

"Hear about the crash in D.C.?"

"We heard something about it on the radio, a Guppy on takeoff out of National?"

"It's been all over the news," Pete said. Matt sat down and watched the continuing coverage.

"Palm 90, an Air Florida 737 bound for Tampa with seventy-four passengers and five crewmembers, crashed immediately after takeoff in a severe snowstorm. The aircraft struck the 14th Street Bridge, crushing seven vehicles and killing four occupants before plunging through the ice-covered Potomac River and sinking. A total of seventy-eight people died."

"Apparently, they were carrying a load of ice on their wings," Pete said. "They're speculating that the engines weren't making takeoff thrust. They barely got airborne."

"Good God."

"I know. I can't imagine what must have been going through those poor guys' minds. Stall warning rattling like a machine gun, airspeed dropping, seeing that bridge in front of them, knowing they were going to die and nothing they could do to stop it."

"I can imagine it," Matt said. Just then the news broadcast showed the many heroic rescue attempts that took place at the scene. At 4:20 p.m., nineteen minutes after impact, a U.S. Park Police helicopter arrived on the scene and attempted to lower a line to the few survivors who were clinging to the tail section. The helicopter crew risked their lives working so close to the ice that, at one point, the helicopter's skids went into the water. When the helicopter crew threw a line down to a stricken passenger, Arland Williams, instead of wrapping it around himself, he passed it to flight attendant Kelly Duncan. On their third trip back over the tail section, pilot Donald Usher and paramedic Gene Windsor lowered two lines to the survivors, knowing they would only have a few more minutes before succumbing to hypothermia. Arland Williams caught one of the lines but again passed it on to a critically injured passenger. The passenger attached the line around his waist and grabbed hold of Priscilla Tirado, who was severely distraught from the loss of her husband and baby. Patricia Felch took the second line. Before reaching the shore, both Priscilla Tirado and Patricia Felch lost their grip and fell back into the icy water. When the line was dropped to her again, Priscilla Tirado was too weak to grab it.

"Check this guy out," Pete said. "They've been replaying this scene all night." A bystander on shore, Lenny Skutnik, stripped off his coat and boots, and in short sleeves, dove into the icy water and swam out to save her. Matt's attention was riveted to the screen.

"He didn't hesitate for a second," Matt said. "I wonder if he even felt the cold."

"He must have felt it, alright, but it didn't matter," Pete said. "Man, that is one lucky lady."

"She lost her husband and baby. I doubt she feels lucky at all. I think Lenny's the lucky one," Matt said.

"Why is that?"

"Because—for the rest of his life, he'll never have to wonder what kind of man he is."

CHAPTER TWENTY-SEVEN

The carpenters had just finished installing the new union bulletin board in Flight Control when Matt came in from the two-day Meridian trip. The first memo was thumbtacked against the blank cork background.

TO ALL LINE-PILOTS

Today the National Mediation Board certified that the Air Line Pilots Association has been duly designated and authorized to represent the pilots of Arkansas Airways. As the newest members of ALPA, you are cordially invited to celebrate solidarity Saturday night down at Hugo's.

Fraternally,

Wendell Steele, (temporary Council Chairman)

"You need to get yourself a pickup," Pete said, as they drove down the dirt road. Freezing rain was hitting the windshield and cold licks of air leaked in from around the Jeep's ragtop. They parked on the square, facing the Old Post Office. The wind was howling out of the north as they walked down the steps to the subterranean entrance to Hugo's. They could hear the crowded conversations before they opened the door. Laughter and gaiety greeted them as Pete and Matt made their way toward the crowd. Ginger was working the taps like a switchboard operator. Waitresses were moving steady streams of chicken wings and pitchers of beer out among the crowd. Wendell, Mark, and Buzz were seated at the bar as Pete and Matt walked up and joined them.

"You don't have a beer. That's against union rules," Buzz said as he reached for the pitcher and poured.

"Congratulations, guys," Mark said. "Y'all are in the big leagues now."

"You too," Matt said.

"Yeah, well, I thought I mentioned I'm about to punch out. It's official. Maggie and I are moving to Ocala next month."

"I didn't think you were serious."

"Doesn't matter, you're in good hands. Just remember, it's all about finding fun," Mark said, raising his glass toward Wendell and taking a deep gulp of beer. His eyes were a bit glassy.

Wendell was looking out across the room. He'd hardly touched his beer.

"I think we owe a deep gratitude to this one sober son of a bitch," Mark said, putting his big arm around Wendell's neck.

"Our first agenda should include forming a professional standards committee, a grievance committee, and campaigning for elections," Wendell said.

"Will somebody tell this man to lighten up?" Mark said, pouring Wendell another beer and setting it next to his first full glass.

"I can't believe we really pulled it off," Pete said.

"But it wasn't the mandate I was expecting," Wendell said. "Ben called me with the results: forty out of seventy-one, just a four-vote victory. I don't understand it. I canvassed up and down the seniority list. My most conservative estimate was eighty-seven percent. I don't know what happened. Maybe we didn't get through to the new hires. There may be guys celebrating here tonight who actually voted against us. People looked me straight in the eye with total assurance and we end up with just fifty-six percent."

"But we still won," Matt said.

"I choose to celebrate as is," Mark said, grabbing the pitcher.

"I like our new bulletin board," Buzz said. "Let's inaugurate it with a big red banner saying, WORKERS OF THE WORLD UNITE, add a little hammer and sickle to our logo, just for yucks."

"Yeah, well, getting Dresden's goat is one thing. I'm not sure we're ready to take on the National Guard," Wendell said. "George is probably down at the governor's mansion in Little Rock, as we speak."

Matt flew his regular line-trips into February. He woke up in Knoxville at 0500 on Friday and turned on the TV news as he was suiting up for the one-day trip home. Freddie Laker, the British airline entrepreneur who dabbled his deregulatory wick in the transatlantic market, betting on cheap fares and low-cost labor, was declaring bankruptcy. Matt had an uneasy feeling as he tied his tie in front of the mirror.

It was late afternoon as Matt drove home from the airport. Snow flurries covered the dirt road in a thin white sheet. Pete's pickup was in the drive and the air smelled like a campfire. Matt saw smoke coming from the chimney as he carried his suitcase and flight bag in through the kitchen door. He dropped his flight bag in the coat closet and saw Pete pacing back and forth in the living room.

"Nice one," Matt said, nodding at the fire. Pete barely acknowledged the comment. "Something wrong?"

Pete took a deep breath, then dropped into the reading chair. "I don't know," he said. "I was over at Rita's last night. We were just kicking back, watching the news on TV. They were broadcasting a story about how the cost of raising an average child from birth to four years of college is almost four hundred thousand dollars or something. I was hardly paying attention. Next thing I know, tears are streaming down Rita's cheeks, and she turns to me and says, 'But there's no such thing as an average child.' I swear, she's been acting downright loopy lately. Then she tells me she's pregnant and I just freeze. Man, it just shocked me. I might have even panicked. I didn't know what to say except, 'Are you sure?' I don't think it was the response she was looking for. She just broke down and cried. No matter what I tried to say, she was inconsolable. I even offered to marry her but that only made her cry more. Where are you going?"

"To grab a couple of beers."

"I mean, Rita's great. She's the best woman I've ever known. We're like peas and carrots together."

"So, what's the problem then?"

"The problem is I don't want to be forced into anything. I wanted to take my time."

"That's understandable. Who says you have to get married?"

"Oh, come on man, we're not movie stars." They drank their beers, and Pete threw another log on the fire.

"Well, for what it's worth, I think you'll make a great dad."

"Thanks. It's just like they say, life's what happens to you when you're making other plans."

On Monday, March 8, Matt suited up for the easy one-day trip to Fort Smith–Little Rock–Memphis and back to Fayetteville.

It was 9:00 p.m. when he drove home and parked next to Pete's pickup. Pete had been on the sick-list for his last trip due to a cold. The air was humid and scented with eucalyptus as Matt walked into the den and found Pete seated on the sofa with a towel over his head, bowing before a vaporizer.

"How're you feeling?"

"Miserable," Pete nasaled from under the steaming canopy.

"Can I get you anything?"

"No, thanks," Pete said, coming up for air. "I've got a tea with lemon and a shot of whiskey. How was your trip?"

"Good. I flew with Jackson. He said to say hi."

"You're not going to believe what I found today. Rita came by and brought me some chicken soup. I had nothing to do after she left, so I decided to put revisions in my flight manual. I went to the coat closet to get my flight bag. When I opened it, I realized I'd grabbed Grayson's bag by mistake. Then something caught my eye. It was an open letter between Grayson and Barry Dresden. Here, read it for yourself."

Dear Barry,

I found this article in the *Wall Street Journal* the other day and thought I'd pass it on. It appears that a union dispute arose recently between the Railroad Yardmasters of America and the Yardmasters Steering Committee. At issue was the question of which organization should represent the Yardmasters of the Union Pacific Railroad. The National Mediation Board intervened, conducted an election and, despite protests from the RYA, certified the YSC as the organization designated and authorized to represent the workers.

Somehow the RYA found out that the National Mediation Board had only one acting member when the vote was counted, and that a minimum of two of the three members is required to constitute a legal quorum. The RYA sued to have the Board's order invalidated. The District Court sided with the RYA and held that the order had been issued in violation of the Board's quorum requirement, so the election was nullified.

Barry, the time frame of the election and vote count was the same as our union vote. Maybe our attorneys could act to nullify our election based on the same precedent. I just thought you should be aware of this. I hope all is well.

Respectfully,

Bob Grayson

Barry Dresden's response was on the back of Grayson's letter.

Dear Bob,

Thank you for your letter. I read the article with great interest and passed it on to George, who immediately contacted our attorneys in Little Rock. Let's all hope for the best. I want to thank you again for all your hard work, educating our new hires. If more pilots displayed your dedication and loyalty, there would be no limit as to what this airline could achieve.

Best regards,

Barry

Matt put the letter down and let out a low whistle.

"I knew he was a scab all along," Pete said. "Who does he think he is, reading the *Wall Street Journal?* I called Wendell right away. He said he'd get in touch with Ben Weinberg immediately."

"Do you really think anything will come of it?" Matt said.

"I don't know. I'm sure, as far as they're concerned, it won't be over until they've won. The one thing I do know is, I'm not living with a scab."

CHAPTER TWENTY-EIGHT

Early Friday morning, March 12, Matt walked into Flight Control for the Kansas City turn with T-Ball. There was a note from Barry Dresden in his mailbox.

> Due to attrition, and the acquisition of two additional Metroliners from Air Wisconsin, the following first officers are awarded captain bids:
>
> Don Bishop, Pete Sutherland, Andy McShane, Matt Lavery, and Bob Grayson.
>
> Please report to conference room 101 on Monday, March 22, at 0800. The normal course syllabus calls for five days of ground school and five days of flight training, followed by initial operating experience with a line check airman. Your schedules for the remaining month will be adjusted accordingly. Good luck and congratulations in advance.
>
> Barry Dresden

That night, Matt met Pete down at the Whitewater Tavern. "Evening, Captain," he said as he walked up to the bar.

"Same to you," Pete said, saluting with his beer bottle.

"Just imagine, our salary's going to double. We'll be making twenty-thousand dollars a year; we'll be rolling in dough."

"I'll be rolling in diapers is more like it."

"Yeah, but at least you'll be a wealthy man. How's Rita doing?"

"She's fine. A little morning sickness, that's all."

That night, Matt lay in bed and called Olga. "That's fantastic," she said when Matt told her about captain school and that Pete and Rita were expecting a baby. Pete never told Matt to keep it a secret, and Matt wanted to share everything with her, knowing she'd be discreet with the news. "Will I have to salute when I see you?" she giggled.

"I'm not sure how much longer we'll be in the house," Matt said. "Neither of us wants to live with Bob, and I'm sure Pete and Rita will be getting their own place soon."

On Thursday, Matt flew his last trip as a first officer. It was the two-day Kansas City–Dallas trip with Buzz. When they walked into Flight Control there was a new memo on the union board.

To All Line-Pilots

Be informed that Arkansas Airways has just filed a lawsuit against the National Mediation Board. The company claims that the order of the NMB certifying ALPA as bargaining agent is invalid, and they deny that ALPA is the legally recognized bargaining agent for its pilots. At issue is the fact that the NMB had only one acting member when the vote was counted, an apparent violation of its quorum requirement.

In response, ALPA has counterclaimed for an injunction to require the company to bargain with ALPA and for damages resulting from Arkansas Airways' refusal to bargain. ALPA claims that the NMB's order was valid, and that Arkansas Airways has a legal obligation to bargain with it, entirely apart from the Board's action because it had the support of a majority of pilots.

The NMB is also appealing. Please rest assured that every legal strategy will be employed to protect your right to representation. Don't be distracted by outside events. Continue being the consummate professionals that you are. Fly safe.

Fraternally,

Wendell Steele

"Those bastards," Buzz said. "We voted, fair and square. We won and they lost. How can they overturn a legal election? Why can't the NMB just assemble a legal quorum and recount the ballots? And how in the world did their attorneys find out how many NMB members actually counted the votes?" Then Matt told Buzz about Grayson's letter to Dresden. "That scumbag," Buzz said. "Just wait till the word gets out, that ass kisser's going to pay."

On Monday morning, March 22, Pete and Matt carried their flight manuals into conference room 101 in the main terminal. Andy McShane and Don Bishop were already there. Andy's wife, Sandy, had given birth to a baby girl back on Thanksgiving Day.

"So, how's fatherhood going?" Pete asked. "Are you getting any sleep?"

"It's wonderful," Andy said. "I highly recommend it." Just then, Bob Grayson walked in and took a seat next to Pete. Pete looked at Matt, picked up his flight manual, and moved to the opposite side of the room. Then Tom Tomlinson walked in, and the five days of ground school began.

At the end of the third day, Matt and Pete had been home for an hour when Barry Dresden's Buick pulled into the driveway. Matt looked out the window and saw Grayson get out and storm toward the kitchen door.

"I want to know which one of you bastards slashed my tires!" Grayson shouted as he walked into the den. Pete got up from the sofa.

"I don't know a thing about it. If I did, I'd go right out and buy him a beer."

"Very funny," Grayson said. "Well, two can play at that game. If I were you, I'd lock up that precious stereo of yours."

"What's that supposed to mean? I told you, I don't know who cut your tires. You so much as lay a hand on Mary's knobs, I'm calling the police and filing charges, you pathetic little scab." Matt was watching the exchange from the open doorway.

"Do that, and I promise you won't have a job here for long," Grayson said.

"Trying to threaten me with your boyfriend, Dresden, are you?" Just then, Grayson lunged at Pete and knocked him against the wall. Pete lunged back at Bob and punched him hard in the nose. Blood burst over Grayson's face and he let out a cry, covered his nose with his hands, and ran upstairs.

"Well, that was fun," Matt said, handing Pete a cold beer. "I never took you for the gladiator type."

"I'm not," Pete said as he dropped onto the sofa. "That son of a bitch had it coming, though. I guess I just lost control."

"Probably no point in shaking hands and making up."

"Nope. I'll give him one week to move out. If he's not gone by next Wednesday, I'm out of here."

Bob wasn't in ground school the next day, to Matt's relief, and when he and Pete got home, they found that Grayson had moved out. Pete ran over and turned on the stereo and breathed a sigh of relief.

"Well, good riddance," he said.

Flight training was routine; the same maneuvers with the opposite hands, just something to get used to. Matt and Pete took their uniform jackets to Lori's to have the fourth stripe sewn on, then picked up their new captain hats from Janice in the flight office.

After they'd passed their check-rides, all that was left was an initial operating trip flown with a line check airman. Matt was paired up with Wendell to fly the two-day Knoxville layover with five intermediate stops. Along the way, Matt told Wendell about the fight between Pete and Bob and that he was afraid Barry would come gunning for Pete in retaliation.

"I'll call Pete tomorrow," Wendell said. "I wish he hadn't provoked him. He needs to keep his distance and not give Dresden due cause. That's the last thing we need right now."

Late that afternoon, when he'd finished his trip, Matt drove down the dusty dirt road in a state of elation. He parked in the driveway and went up to his room to unpack. Through the open window he heard the sound of a shovel pounding at the earth. He looked down and saw Pete working in the garden. Instead of his usual slow and steady pace, Pete seemed obsessed, cranked into overdrive like a madman gone berserk. He had a pickaxe in his hands and was savagely thrusting it at the ground, repeatedly striking it with all his might. Matt went outside and watched in confusion as sweat poured from Pete's brow. Pete was grabbing handfuls of seeds and throwing them at the ground.

"I've never heard of power-gardening before," Matt said. Pete looked up and stared at Matt as if he were a stranger. Then he picked up a hoe and leaned on it for support.

"Are you alright?" Matt tried again. Pete looked like he was on the verge of collapse. It had been unseasonably warm for the last few days. "How long have you been out here in this heat?"

"Matt … Rita, I mean we … we lost the baby," he said with a pained expression.

"I'm sorry."

"Rita's completely inconsolable."

"You want some water or a cold beer or something?"

"A beer, I guess," Pete said. Matt went in to grab two beers from the fridge. When he came back out, he found Pete sitting on the front porch, staring out at the dirt racetrack across the road. "It just broke my heart to see her crying like that," he said. Matt sat down on the porch and leaned against one of the white columns.

"I guess it just wasn't meant to be."

"Who knows?" Pete said.

"You can always try again when the time is right."

"Time is right?"

"Yeah, like when you're really ready. I mean, it does sort of let you off the hook, so to speak, right?"

"I can't believe you could say a thing like that. Our baby just died. You think I feel relieved about that?" Pete stared at Matt and shook his head in disgust.

"I'm sorry. I just thought you weren't really ready, that's all."

"That was just my initial reaction, but I quickly warmed up to the idea. Rita and I have been picking out names and looking at baby clothes and furniture and everything."

"I had no idea," Matt said, staring out across the dirt road, trying to avoid Pete's glare. "But what if it didn't die at all?"

"What are you talking about? I told you, we lost our baby."

"I read somewhere that some religions believe that when a baby is conceived, it creates a vehicle for the soul to enter, a vehicle to journey through life in this physical plane, like getting in your car in preparation for a long road trip. But let's say your plans change at the last minute, or just when you get in the car, you realize there's a problem, so you get out and postpone your trip. It doesn't mean you died; it just means the time wasn't right."

"Who believes this?"

"Hindus, I think."

"But how do they know?"

"I don't know. How do we know there's a God and heaven and an afterlife and all that? I don't know if it's true. It's all a matter of faith."

"Doesn't matter," Pete said, getting up from the porch. "I'm going to call Rita and tell her what you said."

The sun was painting an amber glow behind the trees off to the right. Dark shadows covered the dirt road and the racetrack beyond. The heat in the spring air was fading and a slight chill took its place. Matt was about to go inside when Pete appeared in the doorway. He had a smile on his face as he sat down and leaned against the column.

"Rita was still crying when I called, but I told her what you said, and we talked about it. By the time we hung up, she'd stopped crying and we both tried to laugh a little."

"I'm glad to hear that."

"Hey, I didn't mean to snap at you like that."

"No, it was my fault," Matt said. They touched their beer bottles together and took a sip, then they both stared out at the bucolic scene turning to shadows before them. Then Pete looked at Matt, who was still in his uniform.

"Man, look at you, four stripes and all."

"Yeah, well it's your turn tomorrow, Captain."

CHAPTER TWENTY-NINE

On the evening of May 31, Matt picked up the phone by his bed and called Olga.

"I'm so excited I don't think I'll be able to sleep," she said. The next day was her twenty-first birthday, and Matt had been planning for weeks, wanting to make it a day she'd never forget. "Just give me one hint," she pleaded.

"You're too clever; I'm afraid you'd figure it out. Go to sleep and I'll knock on your door at seven."

Matt checked the forecast for the next day and smiled to himself: clear skies with morning temperatures in the mid-seventies. Perfect, he thought.

"Feliz cumpleaños," Matt said as Olga opened the back door and was greeted with a kiss.

"Gracias. Are you hungry? Can I get you anything?"

"No, I'm fine. Are you ready?"

"I'm ready," Olga said as she closed the door behind her. She was wearing brown leather shoes with beige linen slacks and a green silk blouse. Her Calvin Klein sunglasses hung around her neck from thin leather laces.

"Is it Devil's Den?" Olga asked as Matt turned south on Highway 71.

"You'll see," he said with a smile. As they approached the airport and passed the first hangar, Matt switched on the left turn signal.

"I see, you're taking me to work for my birthday," she laughed. "I never would have guessed." Matt helped her down from the Jeep and took her hand as they walked toward the little building south of the Flight Service Station. He opened the door and ushered Olga inside.

"Morning, Matt," Gene Crandall, the senior flight instructor said as they appeared. "She's all gassed up and ready to go."

"Gene, this is Olga Vargas," Matt said.

"I've seen you down at the ticket counter," Gene said.

"Don't tell me," Olga said to Matt.

"Remember how you said you wanted to fly with me someday? Well, be careful what you wish for."

"This is so exciting," Olga said. "I should have brought a camera."

"For you," Matt said, as he reached into his backpack and took out the little 35mm camera wrapped in red ribbon. "Happy birthday."

Matt opened the door to the ramp, and they walked out to the little white Cessna with red trim that sat gleaming in the morning sun. Matt opened the left door, reached in, and removed the control-wheel lock, turned on the master switch, lowered the flaps to ten degrees, and grabbed the fuel strainer tube from the door pocket.

"Don't worry, I'll show you exactly what you have to do."

"What *I* have to do?" Olga said, the smile somewhat wiped from her face.

"You're going to fly," Matt said, "if you want to."

"Are you serious?"

Matt walked Olga through the exterior inspection, then helped her strap into the left seat before shutting his door and calling out "Clear" before engaging the ignition switch. The propeller started turning as the engine burst to life. Matt called ground control for taxi clearance, released the parking brake, and they started to move.

"You have to steer with your feet on the rudder pedals. It's easy to forget at first," Matt said when he saw Olga trying to use the control wheel like the steering wheel of a car.

They set the parking brake by the end of runway 16 and Matt showed Olga how to run the engine up and check both ignition magnetos.

Matt showed Olga how to pull the carburetor heat control and checked for a slight RPM drop. Then Matt called the tower for takeoff clearance. He turned the strobe lights and radar transponder on as they lined up with the runway centerline.

"Just follow me through on this one," Matt said as he glanced over and saw Olga's look of total concentration.

"Slowly push the throttle up," Matt said as the plane rolled forward, gathering speed. At fifty-five knots, he gently pulled back on the control yoke and the little Cessna jumped into the air. "We'll climb out at seventy-three knots. Use the yoke to control airspeed. Pull up slightly to slow down, push forward to speed up."

They made a gentle, banking left turn and departed the traffic pattern to the north.

As they climbed, and the rolling hills before them spread out, Matt looked over and saw a smile spread across Olga's face. She was concentrating on the flight instruments and looking out at the panoramic view before them.

"It's so beautiful," she said. Matt felt a surge of pride, remembering the first time he'd broken ground in a high-wing Cessna and felt smitten with the pure miracle of flight—the flight that changed his life.

"Where do you want to go?" Matt said.

"Everywhere."

They flew over Beaver Lake and Horseshoe Bend, looked down and saw the twin wakes of an early morning speedboat towing a water skier. A few minutes later, they were over the rolling green fields of Pea Ridge, and Olga's attention was riveted to the terrain. When she brought her focus back into the cockpit, they were in a shallow, descending right turn.

"It's easy to get distracted," Matt said. "It's something you have to always guard against." Olga nodded. The ground below them looked like a magic toy-land with green hills, sparkling streams, and fertile fields.

Soon they were over the little town of Eureka Springs, and they looked out and saw the white statue of Christ with its arms outstretched.

"This is just like our first date," Olga said, looking over at Matt with a smile. They banked to the left, along the Missouri border, and saw Table Rock Lake glistening in the morning sun.

"Let's go back and practice a few touch-and-goes," Matt said. They turned south and followed Highway 71 over Bentonville and Rogers. Matt called the tower over Springdale, and they were cleared for touch-and-goes on runway 16.

"I'll make this first one," he said as he applied carburetor heat, pulled the power back, and extended the flaps.

"There's the stadium and my parents' house off to the right," Olga said. They slowed to seventy knots on final approach. A few feet above the runway Matt pulled the power back to idle, applied a touch of back pressure to the yoke, and the main wheels settled onto the pavement with a gentle thud. As they rolled out, Matt pushed in the carb heat lever, raised the flaps, and pushed the throttle full forward. Soon they were airborne again.

"Now it's your turn," he said. Olga concentrated on the instrument panel, following Matt's instructions around the traffic pattern. On short final, Matt said, "You're right on the glide path, speed's good. Fly down onto the runway, that's it, now pull the throttle all the way back, pull slightly on the yoke." The Cessna kissed the runway with an almost imperceptible touch. "Tell me you haven't done this before," he said. They went around for one last landing. On the downwind leg, Matt looked over, picked up the camera, and snapped a shot of Olga's face, full of joy.

"That was the nicest birthday present I've ever had," she said as they drove back to town.

"I'll pick you up at your parents' house at six," Matt said as he backed out of the drive.

At 5:00 p.m., he put on his suit and looked at himself in the mirror. A wave of sadness came over him as he remembered how his father had taught him how to tie a Windsor knot so many years ago. He picked up the photo of his father from the nightstand and held it in his hands. "I wish you could have met her, Dad," he said out loud.

At 5:30 p.m., unable to wait any longer, Matt got in the Jeep and drove to Olga's parents' house. He left the bouquet of roses in the back seat, walked up to the front door, and rang the bell. When the door opened, Dr. Vargas stood before him.

"Come in, Matt. Olga and María are out shopping, but they should be home soon." Matt walked in and felt the same change in energy he remembered from last Thanksgiving, a welcoming peace that put him at ease.

"I just got in from Little Rock late last night," Dr. Vargas said. "I've been spending the day trying to catch up. Can I get you anything?"

"No thanks," Matt said. "Please don't let me keep you from your work, sir."

"On the contrary; I welcome the interruption. I've just been reading the latest briefing from Amnesty International. I try to see if there's any news about Leandro and some of our friends." Matt followed Dr. Vargas down the hallway and into the den. "Make yourself at home," he said as he walked around his mahogany desk and sat down in the leather chair.

Matt looked around the den and glanced at the volumes of books on the wooden shelves that spanned from floor to ceiling. He looked at the framed photographs on the walls. There were photos of Olga and her parents through the years, and a photo Olga had shown him before of Eduardo and Leandro when they were teenagers, sitting on the seawall in Havana, smiling into the camera.

"We were so carefree back then," Dr. Vargas said. "We had no idea that a tidal wave was coming."

"Olga told me you recently went back there."

"I've been back twice in the last few years. In the late seventies, Fidel was looking for an opening dialogue with the U.S. He was desperate for dollars and saw Jimmy Carter as the one president he could trust. When we found out about this, we decided that María's father, Alberto, and I would make the trip. We thought it might be too risky for all of us to go.

"When we arrived in Havana, we were met by Blanca Flores, Leandro's female companion. They met years before at San Juan and

Martínez, a farming prison in Pinar del Río. Leandro had been sent there as punishment for refusing to wear the blue uniform of a common criminal and for his refusal to undergo rehabilitation. Blanca was a nurse in the compound's infirmary. Leandro, who was forced to cut cane under the broiling sun, passed out due to heat-stroke and was brought to the infirmary for treatment, not out of any humanitarian concern; the regime just needed all able-bodied hands in the fields cutting cane.

"When he came to, he looked up and saw Blanca's face smiling down upon him. They began to talk. Unafraid that Blanca would report him to the authorities, he told her how much he detested the revolution and how Fidel had betrayed his people. He told her of his dream for a democratic and free society, and how the Cuban people needed to rise up and demand change. He recited poems and quoted the words of José Martí: *Man is not free to watch impassively the enslavement and dishonor of men, nor their struggles for liberty and honor.*

"Blanca then confided in a whisper that she, too, believed the same things but was too afraid to admit it. As the weeks went by, Blanca tried, whenever she could, to secretly bring Leandro an extra ration of water, a piece of bread, a morsel of meat. When the authorities finally caught her in the act, she was fired from her job and forced to move back to Jesús del Monte, a *barrio* in southern Havana. Leandro was immediately transferred far away, to the notorious Boniato Prison in Oriente province. He was locked in a *gaveta,* or drawer, a dark 4x6 foot punishment cell. He was tortured in this rectangle of death, so small he couldn't straighten his legs for months.

"From a friend, Blanca managed to find out where he had been taken. She wrote a letter, addressed to María and I, and gave it to some Canadian tourists she met in Old Havana, to mail once they returned home. She revealed the horrors he endured during his many years of incarceration, his time spent in the punishment pavilion at the Presidio Modelo Prison on the Isle of Pines, where guards walked across the chicken-wire roof with prodding poles. As soon as a prisoner was about to collapse from lack of sleep, they were brutally prodded with the pole from above. Buckets of human and animal excrement were thrown down upon them, with no water and no means to cleanse themselves. Rats scurried across the floor, and what little food they received was rancid and infested with maggots.

"Leandro had suffered a broken leg during a failed escape attempt. Back in the punishment pavilion, racked with pain, a guard jumped down on his leg. The pain was excruciating. He never received medical care, and his leg never healed properly. The night of our crash landing, when I, too, was racked with the pain of a broken leg, it was the example of Leandro's courage that sustained me.

"María could hardly contain herself when she read the letter. A few days later, in the middle of the night, she woke from a terrible nightmare. She told me she saw Leandro calling out to her. He'd been on a hunger-strike and was close to the end. I held her in my arms and made a promise that I would not rest until I was able to secure his release.

"Months later, we received another letter from Blanca, postmarked in Madrid. We were shocked to find out that Leandro had, in fact, been engaged in a hunger strike of some forty days. The last day coincided with the night of María's dream. I wait until I have privacy before reading these reports, to spare her the pain."

"Would you mind if I read some of them?" Matt asked. Dr. Vargas handed Matt the bound notebook. He sat in the leather chair as Dr. Vargas brought his attention back to some papers on his desk.

The articles were cut-and-pasted, much like a scrap album. Matt opened the notebook and started to read.

> **Mrs. Alberto Lazo Pastrana and her three children. Assassinated during an exit attempt in 1971. Location: Caribbean Sea. Alberto Lazo Pastrana. Mysterious death in prison 9-1-78. Combinado del Este prison. Alberto Lazo Pastrana had been a member of Castro's revolutionary army and had fought in the mountains against the Batista dictatorship. When Castro took power, he grew disenchanted and joined the opposition.**

Captured for alleged counterrevolutionary activities, he served a ten-year sentence in Isla de Pinos. After his release, he was denied work, as well as permission to leave the country. Desperate, he built a raft with his family. They left on the primitive vessel but were spotted late at night by a Cuban Coast Guard patrol. Despite their cries for mercy and that children were onboard, the Coast Guard rammed and sunk the raft. The father made it to shore, exhausted; the wife's body washed ashore the next day, partly devoured by sharks. The children's bodies were never found. The father was captured and tortured, despite his devastating grief. He was sentenced to eighteen years in prison. Right before he was to be released, in a general amnesty declared by Castro, he developed a colon ailment and died mysteriously in the prison's hospital.

Firing squad executions of political prisoners and former members of the Batista regime began on January 7, 1959. By the end of the 1960s, 14,000 Cubans had been executed without anything resembling due process of law. On April 7, 1967, the Organization of American States Human Rights Commission issued a detailed report based on dozens of verified eyewitness accounts. "On May 27, 1966, from six in the morning to nightfall, political prisoners were executed continuously by firing squad at La Cabaña prison. Each of the 166 men who were executed on that day had five pints of blood extracted prior to being shot. Extracting this amount of blood often produces cerebral anemia and unconsciousness, so that many had to be carried to the execution wall on stretchers. The corpses were then transported to a mass grave in a cemetery outside the city of Marianao. On 13th Street in Havana's Vedado district, Soviet medical personnel had established a blood bank where the blood is transported and stored. This blood is sold at $50 U.S. per pint to the Republic of North Vietnam."

Matt let out a low whistle. "My God."

"Which one?" Dr. Vargas asked.

"The one about the blood."

"Yes, I could hardly read that myself. Imagine—the democratic blood of innocent patriots coursing through communist veins. Che Guevara had a window installed in his office at La Cabaña so he could personally witness the executions. Working on a college campus, I regularly encounter students wearing some garment displaying that iconic portrait of Che. It is hard for me to contain myself. The man was a cold-blooded murderer who detested the United States. He wanted nothing less than to see the Soviet missiles aimed at New York City. That Christlike image with the heavenly gaze has been manipulated and misinterpreted. Embraced by the Beat Generation, Guevara is seen as an early advocate of counterculture, a proponent of defiance against authority, a champion of the oppressed. Nothing could be further from the truth. Anyone caught disagreeing with the regime or just listening to rock music would be rounded up and either forced into rehabilitation, imprisoned, or put before a firing squad. It's a miracle that Leandro is still alive. I may not have succeeded in freeing him, but it's possible all the media attention I've enlisted has helped him to survive."

"This must be so hard on your family."

"Yes, it is," Dr. Vargas said, with a weary, far-off gaze. "But as disastrous as things have been, Leandro's simple message of defiance and courage inspire me every day. It is not about Batista or Castro, Kennedy or Khrushchev, you see—the enemy is always injustice, Mateo." Then Dr. Vargas went back to his paperwork, and Matt brought his attention back to the notebook in his hands.

Lydia Pérez López, age 25, eight months pregnant and unborn child. Assassinated in prison, 07-07-61. Guanajay National Women's Prison, Pinar del Río province. Kicked in

the stomach by prison guards thirty days before her due date, she lost her baby, received no medical attention, and bled to death.

Owen Delgado Temprano, age 15. Assassinated on 23-03-81 in an exit attempt. Location: G-2 State Security police headquarters at Villa Marista, Havana. Entered the embassy of Ecuador on 13-02-81 with his family to ask for political asylum. Seven days later, on 21-02-81, Cuban Special Forces stormed the embassy and took the entire family into custody. At State Security headquarters, as members of his family endured beatings, Owen yelled for them to stop. He was then brutally beaten, suffering severe blows to the face and head, and had one ear nearly severed. Transported to Pinar del Río hospital, he lapsed into a coma and died two days later. His body was not returned to the family for burial.

Matt read numerous other detailed reports, then skimmed the list of additional abbreviated cases.

Máximo Galán Zaldivar, age 17, 01-20-79, State Security office in Guantánamo. Leader of a youth group of rock and roll fans. Assassinated while under arrest for ideological deviations.

Armando González Peraza, age 14, 02-12-61, Las Villas province. Assassinated by police, who claimed he committed suicide.

René Martinez, age 14, 13-06-62, city of Matanzas. Assassinated while under arrest.

Matt looked at his watch. Dr. Vargas glanced up, then back down at his work. "A beautiful woman is always worth the wait, don't you agree?" he said.

Just then, Matt heard a car pulling into the driveway. He handed the notebook back to Dr. Vargas, stood up, and for a moment, felt faint.

CHAPTER THIRTY

They sat across from each other. Their candlelit table was located on the second tier near the back of the restaurant, covered by a white linen cloth, surrounded by tall oak paneling under a slowly revolving Moroccan fan. Olga wore her black dress with a white pearl necklace.

"I had the nicest day," she said, smiling. Matt's gaze was drawn into the candlelight. He forced a smile as he tried to bring his thoughts away from some distant place. Olga reached out and took his hand. "Where are you?" she asked.

"Right here," he smiled. "I was just thinking about our flight this morning."

"I've been thinking about that all day myself, but without such a serious look on my face." Matt knew that the only way to be with Olga was straightforward. His feeble attempt at evasion was no match for her keen intuition.

"I like your father very much," he said. "Both your parents. He was telling me more about Cuba and your uncle." Matt paused for a moment, then said, "He let me read one of his notebooks." Olga nodded, a look of relief appearing on her face, happy that she was now hearing the truth.

"Once, when I was a little girl, I found one of his notebooks on the table in his study. He'd stepped out to run an errand and forgot to put it away. I sat down and started to read. When he came back, tears were streaming down my face. I just looked up at him and couldn't utter a word. He put his hand on my shoulder with the most pained expression.

I think he thought it was the end of my innocence, and it was all his fault. I stood and he wrapped his arms around me and just let me cry. When I could speak, I just said, 'Why, Papi? How could anyone treat another person with so much cruelty?' All he could say was, 'I don't know, my love.' Then I asked him if I would ever see my uncle, face-to-face, if he would ever be set free. He looked me straight in the eyes and said yes, but something inside me knew he couldn't be sure. That was the last time I ever saw one of his notebooks." Matt gently squeezed Olga's hand.

"I think he saw a certain end-of-innocence look on my face as well," Matt said. "He tried to rationalize it by reducing it to its root causes, the cruelty and inhumanity, I mean. In the end, he just looked at me and said, 'The enemy is always injustice, Mateo.'"

"He called you Mateo?" Olga said.

"I think he was tired."

"He's never done that before. He's never referred to any of my friends by their Spanish name." Matt wasn't sure if it was meant as a compliment or a subliminal slip that they were still just friends. He looked down and opened the menu.

Later that night they stood on Olga's back porch. The air was still and warm with the chirping of crickets in the dark. Matt and Olga wrapped their arms around each other and kissed each other's lips. Then Olga gently pulled back and looked straight into Matt's eyes.

"I don't know where this is going," she said, but not with the pained expression Matt remembered from last Christmas by the fire. It was more a resigned admission of the mystery of love, an acceptance of the unknown.

"I don't either," he said. "All I know is how I feel." Olga took the key out of her purse and opened the door. She took Matt by the hand and led him down the darkened hallway and into her bedroom. They stood next to the bed and held each other. Bright silver moonlight poured through the window and cast its glow on Olga's face. Matt took his suit-coat off and Olga reached up and started to unbutton his shirt. Matt's heart was racing as Olga took off her dress and stood before him. She lay down on the bed and reached up and took him by the hand, pulling him down by her side.

They took their time, their eyes adjusting to the light, their hands slowly discovering each other's delight.

"I never want to forget this," Olga said. Matt reached up and felt a moist tear on Olga's cheek.

"Me neither."

"It's the end of our innocence together—forever," she said.

CHAPTER THIRTY-ONE

It was 8:30 a.m. when Matt pulled into the driveway and opened the kitchen door. Pete was standing by the counter in khaki shorts and his faded orange Clemson Tigers T-shirt, grinding coffee beans.

"Hey," Matt said.

"Don't tell me you had a job interview," Pete said. Matt was still wearing his navy-blue suit from the night before. "You been to church or something?" Matt sat down at the kitchen table.

"No, I took Olga out for her birthday last night."

"You took Olga out? I didn't think she—"

"Many times, I've wanted to tell you."

Pete let out a low whistle. "You and Olga? Since when? Why didn't you tell me?"

"It's been almost nine months, since just after the crash last fall. I wanted to tell you, like I said. It was like holding this beautiful bird in my hands. I thought if I showed it to someone, it might fly away."

"Oh, come on man, spare the drama. I've shared every detail about Rita and me with you. I thought we could trust each other."

"You're right," Matt said.

"Well, I'm happy for you, son," Pete said, handing Matt a cup of coffee. "Now there's no excuse why you and Olga can't join Rita and me next Friday. We're taking the canoe down the Buffalo River."

It was early Friday morning. The tree-line ahead was shaded in a dark silhouette before the blazing orange of dawn. Matt and Olga were following behind Pete's pickup as they took Highway 16 out of town. Pete was driving slower than usual, the canoe nestled among pads and blankets and tied to the truck-bed. The two red taillights glowed up ahead, and Matt saw Rita through the rear window sitting close to Pete on the bench. They passed through wooded hollows and pastured ridges as they made their way toward Ponca, near the headwaters of the Buffalo River.

On the west end of the low-water bridge, off Highway 43, there was a narrow dirt road marked by a green sign with a picture of a white canoe. Pete slowed and put his turn-signal on, and the little caravan slowly bumped and rumbled down the rut-filled road. Up ahead, close to the water's edge, stood a wooden cabin with a red tin roof. A sign hung over the porch that said River Rat Outfitters, with a painted picture of a rat wearing sunglasses and paddling a canoe. Pete stuck his arm out the side window and motioned for Matt to park. Pete turned around and backed the pickup toward the water's edge. Matt and Olga carried the cooler, quilt, and picnic basket down to the water. Off to the side of the landing stood a rack of six aluminum Grummans and an empty canoe trailer. At the base of a tree stump lay the carcass of a canoe that was dented and smashed and filled with black dirt, ferns, and wildflowers. Matt helped Pete untie the canoe from the truck-bed as the door to the cabin opened and a large man with a black beard came toward them wearing jeans and a green River Rat T-shirt. He wore moccasins, and a knife in a leather sheath was fastened to his belt.

"Mornin' y'all," the man said as Matt and Pete slid the canoe out of the truck and set it on the ground.

"Morning."

"Virgil Potts," the man said as they all shook hands. "Nice little Sassafras."

"Thanks," Pete said. "I was a bit hesitant to bring her. If the water was running too fast or too shallow, I'd have left her home."

"Checked the bands on the pier last night," Virgil said. "Water level's in the green, about twenty-eight inches under the bridge deck. Should be perfect. How far're ya floatin'?"

"Only about ten miles," Pete said. "Just down to Kyles Landing."

"We'll pick you up," Virgil said. "If we're not there on the hour, we'll be there on the half."

"My friend here's going to need a boat," Pete said. Virgil pulled out a new seventeen-foot Grumman from the rack and set it down by the water. Then they all walked back to the cabin.

Inside the cabin stood glass cases of ancient marine fossils and posters that explained the geological timeline of the Buffalo River Basin. Virgil saw Matt gazing at the fossils.

"Hard to believe this whole Ozark region used to be underwater," Virgil said. "Last emerged from the sea some 300 million years ago. Most of those fossils you're lookin' at are extinct marine animals. During the Paleozoic era, due to continental drift, where we're standin' right now used to be south of the equator."

Matt shook his head. "That's hard to believe."

He left a deposit for the canoe and picked up a brochure and a map of the river. Then they went back out and walked to the water's edge, where Rita and Olga were applying coconut oil. Olga wore an olive-green tank suit under a white cotton blouse and khaki shorts. Her dark hair flowed from under a wide-brimmed straw hat. Rita had on denim cut-offs and was just taking off a white Ozark Sports T-shirt that revealed a purple bikini top. Her body was tanned and toned, and her black curly hair was pulled back and held in place with an elastic band.

Pete brought two quilts tucked inside plastic bags. He placed one in each canoe, then loaded the picnic baskets. Olga and Rita grabbed their paddles, and each climbed into their canoe and sat down on the front seat. Matt and Pete slid the canoes into the water and climbed in.

"We're off," Pete said as they started paddling. Soon their cadence fell into place, and the two canoes slid through the cool river water with ease. The sun was higher now, and the air was warm and heavy with humidity. A red-tailed hawk circled above the high limestone bluffs and a whippoorwill called out from an inland tree branch.

"I've loved this ol' river since I was a little girl," Rita said. They passed by a wide pool, curving around to the left, with big trees angling out above its bank. A little farther along, Rita said, "That's Bee Bluff up ahead. A long time ago, a huge swarm of bees lived up there. In 1916, two boys from Ponca blasted open the cavity with dynamite and a wave of honey came streaming down the cliff."

They glided past towering moss-covered limestone bluffs and natural swimming holes, and navigated around boulders. The water still retained the slight aqua-green tint of spring, and the air was warm and moist and smelled of flinty rock, black earth, and wet forest grass. Pete tied two nets around floating Styrofoam rings and attached them to the stern of each canoe with nylon cord. The nets each held a bottle of white wine, assorted cans of beer, and two plastic bottles of drinking water. "Natural refrigeration," he proclaimed.

Two hours later they floated past a large cluster of beech trees along the right bank. Then Rita said, "I'm starving, y'all. There's a nice little gravel bar up ahead. Why don't we haul out and have lunch?"

They paddled straight for the fine gravel shoreline. As the canoes came to a stop, Olga stepped out onto a warm carbonate slab, put on her sandals, and helped pull the canoe a few feet forward onto the gravel. "Let's lift her up so we don't scratch the bottom," Pete called out to Rita.

Up the bar, about forty feet from the shoreline, was a row of flat-faced limestone boulders. Pete and Matt opened the plastic bags and spread the quilts out in front of the boulders. Matt carried the picnic baskets up while Pete untied the nets from the boats.

Pete opened one of the picnic baskets and served out golden fried chicken with fresh radish slices and homemade vegetable samosas stuffed with chickpeas, corn, chopped onion, and coriander. Matt opened one of the bottles of wine using the corkscrew on his knife. "That's a nice sound," Rita said as the tight cork pulled out from the neck of the bottle with a loud echoing pop. Matt poured the pale straw-colored wine into four glasses and passed them around.

"I'll be good for nothing after this," Olga said as she took a sip.

After lunch they went for a swim. Opposite the gravel bar was a deep swimming hole. They walked on the river bottom until they felt the bottom drop out. Then they began to float and swim.

After they'd come out and dried off, Pete grabbed one of the quilts and took Rita by the hand. "I think we'll go for a little stroll," he said. They disappeared along a small footpath that led inland from the bar. Matt pulled the cork out from the wine bottle.

"More wine?" he said.

"No thanks," Olga said. "I'm getting sleepy." She put her wide-brimmed hat on, then leaned back against the face of the warm boulder next to Matt. Matt finished his wine, then nestled next to her and took her hand.

"Wake me when it's time to go," she said.

Off in the distance, Matt heard Rita giggle. Just then, two canoes appeared on the river, gliding past them in silence. Olga looked out from under the brim of her hat. She took a deep breath and sighed.

"It's like time," she said. "The river, I mean. For a brief moment, we've been allowed to step off, to retreat from it and look out upon its infinite flow. Seeing those canoes float by somehow reminds me of our shared humanity, that we're all linked by the common destiny of inhabiting the earth at the same time." Matt gave Olga's hand another squeeze, then pulled the brim down over her eyes. From under the brim of her hat, just before drifting off to sleep, she said, "It's probably the wine."

Olga had her arm wrapped around Matt when she awoke. "Matt, what time is it?"

Matt shook himself out of sleep, craned his head upward, and squinted at his watch. "It's two o'clock. We've been asleep for almost an hour." They both got up and started packing everything into the picnic basket. Olga carried the basket down to the canoe while Matt folded up the quilt. Just then, Olga let out a piercing cry and held the basket out in front of her.

"Matt!" she cried. Matt rushed over to her side, then abruptly stopped. On the flat carbonate slab next to the canoe lay the thick black coil of a large snake. It raised its head and looked around, its coils moving in on themselves.

"Let me think," Matt said, looking around for a large stick or rock. Just then, Pete came running down the footpath. As he approached, his eyes were riveted on the menacing serpent before them.

"Step aside, son," Pete commanded. Pete stopped next to Matt for a split second, then in an almost imperceptible blur, his arm shot forward, and he grabbed the snake around the base of its head. His arm made one continuous motion as he flung it over the canoes where it hit the ground and slithered off through the willow grass along the shoreline.

"My hero," Rita said. "Now you be sure to wash your hands before you touch me, ya hear?"

"Thanks, Pete," Olga said as she reached up and kissed him on the cheek.

"With soap," Rita said. Matt was still standing in the same spot. Then Rita and Olga gathered up the other things while Matt and Pete got ready to launch the boats.

"That was some trick," Matt said.

"My Uncle Everett taught me that on his farm when I was just a kid. He had me practice on a coil of hose, then he bought a fake rubber snake from the county store to practice on. The trick is just not to hesitate. Besides, that was just a harmless water snake. That ol' boy thought that rock slab was the perfect place to soak up some rays."

"But what if it had been a cottonmouth or a rattler?" Matt asked.

"Same technique, less room for error."

Matt was quiet for the rest of the trip. He had to force himself to comment along with the others as they drifted past a beautiful, lush fall of maidenhair ferns cascading down the side of a shallow shoreline bluff. They paddled through a chamber of air filled with the green concentration of chlorophyll perfume. Matt felt emasculated, a coward in front of Olga and the others. He stood paralyzed while Pete didn't hesitate for a second. He thought of Lenny Skutnik on the bank of the icy Potomac. Lenny hadn't hesitated either.

The sun was low on the horizon before them as they followed the country highways back to town. Pete's pickup was up ahead, and Matt saw the red taillights switch on. Olga tried making conversation, commenting on what a nice day it had been. When Matt didn't return his share of words, she joined him in silence, letting him have whatever it was he seemed to be needing. Finally, when it was dark behind them, and they were almost back to town, she said, "When I think of all the attributes I hoped to find in that special someone, you know, that wish list we all have, as unrealistic as it may be; Matt, I want you to know that serpent slinger never even made the cut." Matt reached out and they held hands, a smile spread across his face as they drove down the highway toward home.

CHAPTER THIRTY-TWO

It was Wednesday, October 13, and Matt had just come back from the long Knoxville turn. When he walked into Flight Control, he saw Jackson and Buzz with grim looks on their faces. Jackson nodded at the bulletin board. The succinct message from Wendell was the only note left.

To All Line-Pilots

Please check your mailboxes for an important message.

The news was too disheartening to post in public, too disappointing to display, kept guarded like a bad report-card.

The national Court of Appeals in the Eighth Circuit had just ruled against the National Mediation Board and ALPA, claiming that the NMB acted in violation of its quorum requirement during the election for union representation. Wendell tried to end the message on a high note, stressing that after a couple of months, they'd be allowed to vote again.

"We had it in the palm of our hands, and they just snatched it away," Buzz said.

"You'd think the law would be a reflection of fairness," Matt said.

"Fairness is defined by those who hold the power," Jackson said, shaking his head.

"Maybe we'll win the second time around," Matt said.

Jackson just let out a loud baritone laugh. "Man, you just don't get it," he said.

When Matt got home, he took a quick shower and crawled into bed with the phone by his side. He knew she would be waiting for his call, tucked into the covers with a book and a cup of tea. Just before he reached for the phone, it rang, startling him.

"Matt."

"I was just about to call you."

"Oh Matt, something's happened." Her voice sounded frantic, almost hysterical, a stress and tone he'd never heard before.

"What?" He could hear her sobbing.

"My parents just got a call from my Aunt Miriam in Miami. My Uncle Leandro was just released from the Boniato prison."

"That's fantastic news."

"No, you don't understand. The only reason he was set free is because he's dying. My mother is overcome with worry. My father's been frantically making phone calls, trying to get Leandro medical attention and a visa. My Aunt Miriam said his most recent hunger-strike has left him emaciated and almost unconscious. Matt, he hasn't eaten in fifty-six days. His girlfriend, Blanca, took him to her sister's tenement in Jesús del Monte. She's trying to get him to take some food but he's so weak he can't eat."

"Olga, I'm so sorry. I wish there was something I could do."

"I always prayed that somehow I would finally meet my uncle face-to-face. I'm so worried about what might happen to my mom if he should die. All these years she's held out hope, hope that our family would be reunited. That hope has always sustained her. I don't know what I'll do if anything should happen to her. I'm so scared, I wish you were here."

"I'll come right over."

"No, it's too late. I'm going over to my parents' house early in the morning."

"Try to get some rest. I'll call you in the morning."

Matt was wide awake in the dark. It seemed like his whole life had been spent overcoming obstacles, defying the odds. He wanted desperately to find the key that would open the lock, but there wasn't one. The odds seemed insurmountable. He thought about Dr. Vargas and knew how desperate he must be, trying to use the depth of his intellect, the breadth of his personal contacts, to find a solution before the ticking clock expired. Matt looked at the clock on the nightstand. It was 3:00 a.m. Just before his exhausted mind and body succumbed to slumber, an idea surfaced.

He woke at 6:00 a.m. feeling drained and stiff. He pulled on his sweats, grabbed the swim bag, and drove to the pool.

While his body was working out the kinks, he went over the plan. It was a long shot; it would be risky, audacious—but not necessarily impossible.

He drove home, made a pot of coffee, reached for the phone, and dialed Olga's parents' number. Dr. Vargas picked up on the first ring.

"Dr. Vargas, it's Matt."

"Yes Matt, Olga should be here any minute now."

"Actually, I called to speak with you, sir. Olga told me about Leandro last night. You see, I know someone who might be able to help."

CHAPTER THIRTY-THREE

Matt packed his suitcase, wrote a letter to his mom, another letter to Olga, and a letter to Pete, enclosing the spare set of keys to the Jeep. He sealed them and placed them in the nightstand drawer.

He drove to the airport and caught the next flight to Memphis. In Memphis he boarded a flight to Fort Lauderdale.

He rented a compact car and drove out of the airport parking lot. The air was hot and humid, and graceful green palm fronds swayed under a blue sky. It was just like he'd left it two years before. He drove north to State Route 84, turned left, then shortly after, pulled into the parking lot of the Ramada and saw the familiar green Eldorado convertible. Some things never change, he thought. He checked in at the front desk, went up to his room, and threw his bag on the bed. He took the elevator downstairs, walked into the back bar, and smelled the stale air of old cigarette smoke. It was dark and it took his eyes a few seconds to adjust. He bought a Perrier and a Dewar's on the rocks from Vince who, thankfully, didn't recognize him. Wally was seated in a corner booth, smoking a cigarette and glancing up at the TV news from an overhead screen. Matt took a breath of the rancid air. He'd burned this bridge before, and now he'd have to wade through the water to get to the other side.

"How've you been, Wally?" he said, placing the drink in front of him. Wally stared up at Matt, trying to bring his eyes into focus, the recognition finally taking hold.

"You've got a lot of nerve if you've come asking for your old job back."

"I don't want my old job back, Wally. I'm here to offer *you* a job."

"You've come to offer *me* a job?" Wally's face was full of confusion.

"Wally, look, I'm sorry I left the way I did. I wanted to explain. Things were just out of control. Everything was happening so fast."

"I didn't mind in the least that you left, had you replaced in an hour. What I minded was that Nadine turned in her two weeks' notice that same afternoon, left me high and dry. I have no doubt you were to blame for that."

"How is Nadine?"

"I have no idea. Last I heard she was working for a cruise line. Look, thanks for the drink, but I'm kinda busy right now."

"Wally, remember all those trips in the 310 to Walker's Cay? Landing on a strip not much longer than your driveway, full of chuckholes, where you had to flare out over the water to be able to touch down without running off the far end, where the garbage dump for the whole island was right by the runway, sea birds flapping and flocking all around you, and on either end you could look down through the crystal blue water and see all those sunken airplanes resting on the bottom and…"

"Kid, what in the world are you trying to get at? Don't tell me the Boy Scout has turned to smuggling."

"And remember that charter we did to the Caymans? With the fat man who owned the diamond mine in Africa, and his two female escorts." Wally took a deep gulp of scotch. "We flew right over Cuba at eight thousand feet, right down the Girón corridor."

"So what?" Wally said. Matt looked over his shoulder. Vince was washing beer glasses and there were a couple of half-drunken yachties seated at the bar. "Wally, look, I need your help. I met someone."

"Don't tell me, she's a tall blond with big—"

"No, Wally. She's Cuban-American, just like you." Matt took out the picture of Olga from his wallet. Wally let out a low whistle. "Her mother's brother has been a political prisoner in Cuba. He's been locked away and tortured for the past twenty years, not for committing a crime, only for expressing an opinion. Wally, if you only knew what her family's been through, trying to secure his release, hoping for all these years. They just found out that he *was* released but only because he's dying. He's endured brutal beatings, starvation, humiliating strip searches, solitary confinement, every kind of torture you can imagine. He refused to wear the uniform of a common criminal, so he's spent years in confinement doing hard labor. His last hunger-strike has left him emaciated. They don't think he can last for more than a few days. Look, Wally. I want to take the 310, come in low under the radar, right above the waves, land on a coastal road, pick him up, and beat it back before the Cuban air defenses can do anything about it. I know it's risky, but I know I can do this." Wally looked stunned.

"Oh no you can't," he said. "It's impossible. You'd never get away with it, especially not in *my* airplane. Kid, look, you hightailed it out of here two years ago because you were scared, scared that somehow flying for me was going to jeopardize your big chance with Delta. Don't think I didn't know. Now you want to do something that'll probably get you killed. Right now, you think you're in love. Later, you'll come to your senses, and you can come back and thank me with another drink, thank me for saving your life. Besides, from a strictly business standpoint, my insurance policy doesn't cover getting shot down by a MiG-21 in Cuban airspace. I'd be a fool to sign on to such an act of lunacy."

"Wally, there's money involved, big money. Just name your price."

"I promise, whatever you have would never be enough," Wally said. Matt was trying to keep his emotions in check but felt his anger rising up. Wally was right, and a part of Matt knew it. The desperation of the moment still had the upper hand, making a fool out of Matt and his naiveté.

"Alright Wally, if you won't help me, I'll find someone else who can."

"Forget it, kid, you won't find anyone with fewer scruples than me. Accept it. There's oppression in the world, and people die. There's nothing you can do about it." Just then the door to the bar opened and Dr. Vargas walked in. Matt waved a hand and Dr. Vargas came over and pulled up a chair. He looked at Matt for a sign, but Matt's expression offered little encouragement.

"Wally, this is Olga's father."

"Eduardo Vargas, sir. It's a pleasure." Dr. Vargas and Wally shook hands.

"I'm sorry to hear about your wife's brother, but as I was just telling Matt, I'm afraid you're both wasting your time. It's impossible for me to offer you any encouragement."

"I'm prepared to offer you $200,000," Dr. Vargas said.

"I appreciate that, sir, but my answer is still no. Perhaps you could purchase an airplane, but those transactions usually take some time."

"Time is running out, I'm afraid," Dr. Vargas said.

"Look, my family came here from Cuba in the thirties. They fled Havana after my grandfather was gunned down by Machado's secret police. I feel for you. Hitler, Stalin, Mussolini, Machado, Batista, Castro, they're all the same. I wish there was something I could do, but there isn't."

"Matt, will you excuse us? I'd like a few minutes to speak with your friend, Cuban to Cuban," Dr. Vargas said. Matt nodded and got up. He went up to his room and started pacing back and forth. He wanted to call Olga, but he resisted. She'd be overcome with worry if he told her about his plan. But he couldn't lie to her, either. He'd just be vague, omit a few key details. He was just here to introduce her father to someone who might be able to help. He kept pacing, trying to figure out how he could get his hands on a Cessna 310 or similar plane. He'd been in his room for half an hour when he heard a knock on the door. Opening the door, Dr. Vargas stood before him looking effete and forlorn.

"Come in," Matt said. Dr. Vargas stepped into the room and closed the door. He pursed his lips and shook his head.

"Matt, I just want to thank you for trying to help, but you might as well go home. Your friend Wally and I had a conversation. He told me what happened to his grandfather. It started shortly after the stock market crash in 1929 when the price of sugar plummeted. Student-led opposition to the Machado dictatorship was fierce, and Machado retaliated with a reign of terror. Violence escalated out of control. Wally's grandfather, who was a lawyer in Havana, was sympathetic to the students' plight. He joined a group of troubadours who would walk the streets of Havana singing songs of protest against the regime, songs of peace, songs against tyranny. One night, after the group had finished singing, Wally's grandfather joined the others for drinks at a bodega down by the waterfront. When they came out of the bodega, Machado's death squad, the Porra, shot them dead in the street. Wally's father was only thirteen years old when he lost his own father. Wally's grandmother fled Cuba for Miami with her three young children. She worked as a seamstress, trying to keep her grief-stricken family afloat. Then she got a job sewing parachutes for the war department in the early 1940s. As Wally was telling me this story, I got the faint impression that I might be changing his mind, that somehow, he would connect Leandro's sense of justice to that of his own grandfather's. I was hopeful. I thought he might even see this mission as an act of avengement. Then he just ended the conversation. He said he wished there was something he could do but there was not. Then he got up to leave. I haven't given up hope, but I'm afraid there's not much time. I'm going down to Miami to spend the night with María's family. Here's my phone number in case you need to get in touch."

"I'll keep trying to think of something, sir," Matt said as Dr. Vargas turned to leave.

Matt was too restless to stay cooped up in his room. He packed his swim bag, got in the car, and drove past the airport, past the old terminal, his old apartment. He crossed the 17th Street Causeway and followed A1A along the beach. He pulled into the parking lot of the Swimming Hall of Fame pool and swam a mile, trying to rack his brain for the elusive solution. He stood at the east end of the pool as the sun was going down and looked to the west. Towering cumulonimbus clouds were collapsing over the Everglades. The setting sun, radiant with every hue of magenta, was pouring through gaps in the cloud build-ups. Matt pulled himself out of the pool. The sky over the ocean was almost black, and bright, fluorescent lights illuminated the pool deck. He dressed and drank a beer at the Red Button, then crossed A1A to the beach. He took off his shoes and walked across the warm sand, down to the water's edge. The sky overhead was full of twinkling stars, and big hulks of container ships at anchor dotted the near horizon, their decks awash in silver fluorescent light. Matt heard the hypnotic sound of the waves sliding over the sand and lapping at his feet. He looked to the south, past the Yankee Clipper Hotel. Cuba was out there, about the same distance between Fayetteville and Memphis. Matt got back in the car, had dinner at the Cockpit Bar and Grill, then went back to his room and called Olga. He tried to cheer her up. He told her he was optimistic they'd find a solution.

"When are you coming home?" she asked. Olga seemed to know nothing of his plan. Her father must be trying to shield her from worry too, he thought.

After hours of tossing and turning, Matt finally fell asleep. The phone rang at 6:00 a.m. He groped for the receiver and was surprised to hear Wally's raspy voice on the other end.

"I didn't know if you'd left yet," Wally said. "Meet me in my office in an hour." Then he hung up. Matt was stunned. Why would he have called? Wally wouldn't have changed his mind. Matt stopped off at Lester's and bought two large coffees. Then he drove to the Sunny South Air Terminal on the north side of the field. Wally's green Eldorado was parked in his spot by a small palm tree. Matt was filled with memories. He couldn't believe he was back in such a familiar scene. So much had happened in the last two years, but now it seemed like he never left. Matt carried the coffees upstairs and opened the door to South Tropic Airways. Wally was at his desk in the back office.

"Close the door," Wally said. Matt closed the door and placed a coffee on Wally's desk, then was startled to see the presence of a man seated on the small leather sofa.

"Matt, I'd like you to meet Victor Morales." The two men shook hands. Matt sat down on the other end of the sofa. Victor looked to be about the same age as Matt. He had black hair and a youthful face, full of good cheer.

"Victor came into my office looking for a job last year. I told him what I tell everyone: no openings. He told me he had a lot of experience but was still working on obtaining his U.S. licenses. I told him to come back when he had them, not really to offer him encouragement, but to excuse him from my presence. He left with cordiality but came back every month to give me a progress report. We've become friends ever since. I'll let him tell you his story."

"My friend, I was a fighter pilot in the Cuban Air Force, flying MiG-21s out of the air base in Santa Clara. We were sent to Russia for initial flight training. It was my first experience abroad. You see, growing up in the Cuban revolution, we are taught that Russia is the utopian state, the model country where the beauty of socialism is revealed through advances in science and technology. But when I got there, I was filled with disillusion. All I saw around me was a broken bureaucracy, a dysfunctional society rampant with alcoholism, corruption, and immorality. It was nothing at all like we'd been led to believe. When I returned to Cuba, more and more I started questioning everything I'd been told. I saw the iron fist of our government controlling every aspect of the individual's life. There was no freedom to travel or start a business, to worship or speak one's own mind, just a totalitarian state dictated by the whims of a megalomaniac. It was the same cult of personality propagated during the reign of Stalin. I lay awake in anguish for my family's future. A disconnect between such utopian idealism and my reality of despair was growing more and more inside me. I knew I could never live as a free man under such a system, the system I'd sworn to protect and defend with my life. I could never raise my children to blindly accept the same false doctrine, to become obsessed with the struggle against imperialism, to grow up without God, without Christmas, without the freedom to be their own unique selves, only to believe the propaganda of a despot. I felt that a part of me was dying. When I was sent back to Russia to receive advanced officer-training for my assignment to the war in Angola, I started making other plans. Here was Fidel, unable to feed and provide for his own people, draining our island of all its resources to fight a Marxist guerrilla war. Friends of mine were sent there never to return. I soon devised a plan. On our flight home from Russia, our Tupolev-154 transport plane would have to make a fuel stop in Gander, Newfoundland. I decided that, at that time, I would defect. And that's what I did. I ran away and made it to South Florida, where I have family.

"Wally called me late last night and told me about your plan. Making conversation, and on a whim, he asked if it would be possible to do what you proposed. At first, I said no, it would be too risky. Then he asked, if it were *my* own idea, risky as it might be, what inside knowledge of Cuban air defenses might allow one to slip through? I thought for a moment, then I said that for the rendezvous point, I'd use a lightly traveled highway along Siesta Beach, between Matanzas and Varadero. It's a short distance between Marathon Key and the north coast of Cuba. I'd depart late in the afternoon just as the sun was on the horizon. That way, the return flight would be under increasing darkness. The more I thought about it, the more I realized that some things might actually be in your favor.

"The radar is frequently down due to power outages. It's an old, Russian system that was never designed to withstand Cuba's climate. The radar operators are becoming increasingly apathetic, all those years of Fidel crying wolf, preparing us for the inevitable Yankee invasion. But if you are spotted on radar, you would still have about fifteen minutes to get to your rendezvous point and depart. An initial alert would have to work itself up the chain of command, and military forces would still need Fidel's personal command to shoot you down. By the time he is located and issues the command, it would still take time to warm up the anti-aircraft radar. The missile's range is less than fourteen miles. Their MiGs would still pose a threat, but it would be next to impossible for the pilots to locate you at low speed and altitude in the dark. Hopefully, by the time the missiles are ready to fire, you'd already be north of the 24th parallel."

Victor stared at the navigation chart, then looked at Wally. "I think it's possible—risky, but possible. The biggest hurdle is making sure your passenger is at the exact rendezvous point at the exact time. Once you land, you'll have less than two minutes on the ground. If he's not there, you'll have to come back empty." Matt nodded.

"I'll call Dr. Vargas right away," he said. Then he looked at Wally. "Wally, I'm confused, shocked, is more like it. Why are you doing this?"

"Strictly for the money. I've had it. I'm selling the business. It's too hard to make a profit. Mike O'Neil and I have been talking about a partnership. He'll stay in Bimini, and I'll run the dive trips stateside. With two hundred grand I could buy one helluva nice dive boat."

Matt reached for the phone on Wally's desk and dialed Dr. Vargas's number. He relayed all of what he'd just heard. He could sense an immediate change in Dr. Vargas's tone, his feeling of dejection replaced by renewed hope.

"I'll make some calls from here, then I'll join you in an hour. Tell Victor I've heard of him, that he has my deepest admiration," Dr. Vargas said.

It wasn't going to be a simple matter of picking up the phone and placing a call to Blanca, relaying the specific details of the plan. That would be too risky. Calls from the U.S. were routinely monitored by State Security. Dr. Vargas couldn't call and speak in code like so many exiles did; an elaborate code had never been established with Blanca. Besides, there wasn't even a phone in the little tenement where she was keeping Leandro, and Leandro was so weak it would be impossible for him to make the trip to Matanzas on his own. Dr. Vargas picked up the phone, but instead of calling Cuba, he placed a call to Mexico City.

CHAPTER THIRTY-FOUR

"**E**ddy, what a surprise. It's good to hear your voice, my friend."
It was Placido Carillo Rivera, portly Professor Emeritus of
Economics and History at the Colegio de Mexico. He and Eduardo
met in the early seventies during a conference on Trans-American trade
policies. They both gave speeches and found that they shared similar
views. They also shared a mutual bond of admiration forged over many
Brandy Alexanders during evenings at La Nueva Opera Bar on Avenida
Cinco de Mayo.

What impressed Eduardo about Placido was not only his profound
intellect and dedication to human rights, but the fact that this ardent
proponent of capitalism used to be a committed communist. His wife,
Salvadora, was Cuban, and the two of them returned to vacation and
visit family there on a regular basis.

Placido had been a great supporter of Fidel during the early days of
the revolution. He wrote complimentary articles in newspapers, and a
glowing article that appeared in *Bohemia* magazine in late 1959. Eduardo
remembered one of their early conversations.

"I tell you, Eddy, it was great fun being a communist in Mexico in
the thirties and forties. The city was overflowing with exiles from the
Spanish Civil War and World War II. Many of the great artists, poets,
painters, and philosophers were communists: Diego Rivera, Frida Kahlo,
André Breton, Leon Trotsky, and many others. If you were communist,

then you were against fascism, against American imperialism, a champion of the rights of the common man."

Placido didn't mention to Eduardo at the time that the first doubt in his ideology began in 1956, when a transcript of Nikita Khrushchev's secret speech before the delegates at the 20th Party Congress, revealing the atrocities committed by Stalin during the Great Purge, was being made available to journalists in the West. Tens of millions of people executed, experimented on with poisons, sent to work camps in the Gulag, never to return. Placido was outraged. He held Stalin in such high esteem during the heroic fight against the Nazis and was hopeful that the next one to carry the torch would be Fidel. He cheered the revolution and the success of the Cuban military during the Bay of Pigs Invasion.

But then stories started filtering in through exiles in Mexico, stories of firing squads, political prisoners, tortures, forced labor camps, the denial of free speech. Again, Placido was outraged but still held out hope that communism could succeed.

The last straw came in 1970, with the failure of Fidel's grandiose plan to harvest ten million tons of sugar. Sugar production had slumped since 1966, and in 1969, only 4.5 million tons were produced.

Fidel became obsessed with the idea, mobilized the entire country, and enlisted every able-bodied citizen to cut cane, one of the most torturous of manual labors. But not one processing plant had been built since 1930. There were constant breakdowns and production halts. It was an impossible goal, and Fidel was betting the revolution on the outcome. Just from an economic standpoint, half the country's labor force, including highly skilled surgeons, were in the fields cutting cane. The rest of the economy suffered. But Fidel was determined to show the world what could be achieved when the power of nationalism was mobilized for the common good, Che's concept of the New Man put to the test.

But when it failed, there were no consequences. In any other system of government, it would have resulted in a change of power. Fidel had total freedom to fail, but the people had no freedom to oppose him. That's when the words from Placido's pen changed. Instead of supporting Fidel, he wrote articles condemning him, holding him personally responsible for the failure of the revolution, and calling for free and open elections and a return to a market-based economy. In short, Placido had become a capitalist, although he still maintained a deep distrust of American imperialism. His scathing articles were now written under the name of Louis Cabrera Boringuen. He had to protect Salvadora's family and still maintain the right to travel freely, not just to observe first-hand the conditions in Cuba, but to keep their annual vacation to Varadero Beach a viable option.

Eduardo always admired Placido's ability to see things objectively and adjust his views accordingly.

"Plaz, thank God I reached you. I've been calling for two days. I need your help."

"I am at your service, as always, my friend." Placido was aware of Leandro's plight and had tried for years to secure his release. Eduardo told Placido of the dire news and gave him the details of the planned air-rescue. "Leave everything to me, Eddy. I'll pack a bag and be on the next flight to Havana. I'll find Blanca. If I'm successful, I'll place a call to Salvadora here in Mexico City. She will call you and give you the word. All communication will flow from me to you through her."

"I knew I could count on you, Plaz. I'll be waiting for her call. And Plaz, one more thing. Be careful."

"No te preocupes, Eduardo," Placido laughed. "I assure you, the hounds will never catch this old fox."

Wally pulled out an almanac that listed the time of official sunset for various cities in the western hemisphere. They calculated that, at a cruise speed of 212 knots, Matt would have to take off at precisely 6:19 p.m. to arrive at the rendezvous point at 6:57 p.m., just as the sun would be touching the horizon.

Victor spread a sheet of legal paper on Wally's desk and drew a sketch of what the topography would look like as Matt approached the coast—the slopes of the Pan de Matanzas mountains off to the right, the power plant, the bay, spanned by the Canímar Bridge, the coastal highway along Siesta Beach. "With the coordinates programmed into the Loran, you should be able to come very close to the exact spot. The bridge is a prominent landmark, keep it just off to your left. There is a little hill that could obscure your visibility. Of course, you'll have to be vigilant for any traffic on the highway, but it shouldn't be too busy at that time of day."

Wally started shaking his head. "Matt, you're not even current in the airplane."

"It'll come back to me, Wally. I can do a couple of practice landings in Marathon."

"Maybe I'll come with you."

"No, Wally, like you said, it's too risky. This is something I have to do myself."

"No, I meant to Marathon. We'll fly down together, and if I don't feel right about it when we get there, we cancel. If you're proficient enough, I'll wait for you there. You might not be in very good shape when you get back—if you get back." Wally grabbed the flight manual to the Cessna and the navigational chart they used to plot the course. "Victor can stay here and wait for Eduardo. Let's you and I go down to the 310. You're going to need the crash course."

Wally and Matt walked down the side staircase to the ramp. Matt looked out on the north side of the terminal building where the jetliners were parked at their gates. The dream was still out there. After all he'd been through in the last two years, he wasn't sure if he was getting closer to it or about to kiss it all goodbye. He looked down on the ramp before him and saw the familiar cluster of airplanes, the de Havilland Twin Otter with its big bush tires that ran shuttles to Walker's Cay, the Learjets and Gulfstreams, and there, in the back row, the same twin Cessna he'd been so thrilled to fly three years ago.

Matt hopped up on the step and stood on the wing. He opened the cockpit door, and the familiar scent of warm leather greeted his senses.

He dropped into the left seat and scanned the instrument panel. Everything seemed so small. He ran his hands over the throttles, the prop and mixture controls, and familiarized himself with the communication and navigation radios. His mind darted back to that first flight with Wally, when they flew out to Andros Island.

"Seems like old times," Matt said.

"Sit here as long as you like. I've got to run some errands. I should be back in the office by 1:00 p.m."

When Wally left, Matt thumbed through the flight manual, refreshing his memory on power settings, stall speeds, approach speeds, and short field takeoff and landing technique. Every time a doubt or fear came into his mind, he canceled it. I can do this, he thought. It's my destiny to do this.

After an hour, Matt got out of the plane and climbed the stairs to the terminal. As he walked down the hall, he heard a muffled conversation in Spanish coming from Wally's office. Eduardo seemed energized, a tone of confidence in his voice. Finally, there was a plan in place.

CHAPTER THIRTY-FIVE

Placido smiled at the young flight attendant for Cubana de Aviación as she set a cup of coffee on his tray-table. He was wearing a white linen suit, his silver hair combed straight back. He gazed out the window through black Wayfarer sunglasses and saw the shimmering whitecaps across the choppy Yucatán Channel.

Retirement had been a mixed blessing. He enjoyed the free time to read, write, and travel, but he felt a growing sense of despair that his best days were behind him, and he was losing his relevance. But now he was on a rescue mission, called upon to play a vital role, and it filled him with a sense of pride and purpose. He could help a dear friend and take a stand against injustice at the same time.

Placido cleared his small travel-bag through Customs and took a taxi to the Habana Libre, where he always stayed. He checked into his room with a view of the sea, then went down through the lobby and out the front door. In a few moments, a pale blue 1958 Cadillac pulled up to the curb. The driver got out as Placido approached.

"It's good to see you, Manny," Placido said as the two men embraced with a firm *abrazo*. "Salvadora sends her love." Manolo Suarez Ruiz, Salvadora's brother, was one of the few fortunate Cubans to have not only a car, but a legal permit to operate as an independent taxi driver. Every aspect of the revolution made it almost impossible to make a living. Most taxi drivers operated outside the law and risked a heavy fine or imprisonment if they were caught without a permit, a permit which cost four hundred pesos a month, the salary of a brain surgeon. Placido and Salvadora faithfully paid for Manolo's permit. It was always a great pleasure for Manny to return the favor and be their personal chauffeur whenever they came to visit. Placido knew Manny could be trusted. Any other driver might report him to G-2. The air of suspicion lurked on every corner. Placido gave Manny Blanca's address in Jesús del Monte, and they pulled away from the curb. They drove south, then bore to the right by the bus terminal. They passed the Plaza de la Revolución, then headed east on Vía Blanca. Manny turned right on Avenida General Lacret, then slowed down to look for Alcalde O'Farrill Street.

"Drop me off here," Placido said. "I'll meet you at the corner in twenty minutes." Manny nodded.

Placido got out of the Cadillac and looked for the address. Everywhere, the old colonial buildings were crumbling from neglect. Hardly any paint remained on the walls, and broken concrete littered the side streets. An old man was leaning against a wooden pushcart, and Placido saw white sheets billowing on a clothesline from a balcony overhead. Even with the sounds of a baby crying, a dog barking, and a guitar and congas coming from one of the tenements, Placido was struck by how quiet the city seemed compared to the old days, before the revolution.

Two stone columns framed a cracked archway that led back to a courtyard with a decrepit, dried-up Italian marble fountain in the center. Placido looked at his watch. It was just 2:15 p.m. He walked through the archway and barely made out the number seventeen by one of the open doorways.

Tears were running down Blanca's cheeks as she rinsed a cotton cloth in a porcelain bowl of water. Before her, lying stretched out on a small bed, was Leandro. He lay with eyes closed in dark, sunken sockets. His black hair and beard were long and gnarled and streaked with gray. The air inside was hot and heavy with humidity. Blanca took the cloth and wiped Leandro's forehead and chest. Leandro was naked except for a small white cloth that covered his loins. His collarbone, cheekbones, and ribs all protruded, giving him the appearance of a skeleton covered with a thin veil of skin. There was a rosary hanging from the bed post, and on the wall hung a painting of the Virgen del Cobre, patron saint of Cuba. On a small table stood a glass of water and a plate with a few slices of mango. Blanca held a mango slice by Leandro's parched lips and said in Spanish, "Take it my love. Please, you must try to eat." Leandro's chest rose and fell slowly as he labored to breathe. He tried to open his mouth and take a small bite.

Just then, a shadow appeared in the doorway. The bright, hazy rays of daylight silhouetted the figure of a large man dressed in a white suit. Blanca felt her pulse quicken. An agent from G-2, she thought, but her thoughts were confused. She was relieved when she heard him say, "Señorita." The simple address was now considered too bourgeois. Anyone from G-2 would have addressed her as "Comrade."

Placido approached her tear-streaked face. He looked down at Leandro's body, and a wave of sadness welled up inside him. He held out his hand to Blanca and said in a quiet voice, "Please do not be alarmed. I am a friend. I come with a message from Eduardo Vargas. I am here to help you." As Placido said these words, Leandro's body quivered, and he strained to open his eyes. The whispered word, "Eduardo," came from his lips. Blanca stood and Placido held her in his arms. Then he knelt down, put his hand on Leandro's forehead, and whispered in his ear.

"You must try to be strong, son. I am here to help you. Arrangements are being made. You are going on a trip." Leandro tried again to open his eyes against tears and fluid that had encrusted around his eyelids.

"A donde?" he whispered.

"To freedom, Leandro, to freedom." Placido reached into a small drawstring pouch and took out a jar filled with guava nectar and guarana. Then he turned to Blanca and whispered in her ear.

"I have a car at my disposal. Can you dress him and try to get him to take this?" Blanca nodded.

"That's all I can tell you for now," Placido said. "I'll return in forty-five minutes to help you."

"Bless you, señor," she said. Placido left the apartment and walked up Alcalde O'Farrill. He hadn't walked far when Manny's Cadillac pulled over at the curb in front of him.

Manny took Placido to the local office of the telephone company. Placido placed the call to his home in Mexico City, where Salvadora picked up on the second ring. Before he left, Placido and Salvadora had worked out a simple set of code words to use in case his call should be monitored. After making light conversation, telling her about the weather, and how Manny was doing, and that he hoped to spend a day at Varadero before his return, he ended the call by saying, "I heard that cane production is on the rise and that Fidel is predicting a most excellent harvest."

"That's wonderful news," Salvadora said. "Give a big hug to Manolito for me. I'll see you soon, my love." She hung up and immediately placed the call to Miriam. Miriam called Wally's office, and Diana, Wally's new secretary, picked up. Eduardo, Matt, and Victor were in the back office. Eduardo picked up the phone and spoke with Miriam in Spanish. A smile broke out on his face, and he gave Matt and Victor a thumbs-up. Then Wally came in carrying a paper shopping bag. He walked into the back office and closed the door behind him as Eduardo hung up the phone.

"It's on," Eduardo said. "They'll be there by sundown. I need to round up a medical team and call a friend who's an immigration attorney. We'll drive down to Marathon and meet you there. We don't have much time."

Wally told Diana to take the rest of the day off and put a message on the answering machine saying they'd be closed for maintenance for a few days. Then he asked Victor to monitor his pager in case they needed to get in touch. Eduardo and Victor left the building while Matt and Wally walked down the side steps carrying the chart kit and Wally's shopping bag.

The tip tanks were topped off with 100-octane and the aux tanks were half full. Matt performed a quick exterior inspection, then climbed up on the wing, opened the door, and sat down in the left seat while

Wally put the paper bag behind the right seat, climbed in, and latched the door. They ran through the pre-departure checklist. Matt pushed the mixture controls to full rich, opened the little side window, and called out "Clear." Then he pushed the start-buttons, and the two big Continental engines sprang to life. Wally called ground control for taxi clearance and Matt released the parking brake.

They took off to the east, crossed the shoreline, proceeded a few miles out over the dark blue Atlantic, then turned south and leveled off at 2,500 feet in order to stay beneath the floor of Miami's terminal control area. Once clear of Miami's airspace, they turned to the southwest and climbed to 4,500 feet. In thirty minutes, they had the Marathon airport in sight.

Matt entered the traffic pattern for runway 07. Wally transmitted position reports on the local frequency as Matt slowed to 140 knots and extended partial flaps. On a five-mile final, lined up with the runway, he dropped the landing gear, extended full flaps, and slowed to 93 knots.

"See if you can put it right on the numbers and be stopped a third of the way down," Wally said. Matt was in full concentration mode, maintaining a three-degree visual glide-path. Approaching the runway threshold, he let the nose drop a bit as he retarded the throttles. A gust of wind caused the airspeed to increase, and they touched down past the numbers and used up more than half the runway's 5,000 feet before coming to a stop. Wally had a frown on his face.

"If this was Walker's Cay, we'd have to swim ashore. You were carrying too much power. Remember, it's not a Metroliner."

"I'll taxi back and try it again," Matt said.

They took off and stayed in a tight pattern. On short final, Matt visualized all those critical landings he'd made at Walker's Cay. No margin for error. He came in low and pulled the throttles back to idle just before the threshold. The airspeed was bleeding back as they dropped onto the runway with a firm thud, just before the numbers. Matt pressed hard on the brake pedals, and they came to a stop less than a third of the way down.

"That's more like it," Wally said. Matt taxied to the ramp area and shut down the engines. They sat in the cockpit with the chart spread out on their laps and programmed the coordinates for Siesta Beach into the Loran. "I still can't believe I'm letting you do this," Wally said. Matt was afraid Wally was about to change his mind.

"When was the last time you took a calculated risk?" Matt said. "Risked everything for something you truly believed in?"

Wally stared out the window. "When I asked Donna to marry me," he said. Matt dropped the subject.

CHAPTER THIRTY-SIX

Manny took Placido back to the tenement. As he walked through the archway, he saw that Blanca had managed to put a pair of old beige cotton pants on Leandro that looked five sizes too big. She tied a piece of clothesline around his waist and turned up the cuffs around his protruding ankles. She placed a pair of worn hemp sandals on the floor by the bed and was struggling to place a clean white shirt around Leandro's shrunken torso.

Placido placed his arm around Leandro's back and held him upright. He cringed when he saw the labyrinth of bayonet scars, the welts and burn marks. Blanca buttoned the front of Leandro's shirt, placed the sandals on his feet, and picked up the sack of fruit and the jar of juice while Placido reached down and picked Leandro up in his arms.

Manny was parked out front with the rear door to the Cadillac open. Placido set Leandro down on the back seat. Blanca slid in next to him, put her arm around him and pulled him close by her side. Placido and Manny got in the front seat and closed the doors. As they drove off, Placido turned around and began to tell Blanca that, if all went as planned, an airplane would soon be coming to take Leandro to the United States. Blanca's eyes lit up with shock. A look of incredulity spread across her face.

"But señor, please, I beg you, I must go with him. He is my life. There will be nothing left without him." Manny looked over at Placido and raised his eyebrows. Eduardo had said nothing about Blanca, and there was no way to place a call to discuss the matter.

"I'm afraid I cannot be the one to make that decision," Placido said. "But if you are not on the plane when it departs, Manolo and I will take you to a place where you can hide. It will not be safe for you in Havana after this." Blanca nodded. "My dear, at the exact moment, we must move very quickly. Come from behind the right wing. Be very careful of the propellers. We'll have to lift Leandro up and carry him into the plane. You know what the consequences will be if we are stopped by G-2?" Blanca nodded. "And you are still willing to …?"

"Yes, of course," Blanca said. They drove through Havana and entered the tunnel that went under the harbor. They continued eastward on Vía Monumental, past the lichen-covered walls of La Cabaña Fortress and El Morro Castle. Leandro's skeletal frame quivered as he squinted through the window and saw the scene of his first incarceration over twenty years ago. In his mind he could see the wooden stake of the firing squad post, the wall of sandbags, the hens pecking at brain fragments in the dirt. He could still hear the blazing dignity of his comrades, just before the end, as they shouted in full defiance, "Long live Christ the King—Down with Communism!"

For a moment, he felt that the regime had finally found its error, that it was a mistake all along that his life had been spared, and that he was being taken back to La Cabaña to face the firing squad. But now it didn't matter. He no longer feared death. He no longer clung to life, only to the arm of this good woman who had been his last link with humanity. But instead of turning into the fortress courtyard, they drove past the laurel trees, continued on Vía Monumental, and passed by Cojímar, the fishing village that modeled for Hemingway's *The Old Man and the Sea*. Manny turned to pick up Vía Blanca, the coastal highway that would take them to the beautiful beaches to the east. They entered the city of Matanzas, crossed the Canímar Bridge, and followed the coastal highway around to the right. A half-mile beyond, they reached Siesta Beach. Manny slowed down.

"This is the spot, right here," Placido said as he looked at his watch: 4:45 p.m. "Keep on toward Varadero. We'll come back in an hour." Just before reaching the pristine beaches, Manny pulled off the highway and stopped outside a tourist shack. "Wait here while I go in and find some food," Placido said.

Blanca placed Leandro down along the seat and rested his head in her lap. Manny looked around and tried to keep calm. He felt vulnerable, sitting immobilized in the car. At any moment, an agent from G-2 could stop him and ask for his papers. He'd have to try to explain that the woman in the back seat was taking her sick brother to the hospital in Matanzas.

In a few minutes, Placido returned with fish sandwiches, mango juice, and two bright orange T-shirts. "These may help the pilot spot you," he said. Blanca held the fish sandwich by Leandro's lips, but he was too weak to take a bite.

They drove back to Siesta Beach. Manny dropped them by some tall grass on the opposite side of the highway from the beach, then drove off toward Matanzas. They moved away from the pavement and hid in the grass. The sun was starting to sink toward the western horizon. Out across the beach, the shimmering water reflected brilliant golden sparkles. They crouched down low as a bus went by.

CHAPTER THIRTY-SEVEN

Matt and Wally spent an hour walking around the little town of Marathon. The sun was just starting to set on their way back to the airport. The terminal building was closing as Matt performed the exterior inspection of the plane. Wally reached into the paper bag and took out a roll of white speed-tape. He cut a piece about twelve inches long. On the aft fuselage, he angled the tape over the first N of the registration number, converting the N into an M. Then he did the same on the other side.

"What's that for?" Matt said.

"N26ST is now M26ST," Wally said. "M26, the name of Castro's revolutionary movement. M for Moncada, the garrison they attacked in 1953. The confusion may give you another five seconds before they aim their Kalashnikovs at you."

"Thanks," Matt said with a drop in the pit of his stomach.

"Hand me your wallet," Wally said. "You can't carry any identification. And here, you may want to wear this. I got it years ago at a little shop on Calle Ocho." Wally reached into the bag and pulled out a black beret with a gold star in front. "They may even think you're a comandante— for another five seconds."

They went over the plan one final time, then Matt looked at his watch. It was 6:00 p.m. Eduardo still hadn't shown up.

"I guess it's now or never," he said as he climbed into the cockpit. Wally climbed up onto the wing and they shook hands. "Thanks again for everything," Matt said.

"Be careful, kid," Wally said. He shut the door, climbed down from the wing, walked over to a small table in front of the terminal building, and sat down. He lit a cigarette and watched as Matt started up and taxied to the runway. At precisely 6:19 p.m., he heard the roar of the engines and watched the Cessna race down the runway, lift off, and retract its landing gear as it banked southward.

A few minutes later, a car pulled through the gate and drove around the corner of the terminal. The door opened and Dr. Vargas got out, looked at his watch, and walked over to Wally.

"What happened?" Dr. Vargas said with a look of confusion. "Where's Matt?" Wally took a last drag on his cigarette, tossed it on the ground, and pointed to the southern sky.

"He just took off, right on schedule."

"Just took off? I don't understand. I thought *you* were going to do this," Dr. Vargas said as his face turned ashen.

"No way, this was all Matt's idea. I thought it was insane from the start. I still do. I never should have let him go. I'm afraid there's nothing to do now but wait."

"My God, what have I done?" Dr. Vargas said as he started pacing back and forth.

Matt's heart was racing and his hands were trembling. Everything was happening so fast. Stay focused, he said to himself. He climbed to one thousand feet and looked out over the Straits of Florida. He saw a cargo ship heading west, leaving a long wake, glistening in the setting sunlight. Probably heading for the Panama Canal, he thought. For a moment, he thought of Karen, then he thought of his mom. Stay focused, he admonished himself.

Matt scanned the instruments. Ten miles before reaching the 24th parallel, he turned off the nav lights and the transponder and dropped down just above the waves, ignoring the readout on the altimeter.

For a moment, Matt imagined the military running the urgent message up the chain of command. Suddenly, Matt was filled with a wave of fear. A near-paralysis was taking over. Too late to turn back, he thought. What if something goes wrong? He could easily be killed, or worse, spend the rest of his life in prison. He would never see Olga or his mom or Pete again, never eat decent food or drink clean water, never be able to swim or even hear the English language, ever. He'd be totally cut-off from everything he knew and loved, forever. Death would be the better option. I should have brought a gun, he thought. Stay focused, he admonished himself.

Soon, up ahead, he could make out some dark hills looming above the purple haze. Maybe the slopes of Pan de Matanzas, he thought. I wonder if they've spotted me on radar. Then the outline on the horizon began to take shape. It *is* Pan de Matanzas, Matt thought, just as Victor described it. The bay should be just off to the left. I'll line up to come right down the middle.

Soon the crests of the mountains grew taller. Off to the right, Matt saw the towers of the power plant, the outline of the coast, and the span of the Canímar Bridge. He was still doing two hundred miles an hour. He throttled back, dropped the landing gear and flaps, and slowed to a final approach speed of ninety-three knots. Passing over the bridge, he banked sharply to the left, dropped down just above the highway, and searched for Siesta Beach. Up ahead, the highway curved to the right. The rendezvous point should be a half-mile beyond the curve, he thought. Then he flew over a car going in the same direction. Matt couldn't see beyond the curve due to his low altitude and some trees off to the right. Then, straight ahead of him, a small truck loaded with lemons appeared from the opposite direction. Matt pulled up slightly as the truck careened off the side of the road, spilling lemons into the scrub. This must be the spot, Matt thought as he pulled the throttles to idle and froze when he looked up and saw a bus with its headlights on, coming straight toward him. There's no room to go around, he thought with his heart pounding in his throat. He was close to stall speed as he dropped the Cessna onto the highway, stood on the brakes, and came to a stop just a few feet from the bus. He looked out through the windshield and saw the sign, *18-Matanzas,* above the driver, who was staring at him with a look of shock and disbelief. Matt donned the black beret that was on the right seat, flashed his landing lights, and waved for the driver to move back. Just then, his peripheral vision picked up two figures dressed in bright orange and a large man dressed in white struggling toward the plane.

The bus was backing up as Matt reached over and opened the door. Blanca and Placido lifted Leandro up onto the wing. Matt set the parking brake, reached back, and grabbed Leandro by the arm. It felt like he was holding onto a stick; there was virtually no muscle to grab hold of. Blanca climbed up and she and Matt positioned Leandro into his seat, then she sat down next to him.

"No, no—solo el hombre!" Matt shouted over the roar of the engines.

"Pleese, señor, I no leeve heem, I no leeve heem!" she cried, imploring Matt with a look of frantic desperation.

"Okay," Matt said. There was no time to lose. Placido gave Blanca a kiss, shut the door, climbed off the wing, and ran back to the high grass. "Cinturones," Matt shouted, pointing at her seatbelt. Blanca looked confused; she had never used a seatbelt in her life. Matt reached back and buckled Blanca and Leandro in. Then he released the parking brake, extended 15 degrees of flaps, and pivoted the Cessna around in a 180-degree turn. He pushed the throttles full forward and started the takeoff roll.

The sun shone like a golden orb, tucked halfway into the horizon. Matt squinted to see the highway ahead. Suddenly, out of the glare, two cars appeared, heading straight for them. My God, Matt thought, we'll never make it. Then, just before Matt was about to swerve off to the side, he saw one car forcing the other to veer off. Matt kept accelerating, and at 82 knots, just as there was no more highway left, he pulled back hard on the control yoke and the Cessna lumbered into the air. Matt retracted the landing gear and accelerated a bit, then pulled back and just cleared the hills ahead. He banked to the right, clearing the tops of the pine trees along Siesta Beach. The sky was darkening, and Matt could barely make out the surface of the water as they headed north, just above the waves. He wondered if the command to fire the missiles had already been given.

He imagined the crews racing to their posts in the silos, the launching ramps, the targeting antenna rotating. He held his breath, expecting to see the ghostly outline of a MiG-21 streaking toward them. But soon, they were crossing the 24th parallel. The sky was almost black. It was too dangerous to fly so low. He climbed to 3,500 feet and turned on the nav lights and transponder, as the lights of the Keys appeared on the horizon like a shimmering string of pearls.

For the first time, Matt turned around and tried to smile. Blanca was holding her arm around Leandro, the look of shock and disbelief still etched on her face.

"Mira," Matt said, pointing forward through the windshield. "Libertad."

In a few minutes, Matt could make out the lights of Marathon. He entered the traffic pattern and lined up with runway 07. A thin film of salt was making it difficult to see through the windshield.

As Matt taxied to the ramp, he saw the headlights of a station-wagon illuminate. A man and a woman were getting out of the car. He parked the Cessna near the car and shut down the engines. Just as the propellers stopped rotating, Eduardo was up on the wing, opening the door. Matt unbuckled Leandro's seatbelt, and Blanca reached under his arm-pits to try to lift him over to where Eduardo could carry him. Leandro was so light and frail, like a scarecrow made of straw. Eduardo wrapped one arm around his back and placed his other arm beneath him. Matt saw Eduardo place his mouth close to Leandro's ear and heard him speak in a low voice. The only words Matt could understand were, *mi hermano*.

The station-wagon was backing up toward the plane. A woman got out, came back, and opened the rear hatch. She was wearing a light blue shirt, and a stethoscope hung from her neck. Two blankets and pillows filled the back of the wagon. A shortened IV stand had been erected behind the front seat. Eduardo and the doctor placed Leandro on the blankets, then the doctor climbed in next to him and started listening to his heart.

Wally was busy peeling the tape off the sides of the fuselage and washing the salt off the windshield. Another man sat in the driver's seat of a second car. As the car doors were closing, Eduardo turned and gave Matt a thumbs-up. Then the two cars sped across the tarmac and out toward the highway. Matt was leaning against the wing. He was in a daze as he watched the red taillights of the two vehicles disappear into the night. For hours, he'd been riveted to the task at hand, but now he seemed confused, not sure what to do next.

Wally came around from the other side of the plane, popped open the wing-locker, and tossed in the dirty rags and tape. He climbed up onto the wing and dropped into the left seat.

"Time to go, Matt. You just sit back, my turn to fly." Matt blinked and came back to life. He climbed up on the wing, sat down in the right seat, and buckled in.

They leveled off at 5,500 feet. All the lights of Miami were twinkling up ahead. Off to the right spanned the black abyss of the Atlantic. Matt was still in a daze. He looked over at Wally.

"You think I'll get a violation, Wally?"

"No, but I might."

"Why?"

"Look, just keep your mouth shut. When the word gets out, I'm sure they'll trace the airplane back to me. If I have to, I'll say I flew it. It'll be our secret."

"Our secret," Matt repeated. "Just like those two hundred hours."

"What?"

"Nothing. I erased them from my logbook, anyway."

Matt was staring at the twinkling metropolis below when Wally reached over and patted him on the knee.

"You gonna be alright, kid?"

"Oh yeah, tomorrow," Matt said.

They shut down on the ramp at the Sunny South Air Terminal and climbed down off the wing. Wally carried the chart kit, and Matt popped the wing-locker open and took out the dirty rags and tape. He flashed back to that night when he reached up into that same wing-locker and found the machine gun bullets. He remembered the anger he felt, the sting in his arm. Then he thought of how fateful that moment had been. If it hadn't been for Jorge Roca and those bandoliers, Matt probably wouldn't have left Fort Lauderdale. He never would have been hired as a flight instructor, where he met Carol and her husband, wouldn't have been hired by Arkansas Airways, and worst of all, he never would have met Olga. And perhaps Leandro's life could be linked to that same chain as well. Maybe Karen was right after all. There was a purpose behind everything, the good and the bad. Maybe it really was his destiny to be standing right back in the same spot where this odyssey began.

Out across the tarmac to the east, a full moon was rising above the ocean.

"Care for a drink?" Wally said, as they climbed up the side staircase and walked down the dark hallway to the office.

"No thanks." Wally put the chart kit under Diana's desk and locked the door. They walked down the stairs and out the front door. Golden moonlight was shining down through the palm fronds. Wally opened the door to his green Eldorado. "I don't know how to thank you, Wally," Matt said as they shook hands.

"Yeah, well, I should be the one to thank you, kid." Wally got in, closed the door, and backed out. Matt watched him drive away as he walked over to his rental car. I wonder what he meant by that, Matt thought.

He drove back to the Ramada and drank a beer at the back bar. Then he went up to his room and opened the door. The red message-light on the phone was flashing.

CHAPTER THIRTY-EIGHT

Matt caught a 6:30 a.m. flight to Memphis, then checked in at the Arkansas Airways gate for his flight home. Pete and a new first officer, Dan Petrillo, were the crew. As Matt walked out across the ramp, Pete came down the airstairs.

"Where ya been, son?" he said with a smile. "I was starting to worry about you."

"I just had some family business to take care of," Matt said.

When they got to Fayetteville, after all the passengers had deplaned, Matt came down the airstairs and was about to pick up his carry-on bag when he looked out and saw Olga racing toward him. He smiled and opened his arms, and she fell into them, crying and laughing at the same time. Pete was coming down the airstairs with his flight bag in his hand.

"I'll never understand it, Lavery," he said with a smile. "Of all the guys—why you?" Matt and Olga didn't even hear him.

"How are you? Are you okay? Promise me you'll never do anything so dangerous again," she said. "My mom and I are on our way to Miami. She's been ecstatic from the news. She can't believe it's real. Our flight's about to depart. I've got to go. I'll call you tonight."

"I'll be waiting by the phone, same as always," he said.

She kept holding him in a tight embrace, then she whispered in his ear, "I love you."

"I love you, too."

"I don't want to let you go."

"I'll be here when you get back," he said. "Then we'll have all the time in the world."

EPILOGUE

A ll these things had been replaying in Matt's mind, more so than usual since he got the call from Rita two weeks ago. Through the years, whenever Pete would call, he liked to have Rita pretend she was the telephone operator. "I have a collect call from a Mr. Bob Grayson on the line," she would say. "Will you accept the charges?" And always, he would hear Pete laughing in the background when Matt said that no, he would not. The prank had long lost its luster, but Pete never tired of it. Two weeks ago, the phone rang. Matt picked up and heard Rita's voice on the line but without the familiar background accompaniment. Then Rita burst into tears when she told Matt that his best friend was dead.

It was a beautiful Sunday morning. Pete got up early to go for a short flight in his vintage J-3 Piper Cub. He finished the flight, towed the little plane back into the hangar, and was driving home in his new pickup when the driver of an eighteen-wheel tractor-trailer fell asleep at the wheel and abruptly swerved into the opposite lane, hitting him head-on.

"I'm so grateful that he left his life doing what he loved best," Rita said.

"He loved *you* best, Rita," Matt said, trying to hold back his tears.

"And I don't think he felt any pain," she said. "One second he was here, the next he was in heaven, just like that."

Matt caught a flight from Miami to Atlanta, then connected to Fayetteville on some new regional carrier; Arkansas Airways had long since gone out of business. Pete decided to stay in Fayetteville, even after he'd been hired by a major airline in Dallas. He and Rita bought Ozark Sports from its previous owner and ran it together for years. They had three children, two girls and a boy, and lived a happy life.

After Matt gave the eulogy at the cemetery, everyone came back to their farmhouse for a barbecue. Pete would have liked it that way. When the guests had gone, Rita took Matt out to the shed in the backyard. She opened the sliding doors, and there, up on the rafters, was Pete's old canoe.

"He always wanted you to have it," Rita said. Matt looked up at the canoe, memories flooded with tears. Friends for life, he thought. It seemed like it would last for such a long time.

Matt looked at his watch. His break was almost over. He raised his seat-back and opened the curtain. Most of the passengers around him were asleep. The eight-hour flight from Rio to Miami was almost over. He went back up to the cockpit and sat down in the left seat.

"Get any sleep, Skipper?" Jack Whitney, one of the two first officers asked.

"A little," he lied. Angie Swanson, the chief purser, was also up in the cockpit, drinking a cup of coffee. Angie had been a flight attendant for almost forty years.

"Can I get you anything, Matt?" she asked.

"Just a cup of hot water, Angie." He reached into his flight bag and pulled out a Kukicha tea bag. After all these years, he'd finally developed a taste for the stuff. As Angie was about to leave the cockpit, she noticed the photograph inside Matt's uniform hat, which was clamped to the bulkhead wall.

"Beautiful kids," she said.

"Thanks," Matt said. "They get that from their mom."

"That's quite obvious," Jack said with a smile.

"What are their names?" Angie asked.

"Mark and María," Matt said. "Mark's a senior at the University of Arkansas."

"Arkansas?" Jack said. "Why there?"

"They spent all their summers there growing up. Their grandfather was a professor there. It's sort of their second home."

Matt adjusted his seat, inserted his Minitel headset into his left ear, and gazed out through the windshield. It was still pitch-dark, but in a few minutes the first hint of an amber ray would appear off to the right.

It was Jack's leg to fly, Matt would be checking in with Havana Center in a few minutes. He picked up the cup of tea, blew the steam off, and took a sip. Up ahead and to the left, he could see the dim lights of Havana, then further up, the Emerald City glow of Miami. Matt saw the graceful curve of the Florida Keys and remembered that harrowing flight from long ago. He remembered how surprised he was when Eduardo told him that Wally refused the $200,000 check. The only payment he would accept was a full tank of Avgas and a case of Dewar's. Thank God for vices.

Matt thought again about the mystery of fate. When Placido came to visit, Matt learned that it was Manny, in his 1958 Cadillac, who saved the day when he forced the other car to veer off and cleared the way for Matt's takeoff roll.

As for Leandro, the mystery of fate held the hint of a miracle, leaving Matt to wonder. Leandro and Blanca moved to Fayetteville, where María nursed her long-lost brother back to health, both physically and mentally. Eduardo oversaw the continuation of Leandro's formal education in matters of economics, political science, history, and international relations. When Leandro's English reached a level of fluency, he was invited to speak at a Rotary Club convention. Leandro recounted the horrors and human rights abuses of political prisoners in Cuba. A reporter for the *Gazette* happened to be in the audience. The morning paper contained a glowing article about Leandro and a tribute to all those who suffered in the name of freedom and democracy.

Over time, more offers came in for speaking engagements. And in 1988, when Ronald Reagan appointed Armando Valladares as Ambassador to the United Nations Commission on Human Rights, Leandro was invited to New York to act as his assistant.

Eduardo watched as Leandro's voice resonated with growing stature and strength. His passion had the power to move audiences to act. And then, on May 10, 1994, the world watched as another political prisoner made history. Nelson Mandela was inaugurated as the first black president of South Africa.

Eduardo knew, at some visceral level, that all of Leandro's suffering had not been in vain. And that the thought of him returning someday as the first democratically elected president in post-Communist Cuba was a very real possibility.

Matt stared out and marveled at how close the distance is between the north coast of Cuba and the Florida Keys. From this altitude, it looked like you could just skip a rock between them.

After Eduardo's prediction came true, and Cuba lost its Soviet subsidy, in the summer of 1994 alone, over thirty-three thousand desperate *balseros* fled the clutches of Castro's communism in rickety rafts and innertubes, risking starvation, dehydration, drowning, and shark attack, across the longest ninety miles on earth.

Matt gazed at the instrument panel. The soft blue and amber light of the electronic flight instruments bathed the cockpit in a warm glow. He counted his blessings every day, something he'd been doing faithfully ever since that fateful flight with Mark Winger.

When Mark told Matt about the updrafts by the cliff wall, and how he didn't think they would have made it without them, Matt thought it was just Mark's characteristic modesty talking. He'd seen first-hand what a gifted pilot he was.

Matt had flown with hundreds of talented pilots through the years, but there would always be a special place in his heart for Mark, Wendell, T-Ball, and Buzz. He thought about Tom Tomlinson's prescient words when he said, "Y'all are going to be flying with some of the best sticks in the business, the finest sticks in the clouds." It seemed so long ago now.

Through all the vicissitudes of life as an airline pilot, especially since that dark day in September of 2001, when the industry lost its innocence, the cockpit of a Boeing 777 still wasn't a bad place to hang your hat.

And Matt thought of Olga, and how his quest to make his dream come true led him to the true love of his life. And in less than two hours, he'd come home and slip in between the cool sheets and feel her warm body breathing softly as she would reach for him and pull him into her.

He was truly a blessed man. He thought, How could I have gotten so lucky in one lifetime? Then he heard the simple words of his father, echoing from his distant memory: "You work hard, you do your best, then wait for Lady Luck to arrive."

Giving a Voice to Creativity!

With every donation, a voice will be given to
the creativity that lies within the hearts of
our children living with diverse challenges.

By making this difference, children that may
not have been given the opportunity to have their
Heart Heard will have the freedom to create
beautiful works of art and musical creations.

Donate by visiting
HeartstobeHeard.com

We thank you.

Made in the USA
Monee, IL
10 August 2022

11318318R00219